Other Titles by Cheryl Brooks

Echoes From the Deep
Dreams From the Deep
Justice From the Deep
Cowboy Delight
Cowboy Heaven
Must Love Cowboys
Unbridled: Unlikely Lovers Book 1
Uninhibited: Unlikely Lovers Book 2
Undeniable: Unlikely Lovers Book 3
Unrivaled: Unlikely Lovers Book 4
The Cat Star Chronicles: Rebel
The Cat Star Chronicles: Wildcat
The Cat Star Chronicles: Stud
The Cat Star Chronicles: Virgin
The Cat Star Chronicles: Hero
The Cat Star Chronicles: Fugitive
The Cat Star Chronicles: Outcast
The Cat Star Chronicles: Rogue
The Cat Star Chronicles: Warrior
The Cat Star Chronicles: Slave
The Cat Star Chronicles Bundle: Slave, Warrior & Rogue
Sharing (Sextet Anthology)
Entanglements (Sextet Anthology)
Occupational Hazards (Sextet Anthology)
Mistletoe & Ménage (Sextet Anthology)
Dirty Dancing (Sextet Anthology)
Small, Medium, & Large (Sextet Presents)
The Lady Takes a Pair (Sextet Presents)
A Tale of Two Knights (Sextet Presents)
Midnight in Reno
If You Could Read My Mind (writing as Samantha R. Michaels

For Stu,

Soul Survivors Book 1

Echoes From the Deep

Cheryl Brooks

CHERYL BROOKS

Enjoy!

DERRYMANE PRESS

Derrymane
Press

Echoes From the Deep
Soul Survivors Book 1
by Cheryl Brooks
Published by Derrymane Press
Copyright © 2017 Cheryl Brooks.
Cover design by Dragonfly Press Design
Cover image by Adobe Stock
ISBN-13: 978-0-9864274-3-5

www.cherylbrooksonline.com

For those whose ideas come to them in dreams

ACKNOWLEDGEMENTS

My heartfelt thanks go out to:

My terrific critique partners, Nan Reinhardt, T.C. Winters, and Sandy James.

My keen-eyed beta reader, Mellanie Szereto.

My buddies in IRWA for their support and encouragement.

My friends and family for their love and understanding.

And Google Earth for helping me find my way around England.

I couldn't have done this without you!

One miraculous survivor becomes a life raft for souls.

Chapter 1

"OCEANA AIRWAYS FLIGHT 2324 TO LONDON'S HEATHROW AIRPORT is now boarding at gate A22."

For the space of perhaps ten seconds, Jillian Dulaine debated the wisdom of ignoring the announcement. She didn't have to leave Newark. She could stay there for the next three weeks and no one back home in Memphis would ever know she'd chickened out.

Her friends and family knew how much she hated flying, and they had all applauded her decision to bite the bullet and make this trip alone—a trip that should've been fun and exciting, not to mention romantic. But now, instead of leaping up with all the eagerness a new bride ought to feel on her honeymoon, Jillian gritted her teeth while mustering every ounce of willpower she possessed simply to rise from her seat.

An air of excited anticipation surrounded her, people chatting and laughing while she took her place in the queue like a mindless drone. No one else seemed to share her mood. No one else was only going through the motions, pretending their entire world hadn't fallen completely apart.

After the gate official scanned her ticket, Jillian walked down the ramp to board the plane, the clack of her new sandals muted by the carpeted floor. Unlike many of the other passengers, all she carried was her purse, preferring to let the baggage handlers deal with the bulk of her belongings. Losing her luggage would be no great loss anyway. Clothes could easily be replaced, and she didn't care what anyone thought of her fashion sense. Especially now, when she was just another body in the herd that moved inexorably toward the door of the huge jet.

A smiling flight attendant welcomed her aboard.

The smile Jillian gave her in return contained little in the way of genuine warmth. She wasn't the least bit thrilled to be embarking on her honeymoon without a husband.

Why am I doing this?

Her sister had insisted she owed it to herself to enjoy the trip, if only to spite Seth Nolan for practically jilting her at the altar. "It wasn't your fault, Jillian," Nicola had said. "He led you on. You deserve better than him."

"Do I?" Jillian asked. What was that old saying? Something about not getting what you deserve but deserving what you get? Or was it the other way around? "Even after being stupid enough to believe he would actually go through with a wedding?" Jillian didn't think that belief was quite enough to recommend her for greater things.

"Even then," Nicola replied. "You're my big sister, and I love you. I want you to be happy."

Jillian smiled to herself, this time with genuine warmth and affection. Nicola was such a sweet girl. If anyone deserved happiness, she did.

Following the directions from the flight attendants, she made her way past the first class section and all those lovely alcove-like seats that could actually be made into beds. Jillian's last-minute request for an upgrade had been turned down, and she proceeded on through the belly of the 747 to the economy section. Reaching her assigned seat in the center row, she noted that someone was already seated at the opposite end.

Seth's seat.

When she and Seth had first booked the flight, the booking agency had said they wouldn't get to choose their seats, but that families would be seated together whenever possible. Seth probably would have been placed on the aisle so he wouldn't rub shoulders with another woman during the night. Perhaps this woman wouldn't have even been on the plane if he hadn't backed out.

Having canceled so late, he wouldn't get a refund for that seat, which gave Jillian some satisfaction, even if she would be the one footing the entire bill for the hotel.

"Think of it, Jill," he'd said. "Three weeks to explore Britain—London, Liverpool, the Cornish coast, Dover—anyplace we want to go."

Now she was doing it alone, with no desire to see anything.

That wasn't entirely true. She at least wanted to see Stonehenge. No doubt all of Britain would seem fascinating and enjoyable once she arrived. Everyone assured her this trip would be good for her, the perfect therapy for a broken heart. The idea had seemed plausible, if only in theory. At the moment, she wasn't so sure.

However, when her gaze met the smiling face of the older woman seated on the aisle, she revised her opinion.

This might not be so bad after all.

The woman was obviously Indian, right down to her dark brown eyes, chignon hairstyle, and deep purple sari. The satiny folds surrounded her like rippling water, giving her an air of serenity. Simply looking at her calmed Jillian's nerves.

Jillian removed the allotted pillow and blanket from her seat and sat down with a sigh. Already she felt closed in, trapped by the high seat back in front of her. Bile rose in her throat, and she took several deep breaths to force it back down.

"They don't give us much room on these planes, do they?" the woman asked with an accent as native as her style of dress.

"No, they don't." Jillian forced out a laugh. "We'll probably feel like old pals by the time we get to London."

"Then we should introduce ourselves now. My name is Kavya."

"I'm Jillian. Nice to meet you, Kavya. I hope my fidgeting doesn't drive you crazy. I'm not used to sitting still for so long."

"Nor am I. I try to think of other more pleasant things. It helps sometimes."

Jillian knew that to be true. Unfortunately, finding a pleasant thought had been difficult for the past few days.

She should have known Seth would get cold feet. Anyone who'd resisted marriage for as long as he had was bound to be the type to call the whole thing off two days before the wedding.

Seth... It would have been different if she hadn't loved him so much. She couldn't even find it in her heart to hate him for breaking up with her the way he had—only a phone call saying he couldn't go through with the wedding and wouldn't be coming home.

Sleep had been elusive since then. Unaccustomed to sleeping alone, she kept turning over expecting to touch him while he slept, only to find nothing beside her but empty space.

As more passengers boarded, two women took their places to Jillian's left in the four-seat row. She thought it odd that none of them were men.

Then again, perhaps seats were assigned according to gender on overnight flights. She had no idea. She was only thankful not to be seated next to a strange man during what would most likely be a futile attempt to sleep. She reminded herself that if this trip had gone as planned, she would've been sitting next to a very *familiar* man, one on whose shoulder she could've rested her head, perhaps even sharing a goodnight kiss.

Closing her eyes, she was vaguely aware when Kavya shifted slightly in her seat. Perhaps she was as uncomfortable as Jillian.

"First trip to London?"

Jillian glanced up as the woman on her left spoke.

Middle-aged and plump with curly, dark red hair, she held out a hand. "The name's Anna. Figured we ought to get to know one another."

Anna's firm handshake seemed incongruous somehow. Given the woman's appearance, she'd expected a softer grip.

Jillian introduced herself and Kavya before adding, "Yes, this will be my first trip."

"My third," Anna said. "It's a long flight, but definitely worth it. Kate and I adore walking in the Pennines."

Jillian darted a questioning glance at the woman seated next to Anna, a long, loose-limbed woman with short blond hair wearing capris and a sleeveless blouse that displayed her muscular arms.

"Oh, no," Anna said with a chuckle. "Kate's a miniature schnauzer." Whipping out her smart phone, she tapped the screen and aimed it at Jillian. "Placed sixth at Westminster three years ago."

A gray dog with perky ears and fluffy white whiskers stared

back at her from the phone. "Very cute." She paused, frowning. "Where is she?"

"Cargo hold," Anna replied. "Rules, you know."

Jillian wasn't much of a dog enthusiast, but a cage in the hold seemed like cruel and unusual punishment for any animal. "How awful."

"Kate doesn't seem to mind, and they take good care of the dogs. Never had a problem." Anna flapped a casual hand. "Great traveler. Very well-behaved and more easygoing than most schnauzers. Was a breeze to train."

"You're a trainer then?"

"Trainer, handler, groomer, breeder... I do it all." As quickly as she'd retrieved her phone, Anna held out a business card. "If you're in the market for a pup, I'll be breeding Kate in the fall."

Jillian scanned the card, which identified her new acquaintance as Anna Lyles, breeder of champion miniature schnauzers, located in Syracuse, New York. "Not in the market. Sorry."

Anna shrugged. "Hang onto the card. You never know..."

Jillian was pretty sure she would never need a dog, especially one that would probably be priced in the thousands. No wonder Anna could afford multiple visits to England.

The woman at the end of the row leaned forward. "Got any more of those cards?" she asked with an accent that was decidedly British.

"Absolutely." Anna produced another one so quickly Jillian wondered if she moonlighted as a magician.

"Thanks." The blonde took the card and introduced herself as Shanda.

"Pleasure to meet you," Anna said, then repeated the name as though something about it—or the woman herself—struck her as familiar. "Wait...you're Shanda Smythe, aren't you? The champion swimmer?"

That explains the arms.

"*Former* champion swimmer," Shanda said. "Retired from competition. Been living in the States for several years now. I'm surprised you recognized me."

"I'm something of an Anglophile," Anna said with a shrug. "I follow all sorts of British sports. Soccer, rugby, cricket. I seem to recall reading something about—"

Shanda cleared her throat. "Yes, well, I'm in the process of moving back home. Might need a dog to keep me company."

The way Shanda cut off Anna's recollection made it fairly obvious that whatever Anna had read was something Shanda didn't care to discuss.

Apparently Anna got the message. Without missing a beat, she resumed her sales pitch. "My schnauzers are great companion dogs. More like a member of the family than a pet."

Jillian's attention drifted. She and Seth had never had any pets during the five years they'd lived together, which was probably for the best. Dividing up furniture was easy compared to a custody battle over a dog or a cat.

At least we were spared that.

The hours ahead seemed interminable. That speech pilots always gave to the passengers was such a joke. *Enjoy the flight?* She'd never been on a flight yet that she actually enjoyed. Endured perhaps, but never enjoyed.

The safety instructions speech was already under way. Jillian barely heeded it except that it meant they might be taking off soon. Emergency exits. Life jackets under the seats. Oxygen masks. Place the mask over your nose and mouth and breathe normally.

Yeah, right.

An upward glance revealed that she didn't even have her own reading light or air flow control. The air was stuffy, almost unbearably so. She could only hope it would improve after takeoff.

Following a difficult swallow, she inhaled deeply. *I'm not afraid. I'm just... I don't know.* Perhaps it was because everyone else on board had reasons for taking the flight. She had lost hers.

Why am I here? I should've stayed home.

A moment of panic struck her. If she got up now, she could get off the plane. Again, she could stay in Newark. No one would ever know the difference until she returned home without any pictures of London to show her family or the crew at the bank. With no one there to remind her why taking this trip was such a wonderful idea, all the encouragement she'd received was fading fast. Was she the only one on the entire plane who was unhappy?

A baby crying across the aisle answered her question.

Too late. The plane was already moving, taxiing down the runway, picking up speed. The sky outside was dark. She couldn't even see a window, yet she knew it was true. The roar increased, the acceleration pushing her back against her seat. The nose of the huge plane rose into the air.

These things are too damned big to fly. How many passengers? Hundreds, surely.

She clutched the pillow and blanket to her chest like a frightened child, squeezing her eyes shut. The baby wasn't crying anymore—probably too stunned by the strange sensations to make a sound.

The air cooled as the plane gained altitude and speed. Blissful, cooling air. She swallowed around a strange lump in her throat.

I'm okay... I'm okay.

Opening her eyes, she stared at the seat back in front of her where a TV screen showed their location. She could watch a movie at some point—something engrossing and thrilling enough to provide some distraction. Would she be able to hear over the deafening engines? Anna still appeared to be chatting with Shanda, but Jillian could barely even hear her own thoughts, let alone a word of their conversation.

As the jet leveled off, she took stock of the contents of the pocket in front of her. Magazines filled with ridiculously expensive items that no one sitting in the economy section could possibly afford. A tiny bag with a set of ear buds. A large, stiff card printed with the safety instructions. She saw nothing of interest but forced herself to focus her attention on everything she found—anything to pass the time.

After she'd flipped through every magazine and knew everything there was to know about what to do in an emergency, she checked her watch. She'd actually killed an hour.

Only six or seven more to go.

Flying east into the sunrise might shorten the hours of darkness, but nothing would hurry the flight itself, except perhaps a stiff tail wind. Sitting for so long was bound to be bad for the circulation. People got blood clots in their legs on long flights, didn't they? As wedged in as she was, getting up for a stroll seemed impossible and yet sitting still was just as difficult. Her fidgeting was bound to annoy everyone around her. She was used to moving or standing. Not this endless sitting.

A glance to her right revealed Kavya holding a faded, dog-eared photograph of a man standing beside a small boy.

Not quite as high-tech as a camera phone—or as crisp an image—and yet she held it reverently, like some sort of talisman or her most prized possession.

Glancing up, the woman smiled and gestured with the photo. "My husband and son."

Jillian replied with a nod. "Very handsome."

"Yes, he was," Kavya said softly. "He died many years ago."

Jillian's curiosity got the better of her. "Your husband or your son?"

"My husband, Ramesh. I still miss him very much." A sigh escaped her. "My son is grown now and is even more handsome than his father."

"You've been visiting him?" Jillian prompted.

"No," she replied. "I've been to see my sister in Chicago. My son lives in London, as do I."

"You're going home then?"

Kavya nodded. "Yes. I will be glad to get home. My son has had troubles lately."

"Oh?"

"Woman troubles. He will never listen to me." She shook her head sadly. "Marriages should never be left to chance. Something so important should be planned and arranged many years in advance."

Given her own recent brush with marriage, Jillian was beginning to wonder if the Indian culture didn't have the right idea—knowing from childhood whom you would marry. She couldn't decide if there would be comfort in that or dread.

Dread, probably. On the other hand, the whole dating thing would become a non-issue. She tried to imagine high school without constantly obsessing over her attractiveness to the opposite sex.

How liberating.

"My son, Ranjiv, does not believe in the old ways. Perhaps because the marriage his father and I had planned for him was such a mistake. But he hasn't had much luck on his own." She smiled. "Thirty years old, and so very, very British."

Jillian stared at her.

I'm a complete stranger, and she's telling me this?

"That doesn't sound so bad." Then again, Seth had been so very, very American.

"Ah, but my sister's daughter already has two sons."

"And Ranjiv—am I saying that right?—he's your only child?"

"Yes, and he is very dear to me. A good son in so many ways." She tucked the picture into the silken fabric wrapped around her waist. "I must be patient."

Jillian knew all about being patient. She and Seth had been together for five years before becoming engaged, and even then, it had been more of a decision than a romantic episode.

I'd say I was patient in the extreme.

Having had the opportunity to mull it over for the past few days, she concluded that her ticking biological clock had scared Seth away. Still, being twenty-seven didn't necessarily demand immediate conception. She had several more years before it became imperative.

Truth be told, Seth was an excellent boyfriend and fiancé. He adored a good time and seldom failed to cheer her up whenever she felt down—until now. He just wasn't cut out to be a husband or a father. At least he'd realized it before it was too late.

Even so, five years was a long time to waste on a man.

Had that time truly been wasted? She wasn't sure. She loved him so much. They'd had fun, and the sex was great. Something had obviously been missing—but what?

His love, perhaps?

Not that it mattered now.

"But enough about me and my troubles," Kavya went on. "Do you have business in London, or are you on holiday?"

Jillian smiled grimly. "To be honest, this was supposed to be my honeymoon."

"Oh my. What happened?"

Despite the whole "complete stranger" thing, Jillian suddenly found herself telling Kavya things she hadn't even confided to her sister. In many ways it was cathartic, telling her story to someone so far removed from the events, similar to talking to a counselor or a shrink. Either way, she felt better afterward.

Kavya patted her hand. "Well, I am sure you will have a wonderful time in London. Perhaps I should introduce you to my son. He will, of course, accuse me of matchmaking."

Jillian grinned. "Can't help it, can you?"

Kavya chuckled. "It has become something of a habit."

Time passed. Dinner was served. Kavya asked for the pasta. Jillian followed suit, suddenly stricken with an intense abhorrence for eating any part of a chicken.

Lowering her tray table, Jillian took the tray from the flight attendant. Tiny containers of food. So uniform, so precise, so impersonal.

"I'll have the chicken," Anna said. "It smells divine."

Divine? Seriously? A dead bird could smell divine?

Jillian's brain felt like a sponge—filled with holes and air—her thoughts escaping like water through a sieve.

She hadn't shed a tear when Seth informed her of his decision not to marry. Perhaps because deep down, she had expected it. And now, thousands of feet above the Atlantic, her brain chose to go into meltdown mode.

Did they keep straightjackets on board for passengers who went nuts?

Picking up her fork, she was momentarily at a loss to explain its function.

Hours. She had to sit there for hours when another second was too much.

"You're still upset, aren't you?" Kavya's voice sounded odd, like she had already said those words before and was having to repeat them.

Jillian finally found her own voice. "I'm not sure. I feel so strange. I'm not sick. I'm—I can't explain it."

"Perhaps you just need to eat something," the older woman said. "The pasta isn't bad, although it's nothing like my own cooking." She smiled. "I've never made anything remotely Italian in my life."

And I've never made anything remotely Indian, unless you count curried rice.

She squeezed her eyes shut. Rice flavored with curry powder. That was Indian, surely. Opening her eyes again, she asked the only question she seemed capable of putting into words. "Are you a vegetarian?"

"For the most part," Kavya replied. "Although not strictly. I sometimes eat seafood or chicken—never beef, of course—but I'm simply not in the mood for chicken."

"Neither am I." At least, not *that* chicken. Anna might think it smelled divine, but Jillian thought it smelled…wrong—yet another thing she couldn't explain.

Peeling back the cover on the pasta, she inhaled the aromas of Parmesan, tomato, and basil… perhaps a touch of rosemary.

Nope. Nothing wrong with my nose.

Only her brain was messed up.

Jillian picked at her meal until someone finally took away the tray. Closing her eyes, she listened to the jet engines—the dull roar that would fill her ears for the next several hours.

She hitched in her seat, feeling more claustrophobic than ever. With nowhere else to put them except the floor, she held the blanket and pillow in her lap. She didn't need them. The cabin temperature was much too hot. Even with so many sleepless nights behind her, sleep just wasn't going to happen.

Her sidelong glance revealed Kavya sitting quietly, her eyes closed as though lost in thought, perhaps even meditating.

Wish I knew how to do that.

Somehow she didn't think this would be the best time to learn the technique.

The lights dimmed. She could still see, but the idea was obviously to get everyone to go to sleep—or at least allow them to.

The cabin temperature rose even further. Did they seriously think that being hot would make everyone drowsy? Jillian was perfectly miserable. She stuffed her blanket under the seat in front of her and picked up the emergency instructions card to use as a fan.

Time crawled by. She tried to watch a movie but could scarcely hear the words over the drone of the engines, even with ear buds. Now and then, she glanced at the people sitting around her. Every one of them appeared to be asleep. She rang her call light and asked for ice water. She had already learned that among the Brits, one had to specify ice or receive a tepid beverage.

So civilized, and yet they ignore ice. It wasn't that cold in Britain. Granted, their summers were nothing like those back home in Memphis, but the temps got up to eighty degrees or so now and then. She knew because she'd researched it.

Good thing I don't mind drinking hot tea.

But not now.

After what seemed like an eternity, the lights slowly brightened. Jillian heaved a sigh of relief as the seat belt light came on and the announcement was made regarding their approach to the British Isles. Someone handed her another tray with juice and a muffin.

Ah, yes, a continental breakfast.

Odd, on a flight to London. Or maybe it wasn't.

She had just taken a bite of the dry muffin when the plane shuddered, first rising and then falling through the air—straight down in a nose dive.

Plates and trays went flying. Screams sounded all around her. Her own tray flew up and hit her in the face. Oxygen masks deployed, but the rate of descent flung them against the ceiling rather than allowing them to dangle within reach. Overhead compartments exploded, their contents now deadly missiles. Blood splattered on the seat in front of her. She glanced at Anna, whose mouth was open in a frozen scream. Kavya clutched her chest, her eyes wide and staring in blank terror.

Were they over water or land? She had no idea. Either way, with such a steep, rapid descent, they were doomed.

I'm going to die. Right here. Right now.

Seth would read the headlines and know he'd made the right choice.

For some ungodly reason, that thought sent her off in a peal of hysterical laughter—laughing harder than she ever had in her life until tears flowed from her eyes.

She tried to lean forward and couldn't. In fact, she could barely move at all. In a crash, you were supposed to lean forward and clasp your hands behind your head. That was the "crash position" wasn't it? The best she could do was to clutch the top of her head with both hands. Not that it mattered. She was going to die anyway.

Someone shouted something about seat belts and life jackets. A flight attendant, perhaps. Due to her study of the emergency procedures card, Jillian knew precisely where her life jacket was. Not that she would ever be able to actually reach it. Not that it would make any difference.

This was no gentle glide to the surface, no floating freefall that suggested that anyone might survive. Her life didn't pass before her eyes the way everyone claimed it would when death was imminent. All she could see was the bloodstained surface above her head. The plane shuddered again, the screaming engines and screeching metal joints drowning out the cries of the passengers—or perhaps no one had enough breath left in them to scream. She certainly didn't. The air had been stripped from her lungs, as though a heavy weight on her stomach had forced her diaphragm into her throat.

She tried to think about her mother, her sister, and the sadness they and the loved ones of everyone aboard the plane would feel. Kavya's son, Ranjiv, who would never see his mother's face again, never hear her voice or feel her arms around him. So much loss. So much death.

Including my own.

The impact was so horrific it should have snapped her neck, or at the very least collapsed her spine. The crushing pressure from her seatbelt nearly cut her in half, making her heave up what little she had eaten. Seawater gushed in, quickly filling the fuselage, proving that they had indeed been flying over the ocean.

Too late. Now completely submerged, Jillian held her breath in a futile attempt to remain alive. People were dying all around her. She witnessed their death throes and tasted the blood and jet fuel mixed in with the seawater, still not quite believing she wasn't dead.

I'm okay?

For the moment, perhaps, but probably not for long.

Through the eerie underwater silence a voice that was strangely calm amid the chaos spoke to her. *"Unbuckle your seatbelt, Jillian. You're going to make it."*

With barely enough light to see, she turned toward Kavya. Her eyes were open and staring, but were now completely lifeless.

"Tell my son I love him. Now, go."

Chapter 2

IN AN INSTANT, THE PRESSURE IN JILLIAN'S MIND RELEASED AND HER consciousness expanded, stretching out to encompass the doomed jet and everyone around her.

Was she dying?

Was this what it felt like to die?

She had always wondered. But even as she pondered that issue, her sponge-like mind sucked in a cacophony of voices. The admonitions were all the same.

"Do it!"

Without another thought, she fumbled for the seatbelt latch and lifted the release. A huge bubble of air welled up from beneath her, shoving her upward through the tangled wreckage and into the open sea. Lungs nearly bursting, she held her breath.

She wasn't dead yet, but how far beneath the surface was she?

"Watch the bubbles." The compelling voice seemed to come straight from the sea, but that was impossible, wasn't it? Even if someone was right there beside her, they wouldn't be able to speak underwater—at least, not in a way she could understand.

As if following the command on their own, her eyes opened. No one swam beside her in the ocean's depths. She was more alone than she had ever been in her life. Even so, within moments, she had oriented herself and knew which way was up. Looking upward, she was again gripped with fear and the utter futility of trying to save herself.

She had never learned to swim; she sank like a stone anytime she'd tried it. Without a life jacket, she would reach the surface only to be sucked back into the sea to drown.

"No, you won't."

Jillian wanted to tell that strange voice in her head to shut up, but it was the same one that had told her to watch the bubbles. So far, its advice had been good.

Spreading her arms, she began the swim toward the shimmering light directly above her. She didn't need that voice now. The ability was there, waiting for her to use it.

Her head broke through the surface. She spent the next several moments gulping in fresh air, clearing her body of the carbon dioxide that threatened to kill her. Her teeth chattered with the mind-numbing cold, and her breath came in shivering gasps, but the sea itself didn't frighten her. Her arms and legs seemed to know what to do. Her legs pedaled beneath her; her arms stroked through the water and down. The choppy waves weren't making her scream in terror as they normally would.

She turned and saw land. But was it Ireland or England? Had they crashed into the Irish Sea or the North Atlantic?

Brightly painted boats were already heading toward the crash site. *Thank God.* As cold as she was, she wasn't sure how much longer she could remain afloat.

"Keep moving."

She spun around again as two heads bobbed to the surface, gasping for breath. Two women—neither of whom could possibly have been the one to tell her to keep moving—both of them, surprisingly, wearing life jackets.

Bits of wreckage followed. Other people. Other *dead* people— or at least not conscious enough to hold their heads above the water. Jillian swam toward them and discovered that her original assessment was correct. No others alive that she could see. The shock of staring into mangled faces and lifeless eyes kept her from searching further.

A yelp sounded behind her, followed closely by a shout that seemed to come from inside her own mind. A different voice this time, not the same as the one giving her swimming instructions.

"Oh, God, it's Kate! You have to save her!"

Turning again, she spotted a cage bobbing in the water with something underneath it buoyant enough to hold it partially above the surface. *A life jacket.* Someone had at least had the presence of mind to inflate one of them. She swam toward the cage, cutting a swath through the water. The power and sureness in her arms astonished her.

"Katie!" she gasped. "You poor baby."

The schnauzer yelped again as the cage tumbled. The door was now underwater and the life jacket threatened to slide out from under it. Looping an arm through the life jacket, Jillian righted the cage and opened the door. The dog swam out, somehow leaping onto the arm Jillian had hooked over the float. The dog clung there, shivering, as the cage sank beneath the waves.

Could she hold on until one of the boats arrived? Already her limbs were growing heavy as the paralyzing cold sapped her strength, stiffening her muscles. The voices in her head couldn't save her now; only a boat or some floating bit of wreckage—anything to get her out of the water—could do that.

Other buoyant items had begun to emerge from the depths. Odd things like empty water bottles with the caps on them and sealed packages of pretzels. She saw nothing large enough to climb onto or even help keep her afloat. If it hadn't been for the horrific nature of the scenario, she might have laughed.

The crest of a large wave slapped her in the face. Jillian's arm slipped on the life jacket, sending her plunging beneath the surface. The dog scrambled to maintain her tenuous perch, her toenails clawing Jillian's arm. Tugging the float closer, she held it in the crook of her arm, frantically trying to get a better grip. Putting it on wasn't an option; both she and the dog would undoubtedly drown during the attempt. Her hand touched one of the ties. She clutched it in her stiff fingers, kicking her feet in a futile attempt to keep her head above the water.

A suitcase popped up a few yards away. One of the other women grabbed it and shouted something.

Moments later, a sort of balloon exploded from the case, quickly inflating to become a raft. With a cry of relief, Jillian began swimming toward it. The distance was short, but the icy water dragging at her legs and arms made it seem much farther.

Searing pain knifed through her side as she swam, her throat raw from saltwater and jet fuel. Nearing the exhaustion point, she was about to give up when a scene from *Titanic* flashed through her mind—dead people in life jackets drifting silently on a flat calm sea. Those people hadn't drowned. They had frozen to death. While these waters probably weren't as frigid, even in late May, the temperature was still shockingly cold. The admonition to "keep moving" had definitely been sound advice. With one last, desperate surge, she grabbed the hand-hold on the outer edge of the raft and shoved the dog up over the side. Then, with every ounce of her remaining strength, she heaved herself onto the raft.

For a long moment, all sounds ceased, save for the cries of seagulls and waves lapping against the raft. Even the dog was silent.

Hoarse cries roused her as two pairs of hands reached up from the water. With fingers still chilled and stiff, Jillian hauled them in, one after the other, each woman collapsing in a heaving, sodden heap once she was aboard.

No one else swam toward the raft. Nothing moved—at least, not with any sort of purpose. Only a fishing boat with a blue and white hull cruising toward them at what was probably its top speed, its flags snapping in the morning breeze. Another boat, a red one, came from the opposite direction.

Her fellow survivors were both relatively young women—one apparently another passenger, the other a flight attendant—each of them wearing the same stunned, incredulous expression that Jillian's own face undoubtedly displayed. Jillian had never seen either of them before and could only assume they had been in different sections of the plane.

The flight attendant was the first to speak. "Are you two okay?"

Jillian nodded, as did the other passenger. "I think so."

Twisting sideways, the attendant gazed out over the side of the raft at the sea. "I don't see anyone else. Do you?"

"No, I don't." Jillian's heart seemed to sink, just as the plane had done. All those people. Gone…

The attendant slumped back down into the raft, expelling a ragged breath. "That was no accident."

Jillian stared at her, waiting for her to explain. A long moment passed without another word being spoken. "How could you possibly know that?" Astonishingly, her voice sounded normal, as though she had survived a dozen crashes without a scratch.

A fit of coughing delayed the woman's response for several moments. She blinked, pushing back a lock of dark red hair cut in what would have been a perfectly straight bob when dry. "Planes don't nose dive like that unless someone does it deliberately. They tumble or glide down. The engines didn't cut out. That dive was under power."

Jillian frowned. "Are you saying a terrorist did it?"

"Either that or a suicidal pilot." She bit her lip as though stopping herself from saying more. She glanced toward the approaching boat. "Looks like we're saved."

"Thank God." The other woman shuddered. "I feel so strange. Like I'm—I'm not sure what I feel. Just…strange."

"Yeah. I know the feeling," Jillian said. "Like you'll never be the same again." She paused, shivering. "Or ever feel warm again." *Or safe.* Wiping a hand over her face, she looked down at the dog sitting by her feet. Her *bare* feet. Her pricy honeymoon sandals were already well on their way to the ocean floor.

The little dog fixed her with an expectant gaze, moving closer as Jillian held out a hand, her whole body quivering as Jillian stroked her head.

Jillian had never cared for dogs. The smell of dog breath and dog feces made her physically ill. Yappy lapdogs irritated her beyond belief, and big dogs frightened her. And yet, this tiny creature looked at her as though seeing something Jillian wasn't even aware of herself. For the first time in her life, she understood why so many people loved their dogs.

"You're a good girl, Katie," she said. "I'm so sorry your friend Anna didn't make it."

The other passenger—a small, dark-haired woman—gasped. "You mean that isn't your dog?"

Jillian shook her head. "I was seated next to her owner. She showed me the dog's picture."

"But I watched you rescue her. You even called her by name."

The woman's tone was simultaneously disbelieving and accusatory.

Jillian wondered why it mattered. Perhaps focusing on minutiae was the woman's way of distancing herself from the shock. "Did I? I guess Anna must've told me her name."

"Seems strange, though. I mean, the way she's *looking* at you..."

"That's only because I'm the one who saved her."

Jillian was hesitant to say more, especially about the voices in her head that told her how to swim and when to unbuckle her safety belt. And a third voice that had informed her unequivocally that this dog was Anna's cherished pet. She gestured toward the water, hoping to divert the conversation to a topic that was less...surreal.

"See anyone else out there?" Although that question had already been asked, it was bound to be first and foremost in each of their minds. Jillian still couldn't quite grasp the absolute finality of so many deaths, so many violent, needless deaths...

The other passenger shook her head. "Three women survived and none of the men. How...peculiar."

"It's *all* peculiar," the flight attendant said.

Recalling her comment about the crash being deliberate, Jillian stared at the woman, noting that her name pin was still firmly attached to her sodden shirt. "Susan," she read aloud. She waved a hand that seemed suddenly weak—a hand that had somehow helped her rise up from the depths of the sea when normally she couldn't swim a stroke. "Nice to meet you. My name is Jillian."

The absurdity of making introductions at such a time was overridden by Jillian's need for normalcy. Some shred of culture or politeness demanded it, if only as a means of reestablishing some semblance of order to this one tiny corner of a chaotic universe.

"I'm Cleona," the other woman said. "I can't believe we're alive. Just can't believe it."

Jillian directed her gaze toward the fishing boat that was now less than fifty yards away. "Yeah. We crashed into the ocean with several boats right here to pick us up. A raft popped up, just when we needed it. If I didn't know better, I'd say this was—" She stopped, unwilling to say the words aloud.

"Go ahead and say it." Susan's voice had seemed harsh before, but was now almost childlike in its softness. "It was a miracle."

Cleona frowned. "But don't miracles happen for a reason?"

"Not sure this counts as a miracle," Jillian said slowly. "At least not to anyone else on that plane." Her heart sank as she realized that the baby she'd heard crying had drowned along with the rest. Entire families must have perished. And yet, here they were, the three of them—four, counting the dog—drifting on a raft, their rescuers already approaching mere minutes after disaster struck.

When the blue and white boat reached them, a man with a grizzled gray beard tossed a rope to Jillian. "Make that fast to the handle, there, miss," he said. "We saw the plane coming down. Nearly swamped the boat when it hit."

Her fumbling fingers somehow managed to accomplish the task before a younger man with tanned skin, dark brown curls, and eyes that appeared to be in a permanent squint climbed onto the raft.

"A blonde, a brunette, and a ginger," he said with a touch of awe. "What are the odds?"

His brogue marked him as an Irishman. His sense of humor…well, Jillian wasn't sure about that. Perhaps the time had come for hysterical giggles, the overwhelming and inevitable result of realizing that they were, indeed, still alive.

No. Not yet. Maybe never.

He held out a hand to Susan. "Seamus Quinn at your service. Always been partial to ginger hair." He even winked at her. "Fierce women, gingers are."

Susan aimed a scathing glance at her rescuer, but the softness of her tone took the sting from her words. "You've obviously been kissing the Blarney Stone."

Grinning, he shot her another wink. "I wouldn't say that. In fact, don't believe I ever have. That's for the tourists."

How could anyone be so flippant and cheerful in the wake of such a catastrophe? His attitude seemed callous, uncaring, and blatantly inappropriate.

"Do not judge him too harshly," a woman's calm voice said. *"He is only trying to help you forget the horror."*

Jillian twisted around so quickly, the raft dipped, nearly sending her back into the sea. That voice hadn't come from anyone on the raft, and it certainly didn't sound Irish. Was there another survivor?

She stared out at the ocean, shading her eyes against the glare from the rising sun. Nothing but a few bits of flotsam and another fishing boat on approach. Somehow, she thought this first boat would be able to handle three additional passengers without sinking. The young couple who must have hired the boat for the day clung to the rail, clearly at a loss for words.

Only three... There would be no other survivors. Too much time had passed for anyone to hold their breath long enough to escape the wreck and swim to the surface. No waving arms or desperate shouts, and the voice that had spoken to her had been calm in its admonishment, almost motherly.

She did her best to suppress the notion that the voice had been Kavya's. That was impossible.

Unless she was being haunted—or had gone insane.

Insanity was understandable. No one could survive such a crash without losing at least a few of their marbles.

"D'you see anyone, miss?"

Jillian glanced up at the elder fisherman. His eyes reflected her own shock and concern as the breeze sifted through his graying hair. "I thought I heard something... But, no. I don't see anyone."

Would bodies wash up on the shore? She turned toward the land. The way the sea crashed against the Cliffs of Moher, there wouldn't be much left of any people that might end up there, alive or dead. *Nice treat for the tourists.* She could see O'Brien's Tower from where she sat.

How the hell did I know that?

Someone must have suggested that she and Seth visit Ireland during their honeymoon and given her a few details or showed her some pictures.

She stared at the cliffs. Despite the early hour, a number of people were gathered at the edge. They must have gotten quite a show when the plane came down—or peed their pants thinking it would hit them.

The other man, Seamus, was already helping Susan onto the boat. The *Branwyn Eostre* rocked with the waves as he fussed over Susan, first finding her a place to sit near the bow, then stripping off his sweater and wrapping it around her shoulders.

So gallant. So sweet. Jillian couldn't find fault with him anymore. The voice, whoever it belonged to, had been correct. He was doing his best to keep them from falling apart.

And God knows we have every right to do that.

The surprising thing was that she hadn't. None of them had. Perhaps that would come later, a delayed reaction in the wake of the disaster.

Katie nudged her hand as Seamus stepped back onto the raft and eased toward her.

Jillian shook her head. "Get Cleona first. Katie and I can wait."

Katie. Anna had called the dog Kate, but Jillian couldn't quite go there. It seemed too short a name for some reason, too abrupt, and not nearly as friendly as Katie. After the initial shout, she'd been calling her Katie—had said it aloud twice now—and thought of her as such. Had she already renamed the dog? Did that mean she'd claimed her? She gazed into Katie's deep brown eyes and something clicked.

Yes, she *had* claimed the dog. That is, if Anna had no next of kin who wanted her.

Somewhere in the back of her mind, a deep sigh sounded, swelling in volume before fading slowly into silence.

Tears stung her eyes as she felt a tiny twinge near her temple. Anna's other dogs were breeding stock. This one was special and needed to be loved.

I can do that.

With a gesture completely foreign and yet at the same time as natural as breathing, she swept her right hand toward her left shoulder. Katie immediately jumped onto her lap, licking her face in a manner that could only be described as relieved.

The raft dipped as Seamus helped Cleona onto the boat. "Ian," he called out to his crewmate, "we'd best use a net to get the wee dog aboard."

Gathering Katie in her arms, Jillian rolled onto her knees and watched as the two men created a makeshift sling out of fishing net hooked onto a rope. She gave the dog a quick hug before placing her in the sling. Seamus fastened the net securely, and Ian lifted her onto the deck.

"Your turn, miss," Seamus said.

Jillian grasped the rope and pulled herself upright, stepping from the raft onto the gunwale with minimal assistance and, surprisingly, no fear whatsoever.

"The *Branwyn Eostre*," she muttered as she reached the deck. "I suppose the name has some significance?"

"Aye, she's named for two goddesses," Ian replied. "Branwyn, the goddess of love, sexuality, and the sea, and Eostre, the goddess of spring, rebirth, fertility, and new beginnings."

"You say that like you've said it before."

"Many times, miss," he said. "Many times."

"New beginnings," she mused. *Or endings.* "Seems appropriate somehow."

She glanced at Cleona. The morning sun shone down on the deck, but the breeze was lively enough that the poor girl was still shaking like a leaf. With eyes that were wide with shock, Cleona didn't seem to be bouncing back quite as quickly as Jillian and Susan had. Then again, if she'd had a similar mind-melding experience, her reaction was understandable. Jillian opted against discussing the possibility. It was bad enough that *she* thought she'd gone nuts. She didn't need anyone else thinking it.

"Don't suppose you have any blankets, do you?" she asked.

"Oh, aye," Seamus said. "Got a couple of macs, in any case. They'll cut the wind."

As he hurried off, Jillian suspected Susan's presence might have something to do with the fact that he hadn't already gone in search of a coat for Cleona. If his behavior had only been a display of Irish charm, he would have been equally attentive to everyone.

Katie barked admonishments at him as he disappeared into the tiny cabin in the center of the boat as though she too wanted a coat.

"The nearest airport is at Inisheer in the Aran Islands," Ian said.

"From there they can fly you to Connemara and then on to wherever ye were bound."

"Fly?" Cleona's shivers increased visibly. "Not sure I ever want to fly again."

"'Tis a small plane," Ian said gently. "Not like the one that went down with ye."

As if that made a difference. It was still a plane. Although probably not, as Susan had suggested, with a suicidal pilot.

"What about Shannon?" Cleona asked. "That's where I was supposed to end up, but probably not for a few hours." Lifting her hand, she gaped at her watch. "I can't believe it still works."

"Mine too," Jillian said. "Probably the only battery-operated device that would work after a dip in the sea." Her thoughts touched briefly on the amount of data she'd lost along with her phone, a thought that was dismissed as quickly as it came. Unlike lives, cell phones and computers could be replaced.

The horror descended upon her once again. How were people supposed to behave after such a calamity? What kinds of conversations were appropriate? Her sister had been in a car accident while driving back to college late one night. A dozing trucker had clipped her fender, sending her car spinning out across the median where it was hit by another truck coming from the opposite direction. Her belongings had been scattered all over the highway and the car was a total loss, but Nicola and her pet bird had survived without a scratch. Afterward, she and the other driver had hugged each other and joked that they should celebrate by getting married.

When she first heard the story, Jillian had deemed it preposterous. But then, she hadn't been there, hadn't experienced the incredible surge of emotions that demanded some sort of release...

And in that particular instance, no one had died.

She'd seen fire and tornado victims on the news, sobbing in each other's arms, unable to comprehend or even speak of the enormous losses they'd suffered. This was different. There was no wreckage to explore, no personal belongings to find. Looking out to sea, she saw the other fishing boat, its crew engaged in the grisly task of pulling bodies from the water. Divers might be sent down eventually, but for the moment, only those things that had floated to the surface could be recovered.

Jillian had lost nothing of importance in the crash, and certainly no loved ones. How was she supposed to react to actually surviving?

Leaning forward, she stroked Katie's fuzzy gray head. Why had she never appreciated dogs before? Interacting with Katie was simple and soothing, requiring very little thought. She asked no difficult questions, expected no answers, and didn't judge whether a behavior was appropriate. Nor did she demand any explanations as to why her new master could hear the voices of the dead.

Seamus returned with three blankets and wrapped each of the ladies in turn, only then donning his sweater again, depriving them of the only shirtless Irish hunk they were likely to see for quite a while. As if that mattered. Given Jillian's recent jilting—*did I really just think that?*—she doubted hunky man candy would interest her for years to come. She waited a moment for one of her new "voices" to disagree. Save for a muted tsk that probably came from her own mind, they remained silent. Perhaps the insanity had only been momentary.

"We were supposed to land at Heathrow," Susan said to Seamus. "Where's your home port?"

"Round the Hag's Head point and further up the coast at Liscannor." Seamus nodded toward their two original passengers who remained near the stern, still seeming too timid to approach. "We came out early so they could see the sunrise over the cliffs. We were on our way back when your plane crashed."

He said the words so plainly, without any hesitation or hushed tones, almost as if he'd said "landed" rather than "crashed."

Big difference.

"Air traffic control already knows we went down," Susan said. "They'll have alerted the authorities. Better take us to Inisheer since it's the closest terminal. We'll have to have medical exams—they may even insist we spend the night in a hospital—and I'm sure there'll be questions."

Susan seemed to have her shit together and obviously knew more about airline procedures than anyone present. She could decide where they should go and what they should do. Content to follow someone else's lead for now, Jillian closed her mind to the discussion, not caring how much time it took as long as she eventually made it to London.

She had a message to deliver.

Chapter 3

FROM THE MOMENT RANJIV TENALI PARKED HIS RANGE ROVER AT Heathrow, he knew something was wrong. As a reporter for *The London Times*, he'd been to the airport enough to have a feel for the place, and right now, the atmosphere was tense.

Security was always tight, but he couldn't recall ever seeing airport officials posted outside the doors to the baggage claim area, stopping people as they attempted to enter the building. Since they appeared to be allowing everyone to pass on through after speaking with them, he doubted any bomb threats had been made. He could see no damage to any of the buildings, which made an explosion unlikely. Therefore, the problem must have been with one or more of the planes.

Checking his phone messages, he found an update he'd missed. *Oceanus Airlines Flight 2324. Terminal One. Delayed.*

A babble of voices caught his attention. Several people were gathered on the steps around a man holding up a mobile phone that displayed flashing images. Ranjiv's eyes widened in horror as shocked gasps issued from every mouth. His heart skittered and fell, taking his lungs with it.

"It's trending on Twitter," the man said. "It'll be on Facebook next—if it isn't already."

Oh, no.

Ranjiv strode past the group and headed for the nearest security guard. "I am here to meet a passenger arriving from the United States. Can you tell me what is happening?"

"What flight was the passenger on?"

"Oceanus 2324," Ranjiv replied.

As the guard opened the door, Ranjiv experienced one brief

moment of hope, which evaporated when he was handed over to another airport employee waiting inside. "Sir, if you will please accompany this gentleman to the conference room."

Their somber expressions didn't bode well. "What's this all about?" Ranjiv asked as the man led him to a room near the baggage claim area.

"Please, sir, if you'll just have a seat in here, they'll be making an announcement in a few minutes."

As Ranjiv stepped inside, dozens of anxious, dread-filled faces met his gaze, many sobbing as though they had already received bad news—or expected the worst. Two men stood behind a podium at the far end of the stuffy, overcrowded room. Ten long, gut-churning minutes passed before one man asked for quiet while the other looked as though he would rather be anywhere else, doing anything but this.

The spokesman was tall, pale, blond, and perspiring. Mopping his brow, he cleared his throat and leaned closer to the microphone. "Ladies and gentlemen, we deeply regret to inform you that Oceanus Airlines Flight 2324 from Newark to London crashed into the North Atlantic off the coast of Ireland approximately ninety minutes ago. The cause of the crash is currently unknown. We had no notification from the aircraft of any malfunctions. The last radio contact with the aircraft was from the pilot, reporting an on-time approach.

"The crash is already under investigation, and we are in the process of contacting the next of kin of all of those on board. Both of those tasks, you must understand, will take a considerable amount of time. However, airline policy directs us to first make this announcement to those of you who are waiting here at Heathrow.

"The plane sank upon impact, but the crew of the Irish fishing vessel *Branwyn Eostre* has reported having picked up three female survivors."

The crowd began clamoring for the names. Ranjiv didn't bother adding his voice to the din. His mother was not young, nor was she in perfect health. Her survival wasn't even a remote possibility, and yet he waited to hear the words, trying to stay calm, trying to stay sane.

The spokesman held up a hand for silence. "Several other boats are continuing to search the area, and although a number of bodies have been recovered, they are as yet unidentified. There have been no reports of any additional survivors." He glanced down at a piece of paper as he continued. "The three survivors are Jillian Dulaine, Susan Maxwell, and Cleona Mahoney." His gaze swept the room. "Were any of you waiting for them?"

Silence fell. No sighs of relief, no groans of despair—not one single sound. Everyone had been holding their breath, hoping to hear a different name. Everyone, including Ranjiv. Tears slid down his cheeks as he closed his eyes, a death knell pounding in his head.

My mother is dead... My kind, gentle, beloved mother is dead...

The spokesman sighed as though he'd expected the lack of response. Ranjiv's eyes flew open as he continued.

"Ms. Mahoney was booked aboard a connecting flight to Shannon, and Ms. Maxwell is an airline employee." He hesitated. "London was Ms. Dulaine's final destination, and she has asked if there is anyone waiting here for," he consulted his paper again, "Anna Lyles, Shanda Smythe, or Kavya Tenali."

Again. Silence.

Ranjiv's racing heart slowed to a dull thud as he raised a hand. "I am Kavya Tenali's son."

The spokesman swallowed, his prominent larynx sliding up and down so sharply it was a wonder it didn't slit his own throat. "Ms. Dulaine would like to meet with you at your earliest convenience. She and the other survivors appear to be unhurt, but they will each undergo a thorough medical examination and be kept for observation until tomorrow morning at the very least. Barring any further complications, Ms. Dulaine should be arriving in London tomorrow afternoon. Do we have your permission to give her your contact information?"

Sweat trickled down Ranjiv's spine. "Did she say why she wanted to meet with me?"

The spokesman's expression became even more tragic, his voice hushed. "It is my understanding that she was seated next to Mrs. Tenali. The other two women I spoke of were seated in the same row with them."

The last person to see his mother alive… "Yes…yes, of course, you have my permission."

Tomorrow afternoon.

He'd already taken the day off to spend time with his mother upon her return. Clearly he would be allotted several more. Time to mourn her loss instead of rejoicing in her return.

The spokesman nodded. "Very well. The airline will keep you all informed of any new developments. To that end, we ask that you remain here until we have verified that we have your correct information."

The likelihood of any "new developments" was evident in both his tone and demeanor. They might recover a few more bodies, but the plane's flight recorder was at the bottom of the Atlantic. Divers might recover it eventually, but the cause of the crash might never be discovered, unless some terrorist faction claimed responsibility.

One of the spokesman's cohorts approached, a skeletally thin Asian fellow who was so small the top of his cap didn't reach Ranjiv's shoulder. "If you'll step over this way, sir, I'll verify your information."

As stunned as he was by the news, Ranjiv was surprised he could even recall his own name, let alone his address and phone number, and yet he was able to rattle them off without hesitation.

The man checked the list before handing a card to Ranjiv. "Our hotline number is printed there if you have any questions. I've also written the name of the survivor who wanted to see you on the back. We don't have a current phone number for her as yet, but she will be contacting you."

Ranjiv acknowledged the particulars with a nod and pocketed the card.

Only then did his mind go blank. His body seemed to know what to do, his feet taking him steadily toward the door, his muscles somehow recalling how to keep him upright, but beyond that…

"Sir, if you wish, we have a lounge set up for use by family members of the passengers who were lost."

Ranjiv blinked twice before realizing he hadn't moved at all.

Other people were queued up behind him and the official was looking up at him from his seat behind the tiny desk. Nodding, he muttered, "Perhaps I should."

He stepped aside as several others gave out their names and addresses. A few minutes later, he joined a small group that was escorted to the lounge. This time he was certain his feet were moving. After an expedited pass through the security checkpoint, they continued on to the executive lounge where they were told they could wait as long as necessary and avail themselves of the facilities and services, free of charge.

The first thing Ranjiv saw was a television monitor replaying a video of the crash. According to the commentator, the view of the tragedy from the Cliffs of Moher had not only been spectacular, it had been recorded by no less than thirty different cameras.

Thirty cameras that all showed the same thing: an enormous jet plane diving straight into the sea.

With shaking hands, Ranjiv poured himself a cup of tea, then found an empty chair in the corner farthest from the television and sat down heavily. He was about to call his Aunt Girisha in Chicago when he realized she would still be asleep.

Better to wait. He had no desire to disturb her slumber with such heartbreaking news. Not yet.

The delay would give him time to plan what he would say to her, although there wasn't any good way to phrase such a thing. At least his aunt had gotten to see her sister before she died.

Ranjiv had taken his mother to the airport on the day she left for America. She'd been so excited at the prospect of seeing Girisha again. With a kiss goodbye, he'd sent her on her way.

That was a month ago. Aside from his mother, Ranjiv's only family in England was his father's brother, Pratap, who lived in London with his family. The rest of his relatives were in India.

Kavya had chosen to remain in England and work in Pratap's import business after her husband's death, saying that it was his wish that Ranjiv be educated in Britain. She had sacrificed so much for him, and now he couldn't even give her a proper funeral. A memorial service, perhaps, but without a body, there could be no cremation, no scattering of her ashes—unless her body was recovered. He had no idea what sort of funeral could be held without it. Perhaps a service on the cliffs overlooking the crash site.

He reached into his pocket for his phone to call Pratap just as it rang. A glance at the caller ID was enough to convince him that his uncle had been watching the news.

Switching on the phone, he held it to his ear. "Hello, Uncle." The slip into the Telugu language was automatic, even if Ranjiv's accent was slightly British—a quirk his mother had often teased him about.

"That was Kavya's plane that crashed, wasn't it?" His uncle sounded as though he had already accepted the truth, his tone brisk to the point of terseness.

Ranjiv replied with a nod before it occurred to him that Pratap couldn't see the gesture. "Yes. Mother wasn't—" He paused as his voice cracked, then blew out a breath, doing his best to regain control of himself before continuing. "S–she wasn't among the survivors. I'm still at the airport. They've put us in a lounge for a bit to recover. To be perfectly honest, I'm not sure I can drive home just yet."

"I see… Do you want me to come there?"

Pratap was a wonderful man. Intelligent and kind, he'd been more like a father than an uncle to Ranjiv, but at the moment, familiar faces were something to avoid—unless Ranjiv wanted to break down in the middle of one of the world's busiest airports. Someone would undoubtedly take pictures that would wind up in *The London Times* or be posted on the Internet as quickly as the crash videos had been.

"No. I'll be better after I've sat for a bit. One of the survivors has asked to meet with me."

"That's odd. She asked for you in particular?"

"Not exactly. She wanted to meet with anyone connected with three of the other passengers. The spokesman said they had been seated together. Apparently Mother was the only one of those three who was being met at Heathrow by a relative. They said the woman is supposed to arrive in London tomorrow afternoon." With a mirthless laugh, he added, "Guess I'll wait here for a while and then just go on home."

Despite the early hour, he was already exhausted. Even moving from his current position seemed too much of an effort. As a reporter, Ranjiv was tireless when it came to taking notes, compiling facts, and conducting interviews. Just this once, he hoped his editor would understand his reluctance to report a breaking story. Waiting in a lounge beyond the security checkpoint enabled him to remain anonymous for a while, but a reporter would find him eventually. They always did.

"You *will* go back to speak with her, won't you?" Pratap asked.

"Of course." For curiosity's sake if nothing else.

"Good," Pratap said. "Call me if you hear any more news—and even if you don't. And Ranjiv, remember, Kavya is with God now. God and Ramesh."

Raking a hand through his hair, Ranjiv nodded. "I know. I just didn't expect to lose her so soon. She wasn't that old. I know she had a bad heart, but—"

"These things are with God."

"Yes, Uncle. You're right. I'll call you if I hear anything further."

Switching off his phone, he put it back in the pocket of his jacket. He'd dressed up a bit to meet his mother's plane. She would've commented on how nice he looked. She always did when he wore a suit. Why would today have been any different?

But it *was* different, and tomorrow he would be meeting a woman who was perhaps the next best thing to seeing his mother again. The last person to speak with her.

Seen in that light, whether he'd worn a suit and tie or a pair of ragged jeans really didn't matter. Nothing did.

Chapter 4

JILLIAN SUSPECTED THE BOAT RIDE TO INISHEER WOULD TURN OUT TO be the only respite she and her fellow survivors would receive. Ian and Seamus had provided them with warm blankets and a cup of the hottest, sweetest tea Jillian had ever tasted, soothing her soul as well as her nerves. The two men had also been tactful enough not to bombard them with questions they couldn't possibly answer.

The staff of the Inisheer hotel had been equally accommodating, allowing them to use their facilities to get cleaned up before the flight to Connemara. Jillian had taken Katie into the shower with her, scrubbing the curly-haired dog with the same shampoo she'd used on her own hair, actually laughing when Katie shook herself dry. However, despite the luxurious soap and copious amounts of hot water, Jillian still didn't feel completely clean— almost as though the contaminants in the ocean had seeped into her pores.

Or perhaps it was only the fear and horror that still clung to her like a second skin. There wasn't enough water on the entire planet to wash that away.

The local shopkeepers had donated clothing—Aran sweaters knitted from soft merino wool with skirts to match—and sensible leather shoes. Everyone had been so kind, from Seamus and Ian to the young girl at the dock who had given them each a flower and had petted Katie with unabashed enthusiasm.

The problems began in Connemara. Several reporters and photographers met their plane, snapping pictures and asking ridiculous questions. How did it feel to be alive when so many others had died? What was it like to crash into the sea? The answers were so obvious. Yes, they were happy to be alive, but very sad that so many lives were lost, and the crash was horrible. What else was there to say?

"How could anyone possibly know we would be landing here?" she whispered to Susan as they were escorted to a private office. "I can't believe the airline would tell anyone."

Susan's lips tightened into a thin line. "Seamus told me they'd radioed ahead that we would be docking at Inisheer. That information must've gotten passed on. Since the flights from Inisheer only land at this airport, it was safe to assume we would show up here eventually."

Both airports had been tiny enough that Jillian should have guessed that. Then again, her brain function hadn't been what anyone would call normal.

At least the voices were quiet now. Funny, she'd expected them to vie for control, similar to the way Paul Atreides's ancestral memories had done after they were "awakened" by the spice *melange* in Frank Herbert's *Dune*. Thus far, they seemed content to allow her to direct her own thoughts and behaviors in the more commonplace matters, only chiming in for something really important.

Nice voices.

Her scalp tightened, creating a headache that throbbed with every beat of her heart. She took a seat in the corner of the cluttered office, massaging her temples. Was the pain the result of what she was beginning to think of as a psychic phenomenon or had she sustained a concussion? She'd certainly been through enough to have acquired one.

Concussion, hell. I should be dead.

Cleona sat down in a chair in the opposite corner, still wearing the same haunted, stricken expression Jillian had seen on her face in the life raft. Jillian felt the same way, but seemed to have internalized it. At least, she thought she had. Perhaps her headache resulted from the stifling of those emotions. She glanced at Susan, who stood beside the desk. Her jaw was set, her eyes hard and determined. What was she thinking? Was this her way of coping? Or was it simply the result of her training?

Jillian reminded herself that everyone reacted to stress

differently. Some people fell apart while others rose to the occasion, performing acts of heroism as though they dealt with catastrophes on a daily basis. Susan seemed to be one of those people. Her baby-soft voice belied a firm, take-charge attitude. Hearing her talk, Jillian never would've guessed she possessed nerves of steel, whereas Cleona had required sedation to get her on the plane at Inisheer. The flight was relatively short, but it *was* over water. Jillian could've done with a Xanax or two herself, but quickly realized that holding a dog in her lap had practically the same effect.

She leaned down to stroke the dog's head while the airport officials debated whether to fly them on to Galway—which, aside from being the largest city in the county, boasted a large teaching hospital—or take them there by car.

"Oh, please," Cleona groaned. "Not another plane."

"I agree," Susan said, obviously recalling Cleona's anxiety during the previous flight. "We could do with a nice, scenic drive along the coast."

"Same here," Jillian said. "Especially since we aren't in dire need of medical attention."

Transportation was arranged with a driver called Ronan whose mini-van accommodated them comfortably while he pointed out various landmarks as though accustomed to shuttling tourists back and forth from Galway. His lilting accent was like a balm to Jillian's ears—ears that were still suffering from the hours they'd been subjected to roaring jet engines, followed by terrified screams and the screeching death throes of the disintegrating 747. True, a flight might have been faster, but traveling over dry land in a vehicle with wheels rather than jet engines was comforting.

The Irish countryside was as soothing as the voices and kindness of its people, perhaps even more so. Its rugged beauty crowded out the visions of blood and gore and death like nothing else could have done.

"You were right about the drive," Jillian told Susan as the green hills slid past them. "This is *so* much better."

Susan nodded. "I've been to Ireland several times. There's no other place like it in the world."

"Does it all look like this?" Cleona seemed genuinely interested in her surroundings—finally losing the deer-in-the-headlights expression that Jillian had begun to fear was permanent.

"The western counties are more mountainous than the east," Susan replied. "Cork and Dublin are distinctively Irish, of course, but without the open spaces you see here. The entire coastline is breathtaking."

Indeed, the sea was beautiful from this perspective—blue, sparkling, and serene—nothing like it had been while Jillian had struggled against it to survive. Nonetheless, she shifted her gaze to the green, sunlit landscape, hoping to dispel the persistent chill that seemed to originate from within. Not surprisingly, even the sunshine didn't help very much, nor did the warm dog curled up in her lap. Her hands were still icy and she was frequently gripped with uncontrollable tremors. Cleona appeared to be having the same problem. Only Susan seemed immune to the aftereffects of the crash.

"L–looks like we've b–both got the s–shakes," Cleona said after a particularly violent bout of shivers. "I can't stop my t–teeth from ch–chattering."

Susan leaned forward and tapped the driver on the shoulder. "Could you turn up the heat a little?"

"Sure thing, miss," Ronan replied.

Jillian gave Susan a grateful smile but found herself wishing for a fireplace and a blanket, along with another cup of Ian's piping hot tea. Somehow she doubted she would have the opportunity to enjoy any of those things anytime soon.

Tea, maybe. "Don't suppose we could stop at a pub somewhere, could we?"

"Oh, God, that sounds good," Cleona whispered. "A pot of hot tea and a bowl of Irish stew."

"And a Guinness—or maybe a shot of Jameson," Jillian added. "You'd think someone would've offered us that before now." She glanced at Ronan who appeared to be following the discussion. "I'm sure you know all sorts of great places along this road, don't you, Ronan?"

"That I do, miss. Were ye wantin' to get totally pissed, or just have a pint or two?"

Assuming that in this part of the world, "pissed" meant the same thing as "shit-faced," she would've preferred the former but resigned herself to the latter. "A pint would be perfect."

Susan blew out a pent-up breath. "We need to be fasting and sober for the physical exams."

Cleona looked like she was about to cry. "Did anyone actually *say* that?"

"Yes, I'm afraid they did." If anything, Susan appeared to be even more bummed about that restriction than Cleona.

"Well, damn," Jillian grumbled. "I was starting to look forward to that pint o' Guinness. Guess you'd better keep driving, Ronan. The quicker we get there, the better."

* * * *

The examinations went far better than Jillian expected. Despite some bruising where her seatbelt had practically gutted her, she was in reasonably good shape. The CT scan of her head was normal—not that she'd expected it to show the three extra voices she'd acquired—and her chest x-ray was clear. Nor did the abdominal x-rays reveal any obvious internal injuries.

The doctors were amazed they couldn't find anything significantly wrong with any of them.

"They seem almost disappointed," Susan muttered.

Jillian had carefully avoided mentioning hearing voices when she talked with the psychology resident. As time passed, she felt less insane and more as though she was a carrier of sorts. For some reason, that viewpoint seemed to help. Aside from that, she felt okay—or at least as normal as any jilted bride who'd just survived a catastrophic plane crash could possibly feel.

Nevertheless, the urgency to get to London was intensifying. Even knowing she would arrive there the next afternoon didn't help much. She was anxious and frustrated, perhaps even a bit resentful of the authorities for making her wait.

That evening, she took another shower and still didn't feel clean. Turning out the light at ten thirty and trying to get comfortable in her hospital bed was almost as pointless. She'd hardly slept a wink since Seth's Thursday evening bombshell. Somehow she doubted that this night would be any different.

What day is it anyway?

She ticked the days off on her fingers. The wedding *should* have been on Saturday. She'd left Newark on Sunday night. Therefore, it must be Monday night. Now that she was fully alert and oriented to person, place, and time, if she didn't admit to hearing voices, the shrinks would leave her be.

Ha.

They never did get their drink at the pub—not even a bowl of Irish stew—although Katie had been given all sorts of goodies. The doctors had all agreed that a liquid diet would be best to start with. They'd had clear liquids for lunch and full liquids for supper. Jillian's insistence that Guinness qualified as a liquid hadn't swayed anyone.

When the aide brought her tray the next morning—a rather bland diet instead of the full Irish breakfast she was craving—Jillian had to admit that she'd slept some, despite a recurring dream that had awakened her several times. Not a replay of the crash itself or the terrifying aftermath, but of Kavya's words to her. Over and over again.

"Tell my son I love him."

"I will, Kavya," she'd whispered in the darkness. "Tomorrow. I'll tell him tomorrow. I promise."

Cleona still couldn't face getting on another airplane, so her cousin drove in from Shannon to pick her up at the hospital. After a tearful goodbye with lots of hugs, Susan and Jillian were driven to the airport at Galway for their flight to London.

"Feels weird to be on a plane and not be working," Susan commented as they boarded the plane.

"Sure it's not just a matter of being scared shitless?"

"I'm not scared at all," Susan replied. "I mean, what are the odds of us being in two successive crashes?"

"I see your point."

Not that it helped much. Still, the first class seats were very nice—unlike the economy version on that doomed 747. Upon further reflection, Jillian had realized that in a nose-first crash, the pilots and the passengers in first class would be the first to go. She'd been seated near the wings. Susan and Cleona had claimed to have been closer to the rear of the plane. If anything could possibly explain their survival, that was probably it.

"Are you happy now, Kavya?" Jillian muttered as she buckled her seatbelt. "I'm flying to London. Should be landing at about one fifteen."

Not surprisingly, Kavya didn't respond. Katie, however, replied with a bark that made Jillian's ears ring.

What was the use of carrying another person's consciousness around if they wouldn't carry on a conversation? There should be *some* advantages—like always having someone to talk to while you were standing in line at the grocery or waiting in a doctor's office.

Realizing that such behavior could get a person committed, she abandoned that train of thought for the more real problem of finding Kavya's son.

She needn't have worried. Once the plane landed in London, the Oceanus officials bent over backward to make the process as smooth as possible. With no passport or identification and certainly nothing to declare, the women's identities were confirmed with astonishingly little hassle. Katie's microchip identified her without question. No one offered to replace Jillian's belongings, but they did provide her with a substantial sum of cash, duplicates of her credit cards and driver's license, a temporary passport, a cell phone, and a new purse that must have cost a bundle.

They also gave her Ranjiv Tenali's phone number.

Unfortunately, she didn't believe the dreams would stop in the wake of a simple phone conversation. She didn't know how she knew she had to meet with him in person. She only knew that she did. Hopefully, he wouldn't ask too many questions because the only answers she could give would sound preposterous. The only truthful answers, that is.

Promising to keep in touch, she and Susan parted after leaving Customs.

Now what?

Heathrow was even bigger than she'd expected. It was practically a city within a city, or at least the world's largest shopping mall. Jillian didn't have to check the price tags in the shops to know the merchandise was above her touch, even with all the pound notes she had stuffed in her designer handbag.

At least they'd been spared the reporters, which left Jillian to assume that the timing of this particular arrival hadn't been leaked to anyone.

Thank God.

Then again, a guide would've come in handy. Surely a reporter would've known the best places to grab a late lunch. Their departure from Galway had been too rushed to stop at a pub, and the bag of chips she'd had on the plane hadn't done much to satisfy her gnawing hunger. Not only was she starving, she had a dog with her—a dog that was probably in dire need of a potty break.

"You never complain, do you?" she asked the dog.

This time, even Katie didn't reply.

She found a bench near one of the restaurants and sat down. Would they allow dogs inside? She had no idea—no idea where to go or what to do.

With a resigned sigh, she pulled out her new cell phone—or "mobile" as the Brits called them—and dialed Ranjiv's number.

What on earth will I say to him? Hello, Ranjiv. I'm the Girl Who Lived? Would he get the Harry Potter reference or would he consider the joke in bad taste?

Just call him.

He answered on the first ring.

"Hello… Mr. Tenali?"

* * * *

Ranjiv had been holding his phone in his hand ever since the flight from Galway landed. That arrival time was the only notification he'd received since yesterday's briefing. Somehow he doubted that very many others had been given that information. Figuring she would call him from the airport, he'd taken it a step further and was standing in the center of the main concourse.

"Is this Jillian Dulaine?" He didn't need to consult the card in his pocket. Having stared at it for so long, he could've called out the name in his sleep.

"Yes. I'm still at the airport. I was wondering if I could meet you somewhere."

"That can be arranged." God, he sounded so stiff. "I mean, I'd like that very much."

"Great. I have absolutely no idea where to go in this town or even how to get out of the airport. This place is so huge, and I–I've got a dog with me. I don't know if—"

"Where are you, exactly?"

"I'm sitting near a restaurant with a picture of a giraffe on the front wall."

Ranjiv scanned the surrounding area, almost immediately spotting the giraffe, the dog, and the girl. "I see you."

"You're here?" Her voice was a high-pitched squeak. "Really?"

Her gaze swept the multitude of people milling about, stopping on him almost as though she'd known precisely who he was and what he looked like.

He hadn't moved, hadn't waved a hand, and he certainly wasn't the only Indian man in the terminal. The only clue she might've had was the phone he held to his ear.

"Yes, I'm here. Be with you in a sec."

Pocketing his phone, he walked toward the pretty blonde, not quite believing his eyes as she stood to greet him. She was slender but curvy, and though her Aran sweater and trim wool skirt marked her as Irish, her accent had been decidedly American.

Jillian Dulaine... An oddly British-sounding name for a Yank. Not knowing anything else about her, he'd expected a fellow Brit. A small gray dog sat at her feet, the picture of perfect obedience.

She held out a hand. "Thank you for coming. I'm so surprised... I had no idea you'd be here."

Taking her hand without hesitation, he found it soft, though slightly chilly. Something in her touch soothed him. "The airline told me which plane you'd be on and that you wanted to speak with me."

"Oh, I see... That was nice of them to let you know, but I'm sorry to put you to so much trouble. I could've taken a cab and met you somewhere."

"No trouble at all." Before he'd actually seen her, he'd been determined to get this meeting over with as quickly as possible. He wasn't so sure about that now. She seemed so lost, so vulnerable. "Won't you sit down?"

Nodding, she resumed her seat on the bench. "I don't know where to begin. I–I met your mother on the plane. She seemed like such a nice lady. I'm so sorry for your loss."

"Thank you. She was—" What did a man say about his mother? One who had sacrificed so much for him, raising a son in a foreign country after her husband's untimely death? "—my only family—immediate family, that is. I loved her very much." Then he remembered that many others had died. "But what about you? Were any of your family or friends aboard?"

"No need to offer me any condolences, if that's what you mean." She reached down to pet her dog. "Not like you two."

"Excuse me?"

Sliding a finger beneath the dog's chin, she lifted its muzzle to gaze into its dark, somber eyes. "Katie lost her owner in the crash. I sort of inherited her."

"I see." He didn't really. But that question could wait for another time.

"I was seated between your mother and Katie's owner. Kavya told me a little bit about you and how she'd lost her husband. She had a picture of the two of you. She was looking at it when we took off."

Ranjiv knew that photograph well. He had seen it in his mother's hand so many times, and her expression was always the same.

Love.

Longing.

Regret.

Her gaze slid from the neutral space between them to become fixed on his face. "You look like your father."

"So I've been told."

She hesitated, chewing her lip in a pensive fashion. "I'm not sure how to say this, but Kavya may have saved my life."

Of all the things Ranjiv expected her to say, this was not among them. "H–how is that possible?"

"She told me to unbuckle my seatbelt and said that I was going to make it." Pausing again, she shifted her gaze back to the dog. "How she knew that, I didn't know at the time. Anyway, I did what she told me to do, and a moment later, a huge air bubble pushed me up out of the plane. But just before that, she told me to tell you she loved you. That's why I'm here—to deliver that message."

Tears stung Ranjiv's eyes. That was so like his mother. For her last thoughts to be of him and probably his father. Pratap was right. They were together now. She was at peace.

But even as those thoughts comforted him, he blurted out a question he shouldn't have put into words. "How is it that you lived and she didn't? Why didn't you—" He stopped, biting back a sudden wave of fury. Fury at this woman for not helping his mother to survive. Fury at himself for blaming her or anyone else for his loss. This woman was no more responsible for his mother's death than he was for putting her on that plane to Chicago a month ago.

Nevertheless, if he didn't ask this particular question, it would haunt him forever. "Why didn't you save her?"

Jillian appeared surprisingly calm in the face of his anger. Drawing in a halting breath, she blew it out before she spoke. "It was too late for anyone to save her, Ranjiv. She was already gone."

Chapter 5

GREAT. NOW HE THINKS I'M CRAZY TOO.

Jillian hadn't said a word to anyone about her bizarre experiences with the dearly departed, and she certainly hadn't intended to tell Kavya's son.

That is, until he'd asked the one question she couldn't answer without telling him the truth—or at least, the truth as she remembered it. Asphyxia did strange things to a person's brain, perhaps even making her hear voices.

But voices with so much knowledge and purpose? She doubted that. The fact that she'd gone swimming in the sea and not drowned and now seemed to know instinctively which hand signals to use with Katie were the best examples. That and the fact that she had recognized Ranjiv.

Granted, she'd seen a picture of him and his father. But the resemblance between a young boy and a grown man wasn't always obvious to the casual observer, no matter how much he looked like his dad.

Not that she felt like a casual observer. On the contrary, she felt as though she'd known him all her life. She could picture him as a baby, as a teen, and as a young college graduate. But despite the fact that those memories had to have come from Kavya, they weren't precisely motherly. Ranjiv seemed more like a cousin than a son, or perhaps the boy next door she'd known since childhood.

A boy who was now a man and looked like he'd just seen a ghost.

"I know it sounds crazy," she went on, "but I'll swear that's how it happened. And no, I haven't told anyone else. If I had, they'd have kept me in that hospital and locked me up on the psych ward instead of issuing me a temporary passport."

"That's impossible," he snapped. "I don't believe it."

"You're entitled to your opinion," she said in a much softer tone. "I'm just answering your question as best I can."

He made no further comment. Apparently being spoken to by ghosts or souls of the dead wasn't a topic he cared to pursue, which was okay with Jillian since she had already told him more than she'd ever intended. She had fulfilled Kavya's last request. Her next job was to discover anything she could about Anna and Shanda.

Did all souls leave an imprint behind when they departed? The seed of some task left undone? Jillian had had plenty of time to ponder that question since the crash. The monotony of long-distance travel was highly conducive to thought—not to mention a sleepless night spent in a hospital—and during that time, she had reached two conclusions. First of all, if this was insanity, it wasn't all that bad. And second, she truly would go insane if she let the gifts they had given her go unappreciated and unacknowledged.

She had an idea that accepting responsibility for Katie fulfilled Anna's task, but Shanda's was murkier. A few days ago, Jillian wouldn't have said that all things happen for a reason. She wasn't so sure about that now.

Was her own reason for surviving only to meet Ranjiv? In view of his persistent scowl, this was doubtful. He didn't seem interested in listening to anything else she had to say and was probably wishing he'd stayed home. She wouldn't have been surprised if he wrote her off as a complete wacko and called the police.

With a sharp exhale, she got to her feet. "Thanks for coming, Ranjiv. I only wish we could've met under happier circumstances. Please convey my condolences to the rest of your family. I'm truly sorry I wasn't able to save Kavya, and I hope her body can be recovered. I know how important that would be to me if my own mother had been on that plane."

Having recently seen a film that touched on Hindu funeral customs, Jillian knew that cremation was considered necessary to release the soul, enabling it to move on to the next life. Perhaps that explained why Kavya's soul had been transferred to a living body.

As if something so bizarre could *ever* be explained.

Ranjiv didn't look at her, nor did he speak. He simply sat there, staring holes into the floor.

Deciding to leave before he told her to get lost, she gave him a brief nod and a tight smile. "Okay, then. It was nice meeting you."

She turned and walked away, mentally kicking herself for being so blunt. After all the time she'd had to think, she should've been able to come up with a reasonable lie. Not everyone could handle the truth, particularly when the pain was so raw, which was something she ought to have considered before opening her mouth. Being one of the fortunate survivors, she hadn't lost anyone dear to her in the crash. Her loss had been incurred before the plane ever took off, and it was nothing like what Ranjiv had suffered.

She'd taken several steps before realizing she had no idea what to do next or where to go. Her need to reach London and speak with Ranjiv had given her purpose, forcing her to keep going when she could've easily succumbed to exhaustion. No one would've been surprised if the stress had reduced her to a mindless mess.

But she hadn't succumbed. She was still able to function. She even remembered the name of her hotel. All she had to do was hail a cab and tell the driver where she wanted to go.

I can do this.

She glanced down at the schnauzer trotting along beside her. "Come on, Katie. Let's find a place for you to pee and then we'll get something to eat. I don't know about you, but I'm starving."

"Jillian, wait!"

Stopping, she turned to face Ranjiv as he hurried toward her.

His expression was contrite, perhaps even a bit sheepish. "Look, I'm sorry, okay? It's just that what you're implying is so strange…"

"No need to apologize. I'm the one who's sorry. I should never have told you that. I know it all sounds crazy, but that's honestly how I remember it. I've been through a lot lately, which might explain that bizarre memory, but I did manage to survive. You lost your mother. All I lost were a few belongings."

And my mind.

He nodded slowly. "Most people who lose a loved one in a

crash don't ever receive a message from the last person they spoke with. I shouldn't have snapped at you."

She cocked her head, studying him carefully. He didn't appear to be a man who'd been raised by an uncaring parent, and having met Kavya, she guessed he'd been showered with affection at every opportunity. "You knew your mother loved you. She didn't need me to tell you that. Did she?"

"No. If there was ever one thing I was certain of in this life, it's that. But thank you for telling me. Believe it or not, it...helps." Silence fell between them for a long, awkward moment until he glanced at his watch. "I shouldn't keep you."

"I'm not in any hurry," she said. "I'm on vacation. Sort of. But you've probably got things to do, arrangements to make and such."

"Not at the moment. I've already called everyone I can think of, and I've scheduled a memorial service for Saturday. My uncle and his family are the only relatives we have in London, and they've already dropped by to offer their condolences. Mother had a lot of friends here, but the rest of the family is in India." His shrug contained a rather defeated air. "All I have to do now is go home."

She was about to ask if he lived alone, but realized she already knew the answer. Kavya had said something about him having women troubles, along with being so very, very British.

She hadn't exaggerated. His accent was as Oxford as it could possibly be. If Jillian had only spoken to him on the phone, she would never have guessed he had his origins outside of England.

Nor had his mother overstated his attractiveness. The hunky Irish fisherman had nothing on this guy. Tall and distinguished—but at the same time quite dashingly handsome—Ranjiv was an appealing mix of ancient Hindu aristocracy and modern masculinity. His dark gray suit looked like it had been tailor-made for him.

"What about you?" he asked. "Are you finished here? Can I drop you at your hotel?"

She didn't respond immediately but stood staring at him for several moments until she realized she was waiting for one of her inner voices to tell her what to do.

Nothing.

Not a single word of advice.

Guess I'm on my own this time.

"Sure. That is, if you don't mind my dog riding in your car."

* * * *

As they left the terminal together, Ranjiv didn't have to think hard to know he'd never met anyone quite like Jillian Dulaine. She'd been involved in a terrible tragedy, and yet she seemed strangely calm while telling him that his mother had spoken to her from…where? The great beyond? The spirit world? A watery grave?

Not that he believed her story. He'd covered enough disasters to know that people often became confused and disoriented in crisis situations. Two people could witness the same event and give completely different accounts of it, even to the point of reaching opposing conclusions.

But something in her demeanor made him hesitant to dismiss her story entirely. His mother had probably spoken those words *before* she died, leaving Jillian's conscience to twist the facts in a way that allowed her to escape the guilt she might otherwise feel.

Survivor's guilt. The "why was I spared?" when so many others around her had perished.

Whatever the cause, she seemed too serene for the circumstances, not to mention unscathed. Plane crash survivors should at least have a few bruises, and she had none. At least none that were visible.

Even her name seemed incongruous. Despite her traditionally British given name and French-sounding surname, her accent was pure Southern drawl. Reaching the door ahead of her, he held it open. "Where are you from?"

"Memphis, Tennessee," she replied. "Home of the Blues." As she passed through the door, she pointed toward a grassy area near the car park. "Do you suppose I'd get arrested if Katie were to potty on the grass over there?"

"Better than in my car," he replied.

As he followed her across the tarmac, he thought perhaps the dog was what kept her from going completely mental. Animals had a way of doing that, calming fears by giving victims something outside themselves to focus on.

"I've never had to deal with a dog before," she confided. "Thank goodness Katie's so well-trained. I wouldn't have a clue what to do with her otherwise."

Ranjiv hadn't heard Jillian issue a single command, but upon closer scrutiny, he spotted the subtle signals she was giving to the dog. Either Katie was incredibly good at reading body language or— "Did you say you were seated next to her owner?"

Jillian nodded. "Her name was Anna Lyles. She seemed very nice, and she was extremely proud of her dogs. Practically the first thing she did was show me Katie's picture." Pointing toward the grassy verge, she tapped her finger in the air twice.

In the next instant, Katie stopped to take a piss in the spot Jillian had just indicated.

"For someone who doesn't know anything about dogs, you two seem to communicate rather well."

Her bemused expression was almost laughable. "What makes you say that?"

Arching a brow, he chuckled. "You don't even realize it, do you?"

"Realize *what*?"

"That dog isn't even on a leash, and she hasn't put a single paw out of line. Until yesterday, you'd only seen a photo of her. And she'd *never* seen you. Don't you think your rapport is a bit odd?"

With an abrupt twist of her head, Jillian turned away, but not before he glimpsed the shuttering of her eyes. "I never said dogs didn't like *me*. I just don't care for *them*."

Throughout his journalism career, Ranjiv had asked a lot of tough questions, and he'd asked enough of them to know when someone wasn't giving him a straight answer. Or had something to hide.

Perhaps her reticence was due to his reaction to hearing that his mother had spoken to her from the grave. Ranjiv had been understandably incredulous—anyone would have been skeptical— but was there something equally unbelievable about her relationship with the schnauzer?

"Anna said Katie was a breeze to train," she went on. "Maybe following orders comes naturally for her."

"Maybe." Ranjiv reminded himself that while his curiosity had been piqued, he wasn't reporting this story and didn't have any right to grill her on the details, except those that concerned his mother. But he'd never heard of a dog that followed orders "naturally." They had to be trained.

Someone had certainly trained Katie.

And that someone had died along with his mother.

He led the way to his car, all the while trying to come up with a topic Jillian might be more willing to discuss.

"You said you were on a sort of vacation," he began. "What constitutes a *sort of* vacation?"

Her pained expression tagged this as yet another taboo topic.

"If you'd rather not say—"

She shook her head before heaving a sigh. "No. I can say it. This was supposed to have been my honeymoon."

"But you said you didn't lose anyone in the crash."

"I didn't." Her voice was as grim as her smile. "I lost him *before* the crash. Just call me Jilted Jillian." Her snort of laughter was completely devoid of amusement. "I shouldn't say that aloud. It's the kind of nickname that's liable to stick."

"I doubt that." Ranjiv hadn't discovered a reason for a man to jilt her as yet, unless it was her tendency to be evasive, a personality trait with which Laksha, his former intended, had been generously endowed. "Are you saying he should've been on that plane?"

She nodded. "Lucky him, huh? No doubt he'll see it as confirmation that he made the right decision." Her eyes grew pensive. "Maybe he did."

"The right decision for *you* or for *him?*" He stopped beside his car—a green Range Rover well past the first blush of youth.

"Both," she replied.

After unlocking the passenger door, he opened it and waited for her to enter.

"You want *me* to drive?" In the next instant, she admitted her mistake. "Sorry. What with all that's happened I forgot about that lefty business you Brits have going." Glancing at the interior, she added, "Good car for a dog."

"Something tells me Katie will make less of a mess in it than I do."

Jillian pushed aside the stack of papers and notebooks that cluttered the front seat. "What sort of work do you do?"

"I'm a reporter for *The London Times*."

"Shit." She couldn't have backed out of the Rover any faster if it had been on fire.

He caught her arm in a gentle grasp. "I'm not reporting this story, if that's your worry."

"I certainly hope not," she snapped. "We got caught by some of those bloodsuckers in Connemara. Guess no one knew we were coming today. Either that or we got lucky and missed them."

"And now you're about to get in a car with another vampire?"

The scowl she shot from the corner of her eye nearly pinned his ears back. "You wouldn't want your mother's name smeared all over the front page, would you?"

"No, I wouldn't."

"Then don't do it to mine."

Was she threatening retaliation? "I won't. But I can't promise you no one else will. This is the kind of story that sells newspapers."

"I know, but—" A stomp of her foot displayed her frustration. "Damn. I should've known the one person I tell about that spooky stuff would turn out to be a reporter."

The longer he talked with her, the less crazy she seemed, and his earlier thoughts about survivor's guilt were rapidly losing credibility. Ranjiv suspected there might be more "spooky stuff" she hadn't told him yet, but he chose to let it pass. For now. "Your secret is safe with me."

"Yeah, right," she said with a derisive snort. "Reporters don't keep secrets. They blab them to the whole world."

"But we never reveal our sources," Ranjiv countered. "You can trust me, Jillian."

Her eyes narrowed in a mutinous frown as her teeth tugged at her lower lip. "How do I know you're telling the truth?"

"The same way you recognized me without anyone pointing me out to you." In view of her other uncanny insights, he didn't think this supposition fell far from the mark, and her hesitation confirmed it.

"I said I saw a picture of your father. And you do look like him."

"That's one explanation," he conceded. "But it isn't the only one. Is it?"

Chapter 6

I'M NOT TELLING HIM THAT. I'M NOT. I ABSOLUTELY REFUSE.

Jillian didn't need the extra voices in her head to warn her that saying more would be dangerous. Dangerous to her credibility as well as her sanity.

"Of course it is," she said. "You said you could see me and you were standing there holding a phone. I simply made an educated guess that proved to be correct."

God, I sound like a schoolteacher.

Had she picked up someone else's aura? Someone who sounded knowledgeable and authoritative and used big words—or little words when explaining something to a child? She hoped not. Having three extra auras was bad enough. If indeed "aura" was the right word.

She had to find some way to make him stop believing the truth.

Now, there's an interesting dilemma… Make him believe the lie because the truth is too hard to swallow.

Except he didn't seem to be having that problem. At least, not anymore. Kavya was his mother, and she had been his only immediate family for most of his life. If he believed she carried Kavya's aura, would he hang onto Jillian like a puppy that had lost its mother?

Interesting analogy, despite the fact that Ranjiv didn't strike her as the momma's boy type.

The trouble was, Kavya's voice had ceased after the whispered—Jillian hated to admit it, even to herself—*"That's him"* she'd heard when she spotted Ranjiv. As far as her interactions with him were concerned, she seemed to be on her own now and was about to get into a rather ancient vehicle with a man who was essentially a stranger. With her new dog. A dog she was going to have to explain to the hotel people who probably didn't allow pets in the rooms, particularly the bridal suite.

She blew out a weary sigh. "I just want to find that damned hotel and get some sleep."

"That can be arranged," he said. "Where are you staying?"

"The Shield and Dagger on Almstead Street."

His eyes widened. "You can't be serious."

"Why? Is there something wrong with it?"

"Slightly dodgy neighborhood," he replied. "But if that's really where you want to go…"

Great. "I should've known it was a mistake to let Seth pick the hotel. He claimed it was picturesque and historical."

"I'm sure it's all that. The location is what concerns me."

"Well, that's where my reservation is, and I'm too tired to go looking for another hotel. Especially since I already paid Seth back for the deposit."

"You don't have any luggage either," he pointed out.

"Lots of people lose their luggage. Airlines are notorious for losing stuff."

"Not as much as you might think," Ranjiv said. "They'll be suspicious of you not having any bags. And you *are* a day late."

"You're a big help," she grumbled. "Just take me there, okay? I've got money and identification. I'll be fine."

With a shrug, he helped her into the car and went around to the other side. He climbed into the driver's seat just as Katie leaped onto the seat between them. Starting the engine, he added, "Don't say I didn't warn you."

She was actually more concerned about the age of his vehicle than she was about the suitability of her hotel. Still, if he considered his car to be trustworthy enough to transport his only parent, it was probably safe enough for her. That frequently cited statistic about planes being the safest way to travel had lost some of its credence— in *her* mind anyway.

She stared out the window, desperate for a distraction. Unfortunately, the drive through London didn't interest her as much as it should have. She felt more like a native than a tourist—one who had stopped ogling the sights long ago.

But whose memories were they? They could have belonged to any—or all—of the three women seated with her on that infamous 747. Every one of those ladies had been to London before, and one had been a current resident. She shuddered at the possibility of having picked up yet another aura. Her mind was overcrowded enough as it was. So many thoughts and memories were jumbled together, simmering just beneath the surface as they scrambled to find a synapse to fire and become permanent. She'd learned enough for three more lifetimes overnight. Thankfully, that pot of knowledge was simmering rather than boiling over.

Not being privy to her thoughts, Ranjiv took on the role of tour guide, pointing out various landmarks, adding in bits of history here and there. She thought it strange that he would know so much about the city until she recalled that, unlike Kavya, he'd grown up in London. He probably knew as much as anyone whose family had lived there for generations, perhaps even more as the result of his job as a reporter.

"Hmm... You weren't kidding about the neighborhood," she commented as Ranjiv stopped the car in front of the Shield and Dagger. The hotel was certainly picturesque and historic and would undoubtedly appeal to anyone who wished to experience a Charles Dickens novel firsthand, but the surrounding structures were pretty shabby. She half expected some street urchin to pop up and offer to sweep the pavement for her.

"Do you want me to go in with you?" Ranjiv asked.

"I'm not sure *I* want to go in," she admitted. "Would you mind waiting a few minutes?" She had a reservation—although she no longer had a confirmation number to prove it—but the means for a quick getaway might come in handy.

Within a few moments of entering the dingy building, she found herself staring at the clerk in disbelief. "I'm only a day late, and my reservation was for the bridal suite. How could anyone possibly need the bridal suite on such short notice?"

"I'm sure I couldn't say, miss. But you must understand we can't hold a room indefinitely."

She suppressed the urge to growl. "Don't you people read the newspapers?"

The clerk stared at her blankly. "How is that relevant?"

"I was on the plane that crashed Monday morning. One of only three survivors? Surely someone would've seen my name and—" Jillian stopped in mid-tirade as she recalled a pertinent detail. "Never mind. My former fiancé obviously made the reservation in his name. You couldn't possibly have known." She blew out a breath. "I suppose my deposit is nonrefundable?"

"Yes. Regrettable, but true."

She was about to ask if there were any other rooms available when she recalled the additional change to her status that was currently sitting quietly at her feet. "I don't suppose you have any other rooms, do you? Rooms that allow dogs?"

The man lowered his head and shook it, his pale face and cringing manner reinforcing the Dickens-like atmosphere by reminding her of Uriah Heep. "I'm afraid we don't have rooms of any kind, miss."

Given the nature of the place, Jillian was surprised to find it so full—and also surprised at how relieved she was that she now had the perfect excuse to stay somewhere else. "No problem. Thank you for your time."

Turning on her heel, she headed toward the entrance, hoping that Ranjiv hadn't given up on her yet.

He hadn't, although his puzzled frown suggested he'd expected her to wave him on rather than approach the car and open the door.

"Know any decent hotels that take dogs?" she asked. "Anna must've known of at least one, although she said something about taking walks through the Pennines. Where *are* the Pennines anyway?"

"Just south of the Scottish border," he replied. "Somehow, I doubt she planned to walk all the way."

"Probably not." She leaned against the doorframe, suddenly feeling as though all the stuffing had leaked out of her. Closing her eyes, she discovered that a few tears were leaking out of her, as well. "I'm sorry to be such a bother. Really. I'm not normally so…" At the moment, she didn't know *what* she normally was, but if she didn't find a place to lie down soon, she was going to conk out right there in the street.

"Exhausted? I'm not surprised. And you aren't a bother. Get in. I know a place where you and Katie can stay, no questions asked."

Jillian didn't really care where he took her but figured a slight show of interest was in order. "Oh? Where's that?"

"My flat. Or my mother's house if you'd prefer. I don't believe she would mind if you stayed there for a while, or even if you borrowed some of her clothes. In fact, I'm quite sure she would insist."

"Can't quite see myself in a sari, but stranger things have happened. And you're probably right about her not minding." She waved a hand and Katie jumped into the car. Jillian climbed in behind her.

He shook his head slowly. "It's like waving a magic wand."

"What?"

"The way you work with that dog. It's like magic."

"Not really. She's bound to be just as tired as I am and wants to go home or to sleep or something." Jillian glanced longingly at the back seat, which was even more cluttered than the front had been. For a man who gave the appearance of a rather fastidious dresser, Ranjiv was a bit of a slob.

His eyes had evidently followed her gaze. "Sorry for the mess. But there *is* a method to my madness. I work more out of my car than I do my office."

"Doesn't bother me a bit," she said with perfect sincerity. At the moment, she didn't give a damn about anything except lying down somewhere for a good, long time. Blessed, blissful slumber—at least three days' worth. "Especially since my entire body is about to implode from lack of sleep."

"You can nap on the way," he said. "My flat is actually closer to the airport than that hotel."

"*Now* he tells me," she mumbled. Katie curled up in her lap, seeming to sense that their journey would be a long one. "Wake me when we get there. If you can."

* * * *

Ranjiv drove into the car park near his flat and spent the next few minutes gazing at Jillian's sleeping form, trying to reconcile his conflicting emotions. The mere mention of her wearing a sari had sent his mind stampeding off in a direction it had no business going. This was not a date, and Jillian was not his lover. She wasn't even a friend. She was a stranger, and this was a time for sadness at his mother's passing, not a time for romance or desire or whatever it was he was feeling.

After a lively internal debate, he had decided that taking her to his flat rather than his mother's home was the best course of action. The dog would undoubtedly need care while she slept, and he didn't mind admitting his reluctance to let Jillian out of his sight—for purely practical reasons, of course.

Keeping tabs on any plane crash survivor was advisable, and Jillian was alone in London. She'd said something about being in a hospital and had obviously been released, but her internal organs might have been jostled and bruised from the impact, causing symptoms that might not show up for several days.

Psychological problems were also possible, although the more time he spent with her, the less crazy she seemed. Her claim that his mother had spoken to her after death had been easy to dismiss at first—he could even rationalize it to a certain extent—but the way she dealt with the dog made him wonder. A lot. Perhaps the dog's owner had also made some sort of psychic impression on her.

His mother's message still had him slightly baffled. Perhaps that was the sort of dying concern any mother might have for her child, but Jillian was right. He already knew his mother loved him. The only thing the delivery of that message had achieved was the meeting between him and Jillian. Had that been her intention? If so, then why? Was she continuing to play matchmaker even after her death?

It was crazy. Impossible. Improbable. And yet plausible in some freakish, bizarre twist-of-fate sort of way. Just because he'd never heard of a similar circumstance didn't mean it had never happened before. And believing Jillian didn't make *him* a nutter.

Did it?

Perhaps it did, but watching her sleep wasn't doing a damn thing for his sanity.

"Jillian," he said quietly. When she didn't stir, the dog began to whine as though afraid she'd lost yet another master. "She's okay, Katie. Just exhausted."

Carrying her was an option, but would the dog follow them?

"Only one way to find out," he muttered.

He got out of the car and went around to the passenger side. Easing the door open, he took Jillian in his arms as the dog jumped onto the pavement.

As she settled herself against his chest, protective instincts he hadn't known he possessed surged in response. Leaning closer to kiss her temple felt perfectly natural and yet wonderfully magical.

Katie gazed up at him with a curious expression, and he nodded toward the building. "Come on, Katie. I don't have any proper dog food, but I'm sure we can find something for you to eat."

He started walking, not the least bit surprised when the schnauzer fell in step beside him. A bit freaked out, perhaps, but not surprised.

Clearly he wasn't the only one who wanted to keep Jillian in sight.

To the best of his recollection, Ranjiv had never carried a woman up two flights of stairs, nor had he ever tried to unlock a door with a woman in his arms. By the time he made it to his flat, he was panting rather hard for a man in reasonably good physical condition. Still, he couldn't help chuckling when he finally carried her inside.

"First time for everything," he told Katie.

His laughter faded quickly when he recalled that, had her wedding and honeymoon gone ahead as planned, Jillian's new husband would have already carried her across the threshold of the bridal suite at the Shield and Dagger.

And I would've spent yesterday evening listening to my amma regale me with the details of her visit to Chicago instead of planning her memorial service.

If Jillian's fiancé hadn't been such an ass. If the plane hadn't crashed. If no one had died…

If, if, if…

Once inside, he was faced with yet another dilemma: where to put her. With only one bed, his own, his choices were limited. The sofa would be best, but—

No. She needs the bed. I can sleep on the couch.

Without another thought, he carried her to his bedroom, pulled back the blankets, and placed her on the bed. After removing her shoes, he pulled the covers up over her.

He started toward the door, then stopped and turned back to where Jillian—this woman who had survived the un-survivable—lay so peacefully. He'd seen the videos of the crash: a straight down, high-speed dive into the sea. No one should have survived that. No one.

And yet this extraordinary woman had lived. What secrets had become lodged in her brain during those moments when death surrounded her? Had the same thing happened to the two other equally miraculous survivors?

Ranjiv had always been a very spiritual person, but this went beyond that. Beyond the cycle of life, death, and rebirth. If what he suspected was true, this was a rebirth within an existing life, with the result that at least a part of the soul of Katie's owner lived on in Jillian.

Despite the inherent insanity of that concept, the belief itself was acceptable enough. Hinduism viewed the world as a whole and acknowledged beliefs in all forms. Therefore, it went against no doctrines for him to believe what he was trying so desperately *not* to believe, which was that a tiny particle of his mother's soul also resided in Jillian.

The reincarnation of Kavya's soul should have been a joyous occurrence for Ranjiv: proof that the cycle was continuing as it should and that his mother's soul had not been lost. He simply didn't want Jillian to be the recipient of that essence. The emotions she evoked in him weren't the sort a man should feel toward his mother, or even his mother's soul. They were protective, possessive, and visceral.

He didn't need to concern himself with that just yet. Jillian was asleep in his bed, but that didn't necessarily mean he intended to join her there. Night was a long way off. Who knew what might happen in the ensuing hours?

Katie let out a soft whine while viewing him with an expectant eye.

"Go ahead," he said with a nod toward the bed. "I'm sure she won't mind."

The dog hopped onto the bed and settled herself in the hollow space behind Jillian's knees.

In that instant, Ranjiv began to wonder if all his ruminations were for naught. Katie seemed to obey him just as readily as she did her new owner. Perhaps there had been no transference of souls, no sharing of the essence of the dog trainer or anyone else.

Perhaps it was all in *his* head rather than Jillian's. Considering the events of the past couple of days, the probability of his own brain being a bit frazzled was understandably high. In that space of time, he had lost his mother and gained a new friend.

Katie opened her eyes, her brow visibly rising as she fixed him with a rather piercing glare.

"Right, then. Better make that two new friends," he amended. "You have a bit of a nap while I see if I can find anything suitable for a dog's supper." His gaze shifted to Jillian. "I certainly hope she likes Indian food."

Katie yawned until her jaws cracked, then huffed out a sigh and snuggled deeper into the blankets.

Ranjiv reminded himself that a large percentage of Americans had never eaten anything more Indian than rice, or perhaps a bit of curry. Would Jillian have the same tastes as the dog trainer, or would she enjoy some of the same things his mother had?

It's all in my head... All in my head... All in my head...

That internal mantra didn't help very much, especially since his next thought was of his mother's somewhat unusual aversion to coriander, a staple spice in Indian cuisine. Kavya didn't care for the seed—coriander—and positively gagged on the plant's leaves—cilantro. Kavya had always blended her own seasonings, and had never used pre-mixed garam masala. At least, not that Ranjiv could recall. She preferred to make her own version, substituting powdered fenugreek for the coriander.

If the two women shared that dislike, he might have to start worrying again, although it certainly wasn't what anyone would call conclusive evidence. Until then, however...

The chant began again, but with even less conviction than before.

Perhaps it *wasn't* all in his head.

Perhaps it was in Jillian's.

Chapter 7

JILLIAN SIFTED THROUGH THE SMELLS THAT SURROUNDED HER—unfamiliar and yet astonishingly recognizable. First off, the dog could stand another bath, a problem that could easily be remedied. Second, from the scent of masculine soap or cologne lingering on the sheets, she deduced that she was in a man's bed. Next came the cooking aromas. Her own mind said curry, but some other entity rattled off the ingredients.

Cinnamon, cloves, fenugreek, black pepper, cardamom, cumin, nutmeg, onions, garlic, ginger, tomatoes, chili peppers.

That was all. No commentary on how good or bad it would taste, just a simple recitation of the components—facts Jillian couldn't have known without help. Even though the "voice" she heard was her own, Kavya's influence remained.

Spookier and spookier.

Opening her eyes, she rose up on one elbow. Despite the shades having been drawn, the tiny chinks of light filtering in around the window's edges enabled her to see quite clearly, although whether that glow was from the sun or the street lamps, she couldn't have said.

Definitely a man's room. Austere. Functional. Sparsely furnished, and yet cluttered.

Like his car.

Ranjiv must have carried her in without waking her. She had already surmised that this was his apartment rather than his mother's house, unless he spent a lot of time there. His scent lingered on the pillow as though he'd been in this bed before—possibly even while Jillian lay there sleeping. However, a quick glance over her shoulder revealed nothing but smooth, undisturbed blankets.

She scanned the room, which contained a chair, a table, and a dresser. The closet door was only partially closed, the clothes within hanging haphazardly while a jumble of shoes littered the floor.

Katie stirred beside her. Lifting her muzzle, she sniffed the air.

"You smell it too, don't you?" Jillian inhaled again. "Chicken."

Her thoughts shifted backward in time. *"I'll have the pasta,"* Kavya had said. *"Not in the mood for chicken..."* Would this strange sense of duality go on forever?

Not just duality. A triad.

No. A quartet.

But with the need to swim no longer a factor, Shanda's presence had become dormant.

"I'm safe now. I don't need your help anymore."

She hadn't realized she'd spoken those words aloud until Katie cocked her head, seeming somewhat puzzled.

"It's true, isn't it? Ranjiv wouldn't—"

"Wouldn't what?" His voice came from the doorway. A moment later, he stepped inside. "Make you eat his terrible cooking?"

"It certainly doesn't *smell* terrible. Smells quite good, actually. What is it?"

He shrugged. "Makhani chicken. Sometimes called Indian butter chicken. It's my mother's recipe, but I'd be the first to admit I can't make it the way she did."

Small wonder Kavya hadn't wanted the chicken that was served on the plane. It hadn't smelled *anything* like this.

"Every cook puts their own spin on a recipe." She ran a hand through her hair, suddenly very much aware that she was in his bed and probably looked like hell. "How long have I been asleep?"

A soft chuckle prefaced his reply. "About six hours."

"Really?" She hadn't slept that soundly in days. "What time is it?"

"Six thirty. I figured it was time you ate something."

The sleep had done her a world of good, but her growling stomach reminded her that she'd missed lunch. "You got that right. I'm starving."

"I'm not surprised."

Katie sprang to her feet, wagging the stump of her tail as Jillian sat up on the side of the bed. "Does she need to go out?"

"I doubt it. I took her for a walk about half an hour ago."

Ranjiv leaned against the doorjamb. He still wore the same dark gray trousers as before, but he'd removed the jacket and tie. His white shirt was now open at the collar and the sleeves were rolled halfway up forearms generously dusted with dark hair. He looked tall and fit—certainly capable of meeting any needs a schnauzer might have, until closer scrutiny revealed the lines around his eyes. He was probably just as exhausted as she was.

And I've been hogging his bed.

"Thanks for taking care of her," she said. "I'm sure she misses Anna something awful." Then she recalled that Katie wasn't the only one who was missing a loved one. "How are you holding up?"

"I've been better," he admitted. "I've been given the rest of the week off, but I'm still not sure what to do with myself."

Was it better to keep busy or sit around and grieve? Never having lost anyone close to her, Jillian didn't know. Seth had effectively removed himself from her life, but at least he wasn't dead. "Any plans for a memorial service?"

He nodded. "Saturday afternoon. Ordinarily, it would've been held today, but I thought it best to wait a bit."

Jillian didn't have to ask why. He was still hoping Kavya's body might be found so that he could give her a traditional funeral, and he certainly wouldn't want to have to go through it twice.

Averting his eyes, he blinked several times in rapid succession. "I–I'd like for you to be there."

"Thank you. I would be honored."

Acknowledging her acceptance with a brief nod, he gestured toward the hall. "The loo is across the hall. Take your time."

No, she thought as his footsteps faded, he wasn't holding up well at all, which made her feel like an absolute heel for leaving him to cope with everything alone. Reminding herself that if she hadn't asked to speak with him, he would have been even more alone than he was now really didn't matter. Perhaps taking Katie out for walks had been therapeutic for him.

Therapy... Would a memorial service give Ranjiv the closure he needed in the wake of his mother's death? This trip to England had been Jillian's means of coping with her broken engagement, although the jury was still out on whether it would do her any good.

Perhaps she *did* know the feeling after all.

Even so, she wasn't feeling that way now. Seth had only entered her thoughts as an example, not someone she truly felt lost without. Surviving a disaster had a way of making a person forget trivial matters like inconsiderate fiancés and broken engagements.

She gave Katie a pat and got up. Several minutes of quality time in the bathroom had her feeling more human. Human enough to appreciate a dog's devotion and a man's thoughtfulness in not only sharing his dinner with her, but also sharing his home and his grief over the loss of his only surviving parent.

Jillian had called her own parents from Inisheer. Thankfully, they hadn't even heard about the crash and had been spared the worry. But what if she *had* died in the crash? How long would it have taken for them to be notified? Surely they would have known by now, and they would be wearing the same expression as Ranjiv—sad, bewildered, stunned—not having fully grasped the truth and finality as yet.

She started toward the kitchen with Katie at her heels, realizing only then that she hadn't thanked Ranjiv for carrying her in from the car. Perhaps he'd had help from a friend or neighbor. She tried not to think of how ignominious she must have looked with her head lolling, arms hanging limply, perhaps even drooling.

Yet another worry that doesn't amount to much in the greater scheme of things.

She had never felt quite so philosophical before. A voice from her past spoke softly to her, asking a question she had never truly understood, an exercise in focusing her attention on the present.

What at this moment is lacking?

For the first time in her life, she knew the answer.

Nothing. Not one blessed thing.

Smiling, she entered the kitchen just as Ranjiv set a plate of butter chicken and rice on the square, wooden table.

* * * *

Ranjiv tried to recall having ever fixed dinner for a beautiful woman who had slept in his bed and couldn't think of a single instance that even came close.

Perhaps that was where he'd gone wrong. If there was any truth in the old adage that the way to a man's heart was through his stomach, the reverse was probably also true. Then again, he'd never dated an American.

Nor am I dating one now.

"Have a seat," he said. "What would you like to drink? Tea? Wine?"

"Tea." She sat down and scooted her chair up to the table. "Although I don't suppose there's any chance I could have it iced?"

A snort of laughter escaped him as he set another full plate in front of her. "You've obviously never been to England before."

"Yeah. I know. Only hot. Just checking. Hot is fine."

She sounded so disappointed, Ranjiv made a mental note to get some ice trays. He set the teapot on the table and handed her a cup. "Sorry. Forgot about you Yanks and your ice addiction."

"I'd like to see you Brits survive a summer in Memphis without it. I never *have* been able to figure out how women survived back when hoop skirts and ruffled petticoats were in style. Thank God for whoever invented shorts, air conditioning, and ice makers."

"We tend to focus more on staying warm here." Taking the seat to her right at the table, he picked up his fork with more trepidation than when he'd gone into the bedroom to check on her. Piping hot tea and spicy chicken normally went down well on a chilly evening. Something had changed, creating a growing attraction to Jillian that had him slightly hot under the collar.

"It gets cold in Tennessee," she said with a touch of defiance. "Maybe not as cold as Minnesota, but it snows once in a while. I own a coat and everything." She paused, frowning. "At least, I *did* own a coat. Now all I have is this nifty Irish sweater."

Ranjiv wiped the sweat from his upper lip. He had already imagined her in a sari, but the "nifty Irish sweater" wasn't bad either. "I guess I need to take you shopping."

"Sounds good. I've had these clothes on for two days now, and I'm not used to wearing wool. It isn't as scratchy as I thought it would be, but I'd much rather sleep in a cotton nightie, preferably flannel." Picking up her fork, she sampled the chicken. "Not bad. Seth and I went to an Indian restaurant once, but it seemed like they put cilantro in everything. This is nice."

The confirmation of at least one of his suspicions regarding Jillian's psychic connection to his mother had Ranjiv aspirating a grain or two of rice from his first bite.

Jillian stared at him in alarm as he succumbed to a coughing fit. "Do I need to Heimlich you?"

He shook his head, wishing he'd had a glass of iced tea to take away the tickle in his throat.

Definitely need to make some ice.

"I'm okay," he said a moment later. "A bit of rice went down the wrong way."

"Hmm... I'm not sure the Heimlich maneuver would help with something that small."

The thought of Jillian wrapping her arms around his waist nearly set him off again.

"You're probably right." Taking a sip of tea, he swallowed it carefully, wishing he had opted to open a bottle of wine instead. "I take it you don't care for cilantro."

"Not at all," she replied with a touch of vehemence. "They put tons of it in the more authentic Mexican food, which is why I tend to avoid those places like the plague. I heard somewhere that the aversion to cilantro is genetic. Guess I've got the gene. Weird, huh?"

Weirder than you might think.

"And you've always had this–this...aversion?"

"Oh, yeah. That is, ever since it started popping up everywhere you go. God knows my mom never put it in her chili."

"My mother never put it in anything she made either." Ranjiv was surprised he could even get the words out. At least Jillian claimed to have disliked those spices *before* she'd boarded that plane.

Coincidence. Only a coincidence.

Her smile seemed the tiniest bit strained. "Your mother and I must have had more in common than I realized."

Until today, Ranjiv would have argued against his mother having *anything* in common with a blond Yank aside from her gender.

Still a coincidence.

She went on with her dinner, only seeming to notice his stares after taking several more bites. "Is something wrong?"

He shook his head. "No. Not at all. I'm just—"

"Tired?" she suggested. "I'm not surprised. You look exhausted. I'll take the couch tonight. That is, if I can sleep again so soon."

At least she wasn't talking about trying to find another hotel. He attempted a smile. "Do I really look that bad?"

"Um...no." Her eyes flicked toward his for a moment, then back down again. "Actually, you look pretty good. Probably a lot better than I do."

"I wouldn't be too sure about that." In his opinion, there could be no comparison. "I'd have expected you to be in much worse shape after all you've been through."

"Yet another weird thing. I should at least have broken an arm or something. I have a bruise from the seatbelt, but other than that, there isn't a mark on me. I'm not even sore."

The prospect of inspecting her for bruises rendered Ranjiv unable to comment for several moments.

What is wrong with me?

His mother's death was still too fresh for thoughts of that nature to be appropriate. But were they truly wrong? Death was as much a part of the cycle of life as conception and birth. Other lives didn't cease because of it. They might be altered or even interrupted, but they did go on.

"About that other thing... You know, your mother telling me that stuff after she had already passed on? Maybe I'm remembering it wrong. I mean, that *is* how I remember it, but it can't really be true, can it?"

He cleared his throat with a significant effort. "Only if you believe in ghosts."

She lifted another forkful of chicken to her mouth, chewing it slowly and swallowing before she spoke again. "I'm not sure belief has anything to do with it. Before all this happened, I had no reason to believe anything of the kind. Never had a single supernatural experience in my entire life."

"Isn't that how it usually goes? You don't believe in ghosts until you actually meet one?" Ranjiv still wasn't sure which side of the argument he wanted to be on, but he'd been around enough to know that the right set of circumstances could make a believer out of anyone.

"I suppose so. But since I don't want people thinking I've gone off the deep end, I'd rather you didn't spread that story around. I saw a video of the crash when I was still at Inisheer, and I'm pretty sure no one else will ever question why I wasn't able to save any of the other passengers, mainly because I shouldn't have survived myself. When you asked me that question, I told you the truth. At least, the truth as I remember it." She paused as her eyes took on a reflective cast. "Don't know why I did that now. I really wish I hadn't."

In a way, he wished the same thing. But she *had* told him, and that knowledge had already taken root in his mind, making it tough to eradicate.

Perhaps the conclusions he'd drawn since then were only a matter of confirmatory bias, and all those strange coincidences could be explained as a matter of chance. If that were the case, he wouldn't have to worry about being attracted to a woman who carried a particle of his mother's soul inside her.

"Let me ask you this," he began. "If my mother hadn't given you that message for me, would you have asked to see me anyway?"

She nodded without hesitation. "I wanted to speak with the families of the other ladies I sat with on the plane. You would've been included in that group."

"Why?"

Her reply took longer this time. "Because we shared something during that flight and because it seemed like the right thing to do. So far, you're the only one I've talked to. I'd still like to find the other families."

Ranjiv tried not to let his relief show. "That shouldn't be too difficult as long as you remember their names."

"Like I could ever forget them." The soft, haunted quality in her voice made him wonder yet again if she'd shared more with those women than she was willing to admit. "I could probably recite them in my sleep." She gave her head a slight shake and then squared her shoulders, sitting up straight in her chair. "You mentioned wine. I think I'll have some after all."

With a nod, he got to his feet. "Red or white?"

A tiny frown creased her brow. "You're supposed to drink white wine with chicken, aren't you? Or is that rule different with Indian food?"

"No. But then, I'm not what you'd call a connoisseur. You can have whichever you prefer." He shot her a wink. "I'll never tell."

"I'll have the white." A smile curved her lips. "Wouldn't want to give the scandal-mongers any more ammunition against me than absolutely necessary."

"Then white it shall be." That bottle of Sula Riesling had been calling to Ranjiv ever since he carried Jillian over his threshold. It was positively screaming at him now. "I'll join you."

Perhaps a dash of alcohol would help eliminate the ghostly soul-sharing suspicions from his thoughts.

Particularly since his mother had preferred red wine.

Even with chicken.

Chapter 8

THE WINE HELPED CONSIDERABLY, ESPECIALLY WHEN JILLIAN'S befuddled brain finally settled on the fact that she was staying in the apartment of a man she hadn't even known for a full day.

Any memories she had of him belonged to someone else and could therefore be discounted. True, Kavya had seemed quite proud of him, and where a lesser man might have taken advantage, Ranjiv seemed gentlemanly and understanding. But had she convinced him she wasn't channeling his mother?

Maybe.

Oddly enough, after his initial rejection of the idea, he seemed to have come to the conclusion that it was actually plausible. Therefore, it behooved her to avoid doing or saying anything that might confirm that belief. His choking fit had followed a comment that pointed to a similarity between herself and Kavya.

I need to watch that.

She hadn't been lying about her aversion to those spices; her own memories substantiated it. Who knew how many other similarities there might be? Would he see each one of those commonalities as further proof?

One thing she definitely could *not* do was to tell him that if he wanted to make butter chicken the way his mother did, he needed to simmer the sauce a bit longer. The way she knew such things was downright creepy.

When I start telling him where his birthmarks are, I'm really in trouble.

Discovering them for herself was an altogether different story.

Kavya's opinion of her son's attractiveness was spot on. The mystery was in why a woman promised to him from childhood would opt to marry someone else. What was his flaw? His mother certainly hadn't seen it or Jillian would probably know what it was. Unless it was that he seemed more British than Indian.

That argument alone wouldn't hold much water. There had to be thousands—perhaps millions—of second, third, and fourth-generation immigrants to Britain from India. There must be another reason. A highly personal one that Kavya had known nothing about.

Was he a terrible lover? Or was he a virgin? Would virginity be a mark in his favor or a demerit of some kind?

She glanced up to find his eyes focused on her face. If his skin had been lighter, she might have seen the blush. As it was, he averted his eyes.

"Sorry," he muttered. "I'm staring again. It's just that—" He stopped and shook his head. "I don't know why."

He might claim ignorance, but Jillian suspected she knew the reason. And if the same were true of him, she would be doing a bit of staring herself. "Checking to make sure the crazy woman isn't going to start screeching like a banshee or speaking in tongues?"

That at least drew a smile from him. "No. Actually, I might feel more at ease if you did."

"Ah, so you *enjoy* hanging out with crazy people."

"Not really. It's more a matter of a crazy person not noticing the fact that I'm staring."

She chuckled. "Prefer your houseguests to be slightly out of touch with reality?"

"Um, no." His hesitation was quite evident. "You see... I get...*nervous* around women."

"All women?" If so, that would explain quite a lot, and it would also prove that channeling his mother wasn't the only issue.

"Not all of them. Just the really pretty ones."

It was her turn to stare. "I wouldn't have thought that would apply in this situation."

A frown furrowed his brow for an instant. "You mean I shouldn't notice an attractive woman so soon after my mother's death?"

That explanation was reasonable enough, but it wasn't first and foremost in her mind. "No. It's not that. It's just that I've never considered myself to be *really pretty,* particularly to men like you."

The frown returned. "Indian men, you mean?"

"No." A smile curved her lips, despite her intention to curb it. "Incredibly handsome men. You put my ex-fiancé to shame."

This time, she actually saw the blush. Subtle, perhaps, but still there. "We're even, then."

Jillian had to think for a moment to draw her next conclusion. She doubted it was true, but thought it might lighten the mood. All these blushes and stares were unnerving, not to mention unnecessary.

"So..." She took a sip of her wine. "The girl you were promised to was a real dog, huh?"

His burst of laughter changed him completely. No longer stuffy or morose, he seemed boyish and approachable. This was the Ranjiv his family saw. Jillian doubted that very many others ever had. His mother hadn't been privy to his deeper thoughts, no matter how close they had been. Either that or she wasn't sharing them with Jillian.

Which is as it should be.

A mother might suspect her child's motivations, but she certainly couldn't know all of them. Therefore, Kavya couldn't have known the degree of disappointment Ranjiv had felt when his promised wife had chosen to marry someone else. Nor would Jillian's own mother know her precise reaction to Seth's desertion, possibly because she wasn't completely sure of it herself.

"Thanks," he said. "I needed that. But no, she wasn't a dog, and I'm guessing your fiancé wasn't either."

She blew out a sigh. "Not really. He just acted like one." She glanced at Katie. "Present company excluded." As her gaze shifted back to the table, she noted a stack of newspapers on the opposite side. The image of the doomed 747 as it dove into the sea was impossible to miss. "I see we made the front page."

"Yeah. There's even a picture of you." He slid the paper across the table.

The woman staring back from beneath the headline certainly had Jillian's features and coloring, but that particular expression was one never before captured by a camera—lost, stunned, otherworldly. She frowned as she scanned the page, and yes, her name was there, along with Cleona's and Susan's. "I guess they aren't releasing the list of those who didn't survive."

"Not yet and maybe never. At least not to the newspapers."

"Has your editor said anything to you?"

"About reporting the story? No. They might ask me to write it up as a personal-experience human-interest kind of story at some point, but not as news—and not anytime soon."

"That's thoughtful of them." She couldn't help injecting a smidgeon of sarcasm into her comment.

Ranjiv either chose to ignore her tone or he truly didn't notice it. "Yes, it is, actually. They're focusing on the why and how of it rather than the identity of the victims."

For once, Jillian was in agreement with the pursuit of that angle, although she hated the idea of a terrorist group getting any press. Those who died should be remembered, but a public list of the names of the dead seemed rather insensitive. "Almost the first thing Susan said was—"

She stopped when she recalled who she was talking to. Any reporter worth his salt would have a field day with Susan's opinion, and given the flight attendant's outspoken temperament, the story wouldn't need any help to circulate. Nevertheless, that was Susan's story to tell, not Jillian's. "I don't suppose any terrorist factions have claimed responsibility, have they?"

"No." Ranjiv's curiosity had obviously been piqued, but several moments passed before he said anything else. When he finally spoke, his voice contained a note of caution. "Do you think that's what it was? An act of terrorism?"

"I don't know. Given the current political climate, I suppose it could have been."

"Susan thought so too. Didn't she?"

Leave it to a reporter to catch a slip of the tongue...

"Maybe. But that isn't what she said. She only said it wasn't an accident, that planes didn't crash that way, and that the engines were still functioning right up until we hit the water. I'm guessing any eyewitness or analyst would say the same thing."

"Possibly."

She arched a brow. "What do *you* think?"

"I think I agree with Susan."

Jillian shuddered as she recalled the way the engines had screamed as the plane plunged into the sea. She also agreed with Susan's assessment, although at the moment, she didn't care to pursue the matter any further. The number of lives lost in an accident was difficult enough to grasp. Mass murder on such a scale was horrifying. "I doubt we'll ever know the truth."

"Not unless you survivors know something."

The remainder of that sentence seemed to reverberate in the air between them. He wasn't accusing her of lying. Nevertheless, his statement still rankled, making her next query sound more like a retort. "You mean something we aren't telling?"

"Not necessarily. It might be some trivial detail you haven't mentioned yet—or haven't recalled."

Putting that spin on it made his suggestion seem less accusatory. Too bad she still didn't know quite how to take him.

Ranjiv came from a different background and culture. The details of his personality and character were somewhat murky. And he was a reporter. Leaving no stones unturned and no questions unasked was a part of his job and possibly his nature.

"Yeah. It might be one of those things we could only remember while under hypnosis or in a dream."

"Or something that hits you very suddenly."

"Out of the blue?" Nodding, she continued. "That happens to me all the time. Stuff I'm trying to remember suddenly pops into my head when I'm thinking about something completely different." She pushed the newspaper aside, not needing—or wanting—any visual reminders of the tragedy. "I never dreamed my picture would be on the cover of a London newspaper, especially not for such a reason. That's the kind of thing that would only happen to me if I won the lottery."

His smile returned, although it wasn't the same broad a grin as before. "Not for becoming a famous film star, you mean?"

"Not likely." She caught herself before inserting "bloody" into her reply. *Sounds much too British.* "I'm only an assistant bank manager from Memphis. Winning the lottery is more probable, despite the fact that I've never even bought a ticket. I've always thought it made the bank look bad for the employees to be playing the lottery instead of investing wisely." She shrugged. "Weird, huh?"

"Not really. Reporters tend to stay out of trouble to avoid getting their pictures in the paper. They understand the price of notoriety."

"I've never thought about it that way." From the look on his face, she suspected he hadn't either. She eyed him curiously. "Did you make that up?"

A rueful smile accompanied his shrug. "Just making conversation."

Probably to keep from crying or screaming. "Gotcha. This is so strange…" She gestured back and forth between them. "Almost like a blind date that really isn't a date. Or freshman-year roommates trying to figure each other out."

He cleared his throat. "Yes, well, I suppose if we were roommates, we would be of the same gender."

"True. This is more like—" *No. I'm not going there. Not going to say that. No way. No need to give him any ideas.*

She didn't have to say it.

He said it for her. "A couple whose marriage has been arranged and are meeting for the first time?"

She blew out a sharp exhale. "Yeah. Like that."

* * * *

Whether Kavya's spirit resided in Jillian or not, Ranjiv was more convinced than ever that introducing him to this bank manager from Memphis had crossed his mother's mind—and probably more than once.

"Does that analogy bother you?" he asked.

"I'm not sure. Maybe."

"Knowing my mother, I'd have to say it was exactly what she intended. If your plane had landed safely, I can see her introducing us at the airport, and then offering you a ride to your hotel, perhaps even inviting you over for dinner."

"Might be best not to play 'what if?' at this point," she cautioned.

Yes, he could have met this lovely woman under happier circumstances, but he wouldn't have carried her up to his flat, she wouldn't have slept in his bed, and he wouldn't have been the one to make dinner for her. His mother would have done that. The chicken would have tasted better, and his only parent would still be alive.

He flipped a hand in defeat. "You're right. Better not." Still, he couldn't help wondering what it would have been like to meet Jillian without this weight of grief and anger weighing him down. Given his previous blunders with the opposite sex, he doubted that their first dinner together would have been anywhere near as relaxed. Or as relaxed as he could ever be in such a situation. "Don't mind me. It's just that Mother had been trying to find me a wife for so long..."

"Oh, I get that," she said. "I'm sure it was second nature to her. But you must admit, she didn't have a very good track record as a matchmaker."

Somehow, he didn't think that was his mother's fault. At least not entirely. "True, but making an introduction isn't anything like arranging a marriage. Perhaps she would've left it at that."

"Then we should probably do the same."

"Right again," he said. "Sorry I said anything." Clearly she wasn't interested, whether she considered him to be "incredibly handsome" or not. "I don't want to make you feel uncomfortable."

She didn't respond immediately, appearing to consider the matter. "It isn't so much a question of comfort as much as it is me being down on men in general."

Ranjiv didn't find that very reassuring. "'It's not you, it's me?'"

"Something like that."

In the space of three heartbeats, he realized he'd blundered again. His mother hadn't been a matchmaking failure. She'd simply had rotten material to work with.

"But I do like you," Jillian went on. "I mean, any guy who would carry my unconscious body up the stairs, put me to bed, take care of my dog, and then feed me a truly awesome dinner—"

"Can't be all bad?"

She chuckled. "Is better than most, is how I would've put it. And yes, that's a compliment."

Better than most and incredibly handsome...

Perhaps he hadn't blundered after all. Perhaps he only needed to keep his mouth shut and do heroic things like taking Katie to the park for a run.

"Thank you—I think."

Chapter 9

Jillian thought she'd dodged the arranged marriage bullet rather nicely. She wasn't about to admit that Kavya had actually considered introducing her to Ranjiv, even though she'd mentioned the possibility before the crash when the spiritual connection between them didn't exist.

Happier times.

Would she always consider her life in those terms? Pre-crash versus post-crash? Ranjiv would think of it as the before and after of his mother's death. His life would never be the same. Jillian had two big black moments—The Crash and the Wedding That Never Was—coming one on top of the other, both of which were life-changing. Whether they were changes for the better remained to be seen.

A whine drew her attention to Katie. The dog sat by her chair, gazing up at Jillian as though coveting every morsel she put in her mouth.

"Oh, you poor thing," she exclaimed. "Here I am stuffing my face when you're probably starving."

"Don't worry. She's been fed," Ranjiv said. "My neighbor, Shalini, gave me some dog food. Katie seemed to like it."

"Thanks. I wouldn't have any idea—" She paused as the mental image of a particular brand of dog food popped into her head.

Damn. Not again.

Maybe she'd seen the commercial. Then she realized it was a brand she'd never even heard of before. "Did you see the bag it came in?"

He nodded. Getting up from the table, he went to the pantry and pulled out a sack that was a perfect match for the one in her thoughts. "There isn't much, though. Shalini was about out of it herself, but she said she was going to the market so she gave me the last of what she had. We can get more tomorrow."

"Sounds good."

If my head doesn't explode before then.

Jillian could only conclude that this was the same food that Anna had bought for Katie when she'd visited England before. Apparently the dog trainer's presence wasn't completely gone, although their communication seemed to be taking place on a less disturbing level than hearing actual voices. She fought the urge to mentally thank Anna for her assistance—but did it anyway and waited for a response.

None came.

That's a relief.

"She loaned me a leash as well." After returning the bag to the pantry, he paused, peering at her with concern. "Is something wrong?"

Pressing her fingers to her lips, Jillian shook her head. "No. Nothing's wrong."

I just have to get used to being possessed by spirits of the dead.

That was probably what most schizophrenics thought. She'd seen *A Beautiful Mind* and understood how amazingly real hallucinations could seem to the mentally ill. But could those hallucinations convey new information? Surely that knowledge had to be tucked away *somewhere* in the affected person's brain.

Guess that means I'm not schizophrenic. While that conclusion should have been of some comfort to her, given the choice between possession and schizophrenia, Jillian wasn't sure which she would choose.

"About the dog," Ranjiv began. "You said you'd inherited her. Does that mean you're her official owner now?"

"I have no idea," Jillian replied. "I won't know until I speak with Anna's family. I left word with the airline that I wanted to get in touch with them. Haven't heard anything yet." A quick glance proved that the dog was still sticking to her like glue. "She seems to like me, though. Maybe I'll get to keep her."

Ranjiv rolled his eyes. "Like anyone could take her from you now. You didn't see the way she watched over you while you were sleeping. I practically had to drag her out to the park."

"You have a park within walking distance?" she asked, grateful for the momentary diversion.

He nodded. "There are parks all over London, some sections specifically for dogs. Dogs are very popular in Britain, you know."

"Dog parks, huh?" Jillian tried to recall if there were dog parks in the States and decided there probably were. She'd simply never needed one before. "Being a non-dog person put me in something of a minority back home." While Katie did seem partial to her, she was also the only dog Jillian had ever rescued from a watery grave. That had to count for something. "How long did you say it's been since she's been out?"

"Not long," he replied. "But I'm sure she'd love a walk— maybe even a good run. I didn't like to stay out for any length of time in case you woke up and needed something."

"That's very kind of you." She doubted Seth would have given the situation that much thought.

Kavya's words came back to her. *"A good son in so many ways."*

So far, Jillian hadn't needed Kavya's input to know that Ranjiv was a kind, considerate man. He'd returned to the airport to meet with her, given her a lift to her hotel, and then took her home and put her to bed. He should have been preoccupied with his own loss. Instead, he'd done his best to look after a woman he barely knew, along with her dog.

Yet, Ranjiv had "woman troubles." Jillian still didn't get that, unless there really was such a thing as being too nice. His happiness had been so much on Kavya's mind, even to the point of discussing it with a stranger. Was Kavya still trying to find a wife for her son? Jillian hated to admit it even to herself, but Kavya's presence hadn't left her completely. Although no longer speaking to her directly, it was still there in some latent form as though concealed behind a veil.

Perhaps Susan was right about their survival being a miracle. Jillian had so easily dismissed Cleona's question about miracles happening for a reason—mainly because of the number of lives lost—but was the answer as obvious as the three of them being spared to carry out some sort of quest?

Jillian didn't believe in miracles. In fact, she wasn't completely sure she believed in anything. Not even luck.

But now she had weird, psychic events going on in her head that she couldn't control. Things she didn't dare admit to anyone, not even this kind, considerate man who was "thirty years old and so very, very British" and was now clearing the table.

He picked up her empty plate and set it in the sink. "How about you? Would *you* like to go for a walk?"

A walk. Had anyone ever asked her that before? If they had, she couldn't remember it. The lump in her throat caught her by surprise. "Yes, I'd like that very much." She couldn't argue the fact that she felt surprisingly at home in Ranjiv's apartment, but a bit of fresh air was quite welcome.

After all, she *was* on vacation. Sort of.

Jillian hoped she could get past that feeling of having seen London too many times before and actually enjoy some sightseeing. Despite the shock of the crash, she had been charmed by what she'd seen of Ireland—a beautiful, friendly country that was even greener than Tennessee. She might take a trip there someday, although she had no immediate desire to see the Cliffs of Moher again. Not even from the other side.

A slight tremor shook her.

"It's probably a bit nippy out," Ranjiv said as though he'd noticed her shiver. "I'll loan you a jacket. I'm not sure your nifty Irish sweater will be enough. We call them jumpers, by the way."

Jillian made a face at him. "I did see *Bridget Jones's Diary*, so I'm well aware of that fact. It's just that in America, a jumper is something entirely different. What you would probably call a pinafore."

"Ah, I see."

"And I also realize that this is a flat, not an apartment, which makes no sense to me whatsoever. It's not like it's actually flat."

He grinned. "I believe it relates to the idea that one's living space is all on one floor."

She hesitated, pursing her lips. "As opposed to a townhouse, you mean. Although God only knows what you Brits would call that."

This time, he laughed. "A townhouse, actually. Terraced houses are similar, but less grand."

"At least we agree on something." She glanced at Katie. "Something tells me we'd better continue this discussion during our walk. Katie looks like she's about to have a cow." The schnauzer had been dancing toward the door ever since Ranjiv mentioned the word "walk," a term she obviously understood.

Unfortunately, "have a cow" was an expression that Ranjiv didn't appear to understand. His bemused frown soon gave way to a chuckle. "Is that anything like having kittens?"

"Close, but not quite." She rose from her chair. "Just give me a sec in the loo and then we'll nip out for a walk."

"You've been studying."

"Damn straight I have," she replied. "This trip has been in the planning stage for quite some time."

He arched a brow. "How long was your engagement?"

"Six months—although we'd been dating for about five years. How long was yours?"

"Got you beat," he said. "I was maybe a year old when my marriage was arranged. Laksha was only a baby."

Jillian gaped at him in disbelief. "How could anyone possibly expect that to work?"

He shrugged. "In our case, it was more a matter of two friends thinking their children would get along as well as they did."

Jillian had heard of young mothers having similar ideas, but those arrangements were seldom more binding than a wish. "I'm guessing both of your mothers were disappointed."

"Yes, they were."

Ranjiv made no further comment, leading her to believe that his former fiancée was the only one involved who *hadn't* been disappointed.

"Laksha... Lovely name."

His expression went from thoughtful to shuttered in the space of a heartbeat, making Jillian wish she'd kept her mouth shut. "Yes, and so was she."

"Plenty of people thought Seth was a hunk too. Oh, well…" She shrugged. "Be right back."

After a quick trip to the "loo," during which she decided that talking about former intendeds was a downer if there ever was one, she returned just as Ranjiv selected a jacket from the front closet.

"This ought to keep you warm."

Expecting him to hand it to her, Jillian wasn't quite sure how to react when he helped her to slip it on.

He gave her shoulders a quick squeeze. "Better?"

"Much." The garment still carried a trace of his scent, evoking warm, comfortable feelings that were oddly familiar.

She gave herself a mental slap. Of course those feelings were familiar. She'd been snuggled up in a bed that smelled the same way.

But that wasn't the only reason. Scent memories had deep roots, and this one went much deeper than it should have.

Pulling the collar up around her neck, she managed to stave off another shudder while attempting to ignore the prickling sensation at her nape. "Come on, Katie. Let's go for a walk."

* * * *

Ranjiv donned a fleece hoodie and then held the door open for Jillian. "Sure you feel up to this?"

"Absolutely." She paused on the threshold, aiming a wry smile over her shoulder. "What's the matter? Afraid you'll have to carry me up the stairs again?"

"No. Just don't want you to overdo." He'd already forgotten how difficult that task had been, only remembering how much he'd enjoyed holding her in his arms. "Be careful. Those steps are a bit steep."

With a hand on the railing, she peered downward. "Oh, God. And you had to carry me up them. I'm so sorry."

"It wasn't bad. Really."

Katie shot past her and scampered down the first flight, uttering a sharp bark when she reached the landing.

"Hush, Katie," Jillian said. "You'll wake the neighbors."

"I doubt it," Ranjiv said. "At least, not that particular neighbor."

He nodded toward the door on the first landing. "Jasraj is elderly and quite deaf."

"That's good to know. Who did you say you got the dog food from?"

"That was Shalini. She lives on the ground floor."

Acknowledging that information with a brief nod, Jillian preceded him down the stairs. "I must remember to thank her. I hope it didn't cause her any inconvenience."

"I doubt it," he said. "Tomorrow is market day, and there are a number of shops nearby."

"Must be nice. There isn't much within walking distance from where I live. You have to drive just about everywhere." She reached down to snap the leash on Katie's collar while he opened the door to the street.

"You don't live in the city, then?"

"In the suburbs, actually. I like the open spaces, but there's a lot to be said for being able to nip down ta the pub fer a pint without having to drive."

Her sudden shift from a Southern drawl to a creditable London accent drew a chuckle. "There is at that."

Ranjiv found it interesting that Jillian could make him laugh so easily when only a day ago, he hadn't believed he would ever smile again. Being informed of his mother's death had been quite a shock—a shock compounded by seeing the video of the crash. The calls he'd made to family and friends afterward—having to relate the same terrible news over and over again—had exhausted him completely. After a sleepless night during which the crash had replayed in his head until he thought he would go mad, he'd come very close to skipping the meeting with Jillian. He almost wished he had after hearing what she had to say.

He felt differently now. When the airline spokesman had announced her name, Ranjiv hadn't known what sort of person to expect. Certainly not anyone like this woman. She had come as a complete surprise—perhaps even more so than her account of how she'd survived the crash.

The hours she'd spent asleep in his bed had seemed just as

interminable as his own sleepless night. He had to keep telling himself that she needed the rest even while fearing she might have lapsed into a coma. Taking the dog for walks and fixing dinner had diverted his thoughts, although neither of those activities had done much to alleviate the dull, hollow feeling in his chest. But now, after only an hour or so in Jillian's company, he felt alive again, despite the painful reminders of the loss of his mother and of Laksha.

He would never forget his mother, nor did he wish to. But even after eight years, he hadn't forgotten Laksha. The pain she'd caused him was still fresh in his mind, and none of the women he'd dated since then had erased the sting of her rejection. In truth, they'd only made it worse, each failure reinforcing his perception of himself as the kind of man no woman could possibly want.

Being told what a preposterous idea that was by his friends was no help at all. They weren't the ones who had taken his measure and found him lacking. His most recent failure had come in the form of Eliza, who'd referred to him as a cold fish—to his face. The worst part of it was that he knew she was right.

And now there was Jillian. Was the connection he felt to her only because of the bond she seemed to share with his mother?

Oh, say it isn't so…

Either way, the timing was wrong. The situation was wrong. Jillian was only visiting England. Her home was an ocean away from his.

Maybe that was why she felt so safe. Nothing could happen between them. Nothing lasting anyway. She would be leaving too soon for that. There was no risk of failure because there was no possibility of success.

Nonetheless, when she hooked her arm through his and leaned closer, it felt natural. Normal.

Perfect.

"I'm so glad you got this leash," she said. "I'm still not sure how well Katie handles traffic."

"She seems to do okay." He doubted she needed a leash the way the dog stayed right with her, matching every step, every pause. He chose not to mention it. A psychic connection to the dog's owner might also suggest a connection to his mother. He didn't want to think about that anymore. "Although navigating through a crowd might be a problem."

She nodded. "Speaking of crowds, you said tomorrow was market day. Think we could go there?"

"Sure. It's open from seven to two. We can walk down the Broadway too. There are tons of shops and restaurants. You'll feel almost like you're in India."

"Can't wait to see it," she said. "Once I get some clothes and a suitcase, I might actually find a hotel and get out of your hair."

Her words hit him like a sickening blow to the gut. "You don't have to do that. I don't mind if you stay here."

"I know, but it's got to feel as weird to you as it does to me. Besides, you wouldn't want your neighbors getting the wrong idea."

Simply walking arm in arm with Jillian was a noteworthy event, and under different circumstances, his neighbors would probably buy a round in his honor if they thought he might be getting somewhere with a woman. No telling what Jasraj might do. The old man had been teasing Ranjiv about finding a wife for years. "You needn't worry about that." His stomach churned again as another thought struck him. "Unless you truly prefer to stay somewhere else."

"I don't, actually, although I probably should. Accepting your hospitality for one night is enough of an imposition." She sighed. "If I hadn't slept so long, I could've found a place today—probably still can." Hesitating, she chewed her thumbnail. "I could make some calls and get a cab to take me there."

"Would you rather stay at my mother's house?"

She shook her head. "That would be worse."

Ranjiv didn't see how, but at the moment, he didn't care. He couldn't help feeling that if Jillian moved into a hotel, he would never see her again. "Then stay with me. I–I want you to stay."

Had he actually said that aloud?

Her pensive expression told him he had. "That's very kind of you, but I don't want to kick you out of your bed, and if it's all the same to you, I'd rather not spend the next three weeks sleeping on a couch."

There was another alternative—two, actually. "We could take turns." He sucked in a breath and fixed his gaze on the pavement in front of him. "Or we could share."

Chapter 10

JILLIAN WOULD HAVE PREFERRED THE LATTER CHOICE IF IT HADN'T been such an incredibly bad idea. Then again, perhaps it wasn't so much that he *wanted* her to stay with him as it was that he *needed* her.

There was a difference.

Could she turn down a man in his situation? After all, sharing a bed didn't necessarily mean he was asking for greater intimacy.

But what if he was?

The warm fuzzies she got from wearing his coat would be nothing compared to curling up with the genuine article. Still, she hadn't slept with anyone but Seth in so long it was hard to imagine getting that close to someone else. At least, not yet.

"I don't think I'm ready to share," she finally said. "I wish I was, but—well, I'm sure you understand."

Ranjiv's reply consisted of a sniff and a quick nod. Clearly her response was the one he'd expected.

As they turned down another street, Jillian could see the gleam of water on the opposite side. "Is that a creek over there?"

"That's the Grand Union Canal. My flat overlooks it."

She'd seen the doors to what appeared to be a balcony, but hadn't ventured out. "Must be a nice view."

"It is." They'd walked another half a block before he spoke again. "I am perfectly willing to give up my bed and sleep elsewhere."

His stilted, overly formal speech surprised her. A glance revealed the tightness in his jaw, his lips pressed into a firm line. He appeared to be grappling with some emotion, although she didn't believe it was anger. Disappointment? Chagrin? Resignation? She wasn't sure.

"I didn't mean to hurt your feelings," she said. "You've already done so much for me. I hate to be a bother."

"Bother?" He said the word with a touch of asperity. "Trust me, you're anything but that."

Once again, she reminded herself that she knew next to nothing about him. "This is important to you, isn't it?"

He nodded. "My mother would want me to look after you, and I—" He drew in an uneven breath. "I don't want to be alone." Squaring his shoulders, he let out a nervous sort of laugh. "Sounds a bit pathetic, doesn't it?"

"Not pathetic at all. I'm still trying to figure out why I decided to come on this trip alone. I've never even been to Nashville by myself." She attempted a smile. "Although now I have you and Katie to keep me company."

"Does that mean you'll stay?"

She heaved a sigh. "I guess so. Dunno about sleeping together, but we'll see how it goes."

"Great." The tension seemed to drain out of him as he pointed toward a gate on the next corner. "There's the entrance to the green. You can probably let her off the leash now."

As Jillian stooped down to undo the leash, she gave Katie a pat on the head, pausing to gaze into the dog's eyes—eyes that were filled with more understanding than those of most humans. "There you go, Katie. Have a good run!"

The schnauzer shot through the gate and scampered off across the well-lit green as though she knew exactly where she was headed.

"I can tell you've brought her here before," she said.

"Yeah. She's a smart little thing. Probably knows the way by now."

Jillian had never been envious of dogs, nor had she ever considered how much easier life would be if humans were as straightforward as they were. Dogs followed their instincts; they loved to eat and adored affection. Why hadn't she ever seen that before?

Fearing the answer to that question would only cause her more worry, she gave some thought to Ranjiv's offer. True, he hadn't actually said anything about a physical relationship, but in this day and age, a man didn't offer to share a bed with a woman without at least considering the possibility. She still thought it was a bad idea. A brief affair with him would certainly be interesting, but it wouldn't solve either of their problems.

Or would it?

It would certainly alleviate their loneliness—at least for a while. Spontaneity wouldn't be a problem. She had an IUD, and she seriously doubted he was carrying any nasty diseases—unless that was the reason for his "woman troubles."

Oh, God. How in the world can I possibly ask him something like that?

The social disease topic generally didn't pop up in casual conversation. Perhaps she could volunteer her own birth control/STD information first. Then again, if he stuck to his side of the bed, there would be no need for any discussion of the kind. About the most they could catch from one another was a cold.

Or fleas from the dog.

"I hope Katie doesn't pick up any cooties in the park," she said. "I have no idea what kind of flea or worming schedule she's been on."

"She belonged to a breeder, right?"

"Yeah. Trainer, handler, breeder... She gave me her card. Guess I could call—" Realizing the sheer stupidity of what she'd just said, Jillian snapped her mouth shut and shook her head. "No, I can't. I lost it along with my purse."

"Yes, but you know her name. Her business would be listed online, and surely someone is taking care of her other dogs."

"True. I could do a search—that is, if I can borrow a computer. The phone they gave me probably has that capability, but I haven't had a chance to play with it much. I'm better on a computer."

"No problem," he said. "I have two."

"Thanks." She watched as Katie nosed about in some nearby shrubbery. "I really wish someone would call me. Anna said she planned to breed Katie in the fall, and her pups were bound to be worth a lot. They may want her back."

"Have you checked your phone for messages? I never heard it ring, but someone may have called while I was out."

"It does have voicemail." She pulled the phone from her pocket, studying the screen. She wasn't very familiar with it yet, but if there was a missed call or a message, she couldn't see it. "Still nothing. They probably have more important issues to deal with."

Just as Ranjiv did. Why he wanted to add a houseguest and her dog to his "to do" list was anyone's guess.

Unless he really did need her.

Ranjiv had said he would be free the rest of the week, and having an acquaintance in London who had a car and knew which side of the road to drive on was a definite plus. He hadn't said how long he wanted her to stay. His mother's memorial service was on Saturday. She could keep him company until then. He probably wouldn't need her after that. She could check into a hotel and finish out the rest of her vacation on her own.

Then maybe she could sort out the weird shit going on in her head.

Unless she really had gone loco. Given all that had happened, temporary insanity was understandable. She was entitled to her meltdown—the one she hadn't had time for as yet. Ah, the bliss of shutting down her thoughts and finally escaping from them. Escape from the total failure she knew herself to be. On the surface, her life wasn't that bad. She had a decent job and earned a reasonable salary. Always doing well enough, but not super. She'd never been one of those beaming people who had their acts together and possessed all the vibrancy she lacked. Where was the peace she sought? There were horrors everywhere she went, no respite to be found.

Perhaps she wasn't the one who'd gone off the deep end. As they strolled further into the park and she watched the small dog that had belonged to a woman who loved dogs more than people, she realized it was the rest of the world that had gone mad. Madness that crashed planes into skyscrapers and into the sea. Madness that killed randomly without remorse. Violence for the sake of violence. Was there a particle of sanity anywhere? What was the point in trying to live when the entire world was disintegrating into bedlam?

For the first time since the crash, she wished she hadn't survived. Drowning would have put an end to the struggle. Survival only made it worse. And now, as if the trials and tribulations of her own life weren't enough to manage, she had acquired those of three others. Didn't they know they'd put their souls on a ship that was already sinking?

Where were they now that she needed them? She had no voices in her head offering comfort and solace. No cheerleaders in the back of her mind urging her to keep fighting. Her nap that afternoon was the only break she'd had since Seth had put the final nail in the coffin of her happiness.

Seth wouldn't have made her happy. She knew that now. But at least she'd had the illusion of joy for a while.

"You're awfully quiet." Ranjiv's voice seemed to come out of nowhere, piercing the maelstrom of her thoughts. "Are you tired? Do we need to turn back?"

Turn back?

Could anyone truly do that? Was there such a thing in life as a replay where the outcome actually changed?

She didn't think so—at least not until she looked up.

Ranjiv's deep brown eyes seemed to liquefy in the darkness, the pupils huge, obliterating the iris, opening a void that sucked her in the way a black hole captures light. Thick, arching brows. The cleft in his chin. The fullness of his lips.

So completely and utterly sane.

A glance toward a streetlight nearly blinded her. "I'm not sure."

"It was a mistake for you to exert yourself so soon," he said, his tone brisk. "You don't appear to be injured, but the toll that sort of thing takes on a body isn't always noticeable at first."

"My body feels okay. It's my brain that's messed up."

"I wouldn't be too sure about that." He took her hand. "My God. You're like ice." Calling to Katie, he took the leash from Jillian's numb fingers then knelt to snap it onto the dog's collar. "Come on, then." He wrapped an arm around Jillian's waist and steered her toward the street.

* * * *

Jillian leaned against him as they headed back to his flat. Ranjiv had no idea why, but she seemed to be growing stronger with each step.

"I feel better now," she said after a bit. "At least I think I do."

"This is my fault," he insisted. "I upset you with all my talk about staying together in my flat and sharing the bed. It was selfish of me. I shouldn't ask it of you."

She shook her head slowly. "It wasn't that. I don't know what it was. But there for a while I felt like—you'll probably think it sounds silly—but it was like the way Harry Potter felt whenever the dementors were closing in on him."

He managed a short chuckle. "So now you're being haunted by imaginary creatures from a children's book?"

"I knew you would laugh. But for a while there, I felt as though all my thoughts and emotions were being replaced with despair."

Closing his fingers around the hand she had placed on his arm, he nodded. "You're warmer now."

Ranjiv wasn't about to attempt to explain it. Not beyond delayed stress syndrome and the cool night air anyway.

"Yeah. Pretty weird, huh?"

"*Definitely* weird." With a nod, he raised her hand to his lips, pressing a kiss to her fingers in a gesture so automatic he had surely done it before.

But he hadn't. In fact, he couldn't recall ever having done such a thing in his life. It wasn't in his nature to be demonstrative with his affections, not with any of the women he'd dated or even his female family members, and certainly not with Laksha. And yet it felt so natural with Jillian. Almost as if he'd done it in another life.

Eliza's cold fish analogy didn't fit with the way he felt about Jillian. With her, the tender touches felt right. He didn't know any other way to describe it.

"You said Kavya's memorial service was going to be on Saturday, right?"

Her question didn't seem to fit with the situation. Perhaps she was trying to change the subject. "Yes. At one o'clock."

"That isn't how Hindu funerals and services are usually done, is it?"

"No. Usually the cremation is the next day and the memorial service is held weeks later. To be honest, I wasn't sure how they would do it without her body having been recovered. At least, not as yet."

He'd been warned that his mother's body might never be found. No doubt the crash site would be investigated—it wasn't as if no one knew where the plane went down—and the sea wasn't as deep there as, say, the mid-Atlantic. But there were no guarantees.

"The service should still give you some sort of closure," she said. "Is anyone coming from India or Chicago?"

"No, but she had a lot of friends here—and my uncle Pratap and his family live in London. Mother worked with him in his import business."

She shivered. "I wouldn't blame anyone for not wanting to fly after hearing about the crash. It probably scares the bejesus out of them to think it might happen again."

"Maybe." He caught himself hugging her more tightly to his side—something else he had rarely done. "What about you?"

"I may have used up all the luck I had coming to me with that last flight—or I would have if I believed in that sort of thing."

"You don't believe in luck?"

"Not really. Although that may be because mine hasn't been all that great up until now, especially in the last week. But I *am* alive, which is more than I can say for nearly everyone else on that plane." She drew in a quivering breath. "It's hard being here with you and Katie knowing both of you would rather I hadn't been the one to survive."

Ranjiv was having similar thoughts, albeit from the opposite point of view. He was very pleased to have met Jillian, and he was even more pleased to have a reason for her to stay with him. The awkwardness resulted from the fact that for the two of them to meet, Jillian had to endure a broken engagement, a plane crash, and the cancellation of her hotel reservation.

And my mother had to die.

"That's not true," he said. "I would rather everyone had survived."

"Yeah. Me too." She spoke so softly he barely heard her.

If he and Jillian had met under different circumstances, he doubted anything would have come of it. He wasn't sure anything would happen now. Not every cloud had a silver lining. Some storms wreaked death and suffering with no redeeming effects whatsoever.

Even reminding himself that positive outcomes were sometimes long in coming didn't help very much. The horrific stories he'd had to report on had taken their toll; witnessing man's inhumanity to man had sickened him to the point of cynicism. His Hindu upbringing should have been a help to him. It wasn't. If souls were indeed striving for perfection, an awful lot of them weren't trying hard enough.

He used to believe that reporting the news celebrated mankind's victories while holding up its flaws as examples of how not to live. Sometimes he wondered if they weren't simply giving ideas to the wicked.

A tug at his arm refocused his thoughts on the woman beside him.

"Now you're the one being quiet," she said.

He shrugged. "Dementors are everywhere."

"They sure are." She heaved a sigh. "Makes me want to have some outrageous fun just to thwart them." A bleak smile touched her lips. "I think I've forgotten how to do that."

"I'm not sure I ever knew. Perhaps that's the task we face—finding happiness in the midst of sorrow."

"Is that a quote?"

Her gaze held his for a long moment.

"I don't know," he finally said. "Maybe." His steps slowed as he closed his eyes, remembering…

"Sorrow prepares you for joy. It violently sweeps everything out of your house, so that new joy can find space to enter. It shakes the yellow leaves from the bough of your heart, so that fresh, green leaves can grow in their place. It pulls up the rotten roots, so that new roots hidden beneath have room to grow. Whatever sorrow shakes from your heart, far better things will take their place."

"You were definitely quoting someone that time."

Ranjiv opened his eyes, only then realizing that he'd spoken those words aloud. "Rumi—a medieval Persian poet and Sufi mystic. He believed souls must evolve in order to achieve perfection." He was oversimplifying the matter, of course. No one could truly explain Sufism or Rumi in one sentence.

Nevertheless, Jillian acknowledged this definition with a quick nod. "Do you believe it's possible to reach perfection? I've never known anyone who even came close."

"Perhaps enlightenment might be a better term."

"Maybe," she conceded. "But that still makes for a pretty tiny minority. Most people don't even seem to try."

He shrugged. "Anything requiring multiple lifetimes can't be easy. And I'm guessing most souls don't want to give up the chance to be born again."

"Too fond of the pleasures of the flesh?"

"Something like that."

Ranjiv had considered the possibility that his soul might be approaching enlightenment because it didn't seem to be terribly interested in those particular pleasures—a possibility he immediately discounted. His lifelong dearth of intimacy had nothing to do with any perfection of the soul and everything to do with a shortage of courage.

No. That wasn't it either.

A far more likely reason was that he'd been suffering from the lack of Jillian Dulaine.

Simply put, he hadn't found the right woman.

Until now.

Chapter 11

Kavya either didn't give a damn about Sufi mysticism or she was keeping mum about everything except how to make idlis and dosas, which was probably for the best.

Jillian still hadn't figured out the origin of those depressing thoughts. Granted, they were topics she'd considered from time to time, but never on such a rock-bottom level.

At the moment, however, she cared less about that than what she would wear to bed that night. She stifled a yawn. "Speaking of the pleasures of the flesh, a good night's sleep is pretty high on my list at the moment. You wouldn't guess it from how long I slept in this skirt and sweater, but I'm kinda particular about my nightgowns."

He winced. "I suppose that rules out wearing one of my shirts."

"Probably. Are there any shops around here open this late?"

"I'm sure we could find something, but we'd have better luck tomorrow."

"True. Maybe we should wait. I can tough it out for one more night." She yawned again. "Damn. You'd think I'd be over my jet lag by now."

The other aspects of the past few days made jet lag seem incredibly tame and insignificant. Despite having voiced the worst of what weighed so heavily on her soul, Jillian still hadn't been able to sort out the awkward feelings she had for Ranjiv. Disregarding Kavya's input about his character, her son was still a virtual stranger. And yet, he was unlike any man she had ever met, a detail that intrigued her. Unfortunately, they had both suffered losses that seemed to prohibit them from throwing caution to the wind and falling into each other's arms.

I should be on my honeymoon.

That was the problem. She'd looked forward to this trip for so long and had made so many plans... Good ol' Seth should have been here to screw her brains out instead of screwing up her life. In the realm of infinite possibilities, there was a chance that if Seth had been on the plane, it might not have crashed at all. And if Seth *had* died in the crash, she would now be a grieving widow and the man walking beside her with his arm around her waist wouldn't have stood a snowball's chance in hell of taking his place.

On the other hand, if the plane hadn't crashed and his mother hadn't died, Ranjiv might have been the one shagging her silly tonight.

Shagging. What a peculiar term. No stranger than the f-word, perhaps, but certainly less universally understood. Or maybe it wasn't. The term popped up in a movie now and then, and she'd watched enough BBC productions to have heard it.

Ranjiv fished his keys out of his pocket as they approached his door. "We've gotten quiet again."

She nodded. "Please don't offer me a penny for my thoughts."

"That bad?"

"I'm not sure. Maybe."

"You might like mine better," he said.

"Oh?"

"Yeah. I just remembered a gift someone gave me a while back. Something I've never even tried on."

"And that would be...?"

"An Irish flannel nightshirt."

"Perfect." It would undoubtedly be too big for her, but when it came to sleepwear too big beat too small by a mile. The fact that there was nothing even remotely sexy about flannel would also eliminate any need for the birth control and STD discussion. "I saw some of those at the shop in Inisheer. Too bad I didn't think to buy one."

Nor had she thought to buy a change of underwear, figuring she would take care of that once she was settled in her hotel. The possibility of borrowing a pair of undies from Ranjiv hadn't existed then, and she wasn't about to ask him now. Tall, lean, and narrow-hipped, his nightshirt might be too big, but she would never fit into his boxers.

"You can keep mine if you decide you like it," he said. "Not really my style."

Okay. I am so not going to ask what he prefers to wear.

He unlocked the door. "This'll be a first. I've never gone shopping with a woman before. Not for clothes anyway."

"You don't know what you're missing," she drawled. "Although there are a few things I'd prefer to buy without any, um, company."

"No worries. I can wait outside."

"Like a chauffeur, you mean?"

In an instant, Ranjiv's smile vanished and his stiff formality returned. "If you wish." Opening the door, he waved her inside.

With a roll of her eyes, she grabbed his arm and steered him up the stairs. "I didn't mean it that way and you know it. Don't be so damn touchy."

Jillian didn't know anything about prejudice against Indian immigrants in Britain. The best she'd ever been able to tell, there wasn't any. Perhaps she'd been wrong about that.

When he failed to comment, she prodded him. "Have you ever been mistaken for a chauffeur?"

"No. But I have been accused of other things."

"Such as?"

"Maybe *accused* isn't the right word, but I've had a couple of people ask me for more tea in a restaurant."

She chuckled. "Probably just looking for an excuse to talk to the best-looking man in the place."

That remark drew a tiny grin. "Not unless they were homosexual. And I don't think they were."

"Ah, well, maybe they were jealous of the way their wives were staring at you and thought they needed to take you down a peg." She gave him a nudge. "Come on, Ranjiv. I was only kidding. And even if you were my chauffeur, I'd—"

She stopped herself before completing that sentence. She

couldn't tell him she thought he was hot. Not when she was about to share a bed with him.

Maybe.

The jury was still out on that decision.

"I mean, this isn't *Downton Abbey*," she chided. "Even in that story, the earl's daughter married the chauffeur."

"True. I'm sorry. It just hit me wrong. Something to do with the sort of comments another woman used to make."

"One you dated?"

He nodded. "The most recent. Eliza didn't do much for my ego."

"Seth just about destroyed mine." The weight of that memory descended one more time. She swallowed hard, then gritted her teeth. "I really wish I could forget that." She wished Ranjiv could do the same and forget all the sadness in his life. Then they might be able to have fun and enjoy each other's company. Maybe even fall in love.

No. The circumstances made it too soon. Too much. Too inappropriate.

Too bad.

He nodded. "Seems like the things you most want to forget are the ones that stay with you forever."

"I have a theory about that." Stopping on the first landing, she turned to face him. "I think it's because a punch in the nose has far more lasting effects than a pat on the back."

His smile did very little to temper his bleak demeanor. "Yet we keep bashing on, never wondering why we do it."

"Oh, I think we wonder. It just doesn't matter because the drive to continue is stronger than the urge to quit." She held his gaze for as long as she could without standing on her tiptoes to kiss him. He needed kissing. Needed a woman to kiss him and love him and make him feel like a king. She suspected he hadn't felt that way in a very long time. Perhaps he never had. "But we all need a break now and then."

A sound from near her feet drew her attention away from the

somber depths of his eyes. Not bothering to hide her feelings, Katie let out a yawn.

"Is that what this is?" he asked. "A break?"

Jillian wasn't sure which "this" he was referring to, although she suspected it was the space of time between the pain of leaving one love behind and embarking upon the exhilaration of the next. That interlude when appearances and behaviors lost their importance and being yourself was all you could manage—the only thing for which you had the strength. Granted, it was a rather selfish period, but it was necessary in order to regroup and soldier on—or bash on, as he would put it, which seemed even more appropriate in this case.

"Yeah," she replied after that moment's pause. "I guess it is." She worked up a fair imitation of a smile. "I should be trying to cheer you up, and all I seem to do is make you sad."

"I'm not sad exactly. I'm not sure what to call it. I feel helpless, ineffective, powerless. Like nothing I can do will ever make any difference."

In that instant, she realized what he lacked. He needed to be needed. She could do that much for him. "You can't bring your mother back, but you *have* made a difference—at least for me." Her throat tightened as her gaze met his. "You don't get it, do you? You *rescued* me, Ranjiv. Maybe you weren't the one who hauled me out of the sea, but without you, I'd be so lost right now I don't even want to think about it."

* * * *

Ranjiv forgot all the reasons why he should curb the desire to touch her. To stop himself before attempting to wipe away her tears and kiss her quivering lips. She didn't resist as he cradled her cheeks in his hands, brushing away her tears with his thumbs before moving on to trace the curve of her cheekbones. The smooth softness of her skin both intrigued and mystified him. Not a speck of makeup adorned her face, and yet it was the most exquisite sight he'd ever seen. Beautiful, serene, with a luminous quality that seemed to impart an added glow to the dimly lit stairwell.

Whether he had moved slowly or with lightning speed, suddenly his lips touched hers. Her hand rested lightly on his shoulder, the one tiny bit of encouragement he needed. Threading his fingers through her hair, he pulled her even closer as she cupped the back of his head and deepened the kiss.

If he'd needed anything to prove that Jillian wasn't the carrier of his mother's soul, this was it. As a child, he'd never received more than the occasional peck on the top of his head. *Nothing* like this. No one had *ever* kissed him like this—not any of the women he'd dated and certainly not Laksha.

At last he understood why men craved a woman's touch—and not just any woman. One particular woman. This lovely woman his mother had sent to him with her dying words.

He should have been crying, but the joy welling up inside him went beyond tears, beyond words. Gentle, sensuous, and so sweet it stole his breath, her kiss sent him soaring to a level of elation he'd never even dreamed about.

And he liked it there.

Katie's soft bark recalled him to his surroundings or he probably would have stayed in that same spot kissing Jillian all night.

"Sounds like she's telling us to get a room," Jillian murmured against his lips.

"Good thing we have one."

Releasing him, she took a step back. "Yeah, well… Maybe we should rethink that."

Had he imagined those emotions or had he blown them all out of proportion? No one could deny feelings that strong.

Or could they?

Never having felt anything of the sort, he had no idea.

Perhaps she was right. Perhaps they did need to reconsider the wisdom of staying together. He hadn't wanted it to stop anymore than he wanted it to end there.

"I'm sorry," he said. "Should I not have kissed you?"

Wide-eyed, she stared at him for a long moment before her swift exhale broke the silence. "I'm the one who should be apologizing. I'm pretty sure that was *me* kissing *you*."

No wonder he couldn't remember closing the distance between them. "Do you hear me complaining?"

"No, but I still shouldn't have done it. You just lost your mother, and my fiancé practically ditched me at the altar. We're supposed to be taking a break from all that relationship stuff."

At least she hadn't referred to it as relationship *crap*. "Really? Well, just for the record, that was the best *break* I've ever had."

Jillian's expression changed so many times over the next few seconds, Ranjiv couldn't even begin to guess her thoughts. He'd almost settled on "bewildered" when she finally spoke.

"You're kidding me, right?"

"No, I'm perfectly serious."

"But you were engaged for *years*. In all that time, didn't you ever—"

"Kiss her?" He shook his head. "Not like that. In fact I—" Ranjiv had never admitted this to anyone he'd dated since Laksha broke their engagement. He wasn't sure he could do it now. "I hardly ever touched her."

"You mean you never slept with her?"

Moment of truth time... "I've never slept with anyone."

Her jaw dropped. "Holy shit. You're a–a—"

Great. She couldn't even say the word.

He said it for her. "Virgin."

Chapter 12

IN ANOTHER DAY AND TIME, JILLIAN'S LACK OF VIRGINITY WOULD have been the anomaly rather than Ranjiv's chaste status. But from a cultural standpoint, it made sense.

Sort of.

The trick now was figuring out how to respond. He certainly wasn't unappealing—damned sexy, in fact. She'd tried to determine his flaws before and hadn't been able to find any. He obviously wasn't gay, nor did he appear to drink to excess. In reasonably good physical condition, he wasn't an aggressive asshole, and if he had any annoying personal habits, she hadn't noticed them yet. He even smelled good.

"I'm surprised no one has caught you before now," she finally said. "Or are you saving yourself for marriage?"

"Partly," he replied. "But that was when I was promised to Laksha."

"I can understand that. I find it hard to believe, but I get it. What I don't get is why none of the others since then— Wait. Were they Indian?"

"Not exclusively. As a reporter, I meet all sorts of people."

And at least half of them female.

There goes that theory.

She could only imagine the kind of looks Ranjiv would draw in a singles bar. He was flat-out gorgeous. *British women must be too picky.*

No. Any woman would be attracted to him—any woman with eyes.

He held up a hand. "Before you wear out your brain trying to figure out why, I might as well tell you. I've had a hard time with it myself—and I've tried to get past it—but I think the whole arranged marriage thing is still stuck in my head."

She nodded slowly. "Your mother didn't approve of the others."

He blew out a pent-up breath. "No, she didn't." His next breath was also held just a touch too long. "But I think she approved of *you*."

The implication was obvious, but she chose to overlook it for the moment. "That really does matter to you, doesn't it?"

"Evidently."

"And her approval is still important, even now?"

"Even now."

Perhaps he was less "British" than Kavya had realized. It was tough to ignore the teachings of childhood even in this modern age. Jillian could understand the influence but didn't consider it a valid reason for embarking on a relationship—especially one in which she didn't see much of a future.

"And here's the weirdest part," he added. "I think she was absolutely right."

She peered up at him through narrowed eyes. "About what, exactly?"

"That you and I would make a good pair."

Whether Kavya still lurked somewhere in the back of her mind or not, Jillian tended to agree. She would have liked Ranjiv no matter how she met him. Even if they hadn't been introduced, she would've found an excuse to talk to him—or at least tried to.

She hadn't needed Kavya's input to spot him at the airport. Her confirmation, perhaps, but that was all. He would have caught her eye anyway.

Now she'd kissed him.

And she certainly hadn't done it out of pity.

"What do *you* think?" he asked.

"I think we need to continue this discussion somewhere else." As Jillian started up the stairs, her downward glance caught the tilt of the Katie's head and her raised brow—in addition to the leash dragging behind her on the steps. Apparently kissing Ranjiv was enough of a distraction for her to have dropped it. "You're such a good girl." Giving the schnauzer a pat, she picked up the leash. "Don't even need this thing, do you?"

Katie responded with a sharp bark.

Jillian waved a beckoning hand at Ranjiv, who had remained on the landing, his expression somewhat bemused. "She's much better trained than you are. Maybe I should put it around your neck instead."

"No need for that. I'm coming." Ranjiv caught up quickly, reaching the door to his apartment ahead of them. Opening the door, he waved them inside with a bow. "Ladies first."

Jillian chuckled. "I don't believe I've ever known such a gentleman before." She aimed a questioning look at the dog. "Have you, Katie?"

Katie gave herself a quick shake and trotted through the doorway.

Jillian froze for a second, then stole a peek at Ranjiv. When their eyes met, she could've sworn he shivered.

"Spooky."

"Please don't start that again," Jillian begged. "She didn't just shake her head. She shook her whole body. Dogs do that a lot." At least she thought they did—especially when they got wet. Katie wasn't wet, but perhaps it was something all dogs did before going inside.

He arched a brow. "Still spooky."

The quirky smile that accompanied his remark stole her breath. How many women had seen that look? Not many, she concluded, otherwise he would've lost his virginity long ago.

Was that why she was here?

She doubted it. Kavya had wanted her son to find a wife, not engage in a casual affair.

"Are you feeling okay now?" he asked.

"Much better, thanks." She took off the jacket he'd loaned her and hung it on a peg by the door. "But I should probably sit down and rest for a while."

"Good idea. You had me worried."

"Glad you didn't have to carry me up the stairs again?"

His lips twitched before stretching into a slow grin. "Not really."

Whether he intended it or not, that smile and his reply seemed openly seductive—or at least flirtatious. Either way, the atmosphere between them had changed.

You can't kiss a man until your toes curl without expecting him to get ideas.

She still wasn't completely sure why she'd done it. Perhaps because she'd been with Seth for so long. She was used to kissing him, which made kissing Ranjiv seem natural.

Maybe.

Then again, she hadn't done any actual flirting in years. Ranjiv wasn't the only one with rusty dating skills.

Taking a seat on the sofa, she leaned back, slipping off her shoes. "That's sweet of you to say."

"I meant it." He hung up his own coat and sat down beside her—not so closely that their thighs touched, but near enough for her to feel his heat. "I don't get to carry beautiful women into my flat every day."

She smiled to herself. Falling for this man would be so easy, requiring far less effort than resisting the temptation.

The dog's barely audible whine drew her attention. "Is it okay if Katie sits on the couch?"

"Sure, why not?"

"Umm…dog hair and fleas?"

"I don't think that breed sheds much, and it's safe to assume that her previous owner never let a flea within a mile of her dogs."

"True." Shifting sideways until her back was against the armrest, Jillian patted the seat.

Katie jumped up immediately, turning around twice before curling up in the crook of Jillian's leg and gazing up at her with adoring eyes.

Jillian cupped a hand beneath the dog's muzzle. "Hear that, Katie? He thinks you're beautiful."

"Did I say that?" Ranjiv's light, teasing tone was as appealing as his smile.

Not daring to look at him, Jillian focused on the dog, stroking her head and fluffing her mutton-chop whiskers. "You let her get up on the furniture. Same thing."

"Right." A moment later, Ranjiv placed a hand on the dog's back, then slid it up to where Jillian toyed with the soft hair on Katie's ears.

Her eyes drifted shut as his hand closed over hers. Wetting her lips, she pressed them together, swallowing around the lump in her throat. Not long ago, he'd kissed that same hand. The memory alone sent a quiver of desire racing through her only to be replaced with a pang of regret.

"I'm sorry," she whispered. "I know what you must be thinking, but it's too soon for that. I don't want to get hurt again. I really, really don't."

She tried to imagine how she would feel if she'd met Ranjiv without the pain of a broken engagement so fresh in her mind. She'd warned Ranjiv not to play "what if." Now she was doing it herself.

"I won't hurt you."

The sincerity in his voice made her open her eyes. "How can you know that?"

"Because *I'm* the one who always gets hurt—never the woman."

She nodded slowly. "And yet you keep 'bashing on.'"

"Yeah." With a wry smile that had a peculiar twisting effect on her heart, he added, "I must be mental."

"No more so than anyone else." If she sat there with him another second, she would kiss him again. The yawn she faked turned into a real one. "Any idea where you put that nightshirt?"

* * * *

Ranjiv didn't know whether to be disappointed or excited at the prospect of Jillian asking for a nightshirt, especially since she still hadn't said where she intended to sleep. Now probably wasn't the best time to ask. "I think so. There aren't too many places it could be."

Getting to his feet, he went to his bedroom and found it in the first drawer he opened—the bottom one—right where he'd stashed it years before. He didn't even remember who had given it to him, nor had he ever dreamed that someone like Jillian might be the one to actually wear it.

With her coloring, the dark green plaid would probably look as good on her as that green and gold sari he'd imagined her in.

Well, maybe not quite as good...

"Very soft," she said when he handed it to her. "Love the color."

"It *is* a rather nice one, which is why I've kept it. I vaguely recall having washed it thinking I might wear it at some point." He shrugged. "Never have."

"Almost makes me wish I lived somewhere colder than Memphis. This is one of those things you wear while curled up by the fire with a cup of hot chocolate."

Ranjiv barely heard anything after the "somewhere colder than Memphis" part. "That could be arranged."

They wouldn't live in this flat, of course. They would need a house in the country with a fireplace and—

"Mind if I take a shower?"

For several moments, all he could do was gape at her.

"Of course," he finally managed to say. "I'll set out some clean towels for you."

The only woman Ranjiv had ever shared a bathroom with was his mother, and he hadn't done that since before going to university. Women's needs were different. Unlike any of his previous roommates, they needed hair dryers and lotions and scented soaps and—

"Great. The last shower I had was at the hospital in Galway, and I'm still not sure I got all the gunk out of my hair."

Gunk? What sort of gunk would she have in her hair?

Then he remembered. Seawater, jet fuel, blood—and God only knew what else.

"I'm thinking it might be best if I spend the night out here on the couch," she went on. "I'm still sorta jet-lagged. I mean, I *feel* tired, but there's no telling if I'll sleep or not. I wouldn't want to keep you awake."

Although he suspected she was only searching for an excuse to keep from sharing a bed with him, being kept up all night by Jillian sounded like a perk. "Whatever you think best. Your choice."

"I'll stay out here then. I can watch TV if I can't sleep."

He wanted to tell her to wake him up if she needed to be entertained. He had all sorts of ideas for how to pass the night—none of which included watching the telly.

"But I will go ahead and take a shower." She rose from the sofa. "That way I won't disturb you."

Clearly that kiss hadn't meant a thing to her. "Jillian, please. You don't need to avoid me."

She blew out a sigh. "I'm not trying to avoid you. I'm trying to— Never mind. Bad idea." Clutching the nightshirt to her chest with both hands, she started toward the bathroom. "I'll try not to take too long."

"No need to rush," he said. "I'm not going anywhere." Then he remembered the towels. "Let me get the towels for you."

She stopped in her tracks. "Oh. Okay."

He hopped up and headed into the bathroom. When he returned, she was standing right where he'd left her.

"All set," he said. "Although the soap and shampoo probably aren't what you're used to."

"Guy stuff?"

"Um, yeah. Guy stuff."

"No problem. I can get some girl stuff tomorrow. At the moment, I'm not in any position to be choosy." She hesitated, biting her lower lip in a pensive manner. "I really appreciate all you've done for me. I feel like I should be paying you rent or something."

If her reservation hadn't been canceled, Ranjiv wouldn't have had any of this time with her, and she certainly wouldn't have needed to borrow anything from him. He would have dropped her off and never seen her again.

Small price to pay...

"No need for that," he said, keeping his tone brisk. "I brought you here and asked you to stay, remember?"

She heaved a sigh. "Yeah. I do. But that was before I, um..."

Frowning, she began worrying her lip again. "...kissed you. It changes things."

"True," he agreed. "But that doesn't necessarily make it a problem."

"Maybe. It's just that I keep saying and doing things I end up regretting—with you, that is."

Ranjiv didn't have to think hard to recall what it was that she wished she hadn't said to him. He felt the same way.

The kiss was a different story.

"I don't want you to feel uncomfortable—and believe me, I understand why you might—but I have absolutely no regrets about that kiss." He summoned up a smile. "In fact, I'd very much like to do it again."

"That's the problem," she whispered. "So would I—and I really shouldn't. I don't think your mother would've liked it." Her gaze drifted downward, coming to rest somewhere on the floor between them. "You may think she intended for us to meet—and maybe she did—but she wanted you to get married, not shack up with someone who'll be leaving the country in a few weeks."

He couldn't argue with that, but the process of finding a wife had to start somewhere. "I think she was more concerned with me being happy."

"I'm sure she was. I just don't think I'll be the one to make that happen. I don't seem to be any good at it."

She was obviously thinking about her fiancé—*an absolute idiot if there ever was one*—rather than the man standing in front of her, a man she'd already admitted wanting to kiss again.

Hearing that tidbit had done wonders for his mood.

"Let's not rule out the possibility, shall we?"

Ranjiv might not know Jillian very well, but he did know his mother. She wouldn't have wanted him to miss out on the chance she'd given him by mourning her loss to exclusion of everything else. Not like she had done in the years after his father died.

Kavya had plenty of room in her heart for her son, but Ramesh had been the one and only love of her life. The fact that theirs had been an arranged marriage hadn't lessened that love. It was there.

Ranjiv saw it every time she gazed at his father's photograph when she thought no one was watching—no one who mattered anyway.

She'd probably been holding it in her hand when she died.

Closing the distance between them, he eased his hand over hers. "After all, there's nothing worse than the regret of a missed opportunity."

"Better to have loved and lost than never to have loved at all?" Jillian quoted. "Maybe. I don't think Seth and I ever had the kind of love that made it worth the pain."

"Yes, but at least you've experienced that much happiness." He raised her hand to his lips. "I'm still looking for it."

"I hope you find it, Ranjiv," she said with a slight quaver in her voice. "I truly do. I'm just not sure you'll find it with me."

Chapter 13

ONCE AGAIN, JILLIAN LISTENED FOR ADVICE FROM THE VOICES IN HER head.

Once again, they remained silent.

"Guess I'd better go take that shower now."

Ranjiv nodded. "Like I said, take your time."

Oddly enough, he didn't even seem disappointed. Was he the type of man who never took no for an answer or was it simply a difference of opinion? She couldn't decide.

If only her hand wasn't still tingling where he'd kissed it.

Once inside the bathroom, she turned on the water, stripped off her clothes, and stepped into the tub. As usual, the hot spray was like a balm to her nerves.

Throughout all the ups and downs in her life, Jillian had learned that if a hot shower couldn't make her feel better, talking to another woman usually did the trick. She might be on the other side of the Atlantic, but she had a phone and plenty of people she could call.

Mom would know what to do. Her parents had been happily married for thirty years. They had the whole relationship thing down pat—most of the time. Her sister Nicola was still in graduate school. Lisa, her would-be maid of honor, was working in the bank back home. They had each applauded her decision to come to London. For their sake, if not her own, Jillian was glad she'd survived and saved them all a tremendous amount of guilt. She shuddered as she recalled that her sister had considered taking the trip with her. Fortunately, in view of her upcoming thesis defense, Nicola hadn't been able to justify the time or the expense.

A call to any of those women would have helped her through most dating disasters. In the days before boarding the jet to London, she'd practically talked their ears off. But *this* dating dilemma was anything but typical. She doubted that anyone short of a psychiatrist could figure it out—or better yet, a psychic. A medium conducting a séance would have a field day with her story.

Perhaps a fortune teller with a crystal ball could tell her what to do. She was pretty sure there were gypsies in England. She could tell Ranjiv that a vital part of her vacation experience was to have her fortune told by an honest-to-God gypsy—although surviving a plane crash had undoubtedly used up her allotment of good fortune for all time.

And yet every twist of fate since the crash had been a turn for the better. The voices telling her what to do, the life raft, the fishing boats, and then she'd met Ranjiv. Her hotel reservation had been canceled, but he'd taken her in like a lost puppy. Claiming that he'd rescued her was no exaggeration.

My knight in shining armor...

On top of that, he was handsome and kind, making Jillian long to throw caution to the wind and dive headfirst into a love affair with no regard for the outcome. Her "better to have loved and lost" comment brought to mind one of her mother's favorite songs—a Rod Stewart tune with a similar theme. Having grown up listening to two generations' worth of rock 'n' roll, she ought to be able to do that. But despite her amazing run of luck, she felt completely gutless.

She reminded herself that she didn't believe in luck. If she had, she'd have hopped another plane to Monte Carlo and tried her hand at roulette or at least bought a lottery ticket instead of plowing on ahead with the London vacation.

What held her back wasn't her own pain, but Ranjiv's. She didn't want her name added to his list of heartbreaks. Her luck in surviving a plane crash might make her invincible, but it wouldn't help him any.

Invincible... Ha!

Jillian had always been the level-headed, sensible type. People who believed in miracles and luck and invincibility were just plain crazy. Not everything had been good. The way she'd felt in the dog park—the horrible, mind-numbing depression—ranked among the worst moments in her life.

That was so weird...

Still, her momentary weakness had allowed Ranjiv to rescue her once again. She'd even kissed him.

Now what?

"No Holding Back."

Yes. That was the name of the song. Her mother must've played it a bajillion times, and usually sang along.

Whoa, shit.

Her mother wasn't a Rod Stewart fan and, as far as Jillian knew, she never had been.

That memory belonged to someone else.

Jillian's heart took a dive and her breathing shortened to tiny gasps as the room began to spin. She closed her eyes in an effort to stave off the dizziness.

Chill, Jillian. Just chill.

She put a hand against the tiled wall. Given the style of the fixtures, the building was relatively modern, but it seemed to have been built to last—solid, substantial, tangible. Not like her spongy brain with its strange, incoherent thoughts.

She'd asked for it and had waited to hear the voices giving her advice.

But whose memories were they?

Somehow Kavya didn't strike her as the rock fan type, which left Anna and Shanda—or someone else on that doomed jet. Again, she wondered if there were others. She'd only interacted with those three women and one of the male flight attendants. He'd been the one to bring her the ice water. She couldn't remember his name, if indeed she'd ever heard it or seen his name badge...

No. It had to be Anna or Shanda, and her money was on Shanda.

Maybe.

Did it matter?

Probably not, especially since whomever it was had been telling her what she wanted to hear.

"Thanks. I needed that."

She wasn't going to hop into bed with Ranjiv. Another night

apart was probably for the best, even though Kavya wasn't screaming at her to keep her mitts off her son. One of the other two entities—perhaps both of them—was telling her to go for it.

Entities. She wasn't sure that was the right word, but it sounded less mystical than souls or spirits and more like something out of *Star Trek.*

Perhaps "katra" would work better—the essence of the Vulcan mind.

Sci-fi rather than a ghost story.

For some strange reason, that made her feel better. She finished her shower and was rinsing off the soap when she spotted a disposable razor sitting on the edge of the tub, a new one with the plastic shield still on it.

Having already seen a razor and a can of shaving cream on the shelf by the sink, she doubted that Ranjiv did his shaving in the shower. He must've thought she would want to shave her legs.

Bless his heart.

Seth would never have done that or even thought of it.

Picking up the razor, she removed the shield and soaped up her legs once more. As she slid the sharp blade over her skin, she caught herself smiling, despite the tears that stung her eyes.

"You raised a fine son, Kavya. You truly did."

* * * *

Ranjiv stared after Jillian's retreating figure. It wasn't until he heard the bathroom door close and the water running that he allowed himself to move, otherwise he might have gone running after her, perhaps even pounding on the door and begging her to let him in.

He shouldn't have been surprised when she opted to sleep on the sofa. She wasn't the type to sleep with a man on the first date—if he could call it that—let alone someone she barely knew.

She wasn't the one behaving out of character. He was. He still couldn't believe he'd mentioned the possibility of sharing the bed. He might have thought it, of course, but he'd never uttered anything that suggestive in his life. Nor had he ever felt so strongly about a woman—one who made him wish he'd spent more time studying the *Kama Sutra.*

Pakshi, one of Ranjiv's school chums, had an illustrated copy. The two of them had pored over it for hours, trying to decide which techniques they would like best, as well as those they thought would give the woman the greatest pleasure. Pakshi had several rather contortionistic favorites, most of which Ranjiv had considered to be physically impossible. Ranjiv's own choices had been simpler, mainly because he didn't believe that having to refer to the instructions would be very romantic.

Guess I should've memorized it.

His friend Janhu had warned against getting too technical—that genuine feelings and spontaneity were more important. Janhu was married with five children. Apparently he'd had the right idea. Thus far, Pakshi had fathered only two.

And I've fathered none.

Clearly studying the techniques wasn't as important as actually making the attempt.

Before he'd met Jillian, Ranjiv had begun to wonder if his window of opportunity had closed for good. Meeting her had flung it wide open again.

His mother had given him this chance, and he was determined not to waste it.

Gathering up the pillows and blankets she'd used the night before, he made a bed for her on the divan. He would have preferred to give her the bed but thought it best to comply with her wishes—at least for tonight. He hadn't forgotten what she'd said about not wanting to spend her entire vacation sleeping on a couch. She'd expected to stay in a hotel with all the amenities.

Damn. She needs a hair dryer.

He glanced at the clock. *Ten fifteen.* Grabbing his phone, he rang up Shalini.

His neighbor was laughing when she took the call. "Need more dog food?"

"No. A hair dryer. Do you have one I can borrow?"

"I might. But I'm betting the dog isn't the one who needs it."

"Um, no. Jillian's in the shower and I just remembered I don't have any way for her to dry her hair."

Ranjiv probably could've heard Shalini's laughter even without the phone. "Tell me again why this woman is staying with you?"

"It's a long story." One he doubted she would believe. "She's been asleep all afternoon, and we figured it was too late to find her a hotel now." It was a lame excuse and he knew it, but it was the best he could do at the time.

"Ranjiv," Shalini said patiently. "Hotels *never* close. Or didn't you know that?"

"Of course I know that. It's just that she's exhausted, and she's been through quite an ordeal. I can't throw her out now."

"You could if it suited you. I'm guessing you'd rather keep her for a while."

Truth be told, he wanted to keep her forever. "Well…"

"Never mind. I'll send one of the boys up." She clucked her tongue a few times before adding, "What would your mother say?"

"Quite honestly, I think she'd be more upset if I'd left Jillian in that dodgy hotel on Almstead Street."

"You're probably right." Shalini sighed. "I'm still having a hard time remembering that Kavya is gone."

"Me too. I keep thinking I should call her and—well, you know."

"I believe I do," Shalini said. "I felt the same way when my mother died."

"I suppose everyone does. Thanks again for the hair dryer. Okay if I bring it round tomorrow?"

"Sure. No hurry."

He rang off, thankful he'd caught himself before adding that the main reason he wanted to call his mother was to voice his approval of the wife she'd chosen for him.

Not girlfriend, not lover, but wife.

Whether his mother's soul was tied to Jillian or not didn't matter anymore. He'd been too quick to believe her story anyway—perhaps because on some level he'd wanted it to be true—but nothing had happened since then to substantiate her original claim.

Jillian's own explanation made perfect sense. He'd come up with the same reasons himself, and the dog *was* very well-trained.

She'd behaved every bit as perfectly for him as she had for Jillian. There was nothing spooky about it at all.

I really need to stop saying things like that.

Perhaps that was why Jillian didn't want to sleep with him. She was afraid he'd freak out if he made love to a woman who'd been possessed by his mother. Or a woman he even *thought* had been possessed by his mother—or anyone else for that matter. Either one was quite enough to send most blokes haring off to the loony bin. If he couldn't shut his brain up, he would be well on the way there himself.

Oh, bloody hell...

Jillian had already given him the best reasons of all for not sleeping together. In less than a week, his mother had died in a plane crash and Jillian's fiancé had dumped her.

Too soon.

Katie let out a sharp bark as the doorbell rang, saving Ranjiv from tearing his hair out in frustration. When he opened the door, Tahir handed him the hairdryer.

"I saw you out walking with her," the boy said, grinning. "She's very pretty."

Ranjiv chuckled. "The lady or the dog?"

"Both. But mostly the lady. Are you going to marry her?"

"I don't know if—"

"You have a girlfriend?" Jillian's voice sounded from behind him.

Ranjiv winced. He didn't see any way to answer that without getting into serious trouble.

When in doubt, answer a question with another question.

"I'm not sure," he replied. "Do I?"

His breath caught in his throat as he turned toward her.

Jillian stood at the end of the hall, her long blond hair curling damply around her face, which was still flushed from the shower. The fact that the nightshirt and dressing gown concealed every curve from her neck down didn't matter. She was still beautiful.

Her color deepened as her lips parted in surprise. "I–I don't know what you mean."

Tahir spoke up from the doorway. "I asked him if he was going to marry you."

She nodded slowly. "I see. Do you think he should?"

"I think it's a smashing idea," Tahir declared. "He needs a wife."

"I keep hearing that," Jillian said. "Considering all the help he's had finding someone, I'm amazed he wasn't taken years ago—not that he really needs any help."

Her slight drawl and the dimple in her cheek hinted that she might be teasing, although Ranjiv wasn't willing to make that assumption.

"None of the others were as pretty as you," Tahir confided. "I can see why he didn't marry them."

Ranjiv cleared his throat. "Thank you for that observation, Tahir." He held up the hairdryer. "I borrowed this from Shalini. Tahir was kind enough to bring it up."

"Great." Smiling, Jillian came forward and held out a hand to the boy. "Nice to meet you, Tahir. Please thank your mother for me, and thank *you* for bringing it. My name is Jillian."

With a smile that couldn't have been broader if he'd just been introduced to Her Majesty, The Queen, Tahir shook her hand. "Jillian," he repeated. "I like that name."

"Thanks. I like your name too."

He quirked a brow. "*You* aren't married, are you?"

"No," she replied. "This trip was supposed to be my honeymoon, but my boyfriend decided he didn't want to go through with it."

"The silly git!" Tahir exclaimed. "What a stupid thing to do!"

"My thoughts exactly," Ranjiv said. "A complete idiot."

Jillian didn't disagree. Instead, she gestured toward the schnauzer who had followed her to the door. "Have you met Katie?"

"Not yet," Tahir replied as he petted the dog's head. "She's nice."

"Yes, she is," Jillian agreed. "What kind of dog do you have?"

"A Corgi. You know, like the Queen's dogs?"

Jillian nodded as though she knew exactly what he was talking about. Perhaps she did—particularly since she claimed to have done some research prior to her visit. She seemed to understand the "git" reference anyway.

"Her name is Bippi," Tahir continued. "She's a good dog, but she's getting quite old. My *amma* says dogs usually don't live much past twelve or so, and Bippi is fourteen."

"I see. And how old are you?"

"Seven," he replied.

"Really? You seem so grown up. I'd have guessed you at closer to nine." She glanced at the clock. "Seems like this would be past your bedtime."

Tahir beamed at her, obviously quite pleased. "I got to stay up late because I did so well at school today."

"Hmm... Well, if you want to do a good job tomorrow, you might want to get some sleep."

"I should," he agreed, nodding. "Good night."

"Good night, Tahir. And thank you again for bringing the hair dryer."

"It was my pleasure." With a wave, Tahir darted off down the stairs.

Jillian chuckled as Ranjiv closed the door. "Don't you just love kids? Their honesty is so refreshing. I would've loved to have seen Seth's reaction to being called a silly git."

"I dunno," Ranjiv said with a wag of his head. "Your reaction to being prettier than my other lady friends was pretty priceless. I think you have an admirer."

"Maybe. Considering my wet hair and lack of makeup, he could've just as easily said I looked bedraggled and plain."

"I doubt it." Even in a man's nightshirt and dressing gown, Jillian was sexy as hell. Ranjiv wished he could be as honest as Tahir, but somehow he didn't think she would want him to be quite that blunt. Not yet anyway.

Why not? It was true.

"Thanks for borrowing that for me."

He stared at her for a long moment, wondering what on earth she was talking about. "Oh, right. The hairdryer... Never use one, myself."

"One of the blessings of short hair," she said with a wry grin. "I keep thinking I'll cut mine, but then I remember how much easier it is to just brush it out and pin it up or pull it back, rather than all that curling and styling. Doesn't look as wild when you first get up in the morning either."

He shrugged. "I guess that depends on what you've been doing all night."

Chapter 14

"ALL NIGHT?" JILLIAN FIXED RANJIV WITH A WARY EYE. "SLEEPING, usually."

Nevertheless, she couldn't help thinking about the possibility of getting her hair seriously mussed. Ranjiv's fingers entwined in the long strands, the friction from the sheets making a matted tangle on the crown of her head. Not to mention everything else that went along with it.

"Uh huh." His slow nod and purring drawl proved he wasn't fooled by her reply. He'd meant exactly what she thought he had.

She'd tried to deny the attraction, but no matter how often she told herself it was wrong—bad timing for him, a rebound for her, to say nothing of the bit about channeling his mother—that magnetic pull persisted. He'd been impossible to miss in a crowded airport. Standing perhaps three feet from her, his appeal was almost palpable.

He waved a hand toward the sofa. "I made your bed for you. Have a seat and I'll dry your hair."

She had to think twice before his words finally registered. "Seriously?"

A smile quirked the corner of his mouth. "Which part don't you believe?"

"All of it."

Had Seth ever done any of those things for her? She couldn't remember exactly, but he must have done something similar at some point.

Maybe. At the same time, the feelings she had for Ranjiv seemed so new. So novel. Like nothing she'd ever experienced before.

"Sit down and I'll prove it."

She'd been sitting on that same couch with him earlier, but there hadn't been any pillows and sheets and blankets on it then. Nor had she been wearing a nightshirt.

His nightshirt. *His* robe.

Seeming to expect her to comply, he set about plugging the hairdryer into an outlet in the base of the end table lamp.

She nodded at the adjacent armchair. "Might be better if I sat there."

"If you insist."

As soon as she was seated, Ranjiv swept her hair over the chair back, his light touch sending thrills racing down her neck. The warm air, the gentle feel of his fingertips on her scalp, the slight tickle as he combed his fingers through her hair all conspired to relax her. With a sigh, she closed her eyes, giving in to the pleasure.

"You missed your calling."

His reply was a noncommittal hum.

"If you'd been with us in Inisheer, you probably could've calmed even Cleona's nerves. She was a total wreck."

"And you weren't?"

"Not really," she replied. "Not like that anyway." Her own reactions had been tempered by the attitudes of the entities she carried. Kavya's presence had helped to calm Jillian's nerves when they first met. Perhaps Ranjiv possessed that same trait.

She had already surrendered to him. She realized that now. All the things he'd done—helping her, looking after her—and she hadn't lifted a finger to stop him from doing any of it. Relinquishing control was something Jillian seldom did, although she'd done the same thing when Susan had taken charge in Connemara. Letting someone else do the thinking, the worrying, and the planning was unlike her.

Her eyes drifted shut only to fly open with a start as her head dipped forward.

"I *told* you to sit on the couch," he chided. "Now you'll have to get up and move over there when you could've fallen asleep where you lay."

She scowled up at him. "Stop complaining. This way is easier for you, isn't it?"

"Perhaps. But that wasn't what I had in mind."

"Just what *did* you have in mind?"

"I wanted to watch you fall asleep." His fingers brushed her cheek as he scooped up a lock of her hair, renewing the rush of tingles. "I've never had the chance to do that before."

She was about to ask why that was so important to him when, suddenly, she understood. It wasn't about how she looked or felt, nor was it a question of increasing her vulnerability. It was a matter of intimacy, something his life had apparently lacked. "I'm sure I'll conk out again at some point."

"I hope so. I enjoy watching you sleep."

"Oh all right." Grumbling more for effect than actual annoyance, she stood quickly, untied the robe, and dropped it on the chair. "But don't blame me if you get a crick in your back from perching sideways on that table." She climbed into the makeshift bed, snuggled beneath the blankets, and flipped her hair over the arm of the sofa. "Have at it."

"Much better."

Her hair was barely damp, but she let him continue anyway. The warm air and his gentle touch worked their magic once again. Within moments, she was asleep and dreaming.

But her dreams were quite different from those she'd had during the previous night, having nothing to do with the crash whatsoever. Ranjiv played no part in them, nor did Kavya. That final message had been conveyed, the task completed. And yet despite Kavya's silence, Jillian still felt like an observer as she watched the nightmare unfold, knowing full well she was asleep and that nothing in the dream could touch her.

The fleeting shadows couldn't startle her. The rustling leaves failed to raise the hair on the back of her neck. She wasn't even bothered by the sound of running footsteps in the dark.

Or the screams.

* * * *

Ranjiv switched off the hairdryer and unplugged it before turning off the lamp. Letting Jillian sleep on the couch was probably a good move. If she'd been in his bed, he would've been tempted to crawl in beside her. Unless he slept on the floor or in the chair, there wasn't room for him here. Both ideas had merit, but she obviously trusted him enough to fall asleep in his presence. Abusing that trust was unthinkable.

Katie jumped onto the couch and proceeded to curl up at Jillian's feet.

"Lucky you."

He couldn't recall having been envious of a dog before—or even a man he'd never met. Seth had been with Jillian for five years. How could a man promise to marry a woman and then suddenly decide not to?

Granted, Laksha had done the same thing to him, but they'd never been intimate. Somehow, he thought that should make a difference.

Perhaps it didn't. After all, he was the one behind the times. The one who'd never taken a lover and had no idea how it would feel to move on to the next.

He certainly didn't want to move on after Jillian. He already dreaded her leaving. Three weeks, she'd said. He had three weeks.

Not enough time.

Not *nearly* enough time.

To hell with what anyone thought about it being too soon after his mother's passing to fall in love. He knew from the depths of his soul that his mother would haunt him for the rest of his days if he let Jillian go. Knew it with a certainty he couldn't even begin to explain.

He turned off the rest of the lights and started down the hallway only to discover that his feet flatly refused to take those next steps. He wanted to stay awake and watch her sleep.

Taking a seat in the chair she'd so recently vacated, he sat motionless, listening to her deep, even breathing, watching the rise and fall of the blankets that covered her. Why did being in the same room with her feel so perfect, as though her presence completed him somehow?

She was wrong about not being the one to make him happy. *So* wrong. So totally and utterly wrong. But a long-distance relationship didn't stand much of a chance.

He needed more time.

Given the horrendous crash she'd lived through, he could easily understand why she might hesitate to board another transatlantic flight. But that was ridiculous. She wouldn't be too scared to ever go home. Besides, he didn't want her to stay with him because she was afraid to leave. Being pen pals or Facebook friends was better than that.

Maybe.

People fell in love on sight all the time in films. Why were audiences so willing to believe that was possible? Perhaps it was because they didn't have time to question the logic the way the reader of a book could. The story moved on, the pace never slacking enough to allow time for rational thought to creep in. He'd scoffed at the concept of insta-love many times before. The Indian custom was to take a lifetime to get to know someone and to love them. It was never an immediate, explosive reaction.

Nevertheless, the moment his eyes had landed on Jillian in the airport, that attitude changed. Never mind her preposterous story; there was something special about her.

Only her story wasn't preposterous. Not anymore. What Jillian had said was true. His mother really had saved her life. And the reason she'd done it wasn't only for the noble act of preserving a life. Her motives were clear now.

She'd saved Jillian for him.

"Thanks, Mum."

* * * *

Ranjiv awoke to a gentle pressure on his shoulder and a whispered, "Ranjiv, go to bed."

For a moment, it was as though his mother had spoken to him. The same inflection, the same tone. Only the voice was different.

That difference made him open his eyes.

The light from the streetlamps filtered through the blinds, casting a glow that highlighted the contours of Jillian's form as she leaned over him, adding an ethereal quality to her lovely face.

He caught himself before making the obvious *you sound like my mother* comment. Not the right time for that. *Definitely* not the time.

On a sigh, he took her hand and pulled her toward him.

Surprisingly, she eased closer with no resistance whatsoever. He felt only her yielding softness as she sank down on his lap.

I'm dreaming. This is the dog in my lap, not Jillian.

"You don't have to keep watch over me," she said. "I'm okay."

"If you're okay, why are you awake?"

A puzzled frown wrinkled her brow. "I'm not sure. Might've been Katie—or a dream I can't remember—but I woke up and saw you sitting here." She gave him an admonishing tsk. "You wouldn't let me fall asleep in this chair, so I'm not going to let you do it either."

"Ah, but I'm awake now."

"True. Although that isn't what I meant."

"What *did* you mean?" He kept his tone light, teasing. Not wanting to sink into the depths again. Not yet. Not now. There had to be a silver lining to this cloud somewhere. Perhaps this was it.

"I meant for you to get a good night's sleep." She swept the pad of her thumb over his cheekbone. "You need it to get rid of these dark circles—and these lines," she added as her thumb reached the outer corner of his eye.

"I thought I was supposed to be the one taking care of you."

She shook her head. "It's my turn."

Ranjiv held his breath as she feathered her fingers through the hair at his temple.

"You really are quite"—she leaned forward to brush her lips over his cheek, her breath tickling his ear, sending delightful tingles racing down his chest—"adorable."

This time, without question, Ranjiv was the initiator of the kiss. Cupping the back of her head with one hand, he hooked the other behind her knees and pulled her to him. Her lips melted into his as he slid his hand up her thigh. The fabric between them was incidental. He was feeling *her*, just her, only her. The curve of her hip, the small of her back.

Jillian rested her hand briefly on his shoulder before reaching up to curl her fingers around the nape of his neck. She was already in his arms. He had only to stand and take the two steps to the couch.

He could have her lying beneath him in a heartbeat.

Seeming to anticipate his intent, she broke the kiss and drew back. Gazing at him through heavy-lidded eyes, she tapped his lips with a fingertip. "Not tonight." She rose and pointed toward the hall. "Go on now."

Following those instructions was fairly low on Ranjiv's list of preferences. He couldn't deny he'd been the one to pull her down, but she had come willingly and had kissed him like she meant it—or at least enjoyed it. "Don't see the point, really. Falling asleep after that kiss is going to be tough."

"You'll never know 'til you try." She flapped her hands at him, shooing him toward the bedroom.

"That's not the best way to get me to go to bed. Actually *taking* me there might be better."

She shot him a sardonic scowl. "Yeah, right. I've heard that before." She blew out a breath. "Look, let's give it a day or two before we start bouncing each other's bones, okay?"

He gave himself a moment to figure out what she'd meant by that. "You mean no shagging?"

"No shagging."

"Ever?"

"I didn't say that."

Ranjiv knew very well what she'd said. He just wasn't sure he believed it. All he really needed right now was hope. Not only the hope that he might get laid at some point, but that Jillian might actually love him enough to give him a chance. To give *them* a chance.

Was staying together a possibility they needed to discuss? Or would talking about it destroy the likelihood? Too much planning and not enough spontaneity—or something of that nature—and then there was that bit about it being too soon. The last thing he wanted to do was to crush the seed of their relationship before it ever had the opportunity to sprout and grow.

A day or two...

What were a couple of days out of three weeks? Granted, she'd spent the first night in a hospital. She was only working on the second night now. Too bad he didn't have some sort of relationship schedule or timetable or personal history to base it on. Three weeks. Would they eventually reach a critical point where they either fell head over heels in love or decided they couldn't stand each other?

Ranjiv reminded himself that he'd reached that "can't stand each other" point several times in the past—usually on the third date, sometimes the second, and on at least two occasions, at the first meeting. One thing he knew for certain, Jillian was the only woman he'd ever actually *wanted* to shag on the first date or first night or whatever this was. Most dates didn't last more than two hours or so. He'd been with Jillian since early afternoon. Sure, she'd slept part of that time, but he wasn't anywhere near to deciding they wouldn't suit each other.

But what if she had already reached that conclusion?

Not if she thinks I'm adorable.

With that cheery thought in mind, he gave her a wink. "Right, then. See you in the morning."

Chapter 15

JILLIAN AWOKE TO A TRULY HEAVENLY SMELL.

Mmm... Masala dosas.

Her nose had taken in the aroma and her brain processed it, just as it would have done with any other scent memory—despite the fact that she'd never eaten a masala dosa in her life.

Might be best to play dumb on this one.

Opening her eyes, she spotted Ranjiv standing in front of the stove, looking endearingly rumpled in a pair of dark blue plaid pajamas, his hair uncombed, his face unshaven.

Oh, yes. Quite adorable.

She gave Katie a quick pat before tossing back the covers. Getting up from the sofa, she went over to the kitchen alcove, doing her best to ignore the urge to press her body against Ranjiv's back and wrap her arms around his waist. "Smells good. What is it?"

"Masala dosas," he replied. "Crispy pancakes filled with potato curry. They go great with mango chutney and a dab of ghee."

Her gaze touched on the jar of chutney and the bowl of ghee, which she recognized as being a type of clarified butter. He spread the batter in a large skillet, then flipped the thin "pancake" over with a metal spatula. "They look more like crepes than pancakes."

"Similar," he said. "Mother always made them with idli batter. I cheat and use a mix."

The empty package sat on the counter. Jillian had never seen anything like it before, and yet it too, was strangely familiar. "She probably used a mix once in a while herself."

"Maybe. She would never admit to it, though. She would soak the rice and urad dal for hours and then grind them into a batter and let it ferment overnight. What she didn't make into idlis, she used to make dosas." He chuckled. "Don't suppose you've ever had idlis either."

"Well, no. I haven't." She knew what they were, though. Fluffy rice and lentil cakes made from fermented batter and cooked in a special steamer. She even recognized the idli pot on a shelf near the stove.

"Maybe I'll make those tomorrow."

"Sounds good." She glanced at Katie, who had followed her to the kitchen. "Guess I'd better get dressed and take her out."

"No need. Tahir came up a while ago to get the hairdryer and volunteered to take her out along with Bippi."

"That was sweet of him." Jillian had plenty of friends back home, but there were people living in her apartment building she'd never even spoken to. The sense of community here was completely different—closer knit, more supportive.

"He's a great kid. Very helpful to his mother. Smart too."

Jillian didn't have to ask if Ranjiv had been a help to his own mother. She already knew it, although not from any memories acquired from Kavya. That trait was part of his character, clearly evident in everything he did.

"Dunno how I managed to sleep through all that." Cocking her head, she arched a brow. "I wasn't snoring, was I?"

"Never made a sound."

Somehow she doubted that. "I must've been"—she caught herself before saying *dead to the world,* deeming it tactless under the circumstances—"sleeping like a log." She studied his face for a moment. "You look better this morning. Less puffy around the eyes."

His smile eliminated the last evidence of strain. "I slept fairly well, actually."

"I'm glad to hear it." Considering his state of arousal when he'd gone off to bed, she'd had her doubts. When sitting in a man's lap, some things were hard to miss.

He added the potato filling to a dosa, folded it, and put it on a plate. "Here. Eat this while it's hot."

Since he'd already mentioned the chutney and ghee, it was safe to assume she could put some on the dosa without freaking him out.

Nevertheless, she opted to try it plain first. Taking a seat at the table, she poured a cup of tea before tasting the dosa.

Scent memory was one thing. The actual flavor was another. "Oh, yum…"

Ranjiv seemed pleased. "It's even better with a dab of ghee and chutney."

After following his suggestion, she took another bite. "Damn. You weren't kidding. This is amazing."

"Glad you like it. Think you could eat another one?"

"Sure. No problem. Aren't you having any?"

"I always eat the first one while I'm frying the second. They're best right out of the *tava*—um, skillet. They get a bit soggy if you let them sit."

I knew that too.

He hadn't even needed to translate *tava* for her, although she probably could've guessed what he meant from the context. She was having hot tea and masala dosas for breakfast for the first time, and yet it didn't feel that way at all. It was as familiar and comforting as eating biscuits and gravy or bacon and eggs.

"This sure makes up for missing out on the full Irish breakfast while I was in Galway," she said. "They only let us have liquids at the hospital."

"No worries." He dropped another dosa on her plate. "The full English breakfast is about the same—black pudding, sausages, eggs, bacon, baked beans, fried tomatoes, and toast."

"Sounds like an awful lot, doesn't it?" She smiled as she smeared ghee and chutney on the dosa with a spoon. "Never thought I'd be having this sort of breakfast in London. I think I like it better than baked beans, though. Seems an odd thing to eat in the morning."

"The potatoes in the dosa don't seem strange?"

"Not at all. We have fried potatoes or hash browns with breakfast at home. Not with curry, of course, although now that I think of it, that would be pretty tasty. Baked beans are for dinner or cookouts."

"I'll take your word for it." Chuckling, Ranjiv sat down and began to eat the rest of his own meal.

Jillian finished her dosa and sat sipping her tea. She recalled hurried breakfasts that she'd barely had time to swallow before she and Seth went off to work. Even weekends were never this relaxed.

I could get used to this.

"So you've never tried much in the way of Indian food?"

"My mom used to make a creamy curry chicken with apples and onions served over rice. She said—" Jillian stopped, wincing as she realized that was yet another memory about someone else's mother. Ranjiv probably wouldn't know the difference but she really needed to keep her stories straight, for her own sanity if nothing else. Too bad she wasn't sure whose memory that was.

"Said what?" he prompted.

"Um…she said it wasn't very authentic, but my family liked it a lot." She was fairly certain that was true about someone's family. Just not hers.

"You haven't talked much about your family," he began. "I'm sure they were all relieved to hear you survived the crash."

Yet another touchy subject. Ranjiv couldn't have felt any relief in the wake of the crash. At least he'd been the one to bring it up. "My parents hadn't even heard about the crash when I called them, which was a blessing. My sister, Nicola, had thought about coming with me on this trip. Thank goodness she couldn't justify taking the time off from school."

"She's younger than you?"

She nodded. "By about four years. She's a sweet girl and very talented—she's finishing up her master's degree in art." She started to say more about her sister, but thought it might be best not to. Ranjiv didn't have any relatives left—no immediate family anyway—and he'd never had a sibling. "You said you had an uncle living in London. Do you have any cousins here?"

"Three," he replied. "They're all married with children."

So many younger cousins, but no children of his own.

Had that thought been her own or Kavya's? Jillian pondered that subject for a few moments—until she realized it didn't matter where the idea came from. Either way, it was still true. "I have quite a few cousins, but most of them have moved away. I don't see them much anymore."

He nodded as though he understood the reason. "Most of my people are in India—near Hyderabad."

"Have you ever been there?"

"Twice. Once before my father died—I was about five years old at the time—and again when I was sixteen. I met dozens of cousins and aunts and uncles, but I haven't seen any of them since that last visit."

"I'm not surprised. That's quite a trip."

"Almost ten hours from here—and that's flying nonstop."

"Tell me about India."

He smiled. "It's different from England in every possible way. Different culture, different landscape. The climate is almost the exact opposite from what we have here, and there are nearly thirty different languages. Bustling cities, teeming with life, vivid colors. The cities are modern in many ways, but you never forget you're in India, even when you're standing inside a new office building. In other places, you feel as though you've taken a leap back through time."

"That's the way Britain seems to me. It has this old world flavor we don't have in America. I saw farmhouses in Ireland that our driver said were two hundred years old—some of them even older—and were still in use. Back home, we have plenty of traditions and historic sites and such. But nothing as old as some of the castles here, except for Native American artifacts, and they tended to live in harmony with the land as opposed to leaving their mark on it."

"I suppose America *was* built on change."

She snorted a laugh. "Planned obsolescence, you mean. Not sure it's the best way. There's a lot to be said for stuff that's made to last. It's appalling the number of things we just throw away."

* * * *

Ranjiv certainly couldn't argue that point. Sometimes even people got discarded, and the Yanks didn't have a monopoly on that. "I know what you mean. My mother has cookware that's been in her family for generations."

Jillian nodded. "Must be nice. So many things are disposable now, worthless after one use."

He had an idea she wasn't only referring to paper plates. "True." He drew in a difficult breath. "Speaking of my mother's things, I really need to check on her house. There are people who watch the obituaries looking for places to rob."

She grimaced. "After my grandmother died, a friend of hers volunteered to stay at her house during the funeral for that same reason. I guess England isn't quite as civilized as it seems."

"Not at all." The change in her mood made him wish he hadn't mentioned the possibility of theft. At least she understood the problem. "Right, then. We'll stop by there first and after that we can go anyplace you like."

"I should probably try to find something else to wear." Her mouth formed a moue of distaste. "Ordinarily I hate shopping for clothes, although that market you mentioned sounds interesting."

"They have plenty of clothes for sale there. Probably not what you're used to, though." He might've been anxious to see her in a sari, but he wasn't about to say so. Not yet anyway.

She shrugged. "We'll see. I've never had to start completely from scratch before. Maybe this'll be the start of my new look." She took a sip of her tea, seeming to consider her words before continuing. "You asked me to go to Kavya's memorial service. I don't know what would be appropriate—to wear, I mean."

"We tend to dress down for funerals," he said. "You won't need anything fancy."

She acknowledged that information with a tiny nod, her expression still pensive as she stared off into space. "Strange how things happen, isn't it? I never would've guessed that I'd be doing any of this in a million years, and yet here I am, sitting at the breakfast table with you, planning the rest of the day, discussing what I should wear to your mother's funeral. It's so... surreal, and yet it seems sort of—" She blew out an exasperated breath. "I can't explain it. Just...can't."

"Natural?" he suggested.

Giving him a sideways glance, she nodded again. "You feel it too, don't you? Like we've done this before—or something very similar."

"Well…we did have dinner together last night. We're even sitting in the same places."

"Maybe that's it." On the surface, she seemed to agree, but her voice contained a note of uncertainty.

Ranjiv reminded himself that Jillian had recently endured a great deal of physical and emotional trauma. These momentary lapses were to be expected—as long as they didn't get any worse. "We've both had a lot to deal with. Maybe we should take today off and see if we can't get back to being more…normal."

Jillian surprised him with a chuckle and a roll of her eyes. "Whatever *that* is."

Normal. She was right about that. What was normal? Would he ever feel that way again? His mother was gone. He was faced with the task of going through her belongings. What he couldn't use himself, his cousins might want. The rest he could either sell or donate to charity. Then there was the matter of what to do with the house. Should he sell it or move into it himself? His flat was spacious and modern, but he'd grown up in that cozy terraced house and had played in the tidy garden that had been his mother's pride and joy. So many things to be done, so many decisions to be made before normalcy could ever return to his life, and even then, nothing would ever be the same.

Especially if he were to lose Jillian now that he'd found her.

She obviously didn't understand how he felt about her, probably because she didn't share the same opinion. She might think he was adorable, but in the greater scheme of things, was that enough? Enough for her to want to make a home with him so far from her own family?

His mother had done it. Left everyone behind and moved to England with her husband. Pratap was his father's brother, not hers. She'd had no blood ties in Britain. How alone she must've felt when his father died—and even before that. Living in a strange country with a vastly divergent culture. He hadn't exaggerated when he'd described the differences to Jillian. There was scarcely any comparison at all.

And yet there was a strong Indian presence in London, even if there was still some prejudice. Jillian didn't seem to share that attitude. He'd been offended by her chauffeur comment. He shouldn't have been. She hadn't meant it that way. He knew that now.

"You're awfully quiet."

Startled from his reverie, he shrugged. "Sorry. Still trying to figure out what normal means."

"Found the answer yet?"

He shook his head. "Have you?"

"No. But I do know we'll never find it sitting here. What do you say we get cleaned up and do this thing?"

Chapter 16

RANJIV HAD BEEN DEVASTATINGLY HANDSOME IN A SUIT AND TIE. He'd been adorable in pajamas. Fresh from the shower in a cream-colored wool sweater and faded jeans, he was irresistible.

Jillian let out a low whistle. "You might've warned me."

"About what?"

The fact that his expression was still endearingly blank spoke volumes. In that moment, Jillian was, to put it mildly, smitten. Not because he was gorgeous, but because he didn't *realize* he was gorgeous.

"I'd better not say. Wouldn't want you to get too cocky."

A quirky grin added even more to his appeal. "No danger of that." His gaze swept her from head to toe, leaving a warm glow in its wake. "Ready?"

"Ready as I'll ever be. Doesn't take long when you don't have to decide what to wear."

Thankfully, her skirt and sweater were none the worse for having been worn three days in a row and the panties and hose she'd washed out the night before were dry. She'd washed her face in the kitchen sink—patting herself on the back for having stashed her hospital-issue toothpaste and toothbrush in her purse—and combed her hair using the window as a mirror.

The moment Ranjiv pulled his keys out of his pocket, Katie trotted toward the door, tossing a sharp bark over her shoulder.

"Either she knows what we're planning or she really needs to pee," Jillian said. "Seems like she hardly ever barks much."

"I've never known a schnauzer to be that quiet. She must've had an awfully good trainer."

Jillian had to bite her lip to keep from blurting out the first words that popped into her head. Counting to three, she collected her thoughts enough to say "I'm sure she did" instead of *You're damn straight she did!*

She couldn't even fuss at the "Anna entity" for that lapse. Those words had come from Jillian's own mind as though she'd been the one to actually train the dog and was not only proud of that fact but wanted credit for it.

Weird.

For someone like Jillian, who'd never even considered dog ownership, it was even weirder.

Shaking off the latest in a series of eerie feelings, she stooped down and snapped the leash to Katie's collar. "How far is it to your mother's house?"

"Not very far," Ranjiv replied. "We can drive over and then walk to the market from there. If you want, we can make a pass down the Broadway before we head back to the car."

"If it's as interesting as it sounds, that might take all day."

"Maybe, but if it doesn't, there are plenty of other places we could go."

"True." She was about to thank him for his trouble when she remembered that he needed this outing as much as she did.

After all, they were both in search of normalcy.

The problem was with all these new memories popping up, Jillian wasn't sure she would ever feel normal again. Would there come a point when they were all incorporated into her own mind enough to seem as though they belonged there? If so, how would she ever know which thoughts were whose? She'd heard memory experts recommend placing various facts in specific rooms inside the mind. Perhaps that was what she needed to do. Too bad they weren't tagged so she would know which room to put them in. She could safely assume that dog memories were Anna's, swimming memories were Shanda's, and anything to do with Indian cuisine or Ranjiv belonged to Kavya, but others were more difficult to categorize.

Yeah, right. And by the time I get them all sorted out, they'll disappear.

The loss of those memories wouldn't be a bad thing. At the moment, the only memories she needed were her own. She didn't need an inherent understanding of Indian culture, nor did she need a map of London in her head. Ranjiv would help her learn those things. While knowing how to train a dog might prove useful at some point, Katie was already trained, and Jillian had no plans to become a dog breeder. As for Shanda's accumulated knowledge, Jillian had lived this long without knowing how to swim. All she had to do was continue to avoid large bodies of water.

And transatlantic flights.

Thus far, however, swimming was the most useful skill she'd acquired. It had certainly saved her life. She could impress Ranjiv with her cooking ability, but was that wise? No doubt he would see it as confirmation that his mother's spirit had taken up residence in Jillian, which was something she was trying very hard to make him forget.

She gave herself a mental shake, reminding herself that she needed to stop thinking and live in the moment. At that particular moment, she was heading out to explore London with her new dog and her new boyfriend, hopefully to find some new clothes.

After two rather remarkable kisses, Jillian figured she had sufficient grounds for claiming Ranjiv as her boyfriend. Aside from the fact that it made things easier.

Hear that, Kavya? He's my boyfriend.

Upon receiving no objections whatsoever, she followed him out the door to the parking lot behind the building.

They were approaching Ranjiv's car when her phone began to vibrate, playing a ringtone that set her teeth on edge.

"I really need to change that," she muttered as she retrieved the phone from her purse and answered it.

"Hello, Jillian? Is that you?"

Hearing her sister's voice helped her take a giant step forward in the pursuit of normalcy. "Hey, Nicola. Yeah, it's me."

"Are you okay? Mom thought one of us should check on you since you didn't call us when you got to your hotel. What time is it there?"

"Ten in the morning," Jillian replied. "Sorry I forgot to call."

"Having too much fun?"

Jillian had yet to decide whether everything that had happened since her plane landed could be considered fun. "The jury's still out on that. The hotel Seth booked was not only creepy, by the time I got there, they'd already canceled my reservation."

"That was pretty crappy of them. Where are you now?"

Jillian couldn't help chuckling. "To be perfectly honest, I don't know. Somewhere in London, um…near a park and a canal and not too far from the airport." Trust the extra entities to keep quiet on a simple but pertinent detail like her current location.

Ranjiv, on the other hand, had obviously been listening. "Southall."

"Southall," Jillian repeated. "If that means anything to you."

"That's the name of the hotel?" Nicola asked.

"No. It's…" She glanced at Ranjiv.

"A suburb of West London in the borough of Ealing." His amused expression dared her to repeat it.

She opted not to try. "Did you hear that? West London somewhere. I'm not—" *How in the world can I say this?* "I'm not staying in a hotel. I'm with a–a friend." She might think of Ranjiv as her new boyfriend, but somehow she thought it best not to describe him as such to her sister. Nicola seemed worried enough as it was.

"You have friends there?" Nicola sounded properly incredulous. "Since when?"

"Since yesterday. It's a long story. I'm staying with the son of one of the ladies I sat next to on the plane. His name is Ranjiv. I met him at the airport."

"You're freaking me out here, Jill," Nicola said. "Let me get this straight. You're staying with a guy you met *yesterday*?"

"That's right. We're on our way to his mother's house. Ranjiv wants to make sure everything's okay there."

"Hmm… Sounds like someone needs to make sure everything's okay with *you*. How much can you possibly know about the guy?"

"His mother told me a little bit about him, and he's been very kind. Not sure what I would've done without him." She paused, aiming a warm smile at Ranjiv. "We've been helping each other out. He lost his mother in the crash."

The last call Jillian had made to her family had been from the Galway airport, and she'd opted not to mention Kavya's request. Telling Ranjiv had been difficult enough. Of course, she hadn't known then just how important the delivery of that message would turn out to be.

"I'm sorry to hear that," Nicola said. "But please be careful, Jill. We nearly lost you once." Her voice broke on a sob. "I–I can't stand the thought of anything bad happening to you."

In light of Jillian's recent brushes with marriage and death, she had to wonder just what Nicola would consider bad. "I'm okay, Nic. Really. Ranjiv has been taking good care of me—and Katie too."

"Katie? Oh, yeah, right. The dog. I still can't picture you with a dog."

"Better get used to it. Katie is absolutely adorable." Her smile became a grin. "And so is Ranjiv."

He grinned back at her, looking more irresistible than ever.

"Ranjiv," Nicola repeated slowly. "That sounds Indian."

"Yes, and he's a real sweetie. Listen, I've got to go. We have a lot to do today."

"Sounds like it," Nicola drawled. "While you're at it, you might want to find someplace to have your head examined."

"Already have. They didn't find anything wrong with it." Nothing visible on a CT scan anyway.

"Sure they didn't." Nicola's eye roll was clearly evident in her tone. "Call me later, okay?"

"Will do. Bye now."

Jillian switched off the phone and stuck it back in her purse. "That was my fault for not calling her like I was supposed to. I'm surprised she hasn't tried to call me before now."

"You two must be pretty close."

"Not as much since she went away to college, but, yeah, we're pretty tight. Always have been."

"Would your marriage have changed that?"

"Maybe. Nicola never cared much for Seth." Preferring a less sensitive topic, she said, "So we're in Southall, huh? Is that anywhere near Hounslow?"

* * * *

Ranjiv couldn't decide whether Jillian didn't want to talk about her sister, her former fiancé, or both, but he knew an evasion when he heard one. As close as she claimed to be to Nicola, and most likely her parents as well, would she even consider the possibility of staying on in England? Perhaps not, but at the moment, he was glad she'd changed the subject. He really didn't want to know.

"Hounslow is to the south," he replied. "That market I told you about is north of here."

"Any cool tourist attractions in Hounslow?"

"A few, but it's mostly residential with several parks and golf courses. On the other hand, we're only a twenty-minute drive from Windsor Park. They have some nice shops there." He grinned. "Even a castle."

"I believe I've heard of that one," she said with a sardonic smile. "The Queen's favorite?"

"So they say," he replied. "I've never asked her myself."

"Maybe we could go there tomorrow. Between the market and all the stores you mentioned, I feel a shopping spree coming on." She glanced at the dog and then at the surrounding pavement. "Guess we'd better take Katie over by the canal to pee before we go anywhere."

"No problem." Ranjiv led the way between the buildings to the canal. "I've hardly been down this way since I moved in here. Having a dog changes things."

"No kidding. Definitely breaking new ground for me."

As always, Katie did exactly what Jillian motioned for her to do. Granted, the dog had done just as well for him, but that was only because he'd used the same signals he'd seen Jillian use. Wondering how she knew them still triggered a slight prickling at his nape.

Best not to dwell on that.

As they headed back to the car, he resumed his host and tour guide persona, threading his arm through hers to help her up the bank. "After we see Windsor Park tomorrow morning, we could go on to Stonehenge if you like. It's about another hour and a half drive from Windsor."

"Sounds good. Stonehenge is the one thing I wanted to see most. It's what got me on that plane, or at least kept me from getting off." Her voice dropped to a harsh whisper, breaking on the last word. She wiped her eyes with the back of her hand. "I came so close to chickening out." On the surface Jillian might pretend to be the eager tourist, but she'd been hurt too badly to bounce back so soon.

So much pain. So much loss.

If Jillian had stayed home, she might have been spared such a terrible ordeal, but she and Ranjiv would never have met. He didn't delude himself into thinking his mother would've survived in her stead. Someone else, perhaps, but not his aging parent. "Thank God for Stonehenge, then."

He didn't have to ask if she grasped his meaning. The tiny squeeze she gave his arm said it all.

Jillian's pensive mood persisted throughout the short drive to his mother's house on Abbots Road. He didn't mind the silence; he only wished he could help her forget.

Jillian had told her sister that she and Ranjiv had been helping each other, but he suspected she'd done more for him than he had for her. Prior to her arrival, he'd coped by making calls and arrangements. He'd met the temple priest at his mother's house and waited outside while the purification ritual was performed. However, once those tasks were completed, he hadn't known what to do with himself. Eventually, he wound up out on the balcony, watching as the rippling water flowed between the grassy, tree-lined banks of the canal. The view was as beautiful as ever and should have eased his mind, but as he sat there attempting to reconcile himself to such a senseless tragedy, he found he couldn't do it. Couldn't find a single scrap of logic or meaning in any part of it, a discovery that only served to make him feel useless and ineffective.

The meeting with Jillian at the airport had given him purpose. Too bad his grief had been too fresh for him to accept what she'd told him with good grace.

Since then, looking after her and Katie had diverted his thoughts like nothing else could have done, but his chest ached with an emptiness that grew stronger as they passed by the familiar rows of terraced houses. He hadn't been inside the house since hearing the news and wasn't sure he could bear it even now. The echoing stillness in the vacant rooms would haunt him far more than any ghost.

He was glad Jillian was with him. Perhaps that was why he'd offered to let her stay there. If she had accepted, he would've shown her through the house and its tiny garden and given her the key. Dealing with a virtual stranger might have made it easier, less personal.

But she wasn't a stranger anymore, and as they drove through the neighborhood where he'd grown up, the memories flooded back more vividly than they had in years. The school, the park, the streets where he and his friends had played. Those streets were busier now than they were twenty years ago, but the rows of houses had changed very little.

Jillian sat beside him, her expression even more apprehensive than his should've been. He pulled in behind his mother's Fiat and shut off the engine. "Are you okay?"

Her quick nod was belied by her teeth fretting with her lower lip. "It just seems strange coming here."

Whether his mother's spirit resided in her or had only spoken to her, Jillian's reaction was understandable. She'd been sitting beside his mother when she died and had likely seen her body. "I'm sorry. Would you rather not go in?"

"No. It isn't that." Pressing the heel of her hand to her forehead, she squeezed her eyes shut. "It's just that all of the sudden, I have this splitting headache."

Again, he chastised himself for forgetting. "Here I am intending to drag you all over London when you should probably take it easy for at least a week. Let's go inside and you can lie down for a bit. We don't have to go to the market if you don't feel like it."

"I was okay until a second ago. Maybe it'll go away."

"Hold on." Ranjiv got out of the car, suspecting that he was about to carry Jillian over yet another threshold. He welcomed the excuse to hold her in his arms, but he would much rather it be for some reason other than illness or injury.

Fortunately, he had the presence of mind to unlock the front door first.

Chapter 17

AT LEAST I'M NOT HEARING VOICES.

Jillian considered that a small consolation after being deluged with thoughts and feelings that completely overloaded her senses. Vivid, swirling images blotted out her sight. Aromas both good and bad flowed in with each breath. Pungent, exotic flavors bathed her tongue. The texture of silks and gossamer-thin veils caressed her skin. Sounds, both discordant and melodic, pounded in her ears.

Her mind worked frantically to process it all, shutting down every nonessential function, which, unfortunately, included walking and talking.

She scarcely felt Ranjiv's arms around her when he scooped her from the car and carried her into the house. She wasn't asleep this time, but she might as well have been. Irritation crept in among the other sensations. Being held in Ranjiv's arms was an experience she'd already missed once. She hated to miss it again.

With no way to fight it, she surrendered to the invasion of her psyche, hoping it would finish quickly. Reality faded into shadows, muffling the world around her.

As time passed, the maelstrom slowly eased and her awareness returned. Cool moisture soothed her brow, Ranjiv obviously having chosen the time-honored method of a cold cloth to the forehead to bring her around.

But had she truly fainted? It must've seemed that way to him, but she had blacked out once before. The pain of a broken finger had dropped her like a rock in the middle of the softball field. Awakening to the anxious faces of her teammates peering down at her, she had no memory of ever hitting the ground. This was different.

She was almost afraid to open her eyes, but when she did, she discovered that her sight had returned. It was even normal. Ranjiv's concerned face filled her field of vision with no distortion whatsoever. Katie nudged her arm, the dog's cold nose contributing yet another measure of reality.

He turned the cloth over, pressing more of the blissful coolness to her skin. "Are you *sure* that brain scan didn't show anything wrong?"

"Mmmhmm..." She drew in a deep breath. The comforting smells of home meshed with Ranjiv's scent, along with something else... Incense, perhaps? "That's what they said."

"Think maybe you need another one?"

"Too much radiation," she replied. "If I have a concussion, I'll recover from that better than I would a brain tumor."

"I can't argue with that, but *still*—"

"Listen, if I ever conk out and you really *can't* arouse me, that'll be the time to call an ambulance." She summoned up a reassuring smile and raised a hand to his face. He felt so real, so solid. "Have you ever considered that I might be faking all this just to get you to carry me around?"

A tiny smile twitched his lips. "Maybe. But all you have to do is ask." The smile blossomed into a full grin. "Or should I just lug you with me wherever I go?"

"That wouldn't be good for either of us."

"True." He leaned over and gave her a quick kiss before rising from his perch on the edge of the couch. "Glad you're feeling better. How about a cup of tea?"

"Sounds good. Tea cures everything."

"Dunno about concussions, but it does have a soothing effect on the soul."

Too bad he didn't realize precisely how many souls he would be soothing with that one cup. "The fishermen who picked us up gave us the most awesome tea." She closed her eyes as the flavor and warmth came rushing back. "I'd never tasted anything that good. Don't think I'll ever forget that."

"Hot and sweet with a dash of milk?"

"Oh, *yeah*..."

"Standard English tea. I can certainly duplicate that."

Turning onto her side, she'd pushed herself up about halfway when Ranjiv took her hand and helped her to sit upright.

"Standard, huh? With all that milk and sugar? It's a wonder the British don't outweigh us all."

"Add a little golden syrup, and, yeah. It's a wonder."

She nodded. "After reading about those treacle tarts Harry Potter liked so well, I found a recipe for them that called for golden syrup. I'd never even heard of it before, but I found some in an import grocery and tried my hand at making the tarts. I couldn't believe how sweet they were. One taste would probably kill a diabetic in seconds."

"Might be just the thing to perk you up, if it doesn't make matters worse. Now that I think of it, both of your 'episodes' happened not long after you'd eaten. Maybe you're allergic to something in the food." He frowned. "Or maybe it's only my rotten cooking."

Chuckling, she shook her head. "I'm not touching that one." Then again, the allergy idea might save her some explaining; she even had a history. "I might be allergic to something growing around here."

"There *are* a lot of things in bloom."

Perfect. "I'm allergic to something back home. I had a sinus infection complete with dizzy spells on the first day of spring for three years straight. Didn't get it this spring because my doctor put me on a steroid inhaler." An inhaler that was in her purse at the bottom of the North Atlantic. She thought it best not to mention that.

"If these spells continue, we might want to see about getting some of that for you here. We can stop by the chemist's and see what's available."

Allergies could explain all sorts of bizarre symptoms. *Why the hell didn't I think of that sooner?* "Must've been something growing in the park or maybe along the canal."

For some reason, that explanation seemed to please him. "Right, then. One cup of tea coming up."

It wasn't until she heard him whistling in the kitchen that she realized why he'd been so pleased. She hadn't blamed the spices or his cooking. Good thing she'd refrained from telling him the truth, which was that his mother was the one to blame.

She gazed around the room, which was now as familiar to her as her own apartment in Memphis. The incorporation of the Kavya entity into her own mind seemed to be complete. No voices spoke to her to tell her that the picture on the wall was of Kavya's husband, Ramesh. She could've easily deduced that, but she knew it for a fact. This visit to Kavya's home had simply brought the assimilation process to a swift and rather abrupt conclusion.

Everything was familiar, yes, but the emotional attachment was lacking. She could look at Ramesh's picture and feel nothing beyond a modicum of sadness for a man who had died so young. She didn't love him any more than she loved the furnishings or any of the other mementos that were scattered about.

Still, she had to smile as she spotted several items that had been produced by the hands of a very young Ranjiv. Anyone could've guessed their source—Ranjiv was Kavya's only child, and these were obviously a schoolboy's attempts at fine art—but she didn't have to guess. She knew.

She also knew that nothing had been disturbed in Kavya's absence. "Doesn't look like anyone's broken in here," she said aloud as Ranjiv returned carrying two steaming cups of tea and a plate of cookies on a tray. "Thieves usually make quite a mess."

He handed her a cup and took a seat beside her. "No. I shouldn't have worried. Her neighbors would've noticed if anything was amiss and reported it."

Jillian was reminded once again of the sense of community here. "My neighbors probably wouldn't notice if I'd been robbed, unless the thieves broke down the door. They might notice that."

"You don't seem to think much of your neighbors."

"It isn't so much that as it is that we only see each other in passing. The people I work with are a different story. We do lots of things together, going out to lunch, movies, that sort of thing."

"Do those friendships last when you change jobs?"

"Some do. Acquaintances with neighbors don't always continue when you move away, though, do they?"

He shrugged. "Depends on where you move to."

Jillian took a sip of her tea. "Mmm... You weren't kidding. This is wonderful."

"Glad you like it."

People said that all the time, but Ranjiv really did seem pleased.

"I'll be able to walk all over town after drinking this." She was laying the praise on a bit thick, purely to see if the effect would be similar.

Ranjiv might have been trying to hide his reaction, but his delight was perfectly clear.

Oh, yes...inordinately pleased.

"It might see you through until lunchtime," he said with a wink.

He was obviously enjoying this opportunity to play knight-errant—not that he would get to do that all the time. Jillian had never seen herself as the fragile flower type, but it was a relief to know that someone was looking out for her. Especially when it was a man who concerned himself with her welfare and enjoyed being an attentive host. Not casually or because it was expected of him, but because it suited him. Those behaviors seemed as natural to him as breathing, and yet from her perspective, so unusual.

Once again, everything boiled down to the simple fact that Ranjiv was a gentleman.

It wasn't only a question of manners. He was...

Oh, God.

All the time. She'd actually thought that. Thought it with the surety of someone who wasn't going anywhere.

Least of all back across the pond to Memphis.

* * * *

What have I done now?

Ranjiv had been looking right at Jillian when her expression changed from smiling enjoyment to stunned silence. He fought the urge to wave a hand in front of her eyes.

"Do I need to call that ambulance?"

"What?" Recalled to her surroundings, she stared at him for a moment. "Sorry. Just thinking. Not comatose or hallucinating.

Besides, I really do think these episodes are my allergies flaring up."

He agreed, albeit somewhat skeptically. "I hope you're right."

She pressed her thumb and forefinger to her eyebrows. "Yeah. That's where the pain usually is. Should've asked one of those docs in Galway for an inhaler and a non-drowsy antihistamine. Might even need a decongestant now."

"I'm sure we can find something to help you today."

"I think you already have. Marvelous tea." She picked up a biscuit and took a bite, then broke off a piece and fed it to Katie. "Nice. Simple, but tasty." She glanced around the room as though searching for a change of topic. "What are your plans for the house?"

"Not sure," he replied. "I could sell it in a heartbeat, but I'm leaning toward living here myself. I like my flat—the view of the canal is beautiful, and I have good neighbors there—but this is home, and it's paid for. I would find it very hard to give it up."

Jillian nodded as though she understood. "You have so much history in this place. The pictures, the furniture and such. I don't think I'd want to sell it either." She paused. "You visited your mother fairly often, didn't you?"

Ranjiv didn't question how Jillian had known that, perhaps because the truth would have been obvious to anyone. "She used to scold me for spending time with her instead of going out in search of a wife. Nor was she above accusing me of only coming here for the food. But it wasn't her company or even a good meal so much as it was being in a place where I felt at ease." He had always told himself his visits were to keep his mother from being lonely. He realized now that it was his own loneliness he'd been trying to keep at bay. His flat was nice, but it had come almost fully furnished. Temporary. Transient. Very little that was truly his own.

"It *is* peaceful here," she agreed. "I could almost forget I was in such a huge city."

"Wait until you see the Broadway. There's hardly room to move on the sidewalks, especially on market day." He laughed as memories of happier times resurfaced. "On my mother's first visit to the States, she called me to tell me what an empty place it was.

'Where *is* everyone?' she asked me." His laughter gave way to a poignant smile. "The streets in Indian cities are always filled with people. I guess it was crowded enough in London for her not to notice the difference as much."

"I'm surprised she would say that about Chicago, although we do have plenty of wide open spaces in America. There are parts where you can drive for hundreds of miles without seeing a soul."

"I don't know if I'd like that." Ranjiv was already lonely enough. He didn't need to have that feeling compounded by living in such a huge country.

"It has a way of putting your life in perspective by making you realize just how small and insignificant you really are."

He didn't need any help with that either. Although Jillian seemed to have the opposite effect, making him feel less like a blip in the ripple of time and more like someone whose life was purposeful, with lasting effects. Perhaps it was the possibility that a relationship with her would lead to having children, which was surely the most eternal contribution anyone could make.

A possibility, yes, but not an absolute guarantee.

Not knowing what to say in the wake of her observation, Ranjiv remained lost in thought until Jillian leaned forward and set her teacup on the tray. Her *empty* teacup.

"Sorry about that," she said. "I didn't mean to put such a damper on the conversation."

"Just made me think is all."

"We've probably done too much of that already. What do you say we give it up and go shopping?"

"I'm game if you are."

"Then let's get going. Katie needs food. I need an antihistamine, a new wardrobe, and some running shoes."

"Trainers, you mean?"

"Yeah. Trainers." She rose to her feet, seeming not the least bit unsteady. It was uncanny the way she could bounce back from those "episodes" she'd been having as though nothing had happened. Ranjiv didn't know if that was a good sign or not.

"What about you?" she asked. "What do you need to buy?"

He thought for a moment. "A hair dryer."

Chapter 18

JILLIAN DIDN'T HAVE TO WORK HARD AT PRETENDING SHE'D NEVER seen anything like the Broadway before. After all, even Kavya hadn't been familiar with every single shop in the noisy, bustling district, nor had she ever gone shopping for American-style clothes, a commodity Jillian was beginning to believe simply wasn't for sale there. Fortunately, antihistamines had been easy enough to locate at the pharmacy. Choosing the right shade of makeup had been much more difficult.

They browsed through the bazaar where Jillian picked out two Punjabi-style cotton nightgowns, complete with elephants printed on the border at the hem. The tunics and trousers were gorgeous, although far more colorful and ornate than anything Jillian had ever worn.

"These are very pretty," she said. "But they're so fancy. All I really need are some T-shirts and a pair of comfy jeans to wear with my nifty Irish sweater."

Ranjiv chuckled. "The airline gave you more money to spend than that, didn't they?"

"Well, yes, but I hate to waste it all on clothes. I'd planned to do some traveling and sightseeing too."

"You might find more of what you're looking for downtown."

"Yeah, right," she said with a snort. "I can really see myself going into Selfridges or Harrods for a pair of Levis. Don't y'all have anything like a Wal-Mart here?"

Ranjiv's reply took the form of side-splitting laughter.

Exasperated, Jillian stomped her foot. "Oh, come on. You know what I mean. Where do the plain ol' Englishwomen buy their clothes?" For that matter, where was the Shanda entity when she needed her? Surely she would've known where to shop. Then again, perhaps Shanda's aura only surfaced when the need to swim arose.

Mighty specific entity.

While Kavya's essence had become fully integrated just as Anna's had done, Shanda's seemed to have faded entirely. Perhaps they would all fade in time. It wasn't as though Jillian could ask an expert in psychic phenomena what to expect after such a transformative experience. For all she knew, *she* was that expert.

During the few moments Jillian took to debate the usefulness of her new auras, Ranjiv's amusement seemed to have tripled.

Jillian's lips twitched into a smile as a new thought took shape in her mind.

This is good for him. Keep him laughing.

Those words of wisdom could have originated with any essence she'd acquired, or even from the depths of her own psyche. She had only to look at Ranjiv to know the advice was sound. Once again, laughter changed him completely, endearing her to him more than anything else could have done, perhaps even more than his kindness or his gentlemanly behavior. While those traits were admirable, the evidence of his glee was quite charming.

"Careful now," she cautioned. "Someone might mistake you for a nutter."

"There's a Marks and Spencer in east Ealing, and an ASDA in Hounslow," he finally said after regaining a modicum of control. "Thought you'd done your research."

"My research didn't include replacing my entire wardrobe," she said with a scowl. "And while I absolutely want to visit Harrods and Selfridges, I seriously doubt I'll have the money to buy anything there."

"You might be surprised," he said. "But before we head off to buy you some sensible clothes, indulge me for a moment, will you?"

She'd already made him laugh. After all he'd done for her, indulging him was the least she could do. "By doing what?"

"Try on a sari."

She hesitated, wondering if it was wise. "Is this a trick question? I mean, you don't think I'll get fussed at for being politically incorrect, do you?"

"Why on earth would you think that?"

"I dunno," she replied. "People are so easily offended by the most innocuous things these days, and I'm so obviously American."

He shrugged. "You're wearing an Irish sweater and skirt."

"Yeah, well, I could pass for Irish in a pinch. Not sure I could pass for someone who belongs in a sari."

"I wouldn't worry about it," he said. "Tourists buy saris all the time, and a green and gold sari would look incredibly beautiful on you." He shook his head slowly. "Not that you aren't incredibly beautiful now. I can't stop thinking about it."

Glossing over the "incredibly beautiful" remark, Jillian focused instead on why he'd phrased his request the way he had. He wasn't asking her to buy a sari. He only wanted her to try one on. With the whole arranged marriage scheme fresh in her mind, she suspected this might be a test to see how well she would fit into his life.

Jillian was loath to admit it, but she would probably fit into his life a damn sight better than he ever dreamed. She'd done her best to play dumb, but she had easily read several signs and posters written in languages she shouldn't have understood. Telugu was very different from many of the other Indian languages, but having lived and worked in Southall for most of her adult life, Kavya must've picked up a smattering of Punjabi somewhere along the way. And so, by default, had Jillian.

"Okay, if you insist," she said. "But there'd better be a helpful saleslady to show me how to wear it." While this was yet another thing Jillian didn't need help with, no way was she going to admit it. She would let the saleslady wrap the spangled cloth around her and show her how to tuck and pleat it. If Ranjiv insisted that she actually buy a sari, she would make a point of pretending to bungle the draping procedure several times before finally getting the hang of it.

"I'm sure there'll be someone to help you," he said. "Like I said, you wouldn't be the first American tourist to try on a sari. After that, we'll have lunch and pick up the car and make a run over to the Marks and Spencer. For all intents and purposes, ASDA really *is* Wal-Mart. You might want to check out something a bit more British."

"To make sure I'm getting the full tourist experience?"

He grinned. "Something like that. We could even take the bus."

* * * *

Jillian's reluctance made Ranjiv wish he hadn't pushed the sari idea, which was more of an erotic fantasy on his part than anything. Perhaps she suspected as much and had used the political correctness argument to cover her lack of enthusiasm.

Not that he would've pursued the matter if he hadn't seen the way she gazed at the fabrics, admiring the colorful cotton prints and caressing the shimmering silks with her fingertips. Comparatively speaking, American clothing was rather plain, being more functional than exotic or alluring. After her first visit to Chicago, his mother had referred to American women as frumpy.

But of course, that was before she'd met Jillian. Would she have said the same about her? Ranjiv had no idea what Jillian had been wearing on the plane, and for the moment, he thought it best not to ask. Not only had the flight ended in a tragic manner, but, for Jillian, it had essentially begun the same way. Her trousseau had probably seemed more like mourning clothes.

He didn't have to think hard to know how a woman might feel embarking on her honeymoon alone. He knew precisely how it felt to be congratulated by family and friends, and then later be forced to endure the pity in their eyes as they offered their condolences. Accepting those same expressions of sympathy was appropriate now. He'd lost someone he could never replace. Laksha, on the other hand, had never truly had a place in his heart.

Jillian was his second and possibly last chance. He knew it as surely as if fate or God or whoever was in charge of such things had spoken to him directly.

When Jillian emerged from the dressing room clad in a sari that matched the colors of her hair and eyes to perfection, he was lost. Completely, utterly, and totally lost.

"Positively stunning," he said when he finally regained the power of speech.

"Not something I could wear every day. At least, not without her help." She nodded toward the saleslady, who, in Ranjiv's opinion, was an absolute artist. He couldn't recall his mother ever wearing a sari in quite the same manner. Jillian slid her fingers through the folds of filmy fabric with something akin to reverence. "And I certainly couldn't wear it while fixing dinner or going to the grocery."

Although her quip made him laugh, he didn't agree. "On the contrary, you could get away with wearing that in any situation. You look like a princess."

Her lips curved into a serene smile as she gazed up at him with an expression he hadn't seen before. Beguiling, provocative, and yet somehow innocent. "Yes, but princesses don't cook or go shopping. They have servants for that."

"I suppose they do." His next question was out before he could catch himself. "Are you going to buy it?"

"Perhaps." Her tone was regal, as befitted royalty. "If for no other reason than to watch you drool."

"Am I? Drooling, I mean?"

"Not quite, but damn close." Even her shrug seemed stately. "Of course, you may choke on that drool when you find out how much this thing costs."

"Doesn't matter. If it's more than you're willing to spend, it would be my pleasure to chip in."

The saleslady piped up with the price, which, in Ranjiv's opinion, was quite reasonable.

"That sounded like a lot," Jillian said after a moment's hesitation.

Her comment and curious expression puzzled Ranjiv until he realized that the amount had been conveyed in Punjabi.

"Fifteen pounds," he translated. "Not bad, really."

"Hmm…about thirty bucks," she mused. "That much, I can afford. Never would've guessed anything so beautiful would cost so little. But then, there isn't much sewing involved, is there?"

He chuckled. "None at all, except for the blouse and the langa—what you would call a slip or a petticoat."

She ran a hand over her hip as though admiring the smoothness of the silk. Ranjiv would have liked to have done the same, albeit for an entirely different reason.

"There's a lot to be said for simplicity," she admitted. "Although it still doesn't seem terribly practical. I mean, nothing beats a good pair of jeans."

"Depends on what you're doing, I suppose." He was starting to repeat himself, and he knew it. The witty banter simply wouldn't flow. But then beautiful women had always tied his tongue into knots.

"True." Still wearing the sari, she drifted over to the racks of tunics. "I might try some of these to see how they feel."

Ranjiv couldn't decide whether she was doing it to please him or herself. Not that it mattered, although he did notice that contrary to his choice of green to match her eyes, she seemed to prefer blue.

She emerged from the dressing room a few minutes later. "How's this?"

Even in the plainer style, she was still— "Gorgeous."

Turning to face the mirror, she again smoothed a hand over her hip. "These are actually pretty comfortable. I think I'll get them."

While she changed back into her skirt and sweater, Ranjiv not only purchased the clothes she'd picked out, he also had the clerk include the sari. Jillian might take him to task for his presumption, but at the time he simply didn't care.

He handed her the bag as she joined him by the doorway, then leaped ahead to the next hurdle. "Ready for lunch?"

"Absolutely." She nodded toward a nearby café. "I don't know what they're frying up over there, but it smells fabulous."

"Pakoras," he said. "A kind of vegetable dumpling. Come on, I'll buy you some."

Ranjiv was about to congratulate himself for emerging from the sari episode unscathed when Jillian fished two twenty-pound notes out of her purse and tucked them into his hand, proving that she knew precisely what he'd bought and how much it cost.

"Like I said, I can afford my own clothes."

"Okay," he conceded. "But I'm paying for lunch."

Her response to that was a barely audible chuckle and a quiet, "Suit yourself."

* * * *

The café was as picturesque, colorful, and authentically Indian as any tourist could've hoped for without being overdone. The artwork was tasteful, as were the snowy tablecloths and elegant water goblets. The food was excellent, and the staff didn't even object to Katie's presence, which Jillian considered to be a mark in their favor.

"Delicious," Jillian said after sampling a pakora. She let her thoughts drift until they arrived at an American counterpart. "Sort of like a spicy hush puppy."

Ranjiv burst out laughing. "A *what*?"

She scowled at him. "You've never heard of hush puppies?"

"Well, no. Can't say that I have."

"They're something of a staple with fried fish. You mix cornbread batter with chopped onions and then deep-fry it a spoonful at a time. The origin of the name has been lost in obscurity, although I've heard that fishermen used to toss them to their noisy dogs and tell them to hush up. No telling how true that is." Jillian glanced down at Katie. "What are your thoughts?"

Katie barked once, wagging the stump of her tail.

"I figured as much."

"Interesting." Ranjiv nodded toward her plate. "Not too spicy for you, is it?"

Jillian dipped a pakora in a dish of tamarind sauce and took a bite before deigning to reply. "Nope. I was raised on my mom's pickled jalapenos. Used to eat them by the bowlful. They taste great with cottage cheese."

This time, she made sure that memory was of her own mother's peppers rather than those produced by someone else's parent before she spoke. She wasn't about to risk taking Ranjiv home to meet the family only to have his mention of pickled peppers be met with a blank stare.

"That Tandoori chicken is pretty awesome too. Kinda reminds me of barbecue. Speaking of which, I'll have to introduce you to Tennessee barbecue at some point." With a wicked grin, she added, "Two can play this game, you know."

He arched a brow. "Ah, so it's a competition to see which of us knows the least about the other's country?"

"Hmm…maybe. If nothing else, it proves how much we each have to learn. I mean, you may have seen some American movies and TV shows, and you may have a McDonald's in every city, but you don't know America until you've eaten corn dogs and funnel cakes at a state fair."

"Touché." Chuckling, he leaned closer. "But tell me this. Why do so many American foods have the words dog or puppy in them?"

"Can't answer that. Maybe it's because we don't eat dogs as a rule, although I know they're a common food source in lots of other places." She pulled off a bit of chicken that didn't appear to have much sauce on it and held it out to Katie. "Sorry, sweetie," she said to her pet. "That's just the way it is."

If the schnauzer was worried about becoming someone's dinner, it certainly didn't show. The chicken went down the hatch without a hitch.

"Might be sorry I gave you that later on, but it's high time you tried some Indian-style table scraps. When in Rome and all that jazz."

Ranjiv wiped his mouth with a napkin, a gesture that struck Jillian as being more sensuous than ordinary. "You probably weren't expecting to spend this much time in Little India, were you?"

"To be honest, it wasn't one of the attractions Seth and I talked about. We were thinking more along the lines of Big Ben and Westminster Abbey." She glanced around her at the hodgepodge of colors and activity. "I really like it here, though. It's beautiful and exotic, and yet… I don't know…" She didn't dare say it seemed homey or familiar. A heartbeat later, she hit on precisely the right thing to say. "I think it's because of you."

"Because of me? How so?"

"You seem to belong here, even though your accent isn't the teeniest bit Indian, and you aren't even dressed like most of the other men."

"But why would my belonging here make you like it?" While he might have been fishing for a declaration of her feelings toward him, it didn't seem that way. In fact, he appeared to be genuinely puzzled.

"I like you. Therefore, I'm inclined to like the places you enjoy."

He leaned back in his chair, smiling. "Guess that means I'll think Tennessee is fabulous."

She chuckled. "It is. Does that surprise you?"

"Not at all."

The inference was perfectly clear. If Tennessee was fabulous, then so was she. She'd already admitted to liking him; he was simply returning the sentiment.

Or did it mean more than that?

The sexual attraction was easily explained. Ranjiv was, after all, a remarkably handsome man. It was the deeper, warmer feelings that seemed strange. Kavya's love for her son was perfectly natural. But this emotion was different, not at all like Jillian imagined a mother's love to be.

In that moment, Jillian realized that Kavya's influence had nothing to do with the way she felt about Ranjiv. Her feelings toward him were entirely her own.

Chapter 19

JILLIAN BOARDED THE BUS WITH ALMOST AS MUCH RELIEF AS SHE'D felt the first time she'd climbed into Ranjiv's car. Unfortunately, by the time she and her aching feet had climbed the stairs to the upper level, she was beginning to regret their decision to take the bus, despite the fact that a ride on the distinctively British double-decker variety was a must for the photo album.

"I had no idea buying an entire vacation wardrobe could be so exhausting," she said as she plopped down in her seat. "I usually pack what I have and only need to buy a few things. Not everything all at once."

Marks and Spencer had provided the essentials, including a hair dryer and shoes, but the other shops along the street had proved too fascinating to ignore. Her nose had even discerned the nearby KFC. Unfortunately, she was still too full of pakoras to compare the British version of the Colonel's chicken with the American standard.

"Can't say I've ever done that myself," Ranjiv said. "Where to now?"

Jillian came so close to saying "home," she nearly choked on the word to stop herself. Home could have meant so many different places; even she wasn't sure which one she'd meant.

"Back to your mother's house, I guess," she said. "You'll want to pick up your car."

"True. Dinner?"

"Surprise me."

Ranjiv settled his share of their packages on the floor in front of him, his thigh brushing her knee as he leaned forward. "You're probably sick of Indian food by now. How about some traditional English pub grub?"

"Sounds great. But just so you know, I'm not sick of Indian

food." Not yet, and probably not ever. Nor would she ever tire of the way his nearness affected her, increasing her appetite for something less nutritious. Diverting her thoughts from how *he* would taste required considerable effort. "I'm anxious to try some real fish and chips, though. My research included reading through scads of menus; things like steak and ale pie, bangers and mash, and sticky toffee pudding have me intrigued."

He chuckled. "How do you feel about beer? The pub experience isn't complete without it."

"I like it okay. Although interestingly enough, gin and tonic is my drink of choice." She smiled. "By the time we've lugged all this stuff back to your car, I'll probably *need* a drink." Then again, the consumption of any alcohol whatsoever would probably be a mistake, unless Ranjiv had a burning desire to lose his virginity in a highly public manner. "I don't suppose the bus stops in front of your mother's house?"

"No, but it's not far." He gave her a wink. "I'm sure we can make it. Besides, it'll give you a chance to work up an appetite for fish and chips."

When the bus finally came to a stop at Abbott's Road, the trick was more a matter of making sure they weren't forgetting anything rather than any of it being particularly heavy, with the exception of the dog food, which Ranjiv carried far more cheerfully than Jillian would have done. Once again, she thanked her lucky stars that Katie hadn't been a Great Dane.

After a pleasant stroll down the street, Ranjiv stowed their purchases in the back seat of the Range Rover. "I need to go inside for a bit. Would you mind?"

Why she would care was a mystery. "I could stand a trip to the loo."

"Me too."

Entering Kavya's house again brought on no ill effects whatsoever. While the antihistamine could easily be credited for the difference in her reaction, she truly felt like she'd come home. Every house had its own characteristic aroma, which tended to become ingrained in the noses of the occupants. This time, if there was such a "nesting smell," Jillian didn't notice it.

She had, however, noticed the surreptitious glances Ranjiv kept darting in her direction, perhaps to reassure himself that she wasn't about to have another meltdown.

"I'm fine," she insisted. "Not a bit dizzy."

Ranjiv's expression was like that of a little boy caught with his hand in the cookie jar, at once mischievous and roguishly charming. "Was I that obvious?"

"Kinda."

"Sorry. Don't mean to hover."

"I've never liked for anyone to hover over me," she said. "Makes me feel like a microbe on a petri dish."

"Petri dish?" he echoed. "Sounds very scientific."

"That's my minor in biology talking. It was my major to begin with; too bad I couldn't decide what sort of career to pursue. Research seemed a bit tedious, and I couldn't see myself as a teacher. I wasn't interested in anything medical either. Can't stand the sight of blood."

She'd seen plenty of that during the crash. The fact that she'd kept one shred of her composure was amazing, along with everything else associated with that event.

"Anyway, I wound up with a degree in banking and finance." She shrugged. "The way new bank branches were popping up everywhere, I figured someone would hire me."

"High finance interests you?"

"Not especially. Although I've always been good with numbers." She glanced toward the stairs. "Bathroom's upstairs, right?"

Ranjiv replied with a nod.

"Be right back."

She climbed the stairs, reminding herself that Ranjiv was only making conversation in an effort to find out more about her. He couldn't know she was feeling the strain of trying to figure out which memories were hers and which belonged to her newly integrated entities. She had to keep telling herself that the Tennessee memories were hers; any others belonged to someone else.

Unfortunately, even that didn't solve her dilemma completely. There were bound to be gray areas.

As she washed her hands, a quick glance at the mirror proved she hadn't magically transformed into someone else. Jillian had known a moment of fear when she'd turned toward the dressing room mirror after the saleslady had finished draping the folds of the sari, fully expecting her reflection to no longer be her own—like in that old movie where Steve Martin saw Lily Tomlin's face whenever he looked in a mirror.

For a long moment, she simply stood there, staring at the mirror without actually seeing anything. Her rational side insisted she was only trying to recall the name of the film. Her *ir*rational side was more honest, admitting it was waiting to see if her reflection would turn into someone else and speak to her.

All of Me.

That was the name of the picture. Jillian quickly reviewed the details of the plot, thinking for one crazy moment that the resolution might actually help her solve her own dilemma. A Middle Eastern psychic had transferred Lily's consciousness back where it belonged. But of course, he'd been the one to initiate the transfer in the first place.

Crap.

Somehow Jillian doubted anyone short of an exorcist could help her. Not that her entities were evil enough to require that sort of intervention.

Only when it finally dawned on her that the release of *All of Me* predated her birth did it occur to her that that particular memory might also belong to someone else. Not daring to check the mirror again, she dried her hands on an all-too-familiar towel and headed downstairs.

* * * *

Ranjiv couldn't help noticing how quiet Jillian was during the drive back to his flat. Was she tired of his company or simply tired? He had to remind himself he didn't know her very well. This sort of behavior might be perfectly normal for her.

Even so, spending the day with Jillian hadn't altered his

impression that she was hiding something. Nothing awful, just something she wasn't telling him or wasn't being entirely truthful about. He also found it hard to believe that any allergy medication could make that much of a difference so quickly. Granted, she'd been feeling better long before she'd taken a dose, but he'd spent the rest of the afternoon slightly on edge, expecting her to have a relapse at any moment.

Arriving at his building, he parked the car and helped Jillian gather up all the bags before heading upstairs. Katie trotted obediently at Jillian's heels, albeit with a tad less energy than she'd displayed earlier in the day. She'd seemed genuinely concerned when Jillian had succumbed to her allergic episode, if indeed that was what it had been. He still wasn't convinced. Jillian had seemed fine afterward, and so had the dog. Perhaps there was a connection. Maybe Katie reflected Jillian's moods.

He'd somehow managed to refrain from mentioning the spooky aspect of a dog's devotion to someone so new to her. He'd even kept quiet when Jillian had shown a liking for pakoras, which had been one of his mother's favorite snack foods. She'd worn her sari differently, although that could have been deliberate on her part or the preference of the shop's dresser. After all, there were about a hundred different ways to wear a sari, and not every woman used the same method every time.

What he really wanted to do was get drunk enough to simply nail her. Just get it out of the way and over with. It wouldn't be a bit like doing it with his mother. He knew that. But there was still the nagging doubt, although as a follower of a religion that believed in reincarnation, consorting with an ancestor was always a possibility.

That's it!

He had a handle on it now. Reincarnation, not possession by a malevolent spirit. He'd never heard of it happening that way, but then again, why would he?

"What's up with you?" Jillian asked. "You're grinning like the cat that got the cream *and* caught the mouse."

"Nothing special. Just a different…perspective on things." Still, having made the decision didn't make the actual act any less difficult to approach. Or even to mention. Did one simply blunder into these things? Never having done it before, he had no idea.

Dinner. We have to have dinner first. He needed to make a reservation at a really nice pub. The Eagle, perhaps? Or the Prince of Wales? It was close, but served mostly Indian food. She wanted pub grub. The Pig and Whistle? Or Kerbisher & Malt for the best fish and chips?

Hmm...

"Fish and chips, right?"

"Absolutely. Bangers and mash tomorrow. Dosas for breakfast, of course. I want to try them with American cheese—the good kind, not that individually-wrapped stuff."

His cheery mood never wavered. "Good luck finding that in London."

"Why am I not surprised? Cheddar will have to do, then. I'm sure you have that here."

"About twenty different kinds, actually."

"Decisions, decisions..."

They had almost reached the door to his flat when Tahir came dashing up the stairs. "My *amma* wants me to ask if you need the hair dryer again."

"Nope," Ranjiv replied. "Bought one today."

"What about a toothbrush?" the child went on.

"Didn't think of that," Jillian admitted. "But I still have the one they gave me at the hospital."

"What about makeup?"

"Got that at the first stop we made."

"Hairspray?"

"Don't use it."

"Dog food?"

"Absolutely."

Tahir nodded. "That'll do then." He grinned unabashedly. "Mum gave me a list."

Jillian laughed. "It's nice to know y'all are looking out for me. But Ranjiv has been doing a fine job. He took me to a dozen different stores, and we went out to lunch."

"What did you have to eat?" Like most growing boys, food was Tahir's chief interest.

"Pakoras and Tandoori chicken."

"I love pakoras! They're great with coconut chutney."

"I'll have to try that next time," she said. "Tell me, what is your opinion of fish and chips?"

Ranjiv could barely suppress his smile. She might have been asking that same question of the food critic for *The London Times.*

Tahir appeared to give considerable thought to his reply. "I like them well enough," he finally said. "Don't like the mushy peas, though."

"Too mushy?"

"Yeah."

"What about sticky toffee pudding?"

"Awesome!"

She nodded gravely. "That's next on my list, then. What else do you recommend?"

This time, he didn't hesitate. "The lamb chops at the Prince of Wales."

"Spoken like a true connoisseur." She glanced at Ranjiv. "Think we can fit all this in?"

Ranjiv's heart took a peculiar sort of plunge. "Between now and…"

"You know…before I have to go home. I'm only here for three weeks."

By this time, his heart was dodging around somewhere near his navel. "I-I'd almost forgotten you weren't staying on indefinitely."

"I think I'd need some sort of visa for that, wouldn't I?"

"I suppose so," Ranjiv replied. If she were to marry a British citizen, she could probably stay on. Unfortunately, he had no idea what the laws were for that sort of thing, nor did this seem like the best time to discuss it.

Tahir, however, had no such qualms. "I thought you were going to marry Ranjiv."

Surprisingly, she laughed. "Even if I did marry him, the wedding wouldn't be that soon. Stuff like that takes a lot of thought and planning. Trust me, I know. Of course, all the planning I did for my last wedding turned out to be a complete waste of time."

Tahir's nod seemed uncharacteristically solemn for a seven year old. "Yes, but you wouldn't be wasting your time with Ranjiv. He's a smashing fellow."

"I agree, but it's still too soon to be talking about marriage." She smiled at the child. "He hasn't even taken me out to dinner yet."

"That's important." Tahir focused his gaze on Ranjiv. "Better take her someplace really special."

"Even if she only wants fish and chips?" Ranjiv asked.

"*Especially* if she only wants fish and chips," Tahir replied, stomping a foot for emphasis.

Ranjiv stroked his chin. "Hmm… Would Kerbisher & Malt meet with your approval?"

"I believe so."

"Are you *sure* you're only seven?" Jillian asked the boy.

Tahir's broad grin displayed the slight gap between his upper and lower front teeth. "I'll be eight in August." He tapped his front teeth. "They're almost in all the way."

"That explains it, then." She held out a shopping bag. "Care to give us a hand?"

"Righto."

* * * *

Heretofore, Jillian's experience with English children had only been through television and movies, but they always sounded so mature.

Must be the accent.

Or better schooling. Any child taught to speak in a country that could count such eloquent fellows as Shakespeare and Churchill among the ranks of its historical figures should have produced reasonably articulate children.

Ha! Diagram that *sentence.* Which, of course, no one did anymore.

She was already starting to feel loopy with fatigue. A nap would've been more welcome than dinner at that point. A glance at her watch proved it was only five fifteen.

Tea time?

No. Tea was at four, although she was fairly certain it wasn't quite the ritual it had once been. "By the way, do the British still do the afternoon tea thing?"

"It's practically extinct," Ranjiv said as he unlocked the door to his flat. "Maybe the rich have time for it, but most people don't get off work until five or even later." He paused, smiling back at her. "Was that a request for a cup of tea?"

"Actually, another cup of tea would go down rather well."

Holy moly, I'm even starting to sound *like a Brit.*

Perhaps that was the Shanda entity resurfacing. Or it might have been the environment. When she lost her Tennessee drawl, she would know she was in trouble.

In trouble of what? Of losing her mind or her own identity?

The stereotypical mystic would undoubtedly see such changes as progress toward achieving enlightenment. Perhaps she was growing as a person or simply expanding her horizons.

No. That couldn't be right. Her experience during the crash had been more a matter of her consciousness expanding than anything to do with her horizons.

Ranjiv dropped several bags on the coffee table, then carried the dog food into the kitchen. "What about you, Tahir? Would you like a cup of tea?"

"No, thank you," Tahir replied, adding his burdens to the growing pile. "I need to get back to my homework."

"Some other time, then," Jillian said. "Thanks for your help."

As the door closed behind the boy, Jillian dumped her purchases on the couch. "I need to get started on the laundry. Gotta wash all this stuff before I can wear any of it."

"Allergic to the starch or whatever it is they put in new clothes?"

Jillian suspected this was a trick question, but decided to give her allergies more credit than they truly deserved. She nodded. "Makes me itch like crazy."

"Well, we can't have that, can we?" Ranjiv's sly smile suggested he would be more than willing to scratch any itch she might have.

A favor she would have been quite happy to return.

Chapter 20

RANJIV'S APPEAL HAD CLIMBED YET ANOTHER NOTCH. SUDDENLY, the kisses they'd shared the night before weren't enough. Not *nearly* enough. Keeping her hands off him was becoming more impossible by the second.

Averting her gaze from his masculine form, she carried her new clothes over to the laundry alcove beside the refrigerator. "Got any scissors? I need to cut off the tags."

"Third drawer from the right," he replied. "Detergent is on the shelf above the washer."

She retrieved the scissors, noting as she trimmed off the tags that the sari was not only in dire need of ironing, the fabric was also marked dry clean only.

Figures.

Dry-cleaning fluid was even more irritating to her skin than the sizing in new fabrics. Then again, something told her the sari was the sort of outfit that might never *need* cleaning. She would only wear it for Ranjiv and probably never for long periods of time.

She had purchased a few such outfits for her honeymoon, most of which had been far more revealing, unless she were to wear the sari without the matching blouse or petticoat. Would Ranjiv like that sort of thing? Granted, he'd seemed quite pleased to see her in it at the store, but—

Pleased, *hell.* He'd practically devoured her with his eyes.

She stole a glance at him as he sifted through his own purchases. She'd pretended not to notice when he left her alone while she perused the antihistamines in the pharmacy, but a man buying condoms was hard to miss. Did he intend to use them soon, or did he simply believe in being prepared?

Nope. Not asking that question. Not now and probably not ever.

Opting to feign ignorance, she dragged out the ironing board and set the iron to preheat before resuming the tasks of reading labels and sorting colors.

When Ranjiv strolled down the hall with the package in question, Jillian's strategic position enabled her to watch him bypass the bathroom to empty the contents into the top drawer of the nightstand. Even if she hadn't known what it was, she probably could have guessed—if for no other reason than his too-casual demeanor.

"Tonight's The Night."

Oddly enough, she didn't *think* those words; somewhere in the back of her mind, Rod Stewart's voice *sang* them.

Okay. Which one of you is haunting me now?

Silence echoed through her thoughts.

"Dammit, Shanda," she whispered. "I know that's you."

"Did you say something?" Ranjiv asked as he returned.

"Just talking to myself." She wasn't sure which would sound crazier: talking to herself or talking someone who only existed in her mind. Opting to nip the insanity notion in the bud, she added, "But don't bother calling an ambulance. That's normal. At least it is for me."

"Been known to do that myself."

His hearty agreement sounded a tad forced. Was he embarrassed for having just stashed a box of condoms in his nightstand? Or was he trying to convince her he didn't think she'd gone completely bonkers?

While she couldn't blame him for questioning her sanity, Jillian's second experience in his mother's house had convinced her that Kavya wouldn't be speaking to her again. Faded, integrated, or whatever label she chose to put on the matter, that separate personality was gone. With respect to her relationship with Ranjiv, she was on her own. The same was true of the Anna entity, at least where dogs were concerned. But Shanda...

Not so sure about you.

Then again, if her relationship with the Shanda entity only pertained to swimming and Rod Stewart songs, she figured she could handle it. In the meantime, exploring her relationship with Ranjiv seemed more important, not to mention more interesting. "I'm doing a load of whites first. Need anything washed?" Perhaps the mingling of their underwear would be the first step toward greater intimacy.

Or maybe I really do need that nap.

Once her clothes were in the washer, she could chill for a bit. Ironing the sari could wait, although she had an idea that Ranjiv would appreciate her taking the time to do it.

"I'm sure I could come up with a few things to throw in."

Moments later, he returned from the bathroom with a hamper. "Not a whole lot here, actually. I did a few extra loads on Monday."

Jillian didn't have to ask why he'd done it then. Making calls and funeral arrangements only took up so much time. He'd probably resorted to catching up on all sorts of household chores to occupy his hands and mind.

She stepped back as he tossed a few T-shirts and briefs into the washer.

Oh, yeah. Definitely *more intimate.*

"I'm glad I have enough to make at least a partial load now," she said as she started the machine. "Washing my one set of undies out by hand every night was starting to get old."

"I'm not surprised." He nodded toward the ironing board where she'd laid the sari. "Want some help with that?"

She didn't have to ask what he'd meant by that either. "Sure. As long as saris are, I don't see how anyone could iron one without it getting all crumpled up on the floor."

She waited half a heartbeat, knowing exactly what he would say next.

He didn't disappoint her. "I used to help my mother iron her saris. I would hold the edges and slowly back away as she finished each section."

In her mind's eye, she could actually see a much younger version of Ranjiv doing just that. The memory triggered an emotion, not arising from the distant past, but from a more recent event. Kavya was right; he *had* been a good son. No doubt he would be just as good at being a husband and father, perhaps even better.

I really shouldn't let this one get away.

She smiled. "I'm sure she appreciated your help."

"Yes, she did." His expression grew thoughtful for a moment, his eyes taking on a misty, faraway appearance before a blink brought him back to the present. He set the ironing board at a different angle. "To give me more room to back up," he explained.

Jillian tested the iron on a small corner of the fabric, which, thankfully, didn't scorch or melt. She dropped the sari on the floor in front of her and draped the upper edge over the board. Ranjiv waited while she ironed the first section, then grasped the corners and took a step backward. She smiled to herself, wishing they were engaged in an activity that required them to get closer together as opposed to putting more distance between them. Still, it was a shared experience, one that had a bonding effect even stronger than washing their underwear together.

"What I can't figure out is how to hang this thing up without getting creases in it again."

He chuckled. "The trick is not to overstuff your closet."

"Not much danger of that. Especially since at the moment, I don't even *have* a closet."

"Sure you do. I'm more than willing to share."

"Hmm… Making room in your closet for me, huh? Sounds serious."

Yet another memory surfaced: the day she'd cleaned out a closet for Seth, whose considerable wardrobe had taken up almost as much space as her own. The emptiness left behind when he moved out still echoed through her mind. They'd shared that apartment for several years, but in the end, the time they'd spent together meant nothing.

Her mood swung abruptly from teasing to morose. "I wouldn't bother if I were you."

* * * *

Ranjiv suspected he had committed yet another dating faux pas, although he didn't fully understand why the thought of sharing a closet would upset her, especially after he'd already suggested they share his bed. Considering the day they'd spent together, he'd been fairly certain she wouldn't insist on separate sleeping arrangements again.

He wasn't sure about that now.

"You would have a closet if you were staying in a hotel," he reasoned. "The least I can do is offer you a place to put your clothes. I mean, you don't even have a suitcase."

She blushed as though she'd been the one to make a mistake, then drew in a long breath as she put down the iron. "Sorry. Should've kept my mouth shut. You've been nothing but kind and accommodating, and I—"

He dropped the end of the sari, waving his hands. "My fault entirely. You were joking. I should've realized that."

"I wasn't joking." With a grimace, she shifted her gaze downward and resumed her task. "Although I wish I had been."

Her sudden slide into the doldrums had him glancing around the room to see if any dementors were approaching. "What's wrong?"

She shook her head. "All that talk about closets got me to thinking about the empty space in my apartment back home." A teardrop slid down her cheek and fell, marring the silky perfection of the fabric she'd just ironed. "At the moment, I'm too tired to fight it."

"Then why are you bothering with this now?" He gave the sari a tug.

"Seemed like the right thing to do." A tiny, mirthless laugh escaped her. "Beats getting plastered. Or should I say pissed?"

"To be honest, getting pissed may be exactly what you need to do."

"Which meaning? Angry or drunk?"

"Both," he replied. "I have a feeling that anger is one of those issues you haven't worked through yet."

"Doesn't seem appropriate now. Not when I'm still breathing, even though I shouldn't be." Her eyes closed as her entire body seemed to sag along with her shoulders. "I'm sorry," she said again. "It's hard for me to be angry at Seth—or even rejoice in being alive—knowing so many others died, especially your mother."

He understood how she felt, but that sort of acknowledgement wasn't what she needed to hear. "You're forgetting what Rumi said about sorrow preparing you for joy."

"I think I need to have that printed on a little card so I can read it about a bajillion times a day."

"That can be arranged," he said. "In fact, I can do it right now. Bring the scissors."

Across the room, he sat down at the desk and opened his laptop. Jillian followed, standing near his shoulder while the words flowed from his heart to his fingertips. A sheet of card stock in the printer, an adjustment to the smallest font, and there it was:

Rumi, the pocket edition.

She handed him the scissors. "I should probably get that laminated."

"Might last longer," he agreed as he trimmed the edges. "Here you go."

She took the card from him and studied it for several moments. "When you told me this before, I was too focused on the stuff about souls striving toward perfection. This was the important part, giving you permission to find joy in the wake of sorrow."

"We *both* need to remember that." He rose from his chair and turned toward her.

"Yeah." Her voice softened to a breathy whisper. "It's hard to accept, though. Even when joy is staring you right in the face."

If he was ever going to take Jillian in his arms and kiss away her sadness, the time was now. Placing his hands on her shoulders, he bent down, brushing her lips with his own. She slipped the card into the pocket of her skirt before reaching up to encircle his neck with her arms. The kiss deepened, growing sweeter with each lingering caress. Heat swirled around him like a cloud—a cloud of desire rather than lust. Longing. Caring. Love.

It was hard to believe, but it was true. No questions, no reservations, and certainly no regrets.

Sweeping her into his arms, he carried her down the hall.

She didn't resist, nor did she protest when he laid her on the bed. He'd done it once before and then had to leave her to sleep alone. This time, he wasn't leaving.

Her fingertips traced the line of his jaw as he covered her with his body. Spearing his fingers through her hair, he held her close, doing his best to convey his emotions with actions rather than words. She was his joy, his salvation, his future and his past. Precious and eternal.

He was too hot, his clothing too confining. She seemed to sense that, pulling his sweater over his head. He did the same with hers. The rest, he wasn't aware of. Any barriers between them simply seemed to disappear.

Her skin was like silk beneath his lips and palms, its flavor unlike anything he'd ever tasted. She touched him in ways he'd never been touched, somehow knowing precisely where to linger and where a feathery stroke would entice.

She reached a hand into the drawer. Had she seen what he'd done? Did she know what was there?

Apparently so. Now sheathed without the fumbling fingers he would have used, he hovered between her thighs.

With a hand on either side of his face, she pulled his head down. "Look at me."

Green eyes swimming with tears met his gaze, surely the embodiment of love. "Please. Say yes."

A move accompanied her affirmative reply, placing him against her in a manner that left him only one choice. A thrusting glide into infinity. A plunge into warmth that thrilled as well as soothed. She held him as he rocked into her, keeping her eyes open wide as though determined to watch as he finally reached the summit. He longed to witness her climax, but his eyes refused to cooperate, snapping shut as he reached his own pinnacle, a rush of exquisite pleasure that obliterated every other sensation.

His body surged into hers as she convulsed around him, prolonging the ecstasy while consuming him with joy. As he spiraled downward toward blissful contentment, he knew Rumi had been absolutely right. A far better thing had indeed taken the place of his sorrow. And not merely the act of love, but the woman who held him in her arms.

* * * *

Jillian had just made a fascinating discovery—not earth-shattering, perhaps, but nonetheless significant. Despite the precipitous nature of their encounter and Ranjiv's apparent inexperience, those few precious moments with him outshone anything else she'd ever done, and she was at a loss to understand why.

Unless he was the one.

She'd never put much stock in the notion that every person had a perfect match. Now, she wasn't so sure, mainly because the way she felt had nothing to do with technique and everything to do with emotion. One emotion. One very important emotion that she now suspected she had never felt for Seth.

Love.

She loved Ranjiv. But how? How could anyone find a place in her heart so quickly? Granted, recent events had rendered her susceptible to damn near anything. But this was…

Okay, so maybe it *was* earth-shattering after all. The only detail lacking was for Shanda to cue the appropriate Rod Stewart tune.

"You Are Everything."

Jillian smiled to herself. Rod Stewart's repertoire probably hadn't covered every possible romantic sentiment, but that particular song said it all. "That works for me."

Ranjiv raised his head, his puzzled expression as endearing as ever. "What works?"

Great. Jillian was mentally kicking herself for not keeping her conversations with Shanda quiet until she realized the answer to his question had already been provided for her.

"Everything."

Chapter 21

THE NEAREST KERBISHER & MALT TURNED OUT TO BE ROCK-throwing distance from the Marks & Spencer, but at least they weren't riding the bus this time. There was even a car park nearby.

Funny how Jillian was already thinking of it in those terms. Back home, she would've referred to it as a parking lot. Car park sounded too much like a place to take your car for a meandering drive through the woods. Then again, having two British entities on board might've had something to do with that.

And now I've had sex with a Brit. Sort of. Or would he be more accurately called an Indian Brit?

Same difference, really. They all lived in the same country. The rest didn't matter very much.

Actually, it *did* matter. Ranjiv was by far the handsomest man she'd seen since her arrival, and the man was put together very nicely indeed. She'd seen him naked now, so she knew. Oh God, how she knew. She had already convinced herself that love was responsible for the greater part of her feelings toward him, but the fact that he was hung like a bull moose didn't hurt—although it could have. She'd been a little surprised when she put the condom on him, half-expecting it not to fit. Thankfully, it did. That was one sexual encounter she wouldn't have wanted to interrupt for another trip to the chemist's to search for extra-large condoms.

A chuckle escaped her as Ranjiv parked the car. "We really should've just hung around here until dinnertime." A moment later, she realized what she would've missed. "Well, no. Scratch that. We did the right thing in going home first."

Ranjiv burst out laughing. "I'm so glad you approve."

"I more than approve. In fact, I demand an encore."

"I believe that can be arranged."

He helped her out of the car and they walked arm in arm along the sidewalk to the corner. A right turn brought them to an unpretentious eatery with large windows facing the street. Several small white tables and chairs sat beneath a blue awning inscribed with the words "Eat in" and "Takeaway."

"Let's eat in," she said. "I want the full chippy experience." And later, she wanted the full Ranjiv experience. Time to linger and explore every last inch of him. What she *didn't* want to do was call her sister for a report on her findings. She wanted the opportunity to immerse herself in the relationship before someone tried to talk her out of it.

He held the door open, waving her inside. "I'm glad Shalini was willing to keep Katie for the evening. Otherwise, we might've had to eat outside."

"Yeah. I'm guessing even Anna didn't take her everywhere. We probably should've left her at home while we were out shopping today."

Ranjiv and Katie had waited outside several of the shops while Jillian went in alone. He hadn't complained—and there were a few things she preferred to buy without an audience—but having a dog along did complicate matters. That being said, sometimes the alternative was even worse. She knew people who left their dogs home alone while they went off to work, only to find the place totally trashed when they returned. She couldn't imagine Katie ever behaving that way, but there was no telling what a lonely dog might decide to do for entertainment.

He nodded. "We never made it that far on the tour, but there's a small garden behind my mother's house. She would've been fine there."

"Tahir seemed pleased to have her for a visit, though."

"That's not too surprising. Their dog isn't what you'd call spry."

Jillian had met Shalini and Bippi when they dropped off Katie. The corgi had moved rather slowly—not on her last legs just yet, but getting there—and she was certainly no match for a lively schnauzer.

As Ranjiv led the way to the counter, Jillian stared at the menu painted on the wall. "Okay. I've at least heard of the different kinds of fish they serve here, but what on earth is a fish finger butty?"

He laughed. "It's just a sandwich made with fish sticks."

"Hmm… Sounds kinda risqué to me. I think I'll stick with the battered cod."

"Mushy peas?"

"I dunno," she said with a trace of caution. "Tahir doesn't like them."

"How about if I get some and give you a taste?"

"Works for me."

After placing their order, they headed for one of the smaller booths.

"Sure smells good in here," she said as slid into the booth. "I promise to try something different next time, but I'm not feeling very adventurous at the moment."

"Is that so? You could've fooled me." His slow, drawling tone and the touch of his hand on her shoulder left no doubt as to what he meant.

"You know what I mean," she chided. "I've already had one meltdown today. I don't want to push my luck, and a fish finger butty might be what sends me over the edge."

He took the seat across from her, shaking his head. "My money's on the dementors."

"Now you're making fun of me," she said, scowling.

"Not at all. I think they're very real. They just don't look like they did in the movies. They're anything that steals happiness from you."

She nodded slowly. "Yeah. That's true. Lots of things—and some people—do that."

"And now they have a name."

One thing for sure, Ranjiv wasn't one of them. Neither were any of her newly acquired entities. Even Anna wasn't berating her for letting someone else babysit her dog. Kavya was probably grinning like the Cheshire cat now that her thirty-year-old son had finally found someone to love. Shanda wasn't exactly playing romantic songs on the iPod of Jillian's mind, but that was okay too, although Rod Stewart *was* starting to grow on her.

When their order was ready, Ranjiv went to get it and brought it over to their table. Jillian doused her fish with malt vinegar and took a bite. "Mmm… This is fabulous."

"Mushy peas?"

"Not yet. I want to savor this fish first." Even the fries were incredible—crispy, hot, and salty. "Okay, I'm hooked now. The fish finger butty will be next."

"You'll really be hooked then, I promise you."

Fish finger butty or not, she was already hooked—on the land, the mishmash of cultures, the history, and most of all, a certain tall, handsome fellow who was no longer a virgin.

After eating enough fish and chips to satisfy her hunger and then some, she tried the mushy peas. "Not bad, but I wouldn't kill for them."

"No worries," Ranjiv said with a shrug. "It's an acquired taste." His tongue passed over his lips in a sensuous, suggestive manner. "Unlike you. You tasted marvelous from the very beginning."

"So did you, but there are some parts of you I haven't tried yet."

Ranjiv swallowed with apparent difficulty before clearing his throat. "I, uh, look forward to that."

"I'm sure you do, and I promise you'll enjoy it." Unable to suppress her smile, she let it stretch into a wicked grin. "Like I said before, two can play this game."

"Yes, well, some of us are better at this than others."

"You'll get the hang of it eventually." She studied him closely. "You're okay, aren't you? We haven't really talked since—"

He raised a hand in protest. "I am *so* much more than okay. You've no idea."

"Glad to hear it." She sighed with utter contentment. "I'm feeling pretty good myself."

* * * *

There were parts of Jillian that Ranjiv hadn't tasted yet, which was yet another thing to look forward to. Already, the custom of arranged marriages and taking a lifetime to learn to love someone seemed easier and more pleasurable than ever before.

That their relationship was similar to an arranged marriage was a fact he no longer questioned. His mother had seen something special in this woman and had sent her to him with her dying words. It was as simple—and mysterious—as that.

He had expected his study of the *Kama Sutra* to have prepared him for sex, but nothing he'd read explained how he would feel after making love with a woman for the first time. It wasn't about being manly and powerful; he was complete—as though the final piece of a puzzle had been fitted into its proper place. Most men probably took such feelings for granted, especially since the majority passed that particular milestone while still in their teens. Ranjiv was old enough to fully understand its significance.

He was glad he'd waited, even though the choice hadn't been entirely his own. Jillian was the right woman for him. He was convinced of that, and he was *not* letting her get away.

He knew how to do it too. He'd told her she looked like a princess in that sari. As far as he was concerned, she *was* a princess, and he would treat her as such, with loyalty, respect, and above all, love. He didn't care if other people considered him old-fashioned. Jillian's opinion was the only one that mattered.

"Aren't you hungry?" she asked, interrupting his reverie. "You're not eating."

"What? Oh, right." He took a bite of a chip. "Just thinking."

She nodded, but didn't press him for the details, possibly because she could've guessed them. Even so, he didn't want her to think he was ignoring her. "I should probably be talking to you instead of sitting here like a lump."

"Not necessarily. I mean, if you have something to say, say it, but I'm okay with gaps in the conversation. I was more concerned that your dinner was getting cold." With a short laugh, she added, "Seth couldn't stand silence. He was always rattling on about something."

"Did you like that?"

"It didn't bother me, if that's what you mean. Although I'll admit to enjoying a little peace and quiet now and then. I read somewhere that dominating a conversation was a control issue, but I can't help wondering if it isn't also a sign of insecurity." She paused briefly. "You don't seem to need to do that."

"So...let me see if I've got this straight. Being quiet means I'm not domineering or insecure?"

She grinned. "No. It means you're the strong, silent type."

"Ah, I see." Resting his elbow on the table, he leaned toward her, chin on fist. "And since you're having dinner with me, I can only assume that's the type of man you prefer."

"I wouldn't say it was the *type* I preferred, but rather the man in question."

A smile tugged at the corner of his mouth. "Guess I should quit while I'm ahead."

"I can keep going if you like. I could describe your masculine attributes."

"Oh?"

She popped a chip in her mouth, chewing it slowly before voicing her reply. "Bigger is better."

"I've heard that. Is it really true?"

"Absolutely. At least in this case—although there *is* such a thing as too big."

"Not too big, am I?" Ranjiv was almost afraid to ask that question, but figured it would be best to know the truth. He hadn't exactly been cautious. Perhaps he should have been.

She shook her head. "Just right."

He threw up his hands and leaned back in his seat. "I'm definitely not pressing my luck any further."

Ignoring his suggestion, she continued with her list. "You're a good cook, even if you *are* kinda messy. I'm okay with that, though. Neat freaks annoy me."

"I'm glad to hear it."

"And you're a nice guy. There's a lot to be said for being nice. People tend to forget that. You're also polite, considerate—"

"Don't forget thrifty and trustworthy."

"Not sure about thrifty, but definitely trustworthy."

He took the plunge before fully considering the consequences.

"So tell me what it is you aren't telling me. You really can trust me, you know."

"Not sure I can, at least, not entirely. This is…different. Someday maybe. But not right now."

Ranjiv wanted to kick himself. In fact, he *deserved* kicking. "Sorry I asked." The trouble was he suspected he already knew what was bothering her. His initial reaction to her story had made her reluctant to say more. The whole idea was too fantastic for him to grasp at the time. Now, well, maybe it wasn't so bizarre after all.

"It's okay, believe me. I'll tell you eventually. I just need to be sure about it myself."

* * * *

Ranjiv's suspicions were Jillian's fault. She knew that. She'd been the one to tell him stuff he never should have heard.

He seemed okay with it though. He'd even had sex with her. Most guys would freak at the mere thought of consorting with anyone bearing traces of their mother's persona, even to the point of choosing a wife who had nothing at all in common with either parent. He'd somehow managed to reconcile the idea in his own mind. Someday she would ask him how he'd done it.

This was not that day.

And it had been such a *good* day. "Kinda spoiled the mood, didn't I?"

"No," he said. "I should've known better than to ask. You'll tell me when you're ready."

"Yeah." She'd said the word aloud, but whether she would follow through remained to be seen. The situation demanded a more neutral topic. "So…Stonehenge. Think we could go there tomorrow?"

"Absolutely. Windsor Park too. We can take Katie with us, although dogs aren't allowed on the field at Stonehenge. She would have to wait in the car."

Jillian glanced down at the floor beside her, half expecting to see the schnauzer gazing up at her in hopes of a treat. Her reaction wasn't too surprising considering the dog had scarcely been out of her sight since the crash. About the only time they'd been separated was during Jillian's stint in the radiology department.

"I'm not sure she would be happy about that. Think we could leave her with Tahir and Bippi?"

"Shalini probably won't mind, but Tahir will be in school tomorrow. Otherwise, he'd probably want to come along."

The image of a small boy accompanying them on holiday tore through her mind. Her child. *His* child.

Oh, my...

Was that a Kavya memory or a foretelling of the future? Quite honestly, she preferred the idea of it being a memory to a prescient vision. Somehow she doubted any of her entities were capable of that.

Then again, Paul Atreides had acquired that capability in *Dune*.

Fiction, Jillian. That was fiction, not historical fact.

She brushed those thoughts aside as they chatted on about other places to visit, easily passing the time while they finished their meal.

Ranjiv wiped his lips with a napkin and dropped it on his empty plate. "Ready to head home?"

"Oh, *yeah*." She started to qualify that response with something about it being a long day, but she didn't need to. His expression told her he'd understood exactly what she meant.

The drive back to Ranjiv's flat didn't take long, even considering how anxious Jillian was to get there. That was one of the nicer things about England. Unlike Tennessee, the distances were relatively short.

They parked the car and headed inside, stopping to collect Katie along the way.

"Did she behave herself?" Jillian asked Shalini as she knelt to snap the leash on the dog's collar. Katie licked her face, displaying her obvious pleasure at seeing her friend again.

"She's a wonderful little thing," Shalini replied. "I would be happy to look after her any time."

"Think she could stay here again tomorrow?" Ranjiv asked. "We're going to Stonehenge and Windsor Park."

"That would be no problem," Shalini replied. "She's such a good little dog. You may want to take her out again before you head upstairs, though."

Ranjiv checked his watch. "The park is about to close, but we can take her for a short walk along the canal."

Jillian nodded her agreement, which was difficult considering all she really wanted was to take a nice, hot shower and climb into bed with Ranjiv. Unfortunately, his neighbors already had enough to tease him about as it was. She didn't want to add any fuel to the fire.

As they left the building, she noted that the streetlights were already on and a number of people were also walking the path by the canal. A group of joggers had just caught up and passed them when Katie finally decided it was time to pee.

"Guess we can head back now," Ranjiv said with a chuckle.

Jillian was about to reply when she glanced toward the street just as a man strode out of the park gate. His piercing gaze shocked her to the core, nearly causing her to trip over her own feet.

Her faltering steps didn't go unnoticed. "I had a feeling this was a mistake," Ranjiv said as he grasped her hand. "You're having another allergic reaction, aren't you?"

If so, it was the most precipitous episode yet—and nothing at all like the others. Not even the episode in the park. What she'd felt then had been depression and despair. This was fear. Mortal, mind-numbing, blood-curdling fear. Anger followed, liberally mixed with hatred.

She shook her head. "I must've stumbled over something on the path."

Jillian was certain she'd never seen the man before in her life. He was simply a random person walking the streets of London. He shouldn't have triggered such a powerful reaction. Nonetheless, his eyes haunted her, even though he was no longer even in view. His high, sharp cheekbones, tousled blond hair, and stylishly cut jacket and trousers were totally foreign to her.

But those *eyes*...

Perhaps he was an actor. She might have seen him in a movie, playing an eerily handsome psychopath or the sort of super-villain who wore a mask or prosthetics to appear alien. British actors were notorious for playing the heavy. Jaguar had even made a car commercial to that effect.

No. Actors were perfectly normal people when they weren't playing a role. They were usually smiling and pleasant during interviews, laughing and joking the way anyone would. This man hadn't seemed like that. Not at all.

"D-did you see that man just now?"

"You mean the tall, blond chap?" Ranjiv asked. "Why? D'you know him?"

"No, but he sure gave me a bad case of the willies."

Chapter 22

RANJIV DIDN'T HAVE TO ASK WHAT SHE'D MEANT BY THE "WILLIES."
Her wide eyes and trembling hands were explanation enough.

"Have you ever seen him before?"

"I don't think so. It was his eyes… They freaked me out. Or maybe I'm just tired. Maybe he startled me or maybe he was mad at someone else and I caught the brunt of it, but I felt like he'd punched me in the face."

"We'll talk about it later. Right now, we need to get you inside. You're shaking like a leaf."

Her lips formed a moue of distaste. "I shouldn't be so upset. Honestly, this isn't normal for me. I don't understand it. Something about this place… I mean, it's beautiful and serene, but I get this really bad vibe here."

"Bad vibe?" That did it. He wasn't buying the allergy explanation anymore. These were psychic experiences, and they were real. He would have bet his life on it. "This has to do with whatever it is you won't tell me. Doesn't it?"

She bit her lip, shaking her head. "I'm not sure."

Still holding her hand, he stopped and turned to face her. "Please. Tell me." He raised her hand to his lips. "I swear, I'll understand."

Her sudden bark of laughter surprised him. "If you do, you'll be the only one."

"Try me." He stood there, waiting.

A furtive glance over her shoulder triggered a shudder. "I think…I think something bad happened here. And I think that man was involved."

"Something bad? What sort of thing?"

"I have no idea, but something left an impression here, like a ghost haunting the place where someone died—or was murdered."

As a reporter, Ranjiv knew that violent crimes had taken place in almost every corner of the city at one time or another. He could search the newspaper files, but for a place rather than a name or a date? Sorting through every particle of news concerning the canal would be time-consuming, although certainly not impossible.

"We could do some research and find out for sure," he said. "But in the meantime, let's get you home. Standing out here will only make you feel worse."

Jillian simply nodded and allowed him to take Katie's leash and lead both her and the dog back to his flat. When they reached the building, he fought the urge to pick her up and carry her. Nevertheless, she came willingly, placing her hand on his arm and keeping pace with him as he mounted the stairs. Opening the door to his flat, he ushered her inside.

With a face devoid of expression, she wandered over to the kitchen table and sat down, her eyes blinking as rapidly as a computer sorting through data.

Ranjiv thought it odd that she would choose to sit there rather than on one of the more comfortable living room chairs or even the sofa. But perhaps comfort wasn't what she needed. Perhaps she required the harshness of bare wood to keep her mind focused on reality. He let Katie off her leash and then pulled up another chair. "This is what happened when we went to the park before, isn't it?" He wasn't going to ask about the episode at his mother's house. Somehow he thought that reply might rattle him as much as seeing a ghost himself.

We're back to that again.

No. His mother was no longer an issue. He'd worked through the reincarnation possibility well enough to carry on loving Jillian as a man loves a woman rather than the way a son loves his mother. He had no doubts—or regrets—on that score. Jillian wasn't his mother, and nothing could change the way he felt about her. Nothing could possibly keep him from wanting this lovely woman for his wife.

But her most recent episode disturbed him more than any of the others. This wasn't about Kavya's spirit. This was something entirely different. "You said Anna had been to England before. What if something happened to her in the park? She might've been there with one of her dogs and been robbed or even assaulted."

Jillian turned toward him very slowly, staring at him as though he'd sprouted horns.

"I mean, I doubt it had anything to do with Mother. I'm sure she visited that park at one time or another, but if something awful happened to her there, I think she would've told me."

He was digging the hole deeper by the second, but at the moment, only the truth mattered. *In for a penny, in for a pound.*

"This is what happened during the crash, isn't it? How you knew me. How you knew the way Katie had been trained."

Her mouth fell open. "You couldn't possibly—"

"Know any of that? I don't. But I suspect that you do." He was flying blind, grasping at straws while desperately trying to fit the pieces together. But with a sudden flash of insight, he knew he was right. "You're some kind of–of soul-collector, aren't you?"

Her attempt at laughter failed. "Sounds like something out of a horror movie."

"But that's what happened to you, isn't it?"

Crossing her arms over her breasts, she rocked back and forth, her gaze unfocused while she fretted at her lip with her teeth.

"How many, Jillian? My mother. Anna. Anyone else?"

A deep breath prefaced her reply. "Three." Her voice was barely a whisper. "There are three of them. Kavya, Anna, and Shanda."

Ignoring the complete impossibility of the entire scenario, he plunged ahead. "Okay. The park isn't far from where Mother lived, and Anna was a dog breeder. Either of them could've been to that park or gone walking along the canal."

"Yes, they could have." She sounded doubtful.

"But you don't think it was anything to do with them, do you?"

She was silent for several moments while he stared at the pulse throbbing in her neck.

"I can't swim," she finally said. "Shanda is the one who saved me after the crash. Kavya told me to unbuckle my seat belt, but

Shanda was a champion swimmer. She told me what to do." She hesitated, frowning. "Something bad happened to her, though. Anna knew about it. I think it was her."

He could scarcely believe she was answering him so readily, almost as though his guesses had been correct. A shiver tickled his spine. "Do you have any idea what it was? Why her soul would've latched onto yours?"

With another deep inhalation, she spoke again. "I prefer to think of them as entities. More sci-fi than ghostly or miraculous. It's…easier that way."

"Entities, got it," he said quickly, then waited for her to respond to the question.

"She won't tell me. Maybe it wasn't her or maybe she still can't talk about it."

"She talks to you?"

"Not anymore. They all did at first. I could hear them in my mind." She raised her head and actually looked him in the eyes. "Anna stopped talking to me as soon as it became clear that I was keeping her dog. Kavya…" She stopped there, wincing. "I thought she wouldn't speak to me again after I met you in the airport, but something happened—"

"When you went to her house, right?"

She nodded. "That was when she became fully integrated. She doesn't speak to me anymore, but I know some things only she would've known."

He waited for her to continue, but she remained silent, gazing at him with an air of expectancy.

Then it hit him. "You said that in Telugu." He raked an unsteady hand through his hair as goose bumps tingled his skin. "Bloody *hell*…"

"Not really," she said. "Hell would be if you turned your back on me and never spoke to me again."

"No danger of that. I just… *Blimey*."

At last, she smiled. "Thirty years old and so very, very British."

He exhaled a laugh, thankful she'd managed to alter the mood without giving him the chance to dwell on the implications. "Sounds like something she would say."

"That was before the crash, when she was looking at the picture of you and your father. She told me about you. How you needed a wife, but didn't follow the old ways. She was wrong about that, though. Wasn't she?"

"In some respects, I suppose she was."

"Are you okay?" Reaching across the table, she took his hand. "Seems like you're the one with the shakes now."

"It's one thing to have such suspicions. But having them confirmed…" He squeezed her hand. "Please forgive me if I've ever seemed impatient or annoyed with you. I can't imagine how—"

"I'm still sane enough to function? Yeah. It's a wonder I'm not bouncing off the walls. I'm sure I'd feel differently if I'd picked up some evil villain's aura. At least my entities are benign—quite helpful, really. I owe them my life."

He nodded slowly. "In return for the privilege of sharing it with you."

"Sort of. Listen, I know your mother being one of them probably has you totally weirded out, but, honestly, it isn't like that. When I was in her house, I knew what certain things were—recognized photographs and such—but the emotions weren't there. Only the facts. Any emotions I feel are my own."

Although momentarily cheered by this, Ranjiv couldn't help noticing the flaw in her assessment, particularly in light of her most recent "episode." "What about Shanda? Are you sensing *her* emotions?"

"I think so—some of them anyway." Jillian frowned and shook her head. "She's different. Most of the time, I don't even realize she's there, but then something happens—a memory or a song pops into my head—and I know it has to be coming from her. In the beginning, I had an idea they each had a task that they'd left undone. Anna wanted someone to care for Katie. Your mother wanted you and me to meet. I think Shanda's task has something to do with that man in the park."

"So…in order to get her fully integrated, we have to find out what that man has to do with Shanda."

"Right. I've been thinking about doing an online search for information. She was apparently a well-known sports figure. There's bound to be something about her somewhere. And judging from the way I react to places in this area, I'm guessing she used to live around here, or at least came here fairly often."

"At least once anyway." He paused, searching his memory for anything he'd heard about a swimmer named Shanda, but came up with nothing. "What was her full name?"

"Shanda Smythe. She'd been living in the States and was moving back here. Like I said, Anna seemed to know something about her, claiming to be an Anglophile and a follower of all sorts of British sports."

"Hmm... How old would you say she was?"

"Shanda? Mid thirties...maybe older."

"If she did live around here, it was probably before I moved into this building. I had a flat in Hounslow before that. My uncle might know something, though."

She snickered. "Yeah, right. I can really see you asking him about the entity I seem to have inherited."

"I see your point." He met her gaze, marveling at the comfort he found there. Her eyes were clear and steady, not shrouded in cunning or madness. "Thank you for telling me this. No more secrets, okay?"

"No problem. You have no idea how relieved I am to be able to talk about it. I'm just glad your first instinct wasn't to have me committed."

"Wouldn't dream of it. I'm keeping you." A smile tugged at his lips. "Even if you are a bit loony."

* * * *

Jillian's first thought was that it was too easy. Her next thought was more along the lines of *he really must love me.*

That notion took several moments to settle in, but during that brief span of time, she convinced herself it was the absolute truth.

If Kavya was ever going to speak to her directly again, this should have been the occasion. But she didn't. No words came through, only emotions that Jillian recognized as being entirely her own. The warmth of his affection enveloped her. "I'll remind you of that someday."

He shook his head. "You won't need to. Trust me, I'll remember."

Such words should have resulted in a heated kiss or at the very least a poignant press of the hand. Unfortunately, exhaustion on top of the shock of seeing that man near the park was blotting out any carnal desires she might have had. Her thoughts drifted back to the night before when Ranjiv had dried her hair. What a sweet, loving gesture. Still fragile in many ways, she needed more of that sort of thing if she was ever going to recover completely.

The forced recuperative time in the hospital hadn't done much to restore her to her usual mental health and stamina. Despite having sustained very few physical injuries, she teetered on the brink of another meltdown similar to the one she'd had when Ranjiv had first brought her to his flat. Reminding herself that she should've been dead, or at the very least in a coma with a dozen broken bones, didn't help the matter any. She felt weak and ineffective—not quite helpless, but close.

Apparently, he recognized the signs. "You look completely worn out. We shouldn't have tried to squeeze so much into one day."

"Yeah. No doubt I'll pay for it tomorrow. Even my jet lag seems jet-lagged."

She wished she'd caught herself before saying something so ridiculous and easily construed as making light of what had happened to that doomed plane.

Thankfully, Ranjiv didn't seem to notice. "What do you say we call it a night?"

"Sounds fabulous. I just hope I can sleep after all the excitement."

"You'll sleep better after a shower. Want me to dry your hair?"

Poor guy. He probably thought he'd get lucky again tonight. *No, wait.* Their little tryst had taken place that afternoon, not the night before.

My brain is so fried...

"That would be lovely." She drew in a breath. "I really am

exhausted. Saying 'I'm tired' isn't the equivalent of 'not tonight, dear. I have a headache.'"

"I didn't think it was. Besides, there's always tomorrow morning. Or sometime during the night if we both happen to be awake."

"I should've expected that," she said dryly. "A guy doesn't lose his virginity and then forget all about repeating the procedure."

My, how clinical that sounds.

"No worries," he said. "We'll get back to that at some point. And probably very soon."

She let out a short laugh. "Sex in the shower?"

"Maybe. Although I'm guessing it isn't as easy or fun as it sounds."

"It isn't. Sooner or later, you either run out of hot water or someone ends up falling on their ass. Oral sex works pretty well, although the spray has to be angled just right. Trust me, I know. I practically drowned once."

To his credit, he laughed. "So a shower is better as foreplay?"

"Not really. At some point you have to get out and dry off. Kinda interrupts the flow."

"I see… What about afterward?"

"Only if you do it in the morning. At night, you just have to get up when you'd rather stay put and conk out for the night."

"My, the myriad intricacies," he drawled. "It's a wonder anyone ever finds the right time."

She nodded. "That's why the sex drive has to be so strong. I mean, we know it feels good, but we also understand the consequences. At least, sometimes we do." She heaved a sigh, hoping he didn't take it the wrong way. "I hate to be such a killjoy, but right now, I need sleep more than anything. Okay if we shower in the morning?"

"Sex first?" He was nothing if not persistent. Not that she blamed him. She was looking forward to another round herself. *Just not tonight.*

"After I pee and brush my teeth."

"Okay. Got that. Trip to the loo, then sex, then a shower

followed by breakfast."

"Perfect."

"It's a date, then." He rose from his chair and held out a hand. "What do you say we get you to bed?"

"Yes, please." As funky as she still felt, she was grateful for his help, although her knees seemed stronger now, certainly in no danger of giving way beneath her.

"Think you could fix breakfast this time?" he asked as he escorted her down the hall.

"I thought you were going to make dosas again." If he wanted to find out whether she'd assimilated Kavya's cooking ability, Jillian would rather not go there. Not yet anyway.

Assimilated. Makes me sound like one of the Borg. She might not have acquired robotic parts like the Borg implants, but there were definite similarities. She was part of a collective now. Fortunately, none of the entities she'd assimilated seemed to be vying for supremacy.

"I could do that," he admitted. "But I was thinking of trying something more American."

"Hmm… How does scrambled eggs with biscuits and gravy sound?"

"Delicious."

She suspected he'd only said that to be kind. Despite the number of American restaurant chains in London, she was well aware that most other cultures looked down their noses at American food—hence the dearth of American cheese. "Don't suppose you have any Tennessee Pride sausage, do you?"

"Well, no. But I do have some traditional English breakfast sausages."

"No problem. I can make do." She shot him a wink. "Although I'm thinking those English sausages would be really tasty wrapped in a dosa with a slice of American cheese."

He dropped an arm around her shoulders and gave her a delightfully lingering squeeze. "A culinary delight we may never have the opportunity enjoy."

Heaving a sigh, she leaned against him, grateful for his

understanding as much as his warmth and support. "Sad, but true. Although as a comfort food, I'm guessing a sausage and cheese dosa would be right up there with beans and cornbread."

If her most recent episode was any indication, comfort food was about to become more important than ever.

Possibly a necessity.

Chapter 23

AM I UP TO SOLVING A CRIME?

That thought swirled so relentlessly through Jillian's mind as she closed her eyes, she was beginning to wish she had agreed to the sex. No doubt round two with Ranjiv could have shoved the idea right out of her head.

She would need help from all of her collective entities and also Ranjiv. But first they had to understand just what sort of crime it had been. Given the location along a tree-lined canal, a rape was the most likely. Robbery wouldn't have left anywhere near the kind of lasting impression it had made on Shanda—certainly not enough to get her to leave the country.

But was it random? Or was he Shanda's own personal nemesis?

Jillian's money was on Shanda having been a random victim. The fact that the man was still at large pointed to an unsolved crime, but had he done it more than once?

The look in those creepy eyes of his screamed an unequivocal and resounding yes.

That's my mission, isn't it? I have to catch him in the act. I have to be the bait.

Simply identifying the man as Shanda's assailant wasn't an option. Aside from the fact that no one would believe her, his eyes had been what captured her attention, which meant that he'd probably been wearing a mask or disguise of some kind. If so, Shanda couldn't have provided the police with a recognizable description of him.

But I can. Even Ranjiv could probably pick him out of a lineup.

So far, they had a suspect, a victim, and a location. Not knowing anything about the crime itself made searching for clues difficult, especially since there had been no further input from

Shanda. Her silence wasn't too surprising; somehow Jillian doubted there was a Rod Stewart tune that would apply in this situation.

Such an obscure method of communication.

The "watch the bubbles" admonition had been much easier to interpret.

But did she really *need* Shanda's help? Jillian knew what the man looked like, and a bit of research would confirm what he'd done. Even posing as bait probably wouldn't be as dangerous as it sounded. Not if she had Ranjiv for backup.

Would he agree to such a crazy plan?

For that matter, what *was* her plan? Should she go strolling along the canal with Katie every night? Or was simply identifying the man via an anonymous tip enough?

Maybe, although it would help if there were other victims or witnesses who could corroborate her story.

Hmm... And Ranjiv was a reporter...

After she'd rolled over for the umpteenth time, Ranjiv cleared his throat. "You aren't getting much sleep, are you?"

"Sorry," she said with a rueful grimace. "Maybe I should've slept on the couch after all."

"I don't think that would help, at least not from my perspective. There's a part of me that has no desire to sleep whatsoever."

Her first instinct was to brush a hand over his groin to verify his claim. *Better not.* "Yeah, right. Between my brain and your other head, we'll never get any rest."

"Possibly. But I believe I know a solution to both of those problems."

"I'm sure you do," she said, although she wasn't convinced that solving his problem would also eliminate hers. "I can't see the clock from here. What time is it?"

The mattress shifted beneath his weight. "Three fifteen."

Despite her best efforts to control it, a whimper escaped her. "And we were gonna see Stonehenge this morning."

Their itinerary had changed slightly when Ranjiv had gone online to book their admission tickets, the nine-thirty time slot being the only one available. An early start had seemed doable at the time, but that was before her brain had shifted into overdrive.

His warmth flowed over her as he lay back down. "We still can."

"Not if we have to spend all day solving crimes."

"We can discuss the possibilities during the drive to Stonehenge and then do some research when we get back. No need to go bonkers over it tonight."

"More like bat-shit crazy."

He pulled her into his embrace, chuckling. "Never heard that one."

"It's very popular back home. I forget where I first heard it, but it's gone viral since then."

"So what do you want to do now?"

"Actually, your 'solution' is sounding better all the time."

"I'm still game—although with incentive like that, I can't help hoping this insomnia of yours is a chronic condition."

"Very funny."

"Just going with the flow." The hug that followed was sweet and filled with promise.

"Okay. Let me go pee and brush my teeth first."

"I'll be waiting."

Jillian hopped out of bed with more enthusiasm than she'd felt in ages, with the result that the trip to the loo was accomplished in record time. Nevertheless, as she climbed back into bed and into Ranjiv's arms, her brain was still zinging like a rousing game of laser tag.

Noting that he had already dispensed with his pajamas and laid out a condom on the nightstand, she pulled off her nightie and went down on him. Surely that would focus her thoughts on something other than Shanda's dilemma.

It didn't. Instead, it made her wonder where Shanda's entity went whenever Jillian was intimate with Ranjiv. Did she enjoy it or was she totally turned off?

Jillian's money was on enjoyment. No entity that was turned off by romance would play Rod Stewart songs in her head. Of course, a sexual assault wasn't anything like making love with a cherished partner, but *still…*

Maybe it wasn't rape. Maybe it was something else. Not murder, obviously, since Shanda had survived, but had she been a witness to a crime? Had she left the country because she feared reprisals of some sort?

This is getting too damned complicated. Just tell me, Shanda. Tell me why that man scared me so badly. Spill it. I really need to concentrate on what I'm doing here or Ranjiv will think I don't like doing this.

He was certainly enjoying himself. His sighs and moans and gentle touches were good clues in themselves, but he was also incredibly hard. He even tasted good.

Even better things lay ahead. Things that would settle her mind and soul.

Snatching up the condom, she ripped open the package and put it on him, also in record time.

"Okay, big guy. Go for it."

Don't look, Kavya!

No worries there. Kavya wasn't that close to the surface anymore. *Fully integrated and assimilated, remember?*

Just as Jillian was now fully penetrated by Ranjiv. *God, he's hot. So totally incredibly hot. And he loves me—I think.*

Awesome…

Energetic too. The headboard thumped against the wall, no doubt apprising his neighbors of the fact that Ranjiv was finally getting some. She didn't care. Reaching up, she grasped his upper arms and urged him on. If any of the voices were still there, they were keeping their thoughts to themselves, which was good because this wasn't your everyday, run-of-the-mill sex. Lovemaking was by far too tame a term, not to mention a gross understatement. Even ecstasy was light-years from an accurate description of the truth.

No. This wasn't mere nooky.

This was *nirvana.*

Jillian's rampant thoughts had finally been silenced, her mind expunged of everything except the man inside her. "Oh, *wow…*"

"Jillian… I—" Ranjiv never finished that sentence, obviously too caught up in his orgasm to speak. The power behind his climactic thrusts astonished and overwhelmed her, but his muffled cry touched her heart.

Heat coiled up inside her like a compressed spring until the rebound sent her soaring, weightless and transparent, spinning off through space and time. The inner peace that followed was a balm to her nerves, a soothing salve to her soul.

As she came back down to earth, her fingers lost themselves in his hair as her eyes drank in the vision of his face. Not the face of a terrifying stranger, but the face of the one true love of her life. If Seth hadn't broken her heart along with their engagement, she would've missed this.

Rumi was absolutely right; sorrow truly did prepare you for joy.

"It's just me and you now, Ranjiv," she whispered. "Just me and you."

Finally.

* * * *

Ranjiv awoke to find Jillian in his arms and sunlight filtering in between the slats in the blinds. He couldn't recall withdrawing from her deliciously warm body, but since he was lying on his side with Jillian's back spooned against his chest, he must have done it at some point. Nor had he bothered to get up and put on his pajamas. Being skin on skin with a woman might have been new to him, but there was no mistaking the feeling.

What had become of the condom was a mystery, although chances were good that it was somewhere in the bed. As much as he enjoyed the silky feel of her bare skin, he knew sex would be far more enjoyable without a condom—if indeed greater enjoyment was possible. Did he really need to use a one? In this day and age, it paid to err on the side of caution, but Jillian had been about to embark on her honeymoon when she began her journey to England. Would condoms be the contraceptive of choice for a newly married couple? Somehow, he didn't think it would be. Then again, birth control was an issue he and Jillian had yet to discuss.

She had been the one to put the condom on him during both of their encounters. Perhaps that meant she didn't trust him *or* her alternative method.

She had no reason not to trust him. Generally speaking, a person had to actually have sex to catch a disease that was transmitted in that manner. Admitting his virgin state should have been proof enough that he could be trusted.

Something else we need to talk about.

However, at the moment all he really wanted to do was watch her sleep.

No. Not watch. He had done that before. This time, he could actually participate in the experience—enjoying her soft warmth and the steady rise and fall of her chest as she breathed, delighting in her occasional sigh.

Unfortunately, his body had other ideas.

Blood was already rushing to his groin, creating an erection so intense it made his head swim and his balls ache. Then he remembered the agenda for the morning.

Small wonder his second head had ideas of its own.

He chuckled to himself as he recalled a meme he'd seen somewhere about sleeping in this position. Great for the woman, but the guy only got a dead arm, a face full of hair, and an awkward boner. He could vouch for two of the three, although he truly wasn't complaining. Experimentally, he flexed the fingers of his left hand and felt the telltale tingles.

Better make that three out of three.

He still didn't care. Especially since said erection had slipped quite nicely between her thighs.

"Something tells me it's time for me to go pee and brush my teeth again."

He swept her hair from her neck and planted a kiss there. "Mmm...yes, I do believe it is. D'you mind?"

Her sharp exhale said she minded a great deal, but her lilting tone betrayed her amusement. "I tell you *what*," she grumbled. "You give a guy an inch..."

"Can you blame me?"

"Well, no. I'd probably have already made my run to the loo if I'd been the one to wake up first." She rolled over to face him. "Last night was incredible."

She'd given him the perfect opening. *It's now or never.* "I can think of something that would make it even better."

A tiny smile took shape on her lips. "Oh?"

"D'you suppose we could dispense with the condom?"

"Ah, yes. Probably so. I have an IUD that has served me well for several years. If you're willing to take the chance that I'm not going to infect you with something incurable, go right ahead. It's your call."

Another kiss followed, this time lingering on her cheek. "Could've saved myself a few quid if I'd bothered to ask."

"True. But I wouldn't have known your intentions."

He pushed himself up on one elbow, gaping at her. "You mean you actually saw me buying them? I just thought you'd assumed any man of my age would have a stash in the nightstand."

"Ranjiv," she began in patient manner. "I not only saw you buy them, I saw you put them in the drawer. Plus, you'd already told me you were a virgin."

"And here I thought I was being so discreet."

"You were. It was very…gallant of you."

Ranjiv probably would have laughed at her choice of words if she hadn't chosen that moment to run a fingertip down the center of his chest—a fingertip that became a splayed hand preventing his attempt to pull her closer.

"Must be off to the loo. Hold that thought."

The image of Jillian from behind as she rose from the bed made holding any kind of thought a complete impossibility. Only when she vanished through the doorway did he regain enough control to ward off his climax, which would have been as embarrassing as it was inopportune.

While she was gone, he made a quick search of the sheets and found the condom. Pleased that he wouldn't need to use another one anytime soon, he tossed it in the bin. Then it occurred to him that Jillian wasn't the only one in need of some morning ablutions.

He waited until she was back in bed, hoping she wouldn't object to the delay. "My turn. Be right back."

Staring at his reflection while brushing his own teeth, he vowed to take it slow this time. The poor girl probably thought he had no finesse whatsoever. Not that she could have expected much of that from someone with so little experience. Even so, she'd obviously enjoyed the hot-and-heavy-in-the-middle-of-the-night version.

Incredible, she'd said. Incredibly what? Good? Bad? Indifferent?

No, she'd meant incredibly good. Believing otherwise would put too much of a damper on the festivities—sex, shower, breakfast, Stonehenge, and Windsor Park, in that order with lunch and dinner thrown in. Then they needed to log some serious computer time, which made him very glad he had more than one. They could run independent searches, which would greatly improve the likelihood of uncovering the truth.

But what if that bloke in the park had been out looking for another victim? Could they afford to take even that much time for themselves? Reminding himself that any crime involving Shanda would have been committed several years previously reassured him to a certain extent, although the possibility existed that someone else might be in danger. The reporter in him itched to begin the investigation, and not only for the sake of any other victims, past or future. Solving this mystery was important to Jillian in so many ways.

The interruption had probably done him some good. His erection had eased slightly, although he knew it would return with a vengeance once Jillian was in his arms. One thing was certain, over-thinking the matter had no aphrodisiac effects whatsoever.

Despite the decrease in the size of his equipment, which was now as clean as soap and water could make it, Jillian seemed appreciative when he returned. Her gaze swept him from top to bottom, lingering somewhere in the middle.

"Your previous girlfriends are idiots," she said in a breathy voice. "Absolute morons."

He couldn't help but grin. "And so is your former fiancé—for which I shall be eternally grateful."

No condom. No nothing. Just Jillian. Oh, *blimey...*

The kisses, the heat, the soft warmth. The taste of her skin, the touch of her hand. Ranjiv kissed his way from her nose to her toes and was fairly certain he hadn't missed any places along the way. "So beautiful…" The flavor of her sex astonished him, drawing him back there, setting fire to his groin while his pulse pounded in his ears.

He licked her with as little inhibition as she had shown with him. Her reactions drove him on—a gasp, a quiver, hands fisted in the sheets before moving on to his hair. If he had ever imagined this to be difficult or that inexperience would slow him down, he quickly concluded that all a man really had to do was pay attention. Patience and persistence might have been required, but he wasn't aware of that because this wasn't a task or a chore. This was *delightful*.

Her muffled cry alone would have proven he'd reached his goal, but the surge of her body was the sweetest result. The one that made him smile and adore her all the more.

A tug on his arm brought him up and into her embrace. Tingles prickled the small of his back as he eased inside her, wholly unprepared for the shock of how love with Jillian could feel without any barriers between them. No boundaries and no taboos. Pure, yet raw and unfettered, the way love was meant to be, the way he'd always dreamed it could be. Her eyes glittered through her lashes as her lips curved into a blissful smile. Although urgent at first, he steadied into a rhythm that made her smile even more.

"Oh, yeah. Perfect."

"Harder?"

"In a minute." Raising a hand, she stroked his shoulder, then down the full length of his arm. The warmth of her touch lingered. "No rush. You'll get there."

Ranjiv had all but forgotten his intention to take it slow. But did it matter so much now that she had already reached her climax? Possibly. Perhaps even more so.

These were the things he wanted to spend the rest of his life exploring. He wanted to learn all the best ways to give her pleasure and joy, and then find some even she didn't know about yet.

A lifetime of discovering Jillian.

His favorite illustration from the *Kama Sutra* flashed through his mind, and he rolled onto his back without hesitation, taking her with him. Almost as though she'd seen the same picture in her own mind, Jillian braced her hands on his chest and rose into a sitting position. Golden hair spilled over her shoulders as she smiled down at him, the vision of her luscious curves and glowing skin lifting him to a level of ecstasy he hadn't even imagined before. Raising her arms over her head, she arched her back and began a sinuous dance for him and him alone.

As Ranjiv watched her dance above him, his mind's eye added a swath of embroidered silk and a web of sparkling beads. He understood it now. That was his ideal, originating from the painting he'd studied as a boy.

But Jillian was no artist's rendition. She was real. The living embodiment of beauty and love.

Her graceful moves were enchanting to the eye, each of them bringing with it even greater pleasure and contentment. The highest plane was almost within his reach when, with another exultant cry, she crumpled forward onto his chest and into his arms.

Thrusting upward with renewed vigor, he drove into her, seeking that glorious moment when passion's release overwhelmed him. Consumed with his love for her, he kept on until there it was at last: the event that transcended all others, reminding him once again precisely how it felt to know joy.

Chapter 24

STONEHENGE...

Ranjiv had actually visited the site only once before, but he'd driven by it many times. Even those brief glimpses affected him, the mystical quality of the stones making his nape prickle.

Apparently Jillian felt the same way. "Oh, my..." she said as she climbed down the steps of the visitor's shuttle. "It's spooky and thrilling all at the same time. Just wish I could touch them."

"You and everyone else who comes here," he said. "Not sure it's worth being arrested, though."

"I dunno." She shook her head slowly, never taking her eyes from the huge stones. "Might be worth it at that."

The biting wind on the Salisbury plain had required her to wear his jacket again. Not that he minded. He only wished she'd purchased a shawl during their visit to the bazaar. As warm as it had been then, she hadn't even tried one on. Nevertheless, like the sari, it was a garment he believed would become her quite well.

They started forward, although as focused as Jillian was on the stone circle, Ranjiv doubted she even noticed when he took her hand.

He studied her from the corner of his eye. Was this another of her episodes? If so, it was different from the rest. Not incapacitating, but energizing. Jillian's walk was purposeful and swift, outpacing even those people who had gotten off the bus ahead of her.

A gust of wind sent her hair flying as she came to an abrupt halt. "Can you feel it? The history, the incredible *age* of this place." Her voice dropped to a hoarse whisper, and she shivered, turning her collar against the breeze. "Like the stones have been here so long, they're actually alive."

As if on cue, the skin on the back of his neck tightened again—

a reaction that had nothing to do with the early morning chill. "You can almost see King Arthur and his knights galloping across the plain," he said, hoping to lighten the mood and diffuse any psychic disturbance of hers before it had the chance to reach its full potential.

"It's so much older than that." Her tone remained hushed to the point that he barely understood her.

He reminded himself that none of her 'entities,' as she called them, had been inhabitants of the distant past. But what did he know about such things? For that matter, how much could *she* know? She could have access to all manner of ancestral memories that even Anna, Kavya, and Shanda weren't privy to.

All their names end in an "a." That thought popped unbidden into his head. He couldn't imagine the spelling of their names having any bearing on anything. Now, if her own name ended in the same manner, *that* might have meant something. As it was, her name only contained one "a" and it wasn't even at the end of the word. It was merely a coincidence. This was simply weirdness from within his own mind.

Weirdness was right. He'd had no firsthand experience with any sort of psychic phenomena. Not real ones anyway. Small wonder that a visit to Stonehenge would bring out more of it. He could only imagine what might happen if Jillian were to actually touch the stones. Standing beneath one of the towering trilithons would probably set off a chain of events that would shock everyone present—beams of light radiating from her eyes or some such thing.

They reached the path that encircled the stones. Jillian seemed uninterested in anything the tour guide had to say, quickly drawing apart from the others.

Might be a good thing.

That way, only he would hear what she said unless she shouted.

He let her take the lead, curious as to which direction she would choose. When she finally stopped and faced the standing stones, he glanced over his shoulder, not the least bit surprised to see the Heel Stone directly behind them. The Summer Solstice was still a few weeks away, and although the sun had already risen, the light was nearly in line with the stone.

He was loath to disturb her, or even ask why she had chosen this place to observe the iconic stones. She moved toward the post-and-chain barrier, placing a hand on one of the posts. In that instant, he wished he had considered the possibility that the power of Stonehenge could be conducted through the ground. He should have guessed it, though. The ground had been shaped into the mounds and ditches that surrounded the stones. Even the sun played a role.

Jillian's face took on an ethereal glow, her golden hair tossing in the wind like a wheat field in the path of an advancing storm. Despite her white-knuckled grip on the post, she again seemed more strengthened than sapped by the contact.

Her lips parted. "I've been here before."

Ranjiv knew of at least one of her entities who could have supplied such a memory, but he never had the chance to point that out as she continued.

"I remember when the circle was complete and fires burned within its confines. I was conceived here. I died and was cremated here. My ashes are buried at the base of the stones. Hundreds upon hundreds of lifetimes…"

Ranjiv's skin tingled as though the sun's rays had stroked a fiery finger up the center of his back. Even if he could have spoken, he had no idea what he would have said.

She turned toward him. "If I have ever been afraid, I no longer feel that fear. And I never will again."

He heard conviction her words—words that hadn't been supposition, but absolute truth.

No doubt every other tourist had come to Stonehenge that morning hoping to experience some type of spiritual event. The best he could tell, the only person who appeared to have gotten their wish was Jillian.

* * * *

Stonehenge had been the one place Jillian had wanted to see the most on this journey. The site would have been the high point of her honeymoon and had remained so for the mere vacation the trip had eventually become. Now, she stood on the Salisbury plain, staring at something that had endured throughout five millennia of human history, just as she had emerged unscathed from a disaster that should have meant certain death.

Perhaps unscathed was the wrong word. Nor was she unchanged. She had survived, just as these great stones had done. No palace or castle or anything to do with the British monarchy, not even the crown jewels, could compare with their mythical past. Governments and rulers had come and gone, but Stonehenge lived on, part of a more ancient history that had its origins deep within the planet's bones, creations older than time itself.

The stones were definitely alive. She could feel them, breathing and pulsating with knowledge far beyond that of anything she had ever encountered. They spoke to her in deep, rumbling tones as though she stood among them, telling her things that any conservationist might have said. Humans needed to respect and care for their world. Otherwise, Earth would destroy them.

She recalled the question as to why she had been spared in the crash: why she had emerged with knowledge she hadn't possessed prior to that event. Was her purpose simply to bring Shanda's assailant to justice? Somehow, she doubted that. This communion with the great trilithons was more far-reaching that that. Was she the instigator, or only the turning point? She had no idea, but the feeling was of something greater than herself. Perhaps even greater than all of humanity.

What was on that doomed airliner that could possibly bring about that kind of change? What person? What ideology? What seed of ecological or political revolution? She didn't even know who else had been aboard that flight beyond the three women whose thoughts she now carried.

No. There were at least two others she knew of. Susan and Cleona. Had they undergone a similar transformation? Time would tell. Their cell numbers were programmed into her phone. She needed to talk to them at some point, but she sensed that solving Shanda's enigma was her first obstacle, the first test of her worthiness to continue.

Having uttered those words to Ranjiv, she saw him for what he was. Her protector, her comrade, her enabler, yet another key to the puzzle she now faced.

I am The Chosen One.

Would he scoff at the idea? Somehow, she doubted that. No one who could quote Rumi verbatim was immune to the effects of spiritualism that encompassed not just one religion, but the entirety of humankind.

Humankind. She liked that word. It meant so much more than one country, one people, or one system of beliefs. It gathered every living person into its embrace.

We should *embrace one another. Not ridicule or attempt to possess, destroy, or dominate.*

She glanced down at her right hand, which still gripped the rounded knob of the post, connecting her to the past and possibly the future. Her head spinning, she reached out for Ranjiv with her other hand. His warm grasp steadied her, bringing her back to the present as she released the post. Pain filtered into her awareness, and she studied the source.

"I broke a nail," she said, amazed that her voice sounded comparatively normal. Each of the fingernails on her right hand had been bent backward as though she had tried to claw holes in the metal post. Her thumbnail was broken and bleeding. She stared at the injury, not quite believing it was real.

"Let me see." Ranjiv's reaction was as astonished as hers had been. "How on earth did you do that?"

Drawing in a deep breath of the rarefied air, she shook her head. "No idea."

He whipped out a handkerchief and wrapped it around her thumb. "Was coming here a mistake?"

"No. It was important. More important than anything I've ever done." She glanced again toward the circle of stones, or the Giant's Dance, as it had once been dubbed. Giants hadn't built it, though. Ordinary people had done it. People who didn't know the meaning of the word impossible, but who had absolute belief in persistence and dedication. Her shadow stretched out across the grass, almost touching the spot where the last of the outer ring of stones stood. The central monolith gazed back at her, patient and enduring.

"There was a reason I survived that crash. A reason Susan and Cleona also survived. Now that I'm here, I can feel it. This isn't as simple as meeting you or saving a dog's life or solving a crime. Something else is happening. Something much bigger than that. Bigger than all of us. We were chosen."

Ranjiv's shocked expression made her smile. "I'm scaring you, aren't I?"

"Not really," he said. "Believe it or not, I've been having similar thoughts."

She nodded slowly. "Yeah. Miracles don't happen for nothing."

"And you being here truly is a miracle." With a reassuring grin, he added, "We need time to process all of this, though, don't we? Time to do something as simple and sane as a stroll through Windsor Park, and perhaps a tour of the castle?"

Jillian agreed with a nod, but secretly felt that nothing would ever seem quite that uncomplicated again. "Sounds marvelous," she said aloud. "But let's not waste the time we have here." Taking his hand once again, she started off, resuming the trek around the ancient shrine, pausing at each point of the compass to study it more closely. She wasn't the first to stand in awe of the stones, and she wouldn't be the last.

Whatever purpose she was there to serve would be shown to her at some point. All she had to do was to wait for it to be revealed.

* * * *

After Stonehenge, Windsor Castle not only seemed simple and sane, it was something of a letdown. She doubted she was the only visitor to both sites to feel that way, but whether she was the only one to be so moved was unclear. Perhaps there were practicing Druids who had felt the same sort of communion with the stones.

No. Probably not.

She had no way to prove it, but she preferred to believe that her experience there had been unique. The barren plain between Salisbury and Amesbury was in complete contrast with the beautifully cultured landscaping at Windsor Great Park. Grace and beauty abounded there, as did the rustic touch of a bygone era, but without the haunting majesty of Stonehenge, which was made all the more spectacular by its simplicity. Also, the ground on the Salisbury plain had been chalk. This was ordinary, everyday dirt—more fertile, perhaps, but not quite as interesting in and of itself.

I'm being silly. This is English history at its finest.

Maybe.

Following the tour of the castle and grounds, they had dinner in a lovely restaurant in Eton that overlooked the Thames and was eons removed from barren plains and standing stones.

Grateful simply for a place to sit down, Jillian slipped off a shoe to rub her foot against her calf. "There's too much to see here. Every square inch of the country has some historic significance."

Ranjiv grinned. "I know what you mean. I've lived here all my life and haven't seen everything. Being a reporter helps me get around some, but not so much to the tourist attractions."

"The whole damn country is a tourist attraction," she grumbled. "I once read a novel about America taking over the UK with the intention of turning it into one gigantic historical resort. I want to say it was written by Daphne Du Maurier, but I wouldn't swear to that. Needless to say, the plan didn't work out and the Americans gave up and left in the end." She reached down to massage her heel, chuckling. "No idea what made me think of that. I must have read the book when I was in high school."

But had she been the one to actually read it?

Oh, here we go again...

In that instant, she concluded that the actual reader was immaterial as long as she remembered the story. This new attitude was a significant departure from her earlier dismay when she'd caught herself relating recollections that weren't her own. Now that at least two of her new entities were fully assimilated, that sort of thing would probably happen all the time. If she kept the source of those memories to herself, no one would ever know.

Then again, Ranjiv was the one person who knew all about what had happened to her—or at least as much as she could possibly tell anyone.

"Or maybe Anna was the one who read it," she said. "Being a

self-proclaimed Anglophile, she's the most likely."

Bless his heart, Ranjiv took this explanation in stride, even taking it a step further. "I'm surprised any of the historic sites seem new to you. You're bound to have some kind of past experience with all of them."

"To be honest, I had a 'been there, done that' outlook toward London when I first arrived. I don't know if the memories have faded or what, but I didn't have the overwhelming sense of familiarity with the places we've seen today."

"Except Stonehenge."

"Yeah. That was different."

"Do you want to talk about it?"

"I might—if I had any idea what to say. That whole processing thing you mentioned…it hasn't happened yet. Or maybe it has. I have this sense of a greater overall scheme—one that I'm supposed to be a part of, but I'm not quite there yet. Like I have to complete my assigned tasks before I can move on."

"What sort of scheme?"

"I'm not sure, but I'm getting a 'save the planet' vibe. Like there was someone on that flight who would have saved the world if the plane hadn't gone down."

"Why not save that person instead?"

She wrinkled her nose at him. "Okay, you've got me there—unless you want me to start trotting out clichés like 'God works in mysterious ways.' I don't know why or how, but that's the only thing that fits the feeling."

The conversation was interrupted by the arrival of their dinner. The soup was deliciously hot and creamy, followed by a steak that was perfectly cooked—flavorful and oddly soothing.

Comfort food.

The tea aboard the *Branwyn Eostre* had affected her in a similar manner. Her thoughts shifted back to that time when something as simple as a cup of tea had helped her realize she was alive and safe. The tea Ranjiv had fixed for her had been every bit as calming. She suspected that from then on, anytime she was in the middle of a meltdown, if tea couldn't fix her, nothing would.

After dinner, they took a stroll through the town of Windsor. Ranjiv was an excellent guide, and if there was a shop they missed, it must have been miniscule and its location obscure. Jillian was surprised but secretly pleased that Ranjiv hadn't attempted to resume their earlier conversation. Mainly because it harked back to the question he'd asked when they first met: Why was Jillian saved when so many others weren't? Now—if her mystical experience at Stonehenge was to be believed—there was yet another person whose life should have been spared, perhaps one whose contributions could have made a huge difference to the world.

She hadn't watched the news or even read a newspaper since that first evening. If a passenger list had been released, she hadn't heard of it. Nor had Ranjiv been notified of any news regarding the recovery of his mother's body. The day of Kavya's memorial was rapidly approaching. Was he still concerned about how the service would be conducted? He hadn't mentioned it since that first discussion, perhaps because he was dealing with the upheaval in his life the same way she had done, taking it one day—perhaps even one moment—at a time. Unfortunately, each day brought something new and disturbing into the picture. At least the press hadn't been hounding her—although it was doubtful that anyone could have recognized her from that front-page photo.

Ranjiv and Jillian had both been through a recovery period. He had come to terms with the loss of his only parent while she had accepted the auras of three women she hadn't known existed prior to that flight. Together, they had taken the first steps toward what she hoped would be a lasting romance. But along the way, a multitude of questions had accumulated.

The time to search for those answers was now.

Chapter 25

DARKNESS HAD ALREADY FALLEN BY THE TIME THEY RETURNED TO Ranjiv's flat. After an exuberant reunion with Katie, Jillian wanted nothing more than to crawl into bed with Ranjiv and sleep the night away. But she had a mystery to solve, and the answers weren't likely to find their way into her dreams. Whatever force was running this show had given her just enough clues to discover the solution on her own. Some effort on her part was required.

Ranjiv pulled a kitchen chair over to his desk, logged Jillian onto his laptop, then began his own search on the desktop computer. As new as she was at this sort of thing—her previous investigations having revolved around missing decimal points or the occasional errant penny—she was sure Ranjiv would have better luck. After all, he was bound to have sifted through far more evidence than she ever had. Nevertheless, simply typing in "Shanda Smythe" on a search engine brought up a plethora of links.

As she scrolled through the links, spotting the articles that had nothing to do with her career as a competitive swimmer was relatively easy. The first one revealed what she'd already begun to suspect. Shanda hadn't been a victim; she'd been a witness. Unfortunately, Shanda hadn't been able to identify the man she'd seen stab Ewan Michelson to death one summer night while she was jogging the path along the Grand Union Canal.

Ranjiv leaned closer to read the article. "I can't believe I didn't know about that—especially since it happened such a short distance from here." His expression grew thoughtful. "Ewan Michelson... I wonder if Shalini knows anything about him—or Shanda. She's lived in this neighborhood much longer than I have."

"Guess we should've asked her if she'd ever heard of Shanda when we picked up Katie." Jillian stared at the screen, shaking her head. "This is completely different from what I assumed in the beginning. I was so sure she'd been raped or assaulted in some manner. She was very hush-hush about it—cut Anna off as soon as she mentioned reading something about it—as though she was as much embarrassed as she was traumatized by the experience. But a *man* was killed. Shanda was the only woman involved, and she was a witness."

"I hate to admit this, but it looks as though the media put her at risk, playing up the sports celebrity angle," Ranjiv said as he scrolled further down the page. "For her own protection, her name should never have been released."

"Maybe it wasn't. Maybe someone recognized her and made the connection."

"It's possible. However it happened, she obviously didn't feel safe in this country—or at least didn't want to deal with the publicity. I can't say I blame her. Just wish we knew why she decided to come back."

"Maybe she didn't like living in the States—or thought enough time had passed for people to forget the story." She glanced at the date. "This article was published eleven years ago. There isn't a statute of limitations on murder in the UK, is there?"

"No," he replied. "Nor is there one for serious sexual crimes. She wouldn't have been safe from Ewan Michelson's killer, although he had to have known she wasn't able to identify him."

Jillian nodded slowly. "But I'm pretty sure I can identify him—and so can you."

"Identify him, yes," Ranjiv conceded. "But not as a murderer."

Her hopes dimmed slightly. "Then how on earth can we ever solve this crime? I considered using myself as bait for a rapist, but—"

"Over my dead body." Ranjiv growled every word.

"Yeah, well, it wouldn't work anyway. The man was a murderer, not a rapist." She clicked on the link to a different report. "Wait. This is interesting... Ewan Michelson was a local politician who supported research into alternative energy solutions."

"That certainly fits with your 'save the planet' vibe. Maybe someone with an interest in current energy technology didn't want him to remain in office or move higher up within the political system."

Deeming it too painful, Jillian had done her best to ignore the more recent news, not wanting to see another photo of the crash or read another eyewitness account. She wasn't afraid now.

This is something I have to do.

"What if there was someone on the plane with similar interests? Someone who had discovered a practical solution to clean energy or world peace or global warming." With no more emotion than she would have felt checking the weather forecast, she typed in a search for the passenger list of Oceana Airlines Flight 2324. No emotion, that is, until the page finished loading.

"Oh, my... There are hundreds of names here. How will we ever find out what any of these people did for a living, let alone discover a connection to Michelson's murder?"

"Unless there's a report on some of the notables aboard, we probably won't—at least, not anytime soon."

Purely as a reflex, she searched for her own name on the alphabetized list. Not surprisingly, it was easy to find, as were Cleona and Susan's names, each of which was marked with an asterisk. The names of her own "passengers" also caught her eye, seeming to jump at her from the screen. Too bad none of the others did.

"We could Google each of the names," Ranjiv suggested. "If you start at the top of the list and I start at the bottom, it might only take us a couple of days. Or would you rather focus on Shanda's case instead?"

Clearly, he hadn't forgotten her comment about Shanda's mystery being her first task. "I would if I had any idea where to start. But unless we go out looking for that man we saw and then follow him home..."

"That might result in him coming after us with a knife too."

"Definitely an outcome we want to avoid." She scrolled through the list of names, and then returned to the top. "Do you suppose there were ever any suspects in the Michelson case?"

"Dunno," Ranjiv said. "Let's take a look." Turning back to his desktop computer, he tapped the keyboard, then studied the monitor. "Nothing. No suspects whatsoever, although apparently the angle of the wounds suggested that Michelson might've known his assailant."

"I got the impression that Shanda only saw his eyes—like he was wearing a ski mask or something."

"Maybe—or it might simply have been too dark for her to get a good look at him."

"But we did." She thought for a moment. "Obviously he's still hanging around here. He might even be a local resident. If we were to start knocking on doors like we were taking a survey, we might actually find him."

"Hmm… There are an awful lot of houses within walking distance of the park on this side of the canal alone. Plus, there's a bridge a few blocks to the west that leads to another large residential area. Might take us months to visit every home."

"And we don't have that kind of time—at least, I don't." She stared, unblinking, at the account of the murder, half hoping some revelation would suddenly appear in a pop-up window. "Then again, we could be totally wrong about all of this."

He swiveled his chair around to face her. "You don't believe that, though. Do you?"

"No. The more I think about it, the more convinced I am that the man we saw at the park was the same man Shanda saw. I can't imagine why else he would've triggered that kind of response."

"That's what I thought you'd say." With an expression of chagrin, he added, "Which means we probably have a murderer living—or at least lurking—in our neighborhood."

"Yeah, although I doubt he would be hanging around the park to find Shanda. He would've known her name—might've even seen it on the list of the crash victims and known he was safe."

"Okay then. Let's think about why villains return to the scene of the crime—especially after such a long period of time."

"To dig up the murder weapon?" She couldn't keep the scoffing note from her reply. "It's a safe bet no one else is looking for that knife. Even if someone did stumble upon it, they probably wouldn't understand its significance."

"Can't argue with that," Ranjiv said. "But what if Michelson's family is keeping the case open? What if they're still searching the park and the canal for clues?"

"I dunno," Jillian said. "Seems like tossing the knife into the water would've been his best bet for eliminating any evidence, although I would imagine the police searched the area pretty thoroughly. They might've even sent divers down to look for it."

What *did* happen to the murder weapon? Surely, it was somewhere in the recesses of her brain. Her eyes drifted shut as she opened her mind to the memories, letting them flow at will.

Silence fell—or was it that sounds became muffled? Her eyelids twitched as she swallowed around the sudden tightness in her throat. In the next instant, the canal was there in her mind's eye, flowing steadily in the darkness, the glow from nearby street lamps gleaming on its rippling surface. Just ahead, a tall man wearing a dark suit and some sort of cap was stabbing his unarmed victim to death. She bit back a gasp of horror—not one of her own, but Shanda's.

She saw it then. The flash of the blade. Light filtered through the trees, illuminating only the killer's eyes—those intense, murderous, terrifying eyes. He wasn't wearing a mask; Ewan Michelson could have seen his face, perhaps even recognizing his killer before he died. The knife wasn't tossed aside or pitched into the canal. She heard no splash or thud to suggest it had landed anywhere. The murderer simply turned and ran. Light from a different source glinted on the knife blade as it spun through the air...

Her eyes flew open. "He still had the knife in his hand when Shanda saw him running away. That place in the park where I had my first meltdown...that's where he ditched the knife. Even after all this time, the horror and despair is clinging to that spot. Why he would be trying to find it now, I have no idea, but the knife is still there, hidden in the bushes. I'm sure of it."

* * * *

Ranjiv's scalp tightened. He wasn't about to disagree, not when

Earth itself seemed to be sharing secrets with Jillian. She knew too much, felt too much, saw too much for anything she said to be false. She was telling the truth.

"You can find that knife," he said. "You've got what amounts to a weapons detector in your head. That is, if you can stand to go there again."

"Remember what I said about not being afraid anymore? I'm not. Not about this."

Despite her firm conviction, which caused his scalp to tighten even further, there was one tiny detail he questioned. "Unfortunately, finding the knife won't necessarily solve the crime. There've been plenty of unsolved murders where the weapon was either left at the scene or was later found."

She hesitated, frowning. "What if we were to catch him while he was hunting for it?"

"Still not conclusive evidence," Ranjiv said, shaking his head. "He could say he was searching for his dog's favorite toy or something equally innocuous."

Her derisive snort left little doubt as to her thoughts on that explanation. "Even if we were to let him catch *us* looking for it?"

"That might be better, but I can't see that it would be enough to get him to confess—or even confront us. Not sure how we could lure him there anyway."

"Well…you *are* a reporter. What if I were to give you an exclusive interview about a conversation I overheard between Anna and Shanda during the flight? Shanda could've been telling Anna something about the crime that she'd only recently remembered—perhaps while under hypnosis—and that was why she was returning to England. Even if she'd told someone else about her plans, she might not have told them the real reason."

He nodded. "The place where you had that first episode was near the eastern fence. There's an alley between the park and the buildings on the other side. The gate to the park would've been locked at the time of the murder, but if the killer ran down that alley and tossed the knife over the fence, Shanda might have seen him do it. Saying she'd remembered something about the location of the weapon might draw him out."

"And no one could dispute the story either."

No one alive anyway. She didn't say it aloud, but he suspected the only reason she hadn't was out of respect for his mother.

"Considering what happened afterward, the fact that you're only recalling the conversation now would be perfectly understandable," he went on. "The only improbability is that Shanda would've told her story to a complete stranger."

Jillian leaned back in the chair, tapping her upper lip. "True," she said after a bit. "But I'm pretty sure Anna already knew Shanda had witnessed a murder. She as good as told her so. Shanda didn't want to talk about it, but who's to say they couldn't have discussed it later on during the night when they thought I was asleep? Again, no one could dispute that. All I would have to do is make the story plausible enough for the killer to believe it. If we get him good and rattled, he might do something stupid."

Ranjiv tried not to think about what sort of stupid things a murderer might do. Hopefully his blunder would only involve incriminating himself, rather than killing again. "There are several businesses nearby. If we were to start asking questions, word might get back to him. I'm sure everyone was questioned pretty thoroughly at the time, and it's been years—"

"Yes, but *he's* still hanging around, isn't he? All we have to do is get people talking." Her searching gaze swept his face. "What's stopping us?"

Clearly, she'd sensed his misgivings. "As much as we would like to investigate this business ourselves, the local police would undoubtedly prefer to take the lead. If you don't tell them what you 'overheard' first, they might see it as withholding evidence. Plus, claiming that the evidence originated with Shanda might put you in danger, even if your name was never revealed. After all, only three people survived that crash. Narrowing the source to down to you would be relatively easy."

Her shoulders sagged. "When you're right, you're right." She blew out a long sigh. "So what do you suggest?"

He thought for a moment. "Suppose you tell the police what

you know and then let them make a statement that some new evidence has been discovered in the case—that a new witness has come forward with the possible location of the murder weapon, perhaps even a description of the killer. Your hypnosis idea might be enough for Shanda to have remembered both of those things, and, having found a sympathetic ear, she could easily have discussed it with Anna. The police don't have to name their source until after the man is caught."

"But can we be sure it would make the news?"

Ranjiv gazed heavenward, waiting for her to make the connection.

"Oh. Oh, yes, I see. I give them an account of what I overheard, they make a statement, and you write the news article." She grinned at him. "Sorry. The ol' brain is a bit foggy this evening."

"I'm not surprised. This has been a rather eventful day."

"That's putting it mildly," she said. "I feel like I've been hit by a truck." She paused, frowning. "Or should I say lorry? I'm never sure…"

"Truck will do," he said. "Let's get you to bed. We have all day tomorrow to work on this."

"We should start off in the park."

"You're sure you can handle that?"

"Oh, yeah. Now that I know what those feelings were about, I can use them. Once we find the murder weapon—"

"Even before we talk to the police?"

"We don't want a bunch of detectives to disturb the evidence—or the communion I have with Earth or the Stonehenge spirits or whoever else is trying to talk to me—until we're positive the knife is there." She closed the laptop and rose from her chair. "In addition to three contemporary women, I seem to be in touch with Mother Earth herself. Or maybe she's Mother Nature. Whatever the case, she's older than any of us."

"She?"

"*Definitely* a she. Why else would she have saved three women?"

"Why else, indeed? Unless *Father* Nature likes women better."

Her glare pinned him in his seat. "You're getting that 'she's gone bonkers, so I'd better humor her' look again."

"What? Me?" He waved his hands in protest. "No way. But forgive me if it takes a moment or two to process everything you're telling me."

Jillian's peal of knowing laughter had his nape prickling again. "Maybe you just need a shot of something to depress your inhibitions and make you more receptive."

"Hmm… I might have a bottle of Bombay Sapphire around here somewhere. Beer or wine probably wouldn't cut it."

"Not much of a drinker, are you?"

"No. Although I'm beginning to question the wisdom of moderation in this case. Something tells me all of this would go down much more easily with a glass of gin."

"I believe it would." She held out her hand. "C'mon, Ranjiv. Get me drunk and do me. Otherwise, the Stonehenge spirits are gonna haunt me all night long."

In all his life, Ranjiv had never received a request of that nature. A smile threatened as he gazed up at her. "We can't have that, can we?"

"There's a lot to be said for getting plastered and laid. Clears the mind like nothing else. I've done some of my best thinking in the immediate post-orgasmic state. It's a lot like those thoughts you have when you're about to fall asleep or when you wake up in the middle of a dream."

"Probably because you're closer to the Earth spirits then."

Her eyes narrowed with suspicion. "Are you making fun of me?"

"No possible way." Taking her hand, he kissed it with considerable panache before getting to his feet. "You've made a believer out of me. I may joke around now and then to keep things from getting too grim, but I most definitely believe." He tucked her hand in the crook of his arm and started off down the hall. "Just don't tell the police everything you've told me. Somehow, I doubt they'd see it in quite the same light."

"Don't worry, I won't. I'll only tell them what Shanda said—or what she would've said if I'd happened to overhear her conversation with Anna." Disengaging her hand from his arm, she slipped it around his waist. "Guess I should write down my 'statement' and practice it a bit so I don't mess up the details."

"Actually, you might want to print it out and sign it. That way you wouldn't have to worry about how you tell the story."

"Good idea. I could say I've been working on getting the wording exactly right before coming forward."

"Nice touch." Since her hand had crept from his waist to the seat of his trousers, his reply could have been in response to either her suggestion or her action.

"Yes, it is." She gave his posterior a lingering squeeze, making her meaning perfectly plain while simultaneously sending a surge of heat to his groin. "On second thought, I think we can skip the booze. A few shots of *you* will clear my head quite nicely, and we wouldn't want to hinder your performance with alcohol."

"Absolutely not. Just tell me what you want."

Her lips curved into a provocative smile. "Surprise me."

Considering everything Jillian had been through lately, Ranjiv suspected that surprising her would be a difficult, if not impossible, task. Nevertheless, he was more than willing to give it a go.

"Will do."

Chapter 26

"YOU'VE BEEN CONSULTING THE *KAMA SUTRA* ON THE SLY, HAVEN'T you?"

Ranjiv shook his head. "No need. I've had a lifetime to memorize it."

Considering Jillian's current position, her laughter did amazing things to him. "Somehow, I think you might have embellished on it a bit."

He reached up and stroked a fingertip down the length of her arm. "Maybe. There's a lot to be said for inspiration."

Seated firmly on his groin, she stretched above him, her body's superb curves and contours filling his eyes with loveliness as stunning as it was entrancing. Blond tresses fell forward to frame her breasts with tendrils of gold. The painting he'd once considered to be the epitome of feminine beauty paled in comparison to the vision before him. He could no longer even picture it when he closed his eyes.

Jillian eclipsed every fantasy and dream he'd ever had.

"Whatever the source, I think we've put the Stonehenge spirits to rest for the night." She stifled a yawn. "I feel like I could sleep for a week."

"Oh, I hope not. We have way too much to do."

"No joke." She shifted her weight, grimacing. "Much as I would love to stay right where I am, I need to move. My hips feel like they're locking up on me even as we speak." She leaned forward to lie on his chest as she straightened her legs. "Oh, yeah... Much better."

Ranjiv rolled her onto her back for a lingering kiss. He really didn't care what she did; any position was okay as long as he could feel her soothing warmth. Even in his most vivid imaginings, he had never come close to the reality of true intimacy with a woman. He felt it now, an inner peace that seemed at odds with the violent events revolving around them.

His greatest fear was the danger in which she was about to place herself by delving further into Shanda's mystery. But then, the fact that she had survived when so many others didn't made him suspect some greater force was protecting her. Nevertheless, he felt they were together for a reason, that some effort on his part was necessary to ensure her safety. He only hoped his vigilance didn't disrupt the overall scheme that the crash had set in motion.

Jillian drew away from him but returned quickly, snuggling in beside him. Sharing a bed wasn't uncommon for her, but did she feel differently with him when compared with her former fiancé? Ranjiv relished every moment of their time together, perhaps because he still wasn't convinced their feelings for one another would endure. What happened to people in the aftermath of the sort of tremendous upheaval he was certain was about to occur? Did their lives proceed as though nothing had happened or did the experience bind them together forever? The nature of what they shared now suggested that forever was a possibility, but theirs wasn't the first romance to emerge from tragedy.

Rumi's words came back to him, reminding him that joy followed sorrow.

But was losing Jillian the sorrow from which a different joy would spring?

* * * *

A nudge from Katie's chilly nose woke him. The room was quiet, save for the comforting sound of Jillian's deep, slumberous breathing. Ranjiv felt a strange sense of promise rather than the foreboding as he'd expected in the wake of his thoughts of the previous night.

He rose from the bed and reached for his clothing, donning it quickly after pressing a finger to his lips to request Katie's continued silence. He doubted the dog understood the gesture, but whatever the reason, she refrained from barking or whining while he dressed.

Walking as quietly as the creaking floorboards would allow, he made his way to the living room, Katie's toenails clicking on the floor alongside him. It was a normal beginning to a typical Friday in London. He and Jillian would have breakfast and enjoy a chat over their coffee as any other couple would.

After that, they would embark on a quest that was anything but ordinary. Although they could easily postpone their inquiries for another day, something told him theirs was a task best undertaken quickly. Solving an eleven-year-old murder shouldn't have been accompanied by such a sense of urgency. Nonetheless, he viewed it as a mission that must be completed before any other steps could be taken. Allowing more time would only increase the accompanying sense of dread.

He snapped on Katie's leash and left the flat, starting off down the stairs with that same compelling haste. They had done their research; the field work was about to begin. That was the part of his job he enjoyed the most. Talking to people. Trying to decide if he was being told the truth. Finding corroborating stories. Sifting through facts. Reaching conclusions. Presenting the specifics, hoping others would arrive at the same conclusions, but understanding that points of view often differed.

Katie knew the way now, leading him toward the bank of the canal rather than the park, almost as though she knew it was too early for the gates to be open. Ranjiv was anxious to search the area near the eastern fence, not quite believing the murder weapon would still be there after so many years, and even if it was, would it even be visible or had the ground been soft enough at the time for the blade to bury itself? Was it hidden in the branches of the trees? Or had it been picked up by someone with no knowledge of the crime?

A yawn from Katie drew his attention to the fact that he was standing perfectly still, staring down at the water flowing through the canal. Despite her yawn, Katie sat quietly as if having done what she needed to do; she was simply waiting for him to move on.

Her eyes met his. "Sorry. Not quite awake yet."

He glanced toward the park, half expecting the enigmatic blond chap to be waiting at the gate.

No such luck.

With his nod, Katie turned toward home, taking a very pensive Ranjiv with her. Even in his newspaper career, he'd never had as much food for thought as he had now. The implications of what Jillian had drawn him into were earth shattering. What if she was right and someone who could actually save the planet had gone down with that plane? He had fallen out of the stream of current events in the past week. It was time for him to fall back into knowing what was going on in the world.

As he climbed the stairs to his flat, he mulled over the possibilities. Electric cars were gradually becoming more feasible. Solar power was growing as an energy source. Totalitarian regimes were being overthrown by the masses brought together by Twitter and Facebook. Even so, world peace was still a fanciful wish in the face of terrorist attacks and brewing hatred. Religions often set people apart far more than geography or politics ever could. Belief systems were very difficult to change, and then there was the whole language issue.

No. No one person could have the solution to that sort of dilemma. Not unless he or she was some sort of messiah. His money was on a scientific breakthrough, particularly in light of Ewan Michelson's political platform. That is, if the plane crash and his murder were connected. There were eleven years between those two events. What was it Jillian had said about Mother Nature taking a hand? If so, she'd waited a long damn time to wake up and smell the coffee.

"Even longer if you look back to the beginning of the Industrial Revolution," he said aloud.

Katie glanced up at him and uttered a sharp bark as though she agreed.

"Yeah. Right. She's talking to Stonehenge spirits and I'm talking to the dog. If we told anyone about all this, we'd be locked up as loonies long before that blond chap is ever nabbed."

A corroborating growl ended the conversation as he unlocked the door to his flat. A week ago he'd been the sort of mild-mannered reporter that Clark Kent had been reputed to be.

Whether he would turn out to be Superman remained to be

seen.

* * * *

Jillian had no idea what kind of coffee Ranjiv stocked in his pantry, but waking up to the aroma was like being reborn.

Well, maybe not quite that good, but almost.

Heading into the kitchen, she paused at the doorway to drink in the sight of Ranjiv's heady masculine form before giving him a hug and a lingering kiss. She poured herself a cup of coffee, knowing that if the day ahead went as she suspected, the coffee and Ranjiv's good morning kiss might prove to be the high points.

"I heard you go out with Katie," she said. "Thanks for letting me snooze a bit longer."

"No worries," he said. "We had a lovely stroll."

After the delights he'd shared with her the night before, she felt like she ought to be serving him breakfast in bed. God only knew Seth had never been that creative. Then again, Ranjiv had certainly had enough time to think about it before ever putting his knowledge into practice. She giggled, recalling the scene from *Revenge of the Nerds* when the cheerleader finally slept with the geek and was astonished by his outstanding performance. His reply that he'd been waiting for that moment his entire life was similar to Ranjiv's comment.

She didn't even bother to try to determine just who among the four entities now occupying her psyche had actually seen that movie.

I'm adjusting.

This was fortunate because she certainly needed to keep her wits about her for the next few days. The sense of impending momentous events was growing with each passing minute. If this was the calm before the storm, she had better enjoy it while she could. A leisurely breakfast now might turn out to be the last thing they could take their time over.

"So, first stop is Shalini, right?"

"Definitely. I have a feeling we could have saved ourselves a lot of angst if we'd asked her about it sooner. She's not exactly what you'd call the local gossip, but she probably knows everyone within a ten-block radius, and people tend to confide in her. I'll give her a call and let her know we'll be dropping by."

"Sounds like she'll be more helpful than the police. I'm anxious to hear what she has to say. Can't say I'm crazy about talking to the cops, though. I feel like I'll be perjuring myself by telling them what Shanda supposedly said."

"You'll be fine. Especially since you won't actually be telling a lie. Everything Shanda knew about the crime is in your head now, along with a description of the killer. The manner in which you 'overheard' the conversation is different, that's all."

She gazed at him with wonder. "Boy, when you start believing in a woman, you really go all the way, don't you?"

"I can't argue with the facts. You know things that can't be explained any other way."

Smiling, she sipped her coffee. "Seems like I'm not the only one adjusting to the idea." She paused as thoughts of her fellow survivors flitted through her mind. "I wonder how Susan and Cleona are adjusting."

His eyes narrowed. "You think something similar might've happened to them?"

"I don't know," she replied. "Maybe. Cleona seemed pretty shell-shocked. Susan was more resolute—angry, even. Like she knew something about the crash that enraged her."

"More so than suspecting it was deliberate?"

Jillian took a moment before she answered. Susan hadn't said anything she couldn't have known without having acquired a few extra entities during the crash. "Maybe not. But it seems strange that I'd be the only one of the three to be affected in this manner. You'd think there would've been a lot more souls wanting to hitch a ride up from the deep."

"Tasks unfinished... Lives unfulfilled..." He glanced at the newspaper, then handed it to her. "Here's the answer to at least one of your questions. There was a prominent solar energy scientist on board who was headed to an energy summit in Paris along with several other delegates. I'm guessing any oil magnates took a different flight."

"My, how convenient," she muttered. "Wonder how they got

the pilots to ditch the plane? By holding their families hostage or threatening them with torture?" The mere thought of such tactics made her shiver. Even so, people had been known to do a lot worse when fortunes were at stake. She gave herself a mental shake and waved a dismissive hand, albeit with very little conviction. "This is all conjecture. Shanda's story is the real mystery here."

"You think solving that crime will contribute something to the greater picture?"

"Possibly." She sucked in a long breath. "But we'll never figure it out sitting here. We have places to go and people to see."

And miles to go before I sleep.

She closed her eyes, remembering…

Stopping by Woods on a Snowy Evening, by Robert Frost. No doubt she'd heard that poem in grade school. However, the accompanying tightening of her scalp and rush of goose bumps suggested someone else had also read those lines, perhaps even recited them in front of a classroom.

She could see it now. Green and white cursive letters posted above the blackboard. Large wooden-framed windows that could actually be opened. Wooden desks in a style that spoke of another era. An electric fan in the corner suggesting the lack of air conditioning. A tiny, gray-haired teacher sitting at a sturdy oak desk. Mrs. Slate's fifth-grade classroom….

Except that her own fifth-grade teacher's name was Mrs. Steck.

In the space of a heartbeat, she made the connection to Anna before opening her eyes. "What do you say we get going?"

* * * *

"Do you want me to look after dear Katie again?" Shalini asked when she answered the door. "She's not a speck of trouble."

Jillian suspected that Bippi required far more looking after than Katie did. Even so, that wasn't the purpose of her visit. This time, however, she left the questions to Ranjiv.

"We'll probably take her with us today. Actually, we were wondering if you remember anything about the murder of Ewan Michelson, the man who was killed by the canal several years ago."

"Such a terrible tragedy," Shalini whispered. She folded her arms, hugging her chest as though warding off a chill. "I remember it well. Poor Nisha was so distraught. I'm still not sure she has recovered from the shock."

"Nisha?" Ranjiv repeated. "You know his wife?"

"Oh, yes. She lives across the canal from here. She's still trying to find her husband's killer." She paused, grimacing. "It's become something of an obsession, but who can blame her?"

"Do you think she would talk to us?" Jillian asked. "I was on the plane with a woman who witnessed the murder. She said she'd remembered some things."

"I haven't seen her lately, but I'm sure Nisha would be more upset if you *didn't* talk to her." Shalini shook her head sadly. "She hasn't been the same since that night. She was always such a happy, confident woman—forward-thinking, like her husband. Now, she fears that his dreams will never come to pass."

Jillian would never have imagined this could be so easy. "I overheard Shanda talking to Anna—those were the two ladies seated to my left on the plane. She told Anna she'd remembered more about what the killer looked like and where he'd tossed the knife."

"Nisha would *definitely* want to talk to you about news like that! Having a witness to the crime who couldn't identify the killer nearly drove her mad with frustration."

"We might be able to help her out some," Jillian said, patting Shalini's arm. "To be honest, I've been a little out of it myself. I only just remembered hearing their conversation last night. Anna—she was Katie's owner—was an avid fan of British sports. She actually recognized Shanda—her name anyway. Shanda didn't want to talk about it when Anna first brought it up, but later on, during the night, I heard them talking. They must've thought I was asleep or couldn't hear them. The jet engines were so noisy, I'm kinda surprised I could hear them at all, but they must've had to talk loudly enough to be heard over the engines."

There. I've said it aloud.

"We were just on our way to the police station," Ranjiv said.

"Oh, please. Go see Nisha first," Shalini urged. "She will be elated to hear this from you."

Jillian glanced at Ranjiv. "What do you think?"

"I think we should see her."

"Her house isn't far from here," Shalini went on. "Shall I call her and let her know you're coming?"

Jillian nodded. If nothing else, telling her story to Nisha would be good practice for talking to the police.

Chapter 27

JILLIAN HAD SEEN PHOTOS OF EWAN MICHELSON IN THE COURSE OF her research; he was a typical pale-skinned, dark-haired British gent. His wife, Nisha, on the other hand, was as Indian as her name and the blue and gray sari she wore. Appearing to be in her mid-forties, she was still quite lovely, despite the lines of strain around her eyes and mouth. Her smile seemed forced as she welcomed Jillian and Ranjiv into a terraced house very similar to Kavya's home.

Nisha settled herself in a chair opposite the sofa where she motioned for Ranjiv and Jillian to sit. "Shalini said you have news?"

"Maybe," Jillian hedged as Katie settled down at her feet. "I met Shanda Smythe on the plane from the States—the one that crashed off the coast of Ireland last weekend. I was one of three survivors. Shanda wasn't among them." At least, not in the normal sense.

Nisha's hand went to her throat. "Oh, no... It can't be. She can't be dead." Her horrified expression changed abruptly to one of utter defeat as her shoulders sagged. "I had such high hopes."

Jillian's tingles returned full force. Even her face felt hot. "What do you mean?"

"Shanda wrote to me not long ago. She said she'd been trying to remember more about Ewan's murder and that a hypnotist had helped her to recall more details of what she saw that night. She told me she had already spoken to the police and was coming here to work with an artist to create a sketch of Ewan's killer."

The blood that had flooded Jillian's face departed even more quickly than it had arrived. Her sight dimmed, and she gripped Ranjiv's arm in an attempt to steady her reeling senses. The possibilities she'd thought up weren't her own ideas at all.

I should've known...

"I'm not sure I'll be much help then," Jillian said after taking a moment to gather her wits. "At least, not any more than Shanda was. You see, I overheard her telling another passenger about the murder." She swallowed hard, wishing she didn't have to ask the question, but needing to be sure. "You said she'd been to a–a hypnotist?"

"Oh, yes," Nisha replied. "She was always so sorry she wasn't able to be of more help solving the crime. She was very excited to have more evidence to contribute."

"And you say she'd already spoken with the police?"

Nisha's nod sent Jillian's spirits plummeting.

Although Shanda might have told the police a few things she hadn't told Nisha, Jillian couldn't shake the feeling that any evidence she might give would be completely redundant. She glanced at Ranjiv. "Should we even bother going to the station?"

He shrugged, obviously doing his best to appear nonchalant when he was bound to be as freaked out as she was by how close her guesses had come to the truth. "It couldn't hurt. The police may not have heard everything she had to tell. Plus, she was going to work with an artist. Maybe she hadn't given them the full description yet."

Nisha nodded. "She only told me that the man was tall, slender, and had the most frightening eyes."

"Then maybe I *can* help," Jillian said, feeling somewhat relieved. "There was more to what she told Anna than that." Did Nisha know about the knife? If so, would she have searched for it? Jillian was almost afraid to ask that too. "What else did she tell you?"

"She said she might know where the weapon was." Nisha shook her head. "After so many years, I don't see how it could possibly still be where he left it, but she seemed to think it was likely."

"Did she say where, exactly?" Ranjiv asked.

"No. And I'm glad she didn't. I would have driven myself mad trying to find it."

Jillian knew that feeling quite well. Now that she understood the reason for her despair when she had been in close proximity to the knife, she was anxious to return to that spot and see if Ranjiv was right about her ability to find it. The police would undoubtedly take a dim view of her disturbing the evidence, but with the murder suspect skulking around the park, she couldn't help but wonder if Shanda had told her story to someone besides Nisha and the police. "Has anyone been asking questions about the murder recently? The police or any of your neighbors?"

"No, but I've been on edge ever since Shanda wrote to me. I had no idea she was on the plane that crashed. I didn't check the passenger list." She reached a hand toward Ranjiv. "I knew your mother was on that flight, but no one else. Perhaps I should have paid more attention. Shanda told me she was coming. I wondered why I hadn't heard from her. I never dreamed she might have been on the same plane as Kavya."

"You knew my mother?" Ranjiv asked.

"Oh, yes. Everyone knew Kavya. She was such a dear soul. I can't believe she's gone. And Shanda too." Nisha picked at the hem of her blouse with trembling fingers. "So much death. So much needless, senseless loss."

As though sensing Nisha's distress, Katie walked over and nudged the older woman's hand. Nisha stroked the dog's head in an absent manner until a muffled bark caused her to look down. Katie's furry brows rose—whether in curiosity or sympathy, Jillian couldn't have said—but the effect on Nisha was profound.

Raising her head, Nisha looked directly at Jillian. The tips of her lashes glittered with tears, but a spark of determination lit her eyes. "You'll tell the police what you heard, won't you? Any tiny little detail might help find Ewan's killer."

"I'll do that."

Nisha's gaze softened. "Thank you. Perhaps Ewan's spirit can finally be at rest." With a sigh, she added, "And I'll be able to sleep again."

Before Jillian could ask if it was Ewan's spirit that had been keeping Nisha awake, Ranjiv cleared his throat. "We should go now. Thank you for your time, Nisha."

A bittersweet smile curved Nisha's lips, making her seem much younger, more like the woman she must have been before her husband's brutal murder. "Time was the one thing Ewan and I never seemed to have. Now I have more than I know what to do with." With one graceful movement, she got up from her chair. "You know what they say about grief having stages? The acceptance stage is one that I've yet to reach. I'm not sure I ever will."

"Finding his killer may help with that," Jillian said. "Please believe me, we will make certain he is brought to justice."

She heard an odd echo in her own voice, and if Ranjiv's peculiar expression was anything to go by, he heard it as well.

The ringing tones of prophesy.

* * * *

Ranjiv was reaching the point where his nape no longer prickled with the more momentous of Jillian's utterances. However, he still recognized them for what they were.

"Guess we'd best be getting over to the police station." He paused, darting a glance at Nisha. "Would you mind giving them a ring to let them know we're coming? Might lend us some credibility."

"Of course," Nisha said. "The officer working the case is Detective Chief Inspector Angus McDougal."

"Ah. A Scot." Ranjiv aimed a knowing grin at Jillian. "Tenacious rascals."

"He is that," Nisha agreed. "His determination has made these past few years more tolerable for me. He'll be so very disappointed to learn of Shanda's death."

"If he doesn't know already." Jillian rose from the sofa and extended a hand toward Nisha. "It was nice meeting you. I only wish we'd had better news."

"Any news is good these days." Nisha gripped her hand. "I'm delighted to have met you, and I'm even happier that you survived."

"We'll keep you informed." Ranjiv suspected Nisha would've been more pleased if Shanda had been among the survivors, but he believed that Jillian's link to the—

The *what?* He wished he had a label to put on whatever was communicating with her. Mother Nature or Earth itself? Perhaps it was Earth. There were those who insisted that the planet was only a great rock spinning through space, but there were others who saw it as a living, breathing life-form. He was beginning to believe it was the latter—a life-form that was finally taking a stand to save itself and the human race from self-destruction.

Or perhaps God was speaking to her, trying to enable the people he'd created to rescue themselves and their world.

Then again, perhaps none of that was pertinent. Perhaps the only thing that mattered was solving this particular crime.

No. There had to be more to it than that. Saving Jillian simply to solve one of the hundreds of London's unsolved murder cases seemed absurd, especially when the purpose would have been far better served by sparing Shanda's life. Jillian's survival only made sense if he believed things happened for a reason, which—without putting too fine a point on it—he did.

However, letting the police get wind of the supernatural aspects of the case would destroy what little credibility they had. With that in mind, Ranjiv kept those thoughts to himself during the drive to the police station, not wishing to sound ridiculous or open a Pandora's Box of discussion that would make little difference in the greater scheme of things.

He glanced at Jillian. Surprisingly, nothing in her demeanor suggested she faced any sort of dilemma whatsoever. She wore serenity like a shawl draped casually about her shoulders. Was she content to let fate blow her wherever it wished? Or was she so assured of the outcome as to simply bide her time as each step was completed?

When they arrived at the station, they were met by DCI Angus McDougal himself, which was a testament to Nisha's connection to him. The chief inspector was tall and slightly built, his tweed jacket a shade darker than his hair, which was combed back from his forehead in light brown waves. He ushered them into his office and waved a hand at a bench situated against the wall—a gesture Katie responded to far more quickly than Ranjiv and Jillian did. Hopping onto the bench, she sat down facing the desk, panting softly.

"Sit, please," McDougal said as he seated himself behind the desk. "Nisha Michelson has apprised me of your visit. I believe you have some new evidence for me regarding the murder of her husband."

Ranjiv felt as though they were on trial for their lives, but Jillian's serenity never wavered. She merely nodded and introduced herself before telling her story evenly and concisely from beginning to end with the embellishments woven seamlessly into the narrative. Even knowing the source of some of her "facts" didn't alter the truthful nature of her speech, and she delivered it without seeming the slightest bit nervous or rehearsed. Her calm still unruffled, she handed Inspector McDougal the signed statement and waited while he read what she'd written.

The inspector had been reading for several moments before Ranjiv realized why truth had rung so loudly throughout Jillian's story. She believed it. Every word. The unassailable accuracy of her account was due to the fact that she had actually been a witness to most, if not all, of it.

"Yes, well... Miss Smythe had already given us several of these details over the phone. Her death hasn't stopped our investigation, although we still don't have an accurate drawing of the man she saw by the canal."

Ranjiv noted the careful nature in which the inspector referred to the murderer, making no assumptions, no accusations.

"Blond, you say?" the inspector went on to ask.

"Yes," Jillian replied.

"Seems odd when she originally testified he'd been wearing a cap."

"I think—that is, I suspect—she may have remembered his eyebrows. He wasn't wearing a mask. She could've seen them."

"I suppose so. She did remark upon his eyes having terrified her, in which case she might not have noticed the brows." Returning his focus to the page in his hand, he studied it as he spoke. "Sharp, angular jaw, cleft in the chin. Straight, narrow nose... That's something for the artists to go on. Pity Miss Smythe won't be here to approve the sketch."

"I'd like to see it when the artist is finished," Jillian said. "I might not be able to recognize him, but I can make sure I haven't missed any part of the description."

"Don't see why not." McDougal leaned back in his chair with a genial smile. "The boys watching the park will be pleased. They didn't have much to go on other than the original description, which was rather vague. Right now, they're only keeping an eye out for anyone who looks suspicious."

Ranjiv was quite certain he and Jillian had already spotted the murderer near the crime scene. What he didn't know was why. "After so many years, why would Michelson's killer be seen anywhere near the park?" The moment those words passed his lips, he knew the answer. "Wait. You've already leaked information about the location of the weapon, haven't you?"

McDougal's smile vanished. "Brought the weirdoes out of the wainscoting for sure. Bit of a problem, though. We never searched the bushes to see if the knife was still there. Probably should have, but we thought it best if we were to catch him red-handed— assuming he knows where it is, himself. Didn't want to make it too obvious in case he happened to be watching." He stopped there and shook his head slowly. "Never expected to lose poor Shanda in a plane crash. Sad to think she'd finally be coming home and not live long enough to actually arrive."

Ranjiv nodded. "My mother also. Very sad, indeed."

"You have my condolences," McDougal said, then turned to Jillian. "You had family on the plane?"

"No," she replied. "Although I did make some new acquaintances, Ranjiv's mother and Shanda among them."

"Terrible tragedy," the inspector went on. "They're saying it was deliberate. Bloody terrorists," he added, growling out the words.

"Terrorists?" Ranjiv echoed. "Has a faction claimed responsibility?"

"Several, actually. None will say why—although I suppose the 'why' is fairly obvious."

Ranjiv doubted the obvious reason was the correct one, and a glance at Jillian proved she agreed with his assessment. The plane might have been deliberately ditched, but that particular disaster wasn't a terrorist act—at least not in the usual sense. Considering there was a solar scientist aboard—if he was indeed the actual target—OPEC was more likely to be behind it than ISIS or the Taliban. For that matter, any oil company could have been responsible. None of them seemed to be the slightest bit interested in preventing climate change and pollution when there was so much profit to be made from oil production. World peace suffered from the same problem, supplying arms to the various combatants being far more profitable than peace and prosperity.

This world is so screwed up.

He liked the idea of being a part of that change for the better, but the odds against them succeeding were astronomical. Perhaps that was why Earth was finally taking a stand.

What an insane idea.

The sound of McDougal's voice snapped Ranjiv from his reverie.

"Unlike the murder of Ewan Michelson," the inspector was saying. "Which, on the surface, seems to have been committed with no motive whatsoever. He was a respected member of the community and generally well-liked. Robbery didn't appear to have been the intention, unless Shanda's arrival prevented his attacker from finishing what he'd started."

"Could his political views have been what got him killed?" Jillian asked.

McDougal pursed his lips. "Possibly, although it seems a bit extreme. More to be had by getting him voted out of office—which is easier said than done, of course, and far less...permanent." He paused, looking down at Jillian's statement before he spoke again, idly flipping the corner of the page. "Still, he wouldn't be the first politician to be silenced in that manner."

Ranjiv was reminded of the danger to Jillian. "For that reason, we would prefer to keep the source of this new information quiet."

McDougal nodded his agreement. "As far as we're concerned, the original source is still Shanda Smythe. Miss Dulaine's testimony might back it up a smidgeon, but her statement would only be considered hearsay."

Ranjiv practically had to bite his tongue to keep from laughing.

For the moment, Shanda and Jillian were essentially one and the same.

If he only knew.

"Surely there's something else I could do," Jillian protested. "I could look at pictures of known felons or something of that nature, couldn't I?"

McDougal shrugged. "Normally, yes. But in this case, we'll do a computer simulation of the suspect based on the description you've given us. Because you aren't an eyewitness, we'll have to tie him to the crime some other way—hopefully with the murder weapon." He blew out a breath. "Still not conclusive, of course, and with the crime occurring so long ago and no other witnesses, we may not get a conviction."

Jillian leaned forward, her expression one of grim determination. "What if you were to say that a new witness has come forward with a description of the murderer and knowledge of the location of the murder weapon?"

McDougal tipped his head to one side, seeming to consider her suggestion. "Aye, we could—although that's stretching the truth a bit, wouldn't you say?"

"What does it matter if it draws him out?" She seemed perfectly calm, not even raising her voice or stomping her foot to emphasize her point. "I mean, you need something to bait the trap with, don't you?"

Knowing precisely what she would say next, Ranjiv held his breath as his heart dropped like a stone.

"It might as well be me."

Chapter 28

JILLIAN WAITED FOR AN "OVER MY DEAD BODY" EXCLAMATION FROM Ranjiv that never came. He might have agreed with the notion, but being stunned speechless was probably closer to the truth.

"Don't you see? If you word it right, it's actually true. I *am* a new witness, I overheard Shanda telling Anna where the murder weapon was tossed, and I do have a description."

"Yes, but—"

"It's all in how you spin it," she said eagerly. "Emphasizing my role rather than downplaying it."

"What you're suggesting might also put you in danger." Toying with his pen, McDougal avoided her eyes. "I could understand if you had a stake in solving the crime, but you really don't." His gaze swept upward, riveting itself to her own. "Do you?"

How could she possibly explain why this was a task she had to see through to the end without sounding completely bonkers? "It was important enough for Shanda to return to England, and Nisha needs some sort of closure so she can get on with her life."

McDougal's eyes narrowed. "I'll grant you that, but these women were strangers to you until very recently. Their lives couldn't possibly affect you enough for you to risk your own safety."

Jillian sat up straighter and drew in a deep, fortifying breath. "'Any man's death diminishes me, because I am involved in Mankind. And therefore never send to know for whom the bell tolls; it tolls for thee.'"

John Donne's quote popped unbidden from her memory. She had never linked the two sentences or even the author's name together before, with the result that she had never fully grasped the meaning. She understood it now. At least one of her entities—again, her money was on Shanda—had known those lines by heart, much like the quote Ranjiv had recited. Fingering the card in her pocket, she came very close to adding Rumi's words to Donne's, but thought it might be overkill at this point. She waited breathlessly for the chief inspector's response.

He cleared his throat in a self-conscious manner. "You're quite right, of course," he finally said. "But what we have to go on isn't nearly enough. However, I do understand your motivation, which is much the same as mine for choosing this particular career." With a nod, he continued. "We'll do that, although admitting we have a description might force him to wear a disguise."

"Gloss over that point, then." Having gotten this far, Jillian wasn't about to let him change his mind. "Say only that you've received additional information regarding the weapon rather than the perpetrator."

To her surprise, he laughed. "Not gonna let it drop, are you, lass?"

"No. I'm not."

He glanced at Ranjiv. "Quite the little firebrand, isn't she?"

"You have no idea," Ranjiv said, smiling.

"Yes, well, we'll get on with it then." McDougal rose from his seat and held out a hand. "It was a pleasure to meet you, Miss Dulaine. Together, we might actually get this case solved."

Jillian hadn't realized how cold her own hands were until she placed one of them in the inspector's warm grasp. Something inside her reacted strongly to his touch, feeling reassured and comforted. A moment passed before she recognized the exchange for what it was. Not an interaction between herself and McDougal, but between him and Shanda. The prickling sensation she should've felt in the wake of that revelation never materialized.

"I certainly hope so," she said. "Is there anything else we can do?"

McDougal didn't hesitate. "If you haven't been to the park yet, you might take a look around. Seeing the actual location could jog your memory for additional details you might've overheard and forgotten. In the meantime, we'll get going on that description." He picked up his phone and punched in a number. "Yes, send Holmes and Fry in, would you?" He put down the phone and smiled. "And no, their first names aren't Sherlock and Stephen."

Given all the weird coincidences she'd encountered since leaving the US, Jillian wouldn't have been a bit surprised if that were true. At least he hadn't summoned Holmes and Watson. The fact that she'd recognized McDougal was unnerving enough.

He'd been a detective sergeant and several years younger the last time she'd seen him, but she would have known him anywhere. The wave of goose bumps she'd missed out on moments before finally arrived.

"Constable Holmes is our resident artist and computer whiz," McDougal explained. "And Sergeant Fry is our best undercover officer. Can blend into a crowd without raising the slightest bit of attention. Dunno how she does it."

As soon as the door opened and the two officers stepped inside, Jillian understood completely. Fry was plump and fiftyish, with short brown hair going gray, a pleasant smile, and nondescript features. In short, she was the "plain ol' Englishwoman" personified. Jillian's next thought was to wonder where she bought her clothes.

"I'd like Sergeant Fry to accompany you to the park." McDougal glanced at Katie. "Take the dog with you and spend as much time there as you can." He handed Jillian's statement to the other officer who, rather than being the typical geek, was a tall, handsome fellow with dimples and a thick thatch of wavy dark blond hair. "How soon can you have something for us?"

Holmes studied the page briefly. "Give me an hour or two."

McDougal winked at Jillian. "It'll be more like twenty minutes, if you'd care to wait a bit."

"Why not?" she said. "We don't have anything else planned for today." She glanced at Ranjiv, somewhat surprised at how quickly their "plans" had progressed. "Do we?"

He consulted his watch before replying. "Just lunch. But other than that—" He ended with a shrug.

"Be nice to see the sketch before we head out anyway." Fry's voice was as grandmotherly as her appearance, leading Jillian to wonder if under that unassuming appearance was the body of a ninja warrior.

Not likely.

Even Holmes didn't fit that mold, reminding her more of a tight end than a jiu-jitsu master.

"How about we take Katie for a little stroll, have some lunch, and come back?" The change in Ranjiv's inflection was slight, but it got her attention. He was trying to tell her something.

But what? That he was hungry? That Katie needed a potty break? Or that there was something he wanted to discuss with her in private?

"Sounds good," she said. "We'll be back at around one or so."

"Perfect," Holmes said.

* * * *

Ranjiv wasn't a bit surprised when Jillian rounded on him as soon as they reached the sidewalk. "Okay," she began. "What's up?"

"Do not, and I repeat, *do not* admit to having seen that blond chap near the park."

"Why not?"

"Because it'll seem like you saw him and *then* made the connection to the man Shanda saw."

"Oh. Right," she said with a slow nod. "I get what you mean. Any comparisons might affect the description I gave."

"Exactly. *I* can say he looks familiar and tell them where I saw him, but *you* can't. I just wanted to be sure we had that straight before we saw the sketch." Taking her hand, he pressed it to his lips. "I was afraid that Holmes bloke was going to whip out a pencil and start drawing right on the spot."

"And there I was, hoping he would," she said, chuckling. "Good thing one of us is thinking clearly."

He gave her a hug as they started off toward the car park. "You were great. If anything, you were too calm. Your 'I am involved in Mankind' quote took me by surprise—and obviously made an impression on McDougal."

She held up a hand, pressing her thumb and forefinger together. "I was this close to spouting Rumi's take on joy and sorrow, which would have been way too much." She was silent for a moment.

"That John Donne thing... I mean, I've heard it before—who hasn't?—but I never could have rattled it off correctly on my own."

Ranjiv didn't have to think hard to come up with the source. "Shanda?"

She nodded. "I'm sure of it. Seems like the sort of thing she would latch onto as a mantra or a pep talk to keep up her courage."

"Witnessing a murder would certainly change a person, although she may have had a philosophical bent even before that."

"True. This business has certainly changed me—even without picking up three "katras" along the way."

"Katras?"

"Vulcan term," she said with a grin. "You know... *Star Trek?*"

Recalling her insistence that it was easier to think of them as entities rather than souls, he didn't argue. Nevertheless, she must have noted his puzzled expression.

"Not a Trekkie, are you?" she prodded.

"Well, no. Not really."

"Actually, it's easier for me to believe in aliens than it is to believe in ghosts. More scientific." She stooped down to adjust Katie's leash. "I've never considered myself to be much of a philosopher. With a background in biology and finance, it seems a bit out of character. But then, I never liked dogs much either." She gave the schnauzer a pat and stood up. "What's for lunch?"

"I dunno. What are you in the mood for? English, Italian, Indian, French—or KFC?"

"Indian," she replied. "The Prince of Wales, maybe? I need to try those lamb chops Tahir was telling me about."

"He's right about the chops," Ranjiv said with a chuckle. "But if you want to try the chicken and the kebabs along with the lamb, you should get the Tandoori mixed grill."

"Sounds great. I'll have that."

"My, you're easy."

Her smile did funny things to his heart, but her words nearly knocked the breath from his lungs.

"Not really," she said. "But you... I *trust* you."

He'd given her no reason not to, but the fact that she did

was…remarkable. She'd trusted him from the very beginning.

"And not only because of Kavya's katra," she added, somehow managing to say it before that very thought even entered his mind. "I would've liked—and trusted—you anyway."

He shrugged. "We'll never know for sure, though. Will we?"

"You'll just have to take my word for it."

By this time, they had reached his car. The flip side of that dilemma occurred to him as he unlocked the door. "Oh, I believe you. What I can't explain is why I trust *you*."

"There are some things you simply have to take on faith." Her teasing smile faded to a solemn expression that wrapped around his soul like a warm hug. "You've shown more faith in me than anyone else ever has, and you only met me a few days ago. That makes you very special." When she spoke again, her voice was so soft, he barely heard her. "A good man in so many ways." She glanced up at him. "Your mother said something similar once, but she saw you as her son. I see you as something completely different."

"And when I look at you, I only see Jillian Dulaine. Not Shanda Smythe or Kavya Tenali or Anna Lyles." The presence or absence of those entities didn't matter. He wasn't in love with them. He was in love with Jillian.

Leaning closer, he kissed her—soft, yet deliberate. "What do you say we drop Katie off at my mother's house while we have lunch? It isn't far from here, and she could spend the afternoon in the garden instead of cooped up in the car."

"I'm sure she'd prefer that." Jillian's voice was steady, but the trembling fingers touching his cheek belied her true feelings. Was she nervous about falling in love with him? Or was it because it was so soon after her broken engagement? He was glad they'd cleared that hurdle—but had they actually cleared it?

Only time would tell. And they did have time. Despite the three weeks of her vacation, he knew their relationship wouldn't end when she boarded a plane for the States. If necessary, he would follow her there. But something told him he wouldn't need to. Even if she left Britain, she would be back. Whatever force of nature was using her as its instrument wouldn't let her go that easily.

And neither would Ranjiv.

* * * *

"Oh my God," she said on a sigh. "You weren't kidding about the food here. This is one of the best meals I've ever eaten in my life."

Ranjiv's delight in her pleasure was perfectly obvious, his quick upward glance and slightly shy half smile proving it beyond a doubt. "Glad you like it."

"Now if I could only get you to say the same thing about dinner at KFC, I'd say we were a perfect match." She let the teasing note in her voice do its work, watching as his tiny smile stretched into a full grin.

"Truth be told, I was already a fan before I met you. The flavor is…unique."

"Uniquely American, you mean? Maybe. It's certainly iconic." With a chuckle, she added, "Do you suppose it will stand the test of time? I mean, Indian food lives on because anyone can make it and put their own spin on it. But a secret recipe? What happens when the franchise folds? Will those eleven different herbs and spices ever be made public?"

"We can only hope." Ranjiv was openly laughing now, which had been her intention all along. She didn't like to remind him of what lay ahead, but a glance at her watch proved they were less than twenty-four hours away from Kavya's memorial service. She still had no idea what to expect during the service and especially not what would happen afterward.

Not claiming to recognize the murder suspect wasn't the only instance where caution was required. Ranjiv's family had no knowledge of her connection to them, and if she was careful, they never would. On the other hand, she was bound to overhear conversations spoken in Telugu, perhaps even some that might cause embarrassment.

Closing her eyes, she could picture Pratap Tenali's face with no difficulty whatsoever. Easily as handsome as his brother, the resemblance was such that she could have picked him out of a crowd simply from having seen a photo of Ramesh, although the memory of him was more direct than that. The images of his wife, Chetna, and their children were just as easily recalled.

"Speaking of secrets, I think you should tell your family that I understand Telugu. I can invent a college roommate who spoke the language to explain why, but they need to know."

"Before they say something stupid, you mean?"

"Not necessarily. Indiscreet, perhaps."

"Nicely put," he said. "I'll be sure to warn them, although I doubt anyone would make any unpleasant comments about you."

She took a sip of her tea before she spoke. "It's the nice ones that concern me. I'm remembering what Tahir said."

"I'm sure there are others who will share his sentiments. They've been anxious for me to find a wife for quite some time. Hopefully they'll be less vocal."

Choosing to ignore the assumption that becoming Ranjiv's wife was the probable outcome of their current relationship, she shrugged. "Tahir obviously didn't mind you teaming up with an American, but your family might not be as tolerant."

"I doubt that." He dipped a lamb chop in the mint sauce. "You're far more Indian than some of the Englishwomen I've dated."

"Maybe. But they don't know that, and I hope they never do." She hesitated. "I kinda wish you didn't know either."

"Trust me, I'm past that. And for the rest of it, I'm glad I do." His expression grew solemn. "We have a connection, you and I. One so special that no one else can share it with us." A flick of his brow signaled his approval. "I like that."

Jillian couldn't have wished for a better response. Simply nodding her acceptance, she ate the remainder of her meal in silence, save for a bit of random chatting. She paid attention to the other patrons. If any of them thought the pairing of Ranjiv with an American was odd, she couldn't see it. In many ways, Britain was as much of a melting pot as America, perhaps even more so. The culture was different, though. Having three entities on board with knowledge—one native, one immigrant, and one self-proclaimed Anglophile—might have facilitated the transition, but remaining in England would be easier for her than it would have been for most

Americans. She was comfortable in both countries, and might even have been comfortable in India if it ever came to that. She might look out of place, but she doubted she would feel it.

After lunch, Ranjiv paid the tab and they headed back to the police station, collecting Katie along the way. McDougal ushered them into his office.

Holmes arrived a moment later and handed a sketch to the inspector. "I've already shown this to Fry. She's gone off to the park."

McDougal grunted his approval as he passed the drawing on to Jillian. "What do you think?"

Apparently Holmes had used a computer program rather than a pencil with the result that the artist's rendition was more like a photograph than the pencil sketch she'd expected. The resemblance to the man they'd seen near the park was so uncanny, she had to stifle a gasp.

"You've certainly captured the scary eyes thing," she said. "I mean, I've never even seen this guy before, and he's giving me the creeps."

Ranjiv peered over her shoulder for a long moment before he spoke. "Oddly enough, this chap looks familiar."

"How so?" McDougal asked.

"We were out with the dog yesterday or the day before. I saw a man leaving the park who looked a lot like this."

"Ever seen him before?"

"Not that I'm aware of," he replied.

McDougal rounded on Jillian. "What about you? Did you see the bloke he's talking about?"

She shook her head. "No—and I think I would've noticed him if I had." Her shudder, though well-timed, was entirely genuine. "He certainly looks like the typical villain."

"You'd be surprised at how many criminals don't fit the stereotype." The inspector shrugged, then added, "And then there are those who have murder in their eyes when ordering tea."

This particular man, whoever he was, fit the latter description quite well. Even a brief glance at the picture made Jillian's skin crawl. "So…what do we do now?"

"You and Mr. Tenali take your dog for a walk in and around the park and keep an eye out for this man. I trust you'll know Sergeant Fry again when you see her?"

"Sure," Jillian replied, although to be perfectly honest, she thought she might not.

"Yes, well, if you do see her, which you probably won't, pretend you don't know her. She's undercover."

"Got it."

Jillian was beginning to envy Fry's ability to blend in with a crowd. Unfortunately, between Katie's exuberance and Ranjiv's tall, handsome form, she had a feeling that Sergeant Fry—and possibly the murder suspect—would spot them first.

Chapter 29

EVEN THOUGH JILLIAN HAD BEEN EXPECTING IT, HER REACTION TO being in the park hit her with even more despair than her previous visit, possibly because she now understood the reasons for it. She clutched Ranjiv's arm as they neared the clump of bushes and trees on the eastern edge, the terrifying images assailing her mind like a mortar barrage.

"It's here," she whispered, unable to keep the tremor from her voice. "I can feel it." Closing her eyes, she could see the knife buried deep in a shrub that ought to have died from that dagger to its heart. Pain pierced her chest as though the blade had been thrust between her own ribs.

Oh, surely not... Didn't she have enough to bear with three women occupying space in her brain? Now a damned *plant* was transmitting feelings to her?

A plant with an important story to tell. Or perhaps it was Earth again, speaking to her of the hurt it had suffered. If so, she would have to make a point of avoiding rock quarries or logging sites. God forbid she should be anywhere near an interstate highway under construction.

The scent of freshly mown grass drew her attention to the turf beneath her feet. The thought of every blade of cut grass singing songs of woe elicited a tiny chuckle, but the blessedly silent grass reassured her. Clearly, not every torn leaf or broken branch would beg her to speak for them.

Ranjiv expelled a breath as though he'd been as anxious as she and shared in the humor, although the fact that she no longer had a death grip on his arm was the more likely reason.

"Can you tell exactly where the murder weapon is?" he asked.

She nodded. "What I can't figure out is how to tell the police without incriminating myself. I mean, I shouldn't know where it is, and yet I do."

"As though you'd put it there yourself? Yeah. I can see that being a problem. Perhaps you could say Shanda had been more specific."

"You mean she would have seen that the knife was stuck in an oak rather than a rhododendron?"

He placed a hand over hers and led her out onto the green. "Seems a bit far-fetched, doesn't it?"

"No kidding. I doubt if any memory of hers would've been that precise, even under hypnosis."

"The killer obviously doesn't know the exact location either. If he did, he would've retrieved it by now." He stooped to let Katie off her leash, then turned to face Jillian as the dog trotted on ahead. "Still, it's likely that any knife thrown from the alley would land in those trees. I know the police want to catch the suspect actually searching for it, but anyone could lie their way out of that situation."

"I dunno. Once the cops spot him, I'm guessing they won't bother confronting him. They'll probably follow him, find out who he is, and then look for a motive." She couldn't tell if it was the distance they'd put between them and the knife or not, but she felt sharper, more decisive, more convinced that they weren't wasting their time—particularly given their new allies. "My money's on Sergeant Fry."

Ranjiv's gaze swept the across the park. If he'd noticed anything unusual, it didn't show. "Seen her yet?"

"Nope, which is why I think she'll be the one to crack the case. She's just the sort of murder-mystery character that no one ever recognizes as playing a pivotal role in the outcome."

"Ah, yes. The elderly housekeeper who turns out to be a former British agent."

"Something like that," Jillian said with a shrug. "Only *we* know her for what she really is."

"Let's hope our man hasn't been one to hang around police stations enough to recognize her."

"Or have a job there." She chuckled. "That would be the

ultimate irony, wouldn't it? The person investigating the crime turns out to be the one who committed it?"

The possibility did exist, but she hadn't picked up any bad vibes from the officers she'd met thus far. No doubt the Stonehenge spirits would have been quick to point out any bad apples. An elected official would have been a far more likely candidate anyway.

"A definite plot twist," Ranjiv said with a grim smile. "Can't see McDougal in that role, though. Not in character at all."

"Me either." Curling her arm around his, she was pleased to note that her anxiety continued to abate as they strolled further into the park. "How long do you suppose we should stick around here?"

"No clue, although I can't see that it matters. The odds of us being on hand when Mr. X shows up are pretty slim."

"Leave the dirty work to the professionals?"

She got the sense that he was hesitating, that the war going on inside him had yet to be decided. When he finally spoke, his words surprised her. "Perhaps. But my money's on you being the one to 'crack the case.' The forces behind you are a lot stronger than the police."

Jillian took several steps before voicing her thoughts. "Maybe. But the police are much better armed."

She remembered one man whose struggles against a superior force had been in vain, and also the hundreds of people who had been plunged into an unforgiving sea. Clearly Stonehenge and the Atlantic hadn't been cooperating with each other or more than three passengers would have survived.

I'm losing my mind again.

The weirdness of having other people's thoughts and memories incorporated with her own was enough to make anyone crazy. Now Earth, the sea, and possibly the sky were vying for a spot. She'd be communicating telepathically with Katie next.

Remember the grass... She drew in a cleansing breath and felt the calm return.

"I can't see that being armed would be a factor at the moment," he said. "What do you say we make a couple of circuits of the grounds and then head for home? We can call McDougal afterward."

"And tomorrow?" The subject of Kavya's funeral service seemed to have been overshadowed by the ongoing murder investigation. She suspected this bothered Ranjiv more than he'd let on.

"We rise early, shower, and then go to the temple. We wear white to funerals, then return home, wash again, and change clothes as a purification ritual."

She glanced down with a grimace. Clearly, her yellow *palazzo* pants and her green and fuchsia tunic, although quite Indian in origin, wouldn't be appropriate. "I guess we need to do some shopping."

"I suppose so." He walked on in silence for a time, his frown suggesting a touch of inner turmoil.

Deciding her best course of action was to wait it out, Jillian stopped to pick up a small stick and called to Katie. The schnauzer seemed positively thrilled, barking her approval as Jillian waved the stick over her head before giving it a toss. The little dog raced after it, nearly catching it on the fly.

Jillian had thrown the stick several times before Ranjiv spoke again. "Many Hindu customs are more relaxed here in Britain, but there are still those who would be critical of me for not mourning Mother's death properly and for waiting so many days after her death to hold the funeral. They would say that even acting as your unofficial tour guide is inappropriate, much less being intimate with you. But I don't feel her loss in the way you might expect. Her body may be gone, but her spirit lives on in you. That fact…changes things."

That Ranjiv had referred to her assimilated entities as a "fact" displayed his faith in her. She still marveled at the ease with which he'd been convinced—even guessing the truth before she admitted to it.

A remarkable man, this Ranjiv Tenali—one whose dilemma she understood completely.

"And you can't explain any of this to them," she said. "Not entirely anyway."

"No, I can't."

"I'm sensing some regrets here."

He shook his head. "No regrets. Only second guesses. But then, pleasing everyone is rarely possible." Ranjiv's gaze, which had been aimed off in the distance for most of the conversation, was currently fixed on her face. "Right now, I wish only to please you." A smile softened the seriousness of his expression. "And by so doing, I please myself."

"Oddly enough, I feel exactly the same way." She tossed the stick one last time, then hooked her arm around his and placed her hand on his sleeve. "So...once more across the green?"

"Absolutely," he replied. "Lead on."

* * * *

The call Ranjiv made to McDougal was anticlimactic, to say the least. He and Jillian hadn't spotted any would-be murderers, and neither had Sergeant Fry.

"We'll keep watching," McDougal assured him. "Since you have a dog and live close to the park, it's perfectly natural for you to take walks there. Go as often as you can and let me know the moment you see that chap."

"Absolutely," Ranjiv replied. *As if we would do anything less.*

After dropping Katie off at his mother's house, Ranjiv kept Jillian's hand firmly on his arm as they walked up the street toward the shops. He liked the feeling—one he'd rarely had the chance to enjoy until now—a feeling that not only completed him but one that also gave him purpose. Prior to Jillian's arrival, his job and his mother were the primary sources of meaning in his life. Jillian affected him in an entirely different manner. He looked forward to the time when being with her seemed normal rather than an unusual occurrence.

Their shopping trip didn't take long. In addition to a casual teal and gray sari, Jillian purchased another pair of *palazzo* pants, a *kameez* tunic, and a *dupatta* shawl, all in white. Even in such austere garb, she would still look like a princess. His own white *kurta* pajamas were even simpler.

What he'd told Jillian about some people being upset— primarily because his mother's memorial was scheduled a full five days after her death instead of the following day—was true. However, with the circumstances being what they were, he doubted anyone within Kavya's immediate circle of family and friends would be overly critical. Even the priest had advised him to wait in the hope that Kavya's body could be recovered for cremation. Having received no word from any authority, he could only assume that recovery and identification efforts were progressing slowly, if indeed they were progressing at all.

In a way, they *were* following tradition and were perhaps even ahead of schedule. Among Hindus, the most common practice was to cremate the body, collect the ashes, and on the fourth day, scatter the ashes on a sacred body of water or a place of importance to the deceased. Granted, no actual ashes had been sprinkled on the Atlantic, but there was nothing anyone could do about that.

Twelve days after the funeral, they would celebrate his mother's *samskara*, or reincarnation, with the ritual feast of Kriya. Then he could get on with his normal life. These days prior to the funeral would have been a period of intolerable limbo had it not been for Jillian's presence. Would she still be there a year later to celebrate Kavya's *Shraddha*? The annual ceremony commemorated a death by offering food to the poor and needy, although the practice was more of a family affair in Britain.

Kavya had never failed to remember the anniversary of his father's death, nor would Ranjiv. March fifteenth—the Ides of March, supposedly the same date as Julius Caesar's death—was forever etched on his mental calendar. He recalled thinking that dying on that day made his father quite special, although he would have sincerely preferred that Ramesh's death be a future event rather than a memory.

"A penny for your thoughts," Jillian said as they turned toward home.

"Just thinking about tomorrow," he replied. "For the past few days, I could almost forget Mother was gone. Even now it seems like she should be waiting for us, going on about how much fun she's had babysitting Katie instead of being the one whose funeral we'll be attending in the morning."

"Going into that empty house bothers you, doesn't it?"

"Some. It's different from being there while she was at work or even while she was visiting her sister. The house already seems abandoned."

"There's a way to fix that, you know."

"Yes, and believe me, I've given a great deal of thought to giving up my flat and living there, sleeping in my old room and such. Still not sure."

She nodded as though she understood. Perhaps she did. Perhaps she knew what bothered him was the thought of moving into the house without her.

"The temple priest texted me earlier," he went on. "Since Mother's body hasn't been recovered, he wants me to provide one of her personal belongings to use in a ritual cremation. I have absolutely no idea what to give him."

"Hmm… Something made of wood rather than metal or plastic, I suppose. Maybe a comb or a hairpin?"

"That's as a good a place to start as any, although she probably had those things with her."

"Yes, but you know the sort of thing I mean, don't you?" she continued. "Something she might not have used or worn in years but couldn't bring herself to part with?"

He nodded. "You're right. I'm sure we'll find something appropriate." Dropping an arm around her shoulders, he gave her a quick hug. "I'm so glad you're here to help me with all this."

She returned the gesture with a hug of her own. "My pleasure."

Deciding it was time to drop the previous topic, he asked, "Any thoughts as to what you'd like to do for dinner tonight?"

"After that huge lunch, I doubt I'll have room for very much. Maybe we should've picked up a bag of pakoras to heat up later on."

"That actually sounds pretty good." He glanced over his shoulder. "And if we're going to do it, now's the time. That café we ate at the other day is only two blocks from here."

"Perfect."

They did a quick about-face and set off for the café.

Jillian inhaled deeply as they approached the restaurant. "Don't know how we managed to get past this place before—or any of the others for that matter. The food smells amazing."

Ranjiv couldn't help but be pleased, although she certainly wouldn't have been the first American tourist with a taste for Indian cuisine. Out there on the street, she seemed an odd mix of being both at ease and out of place. How would she feel in the temple? Would she ever truly feel at home there? Hindu temples often seemed strange to outsiders, particularly to those whose own churches were decorated in a less elaborate manner.

Granted, she had more "inner help" than any other American ever had, but the full extent of it was unknown. Although she understood the language—had even spoken it aloud—Hinduism was difficult to comprehend fully, even to those born and raised in its beliefs and practices.

I should know.

Ranjiv was so deep in his thoughts as he ordered an assortment of pakoras and samosas to take away, he didn't notice that Jillian had also fallen silent until he heard her swift inhale. A glance in her direction revealed raised brows and parted lips—an expression simultaneously excited and shocked. Suspecting the start of another mental meltdown, he placed what he hoped was a reassuring hand on her shoulder.

"What is it?"

"Not what, but who." Her grim smile and quiet tone demonstrated the return of her self-control. "Apparently our 'mark' likes Indian food."

* * * *

A heartbeat later, Jillian spied someone whose presence calmed her like nothing else could have done. The man they'd been searching for might have been seated at a sidewalk table indulging in a plate of Tandoori prawns—easily the most expensive item on the menu—but Sergeant Fry was standing roughly twenty feet behind him, perusing a rack of brightly colored scarves dangling from a street vendor's cart.

"Fortunately, he's under the watchful eye of the local master of concealment."

Ranjiv nodded his understanding. "I'm guessing she'd prefer us to remain as quietly invisible as she is."

"Yeah. Do you suppose she spotted him in the park and followed him here?"

"Possibly." Ranjiv paid the cashier and stepped back to wait while their order was filled, casting a surreptitious glance at the table in question. "He isn't alone."

"I noticed that. Wonder who that other dude is."

"Dunno... Looks like a business lunch, though—briefcases at their feet and suit jackets over the backs of their chairs."

"You're getting good at this," she remarked. "I think you may have found your calling."

"I *am* a reporter," he chided. "We tend to pay attention to such things."

She hated to admit it, but they'd spent so much time together, she'd almost forgotten he had a day job. "Right. My bad."

"No worries. You're a bank manager. Do they look like bankers or bank robbers?"

She studied the two men as well as she could without staring, having to glance away briefly when their suspect actually made eye contact with her. "You already know what the one fellow looks like. The other guy could be anything—white shirt, thinning gray hair, looks like he'd be pretty tall standing upright. A bit jowly, I think. I can't see his face very well."

"Me either." Ranjiv shot another glance in that direction just as the man in question turned his head toward the street as a passing motorist sounded his horn and waved.

This time, it was Ranjiv's turn to gasp in surprise. "I know that chap. He's a London MP."

Jillian didn't have to ask what those initials stood for. She knew.

Member of Parliament.

Chapter 30

"THAT'S TOO EASY," JILLIAN SCOFFED. "WE'VE BEEN SEARCHING high and low for that guy and he's sitting right out there on the street having a late lunch with a politician?"

Ranjiv cleared his throat and made a point of turning his back on their quarry. "It *has* been a while since the, ah, *incident* we've been discussing."

Jillian evidently took the hint. "Gotcha." She was still facing the two men, which made it easy for her to peep past Ranjiv's shoulder for a better look.

"Are you sure he's the same man Shanda saw?" Ranjiv asked.

"I'd bet the farm on it—if I had a farm, that is. Older, yes, but still the same eyes." She paused for a moment. "He gives me the creeps, even when he's smiling. Sort of a superior, calculating smile. Like he's gotten away with murder."

"Yeah. The trick will be getting him to incriminate himself." He drew in a breath, reluctant to voice his doubts on the subject. "To be honest, I can't see him doing that."

"Me either. In fact, I'm surprised he's still hanging around the district—unless skipping town would've pegged him as the guilty party." She took another peek, froze briefly, then gave a barely perceptible nod. "Our mutual friend has just given us the high sign."

The cashier handed Ranjiv their order. Thanking the man, he turned to go. "Think we should do what we decided on before?" He felt as though they were communicating in code, as befit spies or detectives or whatever they were. The true nature of their role in the investigation was still a bit murky.

"That's the impression I got from her just now. She seems to have the matter well in hand, although I really hope she has someone following *her* in a car or she'll lose him if he hops on a bus or hails a cab."

"Something tells me that eluding her would be about as easy as escaping death and taxes." Switching the bag of pakoras to the opposite hand, he offered Jillian his arm, which she took without hesitation.

"I hope you're right about that," she said, leaning close enough to whisper. "Although I'm guessing she's recognized his companion as easily as you did. Now that she has him on our mark's list of known contacts, she'll have someplace to start even if she does lose him—somewhere other than the park anyway."

They crossed the street at the next corner and started off down Abbots Road. Despite Ranjiv's assumption that they could safely dispense with their code—and their whispers—he glanced over his shoulder before continuing. "I'd sure like to know what those two were discussing. Might actually be newsworthy."

"I suppose you know that guy's name," she prompted.

"Oh, yes. That was Unwin Turnbull. He's a prominent Conservative and comparatively popular around London. It's no wonder someone chose to honk and wave at him, although Southall isn't part of his constituency. Our MP is a Labor Party member."

"We'll have to look him up online when we get back to your place. I'm gonna take a wild guess and say he's a friend to the oil companies and is one of those jerks who would have you believe that global warming will make plants grow better because of the higher carbon dioxide levels and that solar panels actively deplete the sun's energy."

"You'd have to be barking mad to believe such nonsense."

"No, just ignorant and gullible," she said, scowling. "Some fake think tank in Wyoming has been dishing out that crap." She gritted her teeth. "I mean, *really*…what could anyone on this planet or any other possibly do that would affect the sun?"

"Nothing, unless we were to launch a barrage of nuclear missiles at it. Even that probably wouldn't do any damage."

"I agree, but I wouldn't put it past some idiot to think that's a good idea—probably the one making the bombs."

The hand she had on his arm trembled, although Ranjiv

suspected she was shaking in fury rather than fear.

No, she wasn't afraid. She was a crusader. Planet Earth and the Stonehenge spirits had made an excellent choice when they selected her to be their champion.

Even so, there was still a good chance that both he and Jillian were the ones who were barking mad.

* * * *

After letting Katie in from the backyard, Jillian went upstairs to find a suitable item for Kavya's ritual cremation while Ranjiv searched the living room and kitchen. With the hairpin idea in mind, she made a beeline for Kavya's bedroom and pulled open the top drawer of the dresser.

Her scalp tightened as her fingertips touched on a small, worn box decorated with gold foil. Inside it, she discovered a wooden mantilla-style comb nestled in the molded satin lining. She glanced down at Katie, who had followed her up the stairs and now sat on the floor at her feet.

"I do believe this is it."

Seeing no need to look any further, she went back downstairs to find Ranjiv dragging photograph albums from the bookshelf.

He glanced up as she entered. "I thought about using Mother's chapati board and rolling pin, but they didn't seem all that personal. I was thinking a photograph might be better. Find anything?"

"Maybe." She held out the comb. "What about this?"

Ranjiv took the intricately carved piece from her hand, his expression a blend of reverence and awe. "My father gave this to Mother on their first anniversary. I haven't seen her wear it since he died."

"I found it in her dresser. Not buried underneath her gloves or scarves, but in the center where she would see it anytime she opened the drawer. From that, I'm guessing it must've meant a great deal to her."

"I believe it did—and you were right about using a hairpin. This is exactly what we need. I'm amazed you found it so quickly."

In light of previous events, Jillian didn't consider finding the comb the slightest bit strange. She waited half a beat for him to revise his last statement, then simply nodded when he didn't. Kavya's entity might not have spoken to her directly, but the knowledge had been tucked away in her subconscious, waiting for the right stimulus to trigger it.

Ranjiv would realize his error soon enough. For the moment, however, he merely slipped the comb into his pocket before returning the photo albums to the shelf.

He gestured toward the door. "Shall we?"

* * * *

Ranjiv spent the evening memorizing the funeral verses from the *Bhagavad Gita*. He'd never studied them to such a degree before, but by the time he went to bed that night, he probably could have recited them in his sleep.

Several of the verses warned against lamenting the loss of a loved one, stressing that, although the body is mortal and will inevitably die, the soul is eternal. Ranjiv hadn't lamented his mother's passing so much as he missed her presence in his everyday life. Her spirit might have taken up residence in Jillian, but Jillian hadn't become Kavya. Everything about his mother as a physical being—from her warm smile to the sound of her footsteps—was gone forever.

He read on, losing himself in the text, seeking solace in the flow of the words and the rhythm of the poetry. No, he couldn't trade Kavya for Jillian, nor would he wish to. In many ways, Jillian was his mother's last gift to her only son, a gift he intended to cherish for the rest of his life.

He glanced over at Jillian as she sat at his desk, scrolling through links to the saga of Unwin Turnbull's career.

"Typical politician," she muttered. "Telling people what they want to hear and then doing whatever benefits him politically. I'm going to guess that Ewan Michelson wasn't like that, which is probably what got him killed."

"An incorruptible man destroyed by the corrupt?"

"Yeah. Like Serpico."

Not having a Yank's katra mingling with his soul, Ranjiv was a bit fuzzy when it came to what was clearly an American reference.

"Who?"

She leaned back in the chair, rubbing her eyes before making her reply. "Frank Serpico. Al Pacino played him in the movie. I'm surprised you never saw it, although it *is* pretty old. The real story happened back in the sixties. Serpico was a police officer who blew the whistle on corruption in the New York City Police Department. Supposedly his partners set him up, and he was shot in the face during a drug bust. He lived abroad for a while after that. For all I know, he may still be alive. Strange that being honest could get a guy into so much trouble."

A trickle of fear tickled Ranjiv's spine. "You may be in a similar situation before long, which is why I'm glad we weren't the ones tailing Turnbull's lunch companion."

"Thanks to McDougal, I'm still flying under the radar. I'll try to stay there, but you never know how these things will turn out." Closing the laptop, she yawned. "I don't know about you, but I'm beat."

"Same here." Ranjiv put a bookmark between the pages he'd been reading. "I'm still not sure how to feel about the funeral, though. Part of me sees it as a celebration of Mother's life, but another part is dreading it, and there are so many unanswered questions. I'm afraid I won't have a sense of closure even when the mourning period is over." He shrugged. "Perhaps never."

Jillian grimaced. "That's my fault, isn't it?"

"No, not at all," he said quickly. "The fact that her spirit moved on should help with closure rather than hinder it. But I never saw her body—never received visual proof of her death. I think I needed that."

"I see what you mean. Sure, *I* saw her body, but that isn't the same, is it?"

"No. Your word should be enough, and it isn't that I don't believe you—" Shaking his head, he stared at the floor, seeing patterns in the carpet he'd never noticed before.

"There's another way to look at it."

Her quiet tone and gentle smile comforted him like nothing else could have done. "How so?"

"You get to remember her life rather than her death. You never saw her body, so to you, she's still the same: the living, breathing person you've known since birth. She's like a soldier whose widow only remembers the kiss he gave her before he left, not the way he would look in death."

The truth of her words warmed his heart and drew a reluctant smile from his lips. "I should've guessed you would know exactly what to say."

She mimicked his earlier shrug as she rose from her chair. "That's the advantage of having access to the collective wisdom of three extra entities." Crossing the room, she held out a hand. "Let's get some sleep. Tomorrow is going to be a very busy day."

"It won't end there either," he said with a sigh. "Settling Mother's estate should be simple and straightforward—my uncle is the executor and I'm her only beneficiary—but it probably won't be. Nothing ever is."

"You got *that* right."

* * * *

The splendors within the temple where Kavya's funeral took place more than compensated for its unpretentious exterior, but since there were no pews, most of the people gathered there were seated on the floor. Even if Jillian hadn't already been familiar with the established customs, the collection of shoes near the entrance would have reminded her to remove her shoes upon entering. A visual sweep of the room proved she was indeed the only blonde, making her glad she'd draped the *dupatta* over her head.

Kavya had apparently worshipped at that temple on a regular basis, enabling Jillian to identify the various deities enshrined there and know them for who they were and what they represented. However, those memories couldn't compare with actually gazing at the ornately beautiful, flower-draped shrines with her own eyes. She and Ranjiv had arranged for flowers to be delivered, but the profusion of blooms demonstrated that Kavya had been loved by many outside her immediate family.

When Ranjiv introduced Pratap and Chetna, Jillian had to remind herself that while she knew precisely who they were, to them, she was an unknown. Both were polite but reserved, as befit the occasion. Would they have seemed more pleased if they had met her at a party? *Perhaps.* She couldn't blame them for their reticence. Jillian might have been a perfectly respectable person, but she hailed from a different country with a vastly disparate culture.

Jillian took a seat on the floor to the left of the altar. Although she felt no glares boring holes in the back of her head, she was still grateful for the shield the *dupatta* provided.

The ceremony passed in a blur of songs, chants, and flickering lamps until Ranjiv began to recite from the *Bhagavad Gita* in a strong, clear voice.

"The soul never takes birth and never dies at any time nor does it come into being again when the body is created. The soul is birthless, eternal, imperishable and timeless and is never destroyed when the body is destroyed. Weapons cannot harm the soul, fire cannot burn the soul, water cannot wet and air cannot dry up the soul.

"It is declared that the soul is imperceptible, the soul is inconceivable, the soul is immutable; therefore understanding the soul as such, it is improper for you to lament. For one who has taken birth, death is certain and for one who is dead, birth is certain; therefore you ought not to lament for an inevitable situation."

Hearing those verses, Jillian wondered why there was a mourning period at all. She thought perhaps it was because human beings, unlike their souls, were not eternal and those who loved a particular incarnation had to be given time to grieve and reconcile themselves to their loss. After all, you didn't stop loving someone simply because they had died.

The ritual cremation followed. Ranjiv placed Kavya's hairpin atop a small pile of wood shavings in the center of a wide brass bowl, then set fire to the kindling. Jillian hated to see such a fine piece of craftsmanship destroyed, especially one so high in sentimental value, but she understood the importance of the ritual. After all, Kavya was far more precious than any of her possessions could ever be.

Since becoming fully integrated, Kavya's spirit had been silent, a circumstance which led Jillian to assume that individual thoughts were no longer needed. She thought that transformation might be similar to what happened when a soul passed into a new body at conception: the awareness of former selves was lost amid the creation of a new persona.

Jillian was different from the person she'd been when she boarded the plane in Newark. She understood facts and concepts she'd never studied, recognized people she'd never met, had emotional reactions to a variety of things that shouldn't have affected her, and had communed with the spirits of Stonehenge, perhaps even with Earth itself. Acquiring a new persona might explain those changes.

Or maybe I've simply gone bonkers from being aboard a plane that took a full-throttle dive into the sea.

She slowly became aware that someone was speaking to her. Glancing up, she saw Pratap extending his hand toward her. He was even smiling.

"You were with Kavya when she died," he said. "You must come closer."

Taking his hand, she rose to her feet as fresh doubts assailed her. Did he know she carried Kavya's soul? Would this ritual cremation remove it?

Oddly enough, she didn't want it removed. She needed Kavya's katra to function in this city and culture. Nevertheless, she followed Pratap, although he didn't exactly give her a choice, keeping a firm grip on her hand as though he expected her to pull away. She didn't bother to try.

Pratap joined hands with Chetna and their children. Ranjiv took Jillian's other hand and together, they moved closer to the fire.

As Jillian stared at the flames, a multitude of memories suddenly vanished from her mind. She couldn't remember anything personal about Kavya, not even her birthday. In a moment of startling clarity, she realized that what she'd assumed was a full integration of Kavya's spirit had only been a temporary fix. This was closer to the way she'd felt when she accepted responsibility for Katie.

And Anna's soul had moved on.

Fear and panic clutched her heart, and she would have fallen had it not been for the two men who held her hands. Her head ached as she tried desperately to hold onto Kavya's essence, but it was like trying to catch the smoke rising above the funeral pyre.

She's gone.

The tiny blaze gradually burned down to embers and then to ash.

Jillian heard voices nearby, whispering prayers in everything from English to Hindi. Although she understood most of them, she chose not to delve any further into the knowledge Kavya's entity had left behind. Whether she could recall how to make Makhani chicken seemed irrelevant now.

Her first concern was for Ranjiv. How would he react when she told him she no longer carried Kavya's spirit? Would he regret the loss or be relieved to know that his mother's soul no longer resided inside the woman with whom he'd been sharing a bed?

That can't have been easy—nearly impossible for the average man.

But then, Ranjiv wasn't average. She peered at him from the corner of her eye as he stood beside her. Did he realize how special he was? How unique? Perhaps not. She vowed to tell him at her earliest opportunity.

The recovery of Kavya's body meant very little now. Alone among the entire congregation, Jillian knew that with absolute certainty. The priest might suspect—or at least *believe* he knew—but she doubted he had actually felt the release of Kavya's spirit.

Ranjiv had been holding Jillian's hand. Had he experienced similar sensations? Possibly. Either way she would have to tell him. But not now. Later, perhaps, when they were alone.

She paused to examine the state of her own soul and found it to be joyful and buoyant in many respects, despite being weighted down in others. Shanda's entity was still there, her closure still in limbo, her task as yet undone.

Amid the murmur of prayers, Jillian promised to do her best to help Shanda's soul find peace and move on. Then she would do the same for the other spirits hovering around her, pleading for her assistance.

Somehow, she thought that job might take a bit longer than solving Ewan Michelson's murder.

Chapter 31

WHEN MCDOUGAL CALLED LATER THAT AFTERNOON, RANJIV WAS glad the inspector had chosen to ring *his* mobile rather than Jillian's. The funeral service had clearly sapped her energy, and she'd opted for a nap after returning to his flat to shower and change. He couldn't blame her for feeling tired; he'd felt somewhat drained himself.

McDougal's brogue sounded even more pronounced over the phone. "I've a bit o' news for you. Sergeant Fry was able to ID the man she followed from the park yesterday afternoon. Name o' Walter Buchard."

"Never heard of him," Ranjiv said. "Should I have?"

"I doubt it." McDougal paused long enough that Ranjiv heard his next breath quite clearly. "No prior police record, which isn't unusual. We've found the basics—birth certificate, vehicle registration, a driver's license, address and such—but his employment status is a bit vague."

"Shady dealings?"

"Possibly. Judging from the type of car he owns, he's on *someone's* payroll—unless he's independently wealthy."

"In which case you'd have a rather extensive file on him."

A smile colored the inspector's tone. "I do believe we would."

"I suppose finding him on a list of known assassins was too much to hope for," Ranjiv lamented.

"True. Then again, if he'd done one murder for money and been paid as well as he appears to have been paid, well, there you are."

"But that wouldn't be conclusive evidence in a murder trial."

"Ach, no. Unless we could track down the source, and I'm guessing the trail will have been hidden rather well. Unfortunately, even sudden wealth doesn't necessarily prove dishonesty."

Ranjiv thought it probably should, but refrained from saying so. "What's next?"

"The usual painstaking detective work. Now that we know who he is, we'll try to figure out what he's been up to for the past eleven years."

"Good luck with that," Ranjiv said, not bothering to hide his skepticism.

The inspector's shrug was as audible as his smile had been. "It's what we do."

"And we're all very thankful for your hard work."

"Yes, well..." Following a self-deprecating clearing of his throat, the inspector continued, "Your friend Jillian put it best when she quoted John Donne. We should have 'I am involved in Mankind' posted on the wall here."

"We *all* should," Ranjiv amended. "Unfortunately, there are some whose involvement with mankind isn't exactly benign."

"If it were, I'd be out of a job, now wouldn't I?" A few seconds passed before he added, "Wouldn't mind that, actually."

The inspector wasn't the only one who'd be out of a job. Nothing sold newspapers quite like murders and disasters.

Sad but true.

"That'll do, then," McDougal said, his tone now brisk rather than introspective. "I'll keep you informed. Let me know if you stumble across anything, ah...*interesting.*"

The undertone of his request was clear; the inspector fully expected Ranjiv and Jillian to do some sleuthing of their own.

But that request was most definitely off the record.

"Will do."

The floorboards creaked as Jillian padded into the room barefoot. "Please tell me that was McDougal on the phone just now."

Ranjiv nodded. "Ever hear of a Walter Buchard?"

She collapsed on the sofa with a yawn. "I'm guessing he's our mark. But no. The name means nothing to me."

"Same here."

"Don't suppose you got an address on him, did you?"

"No. But it shouldn't be too hard to find."

Nodding her agreement, she tucked her feet up on the sofa before tugging her nightgown down to cover them. "Google is a useful, if sometimes disturbingly knowledgeable tool. I Googled myself once. The amount of information that popped up was kinda scary even then. God only knows what would show up now."

"Yet another reason why it's best to keep your name out of the news."

"No kidding."

* * * *

Jillian knew why she'd chosen to take a nap. She didn't want to have to face Ranjiv. Didn't want to tell him that Kavya's soul had finally departed. She had to tell him, but whether it would bring them closer together or tear them apart, she wasn't sure.

She couldn't avoid the rest of the day's events by sleeping through them either. Pratap and his family were to join them for the traditional after-funeral meal at Kavya's house. Not as important as the purification of Kavya's home by the temple's priest, perhaps, but an integral part of the mourning process all the same.

Jillian thought it strange that the purification ritual had even been necessary. It wasn't as though Kavya had died a lingering death from disease, and her body hadn't even been brought back to the house. She'd been perfectly healthy when she left her home for the last time.

Ranjiv's mourning period had begun when his mother's plane failed to arrive at Heathrow. Learning Jillian's secret had interrupted that process because, in a way, Kavya had still been with them.

Not so now. The funeral had changed everything.

"There's something I need to tell you." Focusing on a blank space on the opposite wall, she avoided his gaze, not wanting what she would see there to stop her. "About the cremation…it seems to have worked. I–I felt Kavya's spirit leave me. I still understand the language and culture, but her personal memories are gone." As her eyes finally met Ranjiv's, she felt a surge of grief—a unique, private sadness she doubted anyone else could ever comprehend. "It's as if she's died all over again."

A long moment passed. And another. And another. Silence

pounded at her ears.

Finally, he spoke. "Everything is as it should be now. Her soul has moved on, and so should we."

Jillian nodded, but his meaning wasn't clear. Move on to where? To a new life with him in England? Or did he mean for her to return to Memphis once the murder was solved?

By then, even Shanda will have left me.

That idea didn't please her any more than Kavya's imminent departure had. Within the space of a few days, she'd become accustomed to being a repository of souls. And now, just as quickly, two of those souls were gone. Only time would tell whether she would move on to an even greater purpose in the end.

"I agree," she said. "But our interpretations of 'moving on' may be different."

"Us, you mean?" His pause wasn't as long as the last one had been, but Jillian was no less anxious to hear his reply. "We can decide that before the time comes for you to leave."

"Do you want me to stay?"

He gaped at her with obvious disbelief. "I thought we'd established that."

"But I'm not carrying your mother's soul anymore. Seems like that might make a difference."

He shook his head. "That fact only makes the decision easier." A tiny chuckle escaped him. "The presence of Mother's spirit made our relationship difficult before. Now you would have me believe that the reverse is also true. You can't have it both ways, you know."

"I realize that. I just wanted to hear you say it."

"Well, then. I *have* said it. Now kiss me and go get dressed. Wear a sari if you like."

"I believe I will." Rising from the sofa, she stepped into his embrace. As he pressed his lips tenderly to her own, she was astonished by the amount of comfort such a simple act could provide. "Have I told you how special you are?"

"Possibly," he replied. "But whether you've told me or not is irrelevant. The fact that you *believe* it is what matters."

"Damn," she whispered. "You're even more special than I

thought."

"I hope I can live up to that."

"I'm pretty sure you already have." She gave him another quick kiss. "Give me twenty minutes."

In observance of dressing down for a funeral, she hadn't put on makeup that morning, nor did she deem it necessary now. Even the green and gold sari seemed too festive for the occasion, making her glad she'd thought to buy another one in a more casual style the day before.

The next question was whether she would remember how to wear it. But after donning the blouse and petticoat, she tucked, draped, and pinned the sari as though she'd worn one every day of her life.

Like riding a bicycle.

Ranjiv wore a white shirt and dark trousers, somehow managing to look like a movie star even in such ordinary clothing. She took his proffered arm as they started down the stairs from his flat, something she'd never done with Seth no matter where they were going or what she was wearing. Perhaps it was because Seth had never offered.

That realization stunned her for a moment. Was she more dependent on Ranjiv or was she simply enjoying the closeness his gesture provided? She and Seth had rarely even held hands.

Ranjiv was more of a gentleman than Seth had ever claimed to be. Perhaps that was the difference. Or was it simply a question of love?

On that note, she smiled first at Ranjiv and then at the little dog hopping down the stairs beside her. No bonds of marriage or official ownership bound them together. They were a family because they wished to be.

She waited at the foot of the stairs while Ranjiv opened the door, and together, they ventured out onto the street.

* * * *

As she might have expected, entering Kavya's former home had almost no effect on Jillian whatsoever. No one lived there anymore. No spirits hovered, no voices spoke. The house might have meant a

great deal to Ranjiv, but Jillian felt no emotional attachments. She
was certain her attitude would change if she and Ranjiv chose to live
there together, but those feelings would develop gradually, without
the sudden blast of emotions and knowledge with which she'd been
bombarded on her first visit.

Would a second excursion to Stonehenge be a similar non-
event? A ho-hum, been-there-done-that feeling?

Possibly, although the circumstances were entirely different,
seeming to have nothing to do with any extra souls she might have
been carrying at the time.

Pratap and Chetna arrived with their three children, each of
them carrying a dish for the post-funeral meal. The children, who
appeared to range in age from their early to late teens, didn't seem
somber at all once the initial greetings were exchanged. The eldest
boy was soon off in a corner with his phone, no doubt texting his
friends, while the younger boy and girl went out to the garden with
Katie.

Jillian was surprised at the difference between Ranjiv's age and
those of his cousins. Even Chetna seemed younger than her husband.
Perhaps Pratap had waited until later in life to marry or had simply
been the youngest of several brothers with Ramesh being the eldest.

The realization that she no longer possessed the sort of
knowledge Kavya would have taken for granted disturbed her,
although discovering these details provided her with an excellent
topic for conversation with Chetna.

She helped Chetna in the kitchen, arranging cutlery on the table
and putting out plates that she actually had to hunt for, unlike the day
before when she'd run up the stairs to Kavya's bedroom and
unerringly put her hand on the very item needed for the cremation.
Now she had to search through drawers and cabinets the way she
would have done in any unfamiliar home.

Once the tea was brewed and the various foods reheated, a
warm, comforting atmosphere prevailed. She fell into easy
conversation with Chetna and Pratap, learning the answers to her
questions with no difficulty whatsoever. Her deductions might have
been correct, but unlike so many other hunches she'd had lately, they

didn't contain even the slightest hint of prior knowledge.

Nevertheless, an inexplicable sense of foreboding took root and began to grow, a feeling that seemed to have nothing to do with Ranjiv, his family, or even the house. Pratap and Chetna were delightfully warm, caring people; Jillian could see herself becoming good friends with them in addition to the family ties she hoped would connect them one day. The house itself was an oasis of sorts, a place of refuge and shelter from the troubles that lay just beyond its threshold, troubles that called out to her repeatedly, prodding her to action.

She could easily have passed off her disquiet as stress or fatigue—the culmination of what was surely the most eventful week of her entire life—but she knew it was more than that. The climax was approaching.

And forewarned is forearmed.

* * * *

Ranjiv knew something was up. He wasn't clear on what that something was, but Jillian's anxiety was catching. As fond as he was of his aunt and uncle and cousins, he was very relieved when everyone pitched in to tidy the house before they locked up and headed for home.

A light rain had begun to fall as he and Jillian went out to the car. They were nearly halfway back to his flat when he finally broke the silence. "Tired?"

"A bit," she replied.

Her brief response led him to believe there was more to her mood than fatigue. "That isn't the problem, though. Is it?"

She shot him a sidelong glance. "I honestly don't know what's going on with me. I wish I did. Losing Kavya's spirit was hard enough." She paused, shaking her head. "This is different. Something's just not...right."

Earlier in the week, Ranjiv had felt something similar while on his way to pick his mother up at Heathrow.

A premonition, perhaps?

"Confusing, isn't it?"

"No kidding," she declared. "I should be used to this stuff by now, but I'm not." Pressing the heel of her hand to head, she ground it against her temple. "Maybe I have a brain tumor."

A chuckle escaped him. "I suppose that would be a simpler explanation."

"True, although a tumor wouldn't even explain half of what's happened. The things I know, the things I *couldn't* know." Her voice took on a wistful note as she continued. "Have you ever been in a situation you couldn't see a way out of? Like you were wandering around in an abyss and couldn't find the exit?"

In light of her recent history, her choice of similes wasn't as surprising as the fact that she could say it without shuddering. "Not really."

She turned toward the fogged window as beaded raindrops began sliding down the glass. "Or tried to fix something that's been smashed to smithereens? Your world broke apart the day that plane went down. So did mine. Neither of us will ever be the same. But I wonder... is that what the loss of each entity means? That I'm one step closer to normalcy? Or am I one step further into insanity?" She gazed at him with eyes that glistened with tears. "We've had a few days to recover, but will they be enough? Can we carry on and see this through?"

Ranjiv shrugged. "I think we have to. You said it yourself. You're the Chosen One."

Her derisive laugh fell somewhere between a snort and a sneeze. "Oh, I did not."

"Maybe not in so many words, but it amounts to the same thing." Taking her hand, he gave it a gentle squeeze before pressing it to his lips. "We'll get through this. Nothing lasts forever. Not the good times or the bad."

For a long moment, Ranjiv feared his attempt to reassure her had fallen on deaf ears. When she spoke again at last, her words proved him wrong.

"Funny how we seldom think of things that way. We keep telling ourselves the bad luck will run its course, but good luck does the same thing. In between is normalcy, which is vastly underrated."

He couldn't argue with that, but at the same time, upheaval had brought him and Jillian together, an event that he suspected would turn out to be one of the more important changes his life had ever undergone. "Maybe we'll get back to that someday."

"We can only hope. In the meantime, I'm feeling the need to vegetate for a while. Got any old movies we can watch?"

"Sure. What are you in the mood for?"

She blew out a pent-up breath. "Anything that doesn't contain hatred, violence, and death."

"You get that sort of thing even in fairy tales and cartoons, which pretty much narrows your choices down to romantic comedies."

"I'm good with that."

Chapter 32

VIVID IMAGES PLAYED OUT IN JILLIAN'S MIND AS SHE SLEPT, SOME real, some imagined. The trip to Stonehenge and her experiences there. Even the walk in Windsor Park. Someone had been watching her every step. Every move. She could see it now; a shadow hovering just beyond her waking awareness, one that could only manifest itself in dreams, like the normally straightlaced, uptight schoolmarm type who couldn't let go without a shot of tequila.

The shadow had followed her everywhere. Was it Shanda's ghost, or something else? Her money was actually on the something else. Shanda had never seemed like the type to simply hover; she'd made her presence known by speaking in ways only she would have chosen.

Drifting back down into her subconscious, she saw what it was. The Earth personified—or rather the lives of everyone who had ever lived, oscillating back and forth; first Asian, then Hispanic, then African, and on to Greek, Arabic, and further back in time— Neanderthal, perhaps? Some male, some female. The image at any given moment didn't matter; what she was seeing were the shadowy remnants of humankind calling her to action before it was too late.

The knife called to her—screamed at her to retrieve it right *now*.

She was awake. Despite her better judgment, she could no more have ignored the summons than she could stop her heart from beating.

Common sense warned against it. But sometimes, common sense was simply that: common. Right now, extraordinary actions were required, and a will much stronger than her own was giving her no choice but to act, act now, and act alone.

She rose from the bed, never touching the slumbering Ranjiv, not even disturbing Katie.

Am I a ghost too?

She glanced back at the rumpled sheets and blankets. Her body wasn't there. Unless it was at the bottom of the Atlantic and the entirety of the past week merely a physical manifestation of her spirit, she was still alive.

Donning jeans and her Irish sweater, she stole through the living room to the doorway before putting on her shoes. The jacket Ranjiv had loaned her was the first thing she touched when she opened the hall closet. Her phone sat on the table by the door; she reached for it, unplugging it from its charger, slipping it into her pocket—doing all of this with very little thought.

She had no weapons. No reason to assume she could take on anyone, let alone a known killer, if indeed he was anywhere near.

But Walter Buchard wasn't the one calling to her. This was something *else.*

Unbolting the door, she exited the flat and closed the door behind her, then ran lightly down the stairs. Upon reaching the lower landing, she pushed open the outer door and stepped out into the night.

She rounded the building and headed down to the canal. The soft, moisture-laden air created a billowy fog over the canal, muting the ripple of the flowing water. If there were any other people out and about, they were keeping out of sight. Even the birds were silent.

Running along the path, she reached the place where Ewan Michelson had been murdered. An oscillation in her vision marked the exact spot where his blood had been spilled, drawing her gaze whether she wanted to see it or not.

Street lamps illuminated the entrance to the park where the gate, which should have been locked at that hour, stood open. Not swung wide as it would have been during the day; only a tiny gap betrayed the fact that this was most likely a furtive, illegal entry.

Jillian took her phone from her pocket and pressed the number for the police station. When the night clerk answered, she had only managed to blurt out a brief description of the problem when she heard scampering feet and a soft whine.

"Oh, no," she groaned. "Here, Katie!" She followed that command with a beckoning gesture and called again.

Katie ignored Jillian completely and darted through the open gate and into the park.

Filled with dread, Jillian dropped the phone into her pocket and ran across the street. As she slipped through the gate, beams of light caught her eye, and she headed toward them.

Moments later, Katie let out a growl and snapped at the trouser leg of the tall, slender man who was scanning the clump of trees and shrubs on the park's eastern border with a large, heavy-duty flashlight. If he was a police officer, he wasn't wearing a uniform. His clothing was dark, and he was wearing the same sort of knit cap he'd been wearing the night of the murder.

Walter Buchard.

"Call off your damned dog," he snarled.

Responding to a hand signal, Katie retreated to sit quietly at Jillian's feet. Calm descended upon Jillian like a veil. "Sorry. We were out for a walk along the canal. I was surprised to see the park gate open. It's supposed to be locked at night, isn't it?"

There. Let him talk his way out of that.

He didn't bother to explain. "Yes, it is. You shouldn't be here."

"Probably not," she agreed. "What about you?"

"My business here is my own, and if you've any sense at all, you'll keep out of it." He took a step closer, drawing a growl from Katie. He hesitated. "Wait. I've seen you here before."

"So? I have a dog. Coming to the park is what we do."

"Perhaps... But not only that. I saw you on the Broadway yesterday."

She arched a brow. "Oh, so now it's wrong for me to be seen on the street?"

"No. But it is unwise to poke your nose where it doesn't belong." Narrowing his eyes, he peered at her, his close scrutiny prickling the nape of her neck. "You're the Yank who survived that plane crash, aren't you?"

"I didn't think that picture in the newspaper was a very good likeness. Apparently, it was good enough."

Again, he hesitated. Jillian could almost hear him weighing his options, trying to decide whether confronting her was worth the risk.

Smiling that same calculating, superior smile she'd seen at the café, he apparently decided the risk was too great. "Forgive me. You and your dog gave me a bit of a start."

"I suppose we did." Folding her arms, she met his gaze directly. "But then, I'm guessing you aren't supposed to be in the park at this hour any more than we are."

"Probably not. You see, I lost something here. I was trying to find it when your dog attacked me."

"And this is something you couldn't possibly have found during the *day*?" The note of sarcasm in her voice would have been appropriate, even if she hadn't known the reason for his search.

"I need it tonight."

"Oh. Perhaps you'd like some help then."

His expression hardened, as did his tone. "I can handle it."

"Really? Doesn't seem that way to me. I've seen you here before too. That thing you lost... It isn't cooperating with you, is it?"

"I might say the same for your dog," he retorted.

"True," she said with a nonchalant shrug. "But then, I'm new to dog ownership. Funny thing, though. Up to now, Katie's been amazingly obedient—doesn't really even need a leash. Seems strange that she would take such an instant dislike to you."

"I suppose there's no accounting for taste." He paused, sweeping her from head to toe with an assessing glance, then gestured toward the gate with his flashlight. "Better be getting on, now. You've put yourself in a spot of danger by coming out here tonight."

Jillian couldn't have agreed more. Unfortunately, leaving wasn't an option.

The police were already on the way, and given Katie's timely arrival, Ranjiv couldn't be far behind. Knowing she had backup provided her with sufficient courage to stand her ground, but if help arrived too soon, the only thing Buchard would be guilty of was breaking into the park. He hadn't admitted to being there to retrieve a murder weapon. She had to make him incriminate himself in some other manner. Something that would eventually tie him to an eleven-year-old murder…

She shook her head as though oblivious to his thinly veiled threat. "I wouldn't have thought so. I know Ewan Michelson was murdered near here a while back, but that seems to have been a politically motivated crime. From what I've heard, this has been a relatively peaceful neighborhood since then."

"Yes, well, don't believe everything you hear." With that, he slapped the handle of the flashlight against his open palm and took a careful step toward her—the first move a predator would make toward its prey.

* * * *

Katie's cold nose on his cheek was more than enough to wake Ranjiv, but he was able to ignore it for several moments until the realization that he was alone in the bed jolted him into full alertness. Flinging back the covers, he swung his feet over the side and hit the floor running. In a flat as small as his, there was nowhere to hide, and within seconds, he knew she was gone. Her sense of foreboding—or whatever it was—had been real.

The door to his flat was closed but not locked. He peered down the stairwell. Too late, he saw the sliver of light outlining the door to the street as Katie darted past him and bolted down the stairs, ignoring his urgent command to wait. He ran back to the bedroom and threw on clothing and shoes. Stopping briefly at the hall closet, he grabbed the nearest jacket, noting that the one he'd loaned Jillian was missing. Katie was nowhere to be seen, presumably having long since vanished down the stairwell and onto the street. Switching on his phone, he rang the police station. By the time the call was answered, he had already reached the ground floor.

"There's trouble along the canal near the entrance to the recreation grounds." Ranjiv had no idea who he was talking to, but the response was comforting.

"Officers are already en route."

I should've known. "McDougal and Fry, I hope."

"Both," came the reply. "Plus a few others. I must advise you to stay clear of the area."

Yeah, right. Although what he could possibly do with his bare hands against a potentially armed adversary was anyone's guess. He almost felt like laughing. In a battle between Buchard and Jillian, he knew who had the best backup.

Or maybe she didn't. Perhaps this was a test…

"Sorry. Gotta go," he said and ended the call before the dispatcher could squeeze in another word.

He heard nothing unusual. No screams of terror, no cries for help. Only the sound of his own footsteps echoing off the shadowed walls of the surrounding buildings. He ran through the car park and straight down the center of the street, avoiding the fog-shrouded path along the canal. Unless Buchard had a gun, which was unlikely given his choice of weapons in the past, speed was more important than stealth.

He wasn't surprised to find the gate standing open, but being met there by an army of police officers would've been a nice touch. The place appeared to be completely deserted.

Katie's high-pitched barks and menacing growls spurred him forward. Sprinting across the green, in the shadowy light from beyond the fence, he saw two people locked in a struggle, the man's hands gripping the woman's neck in a stranglehold. When they fell back against the leathery leaves of a huge rhododendron he feared he was too late.

Then he saw the flash of the blade.

* * * *

Jillian feinted toward the gate, then back to where the knife waited for her. She could see it quite clearly, which made her wonder why Buchard hadn't retrieved it years ago.

Unfortunately, Buchard was taller than she, with a much longer reach. He snagged the hood of her jacket as she passed and swung her around, striking a glancing blow to the side of her head with the flashlight. She ducked away from his second swing, nearly ripping the hood from the jacket. Tossing the flashlight aside, Buchard jerked her toward him and wrapped both hands tightly around her neck.

With no other weapon as yet, she used her weight against him.

Falling, she dragged him down with her. She ignored his hands at her throat, reaching back behind her as unerringly as the day she'd found Kavya's hairpin. As her fingers closed over the handle, the blade yielded easily, almost as though it had been ejected from deep within the gnarled trunk. In a flashing arc, she drove the blade downward into muscle and bone.

Buchard let out an anguished roar and grappled for control of the knife. Gasping for breath, Jillian held on doggedly, but he used her own trick against her. As he dropped to his knees, her fingers slipped from the bloody hilt. Seconds later, she was yanked free and shoved aside as Ranjiv delivered a punch to Buchard's jaw that sent him sprawling in the grass.

"Are you okay?" Ranjiv called out.

For a brief moment, Jillian didn't realize who he was talking to, but her aching neck was there to remind her.

"I'm fine," she croaked. She might have been stretching the truth a bit, but she saw no need to divert Ranjiv's attention from his opponent.

Despite the knife lodged in his shoulder, Buchard was back on his feet in seconds. Wrenching the blade from his own flesh, he lunged at Ranjiv.

Ranjiv sidestepped the attack and snatched up the flashlight, wielding it like a baseball bat. The two men began circling one another like a pair of wolves, the one scarcely winded and the other growing increasingly sluggish from the loss of blood. Jillian didn't need to see the growing stain on Buchard's dark coat to know how freely his blood flowed from the wound. She could smell the metallic scent as easily as a bloodhound.

Katie joined in the fight, her flanking movements assisting Ranjiv in his efforts to keep Buchard from making a break for the gate. Jillian was past wondering how the dog could possibly understand Ranjiv's strategy, especially when she didn't fully comprehend it herself.

Shouts rang out as a pack of police officers swarmed through the gate. Outnumbered and outgunned, Buchard dropped the knife and fell to his knees just as Jillian lost what strength was left in her legs. Wobbling toward a nearby oak, she sank down beside the massive tree and leaned against the trunk. The air was laden with the earthy scent of tree bark, and she gulped it in while massaging that same throbbing spot in her temple.

Not a brain tumor or even the blow to the head she'd sustained. Merely the path of least resistance.

I'm losing another one.

She wasn't even granted another Rod Stewart song to mark the event. The Shanda entity simply wasn't there anymore.

Abandoning Buchard to police custody, Ranjiv and Katie rushed to Jillian's aid. Katie opted to lick her face while Ranjiv took the more manly approach of sweeping her up into his arms.

"You are *not* okay," he said, peering first at her face and then at her neck. "Are you?"

"To be honest, I'm really not sure," she admitted. "But I'm guessing there are bruises."

"A few."

The kiss he gave her might have left bruises on her lips if she hadn't been an active participant.

Blaring sirens broke the spell, as did an anxious voice. "Are you all right, miss?"

Jillian looked up to find the English version of an EMT staring at her neck much the way Ranjiv had done a few moments before.

"I think so," she replied. "Just a bit...bruised."

"Best to go to the hospital so they can document your injuries," McDougal said as he approached. "Evidence, you know. Makes the charges stick better when there are pictures and doctor's statements to back them up."

Officer Fry trotted over, looking as grandmotherly as ever. "Chief Inspector? We've found the weapon."

With a nod at Jillian that clearly said *I'll deal with you later*, he accompanied Fry across the green. Ranjiv followed, and since Jillian was still in his arms, she had no choice but to come along.

Drawing a rubber glove from his pocket, McDougal pulled it on before stooping to pick up the knife. "Hmm...a bit rusty." He glanced at Jillian. "Yours?"

"Um, no." She pointed back toward the ancient rhododendron. "It was stuck in there."

"I see."

Jillian didn't understand how the inspector could possibly *see* anything, but she saw no need to discuss the matter.

"And you just happened to find it when that man attacked you?"

She shrugged helplessly. "I can't explain *how* I found it. All I know is, I reached behind me and it was just...there."

McDougal arched a brow. "Miraculously?"

"If you want to put it that way, yes."

"Miracles seem to be your forte lately, Miss Dulaine." Fixing her with a long, penetrating stare, he added, "Yes, well, I won't bother to argue with this one either. Just explain one more thing... Why were you here?"

She shrugged again. "Katie needed to go out. All I did was follow her through the gate."

Ranjiv cleared his throat. "You did tell us to spend as much time in the park as possible."

"Not in the middle of the night." Only then did the inspector's disheveled appearance register—from the misaligned buttons on his shirt to the hair sticking straight up on the side of his head.

"Opportune, though, wouldn't you say?" Ranjiv prompted.

"I do believe it was." McDougal gestured toward the street and the waiting ambulance. "Shall we?"

Another hospital. Another thorough checkup before finally being released. Dawn was breaking when they left there to go on to the police station to review the events with McDougal—or be "debriefed" as Ranjiv had put it.

As it turned out, Fry had gone off shift not long after Buchard had returned to his flat. McDougal didn't come right out and say it, but Jillian suspected the tail he'd replaced her with had been less than attentive—either that or Buchard knew better than to leave his flat by the front entrance.

Jillian couldn't blame the officer for losing his quarry. In fact, his absence had allowed the scenario to play out in exactly the right way, although she could have done without the bruises on her neck, not to mention the blood that had seeped into her nifty Irish sweater. No doubt a good soaking would remove the worst of the stain. However, given everything else she'd become attuned to in the past week, she suspected that the taint of his blood would linger. She had tossed the clothes she'd been wearing when the plane went down for that very reason. Even then she'd known that no amount of soap and water could erase the memories clinging to the fabric.

She replied to McDougal's questions with the same answers as before. No amount of cajoling or badgering would change her responses. Perhaps he sought only to assure himself that she wouldn't crack under cross-examination.

Jillian knew better. After all, she had Planet Earth and the entirety of humankind behind her.

No one, not McDougal or Fry or anyone else, could top that.

Chapter 33

TWO DAYS LATER, DCI ANGUS MCDOUGAL SPORTED A BROAD GRIN as he ushered Jillian and Ranjiv into his office. Closing the door behind them, McDougal sat down at his desk while Ranjiv and Jillian took their seats near the door.

"I see you're recovering nicely, Miss Dulaine."

Ranjiv winced as Jillian brushed a hand over the purplish-yellow bruises on her neck.

"I've had excellent care," she said with a significant glance at Ranjiv.

Ranjiv had been diligently massaging arnica cream into every bruise and sore muscle she mentioned. Their conversations had seldom been about the case, neither of them feeling the need to talk about the altercation in the park as yet. Instead, they'd spent their time trying to regain some semblance of normalcy while also mourning Kavya's death, engaging in quiet, simple activities that required little thought, taking strolls that avoided the recreation grounds and that particular section of the Grand Union Canal.

They had ventured further east along the canal and then north to the neighborhood near the high school Ranjiv had attended, watching children at play in Southall Park and lunching at a tiny pub on High Street. This was the downtime in the wake of high drama, the rhythm of ordinary life diverting the shock of recent traumas, allowing their subconscious minds time to process the raw emotions.

Although she hadn't mentioned the possibility of staying on past her original departure date, Ranjiv had every intention of making the interim so pleasant Jillian would never want to return home. He even had a job in mind for her. Pratap would need someone to replace Kavya as the bookkeeper in his import business. Jillian might not be well-versed in the British monetary system, but having worked in a bank, she was undoubtedly good with numbers, and her facility with languages was another point in her favor. He had yet to broach the subject, but the more he thought about it, the more convinced he became that he'd hit on the perfect solution. Now all he had to do was persuade Pratap and Jillian.

"Turns out that knife was a more significant bit of evidence than we thought," McDougal began. "Seems Buchard had it custom-made several years back. We were able to locate the maker who still had a record of the sale. Stupid of Buchard to use a knife that could be traced—although it might explain why he was so determined to find it once he got wind of the new evidence.

"Anyway, while he does admit to Michelson's murder, he swears he was hired by Michelson's political opponent, Ronald Sympson. Apparently Buchard has been blackmailing Sympson, who of course denies ever hiring Buchard to begin with." McDougal threw up his hands, then leaned forward, smacking his palms on the desktop. "We'll let the courts sort that one out." He smiled at Jillian. "No doubt your testimony will be required at some point, although I'm going to assume they could take your deposition over the phone."

"Or Skype," Ranjiv suggested, hating to admit the possibility that Jillian might not be living in England when the case went to trial.

"Even better," McDougal said with a nod. "In any case, no one would blame you for wishing to avoid another transatlantic flight."

"To be honest, I'm not sure I want to take one now." She toyed with the hem of her skirt. "How hard is it to get a permanent visa?"

McDougal chuckled. "There's a naturalization process, of course." He glanced at Ranjiv. "Although marrying a British subject would certainly chivvy things along."

"The British equivalent of a green card?" she asked with a wry grin.

"Something like that."

Ranjiv's heart warmed with the look she gave him. However, the feeling was short-lived as she directed her next question at both men.

"Is Sympson still in office?"

Ranjiv shook his head. "He was defeated after one term by the current MP, a Labor party member."

"What about Sympson's political agenda?" she went on. "Is there anyone who might have had him in their pocket, so to speak? Any political cronies who might've shared his views?"

McDougal's smile faded. "A few, including Sympson's mentor in the party, one Unwin Turnbull—and I don't have to tell you who *he* had lunch with a few days ago."

"We've been wondering about that," Ranjiv said. "I don't suppose Buchard has said anything about that meeting, has he?"

"Not yet. There may be no connection whatsoever, although I have my doubts." The inspector gave a satisfied nod. "Still, we have our murderer and a signed confession. Never dreamed solving this case would be so easy after all this time."

Given what he knew about Jillian's involvement, Ranjiv suspected the plot was far more intricate than McDougal could possibly imagine. However, the merest mention of her "sources" would only undermine her credibility.

"Not really," Jillian said. "We have Shanda to thank for that."

"Yes...yes, I suppose we do—and you too, of course, Miss Dulaine." With a slow wag of his head, McDougal added, "Still can't fathom how your dog needed to go out at precisely the right moment. It's as if she *knew* Buchard would be there."

"Perhaps she did," Jillian said. "But unless Katie learns to talk, we'll have to chalk it up to coincidence—or luck."

"Like you surviving that plane crash? I suppose so—if you believe in that sort of thing. Seems you've had more than your fair share lately. Let's hope it doesn't run out."

Ranjiv glanced at Jillian and smiled. Something told him her lucky streak wasn't over yet.

"I'll try to stay out of trouble," Jillian promised as she rose from her chair.

"See that you do." McDougal's amused chuckle was at odds with his stern directive. "But if you need me, you know where to find me."

"I certainly do," she said. "Thank you for your help."

McDougal stood and extended a hand. "I should be the one thanking you. No detective chief inspector worth his salt likes an unsolved murder on his turf." He grinned. "Even if I was only a detective sergeant back then."

* * * *

Jillian's mind was awhirl as they left the police station and walked west on High Street. Should she take McDougal's suggestion and marry Ranjiv? Or should she put an end to the affair simply by going home? Did she need to return to Stonehenge for further instructions, or would the Earth goddess find her no matter where she went? Would she collect more souls to replace the three she'd lost? What about Cleona and Susan? Had they been similarly affected by the crash?

These questions and more had been put on hold for a time. In the wake of the meeting with McDougal, they were now vying with each other, clamoring for her attention.

They'd reached the intersection of High Street and South Road when Ranjiv finally broke the silence as they waited for the light to change. "A shilling for your thoughts."

With no desire to blurt out bits of the chaotic jumble bouncing around in her brain, Jillian opted to postpone her reply. "You mean they're worth more than a penny?"

"Absolutely," he replied. "Perhaps as much as a guinea."

"Well then, if you're willing to pay *that* much..." She caught herself gnawing at her lip before she spoke. "I'm not sure where this is going. My extra 'katras' may have moved on, but there's still something... Some presence telling me there's something else I have to do."

"I'm not surprised. Solving one murder case isn't likely to save the world."

She gazed at him in quiet wonder. "You still believe in me, don't you?"

"I love you, Jillian." Taking her hand, he pressed it to his lips. "How could I not believe in you?"

Tears filled her eyes, threatening to run down her cheeks. She blinked and let them fall.

"I love you too, Ranjiv. I just wish being in love was all that mattered right now." She drew in a shaky breath and leaned closer, resting her head against his chest. "But it isn't that simple. I can't help believing there was a reason the three of us were spared. Cleona and Susan... What's been going on with them? I keep meaning to call, but I've been distracted every time. The urge is growing stronger, though."

"Perhaps you need to give in to it."

"To be honest, I'm a little afraid to. We promised to keep in touch, but now... I don't know."

"What's the worst that could happen? That you'd find out you were alone in this or that you'll have help?"

She looked up and smiled at him through her tears. "Whatever's behind this adventure certainly knew what it was doing when it chose you as my cohort."

"Cohort?" he echoed. "I'd like to be much more than *that*."

"Don't look now, but I think you already are." Lacing her fingers with his, she held on tight, never wanting to let him go. "You're my lover, my masseuse, my partner—"

"In crime or in life?"

"Both, I think."

"Why, Jillian," he exclaimed in mock surprise. "Are you asking me to marry you?"

The stoplight turned green. "Actually, I think Inspector McDougal already did that." Chuckling, she added, "And as I recall, so did Tahir."

"Perhaps." With a shrug, he tucked her hand into the crook of his arm as they started across the street. "I've always thought a proposal should be a more private discussion."

"Even if the marriage was arranged by your parents?"

"Even then."

"Tell me, did you ever ask Laksha to marry you?"

"Never got that far," he replied. "An omission for which I shall be eternally grateful."

"Mmm... I see." She hesitated, peering up at him from the

corner of her eye. "Planning to remain a bachelor forever?"

"Only until Mother's mourning period is over. After that, I'm fair game."

"Sounds reasonable. Any idea how long a woman should wait to get engaged after practically being jilted at the altar?"

He appeared to give this some thought, then said with conviction, "I don't believe a waiting period is necessary. Strikes me as the sort thing you shouldn't put off—like getting back on the horse after you've been thrown."

"Never thought of it that way," she mused. "Perhaps you're right."

"I'm sure of it." A few seconds later, he added, "Ready to get back on that horse?"

"Absolutely."

Dropping an arm around her shoulders, he pulled her closer, setting off an unprecedented attack of the warm fuzzies. "Mother would be pleased. Of course, I'm totally thrilled myself, but—"

"A bit gobsmacked, you mean?"

"That too."

Jillian put her arm around Ranjiv's waist and hugged him as hard as she could. "Never dreamed I'd come out of this trip with a new fiancé."

"You're forgetting what Rumi said. *'Whatever sorrow shakes from your heart, far better things will take their place.'* I believe even Mother would agree with that."

"I hope you're right. You're certainly a huge improvement over Seth."

"Really? In what way?"

He was teasing, of course, but it couldn't hurt to remind him. "Bigger is better. Remember?"

"How could I possibly forget?"

Ranjiv kissed the top of her head, and they walked on, enjoying the quiet intimacy. They had just passed the chemist's shop when Jillian's phone rang. A glance at the screen informed her that this wasn't Anna's family calling to contest the ownership of a certain champion miniature schnauzer. Nor was it her sister.

Her pulse pounded in her ears as she answered with a wary "Hello?"

"Hello, Jillian?" the caller began. "This is Cleona Mahoney."

"Oh, Cleona," she said with relieved sigh. "I've been meaning to call you. Are you okay?"

If Cleona thought the question was odd, she didn't let on. "Physically, yes. Otherwise, I'm not really sure *what* to think. Some really strange things have been happening."

"Same here," Jillian said. "Where are you?"

"I'm still in Ireland, at my aunt and uncle's farm near Kenmare." Cleona's swift inhalation was as audible as the quaver in her voice. "I've been seeing things, hearing things, and having the strangest dreams. I know things I couldn't possibly know. I'm either losing my mind or, well…it sounds crazy, but—"

"Trust me, I won't think it's crazy," Jillian said firmly. She glanced at Ranjiv, who nodded his agreement. "Keep talking. I'm listening."

As Cleona told her story, Jillian became more convinced than ever that completing the unfinished tasks of the three women she'd met on that ill-fated flight wasn't the end.

It was only the beginning.

About the Author

A native of Louisville, Kentucky, Cheryl Brooks is a former critical care nurse who resides in rural Indiana with her husband, two sons, two horses, three cats, and one dog. Her **Cat Star Chronicles** series was first published by Sourcebooks Casablanca in 2008, and includes *Slave, Warrior, Rogue, Outcast, Fugitive, Hero, Virgin, Stud, Wildcat,* and *Rebel.* Her **Cowboy Heaven** series, also published by Sourcebooks Casablanca, includes *Cowboy Delight* (a novella), *Cowboy Heaven,* and *Must Love Cowboys.* Look for her new **Cat Star Legacy** series from Sourcebooks beginning in 2018. In addition to the **Soul Survivors** trilogy, *Echoes From the Deep, Dreams From the Deep,* and *Justice From the Deep,* she has one self-published erotic romance, *Sex, Love, and a Purple Bikini,* and two erotic short stories, *Midnight in Reno,* and *Pontoon.* Her **Unlikely Lovers** series includes *Unbridled, Uninhibited, Undeniable,* and *Unrivaled.* She has also published *If You Could Read My Mind* writing as Samantha R. Michaels. As a member of *The Sextet,* she has written several erotic novellas published by Siren/Bookstrand. Her other interests include cooking, gardening, singing, and guitar playing. Cheryl is a member of RWA and IRWA. You can visit her online at www.cherylbrooksonline.com or email her at cheryl.brooks52@yahoo.com

62445751R00177

Made in the USA
Lexington, KY
07 April 2017